CW00518750

ANGELINA'S
SECRET

ANGELINA'S SECRET

Diane Merrill Wigginton

JEWELED DAGGER
PUBLISHING

JEWELED DAGGER PUBLISHING COMPANY
www.jeweleddaggerpublishing.com

© Copyright 2014 and 2017 by Diane Merrill Wigginton

All rights reserved. Except as permitted under the U.S. Copyright Act of 1976, no part of this publication may be reproduced, distributed, or transmitted in any form or by any means, or stored in a database or retrieval system, electronically or otherwise, or by use of a technology or retrieval system now known or to be invented, without the prior written permission of the author and publisher.

Designed by Fine Design

First edition June 28, 2014

Second Edition April 4, 2017

978-1-946146-02-1—Angelina's Secret eBook
978-1-520574-15-8—Angelina's Secret Paperback
978-1-946146-00-7—Angelina's Secret Hardback

To my husband David who believed in me and reminded me that it was my turn to pursue my dreams.

To my mother who taught me, when I was younger, that I could do anything I set my mind to.

To each one of our kids, for always being an inspiration as well as a beacon of light to me.

Prologue

 HAD BEEN BORN THREE WEEKS earlier to a loving home with a mother and father who loved and cherished the arrival of another child into their home and hearts. I was blessed to have twin brothers, Charlie and Jonathan, who had come into this world five years earlier and were as close as two brothers born of the same womb could be. They did everything together and were normal, rambunctious, five-year-old boys unaware of matters and circumstances beyond their little world.

Mother was a beautiful woman in her own right, and in a time when women were revered for their beauty and little else, my mother was a phenomenon. She was a smart, intelligent woman prone to show her witty nature. But Mother had a secret, a sixth sense about things that happened or were about to happen, and she was never wrong.

She told me once that certain gifts ran in our family and that I should always trust my instincts. At the time I was too young to understand what she was trying to say to me. It wasn't until many years later her words to me made sense.

But I seem to be getting ahead of myself in the telling of my story.

Something happened shortly after my birth that changed our family dynamics forever.

Some say that a tragedy changes things for the worse, ripping the very foundation of a family. But I attest to you that tragedy only makes the strong things stronger and can bind a family together forever—eternally linking everyone concerned like stitches of a tapestry tightly woven together for the betterment of all concerned.

And so I tell you my tale of tragedy and adventure that leads to a great love so intricately woven through time that the bonds will never be broken.

I

THERE I SAT IN MY family's sunroom, smiling, politely sipping tea with London's aristocrats—women of the utmost caliber—and all I could think about was, when will the torture end?

The only thing they were able to discuss with a minutia of knowledge was the upcoming season, and who had created scandal during the holidays. And who could forget the season's sought-after eligible males.

I could have bloody well choked on one of those finger sandwiches, and they wouldn't have noticed me lying dead on the floor. Honestly, the way they all carry on was as if they all shared one brain.

Let's be clear. I like fashionable clothes and shoes as much as the next girl. But really, the whole lot of them cared for nothing more than making a good match and bringing more children into this world. One might think that a woman is good for nothing more than sitting around looking pretty, waiting for the man of the manor to come home to tell her how lovely she looks. The thought of such uselessness makes me want to gag on my own tongue.

Why is everyone in such a hurry to marry anyway? I don't see much cause for excitement. I, for one, don't intend on being anyone's property, that's for sure.

As I looked about the room, I spotted Mary Wheatly, the bane of my existence. We went to school together. I thought her mean-spirited then and even more so now. Her father, George, and mother, Prudence, owned two dress shops in the high-rent districts of London along with a millinery factory and two millinery shops: one for men's hat needs, the other for fashionably well-paying ladies. They'd made their money by catering to the wealthy.

Mary was pleasant enough to look at, with her stylish blond curls fashioned high upon her head, and powdered. Personally, I prefer natural hair without all the goopy grease to make the powder stick. But then again, most people refuse to bathe, opting instead to douse themselves in perfumes, finding this a satisfactory option to washing. That's when fans and scented hankies come in handy.

As I was saying, Mary was pleasant enough to look at if it wasn't for her ghastly smile, and voice. Her voice was like two alley cats fighting it out in the middle of the night. It was so unexpected that it grated on the ears. Bad teeth and grating voice aside, my biggest objection of her was her attitude toward the so-called unwashed masses. Those Mary had deemed unworthy of her compassion and of little consequence to society.

The one person I do love beyond all else in this world is Sarah Burgess, my best friend. We grew up together as neighbors in London. Her father, Lord Burgess, was a member of the House of Lords at Parliament. He made his money the old-fashioned way. He married it.

Sarah was presently seated right next to Mary Wheatly, attempting to look interested in something the old girl was saying.

Sarah's delicate blue eyes caught mine from across the room as she pleaded with me to save her.

Feigning as if I were going to leave her in her present circumstance, I broke out the fan and began to fan myself until I noticed the daggers reflected in her eyes shooting my way. Deciding Sarah had endured enough torture for one afternoon, I smiled and nodded to her, giving our well-practiced signal that help was on the way.

I took a turn around the pastry table, picking out a lovely dish with the most scrumptious-looking piece of confectionery delight. With barely a misstep, I picked up the plate, fork, and napkin in one fell swoop and continued on my journey. I was on a mission of mercy and would not be diverted.

"Good day to you, Mary, have you tasted the scrumptious lemon cake yet? It is simply the best I have ever tried. Could I borrow Lady Burgess for a moment? I am in dire need of her opinion on something very important. Thank you so much." Ambushing Mary quickly, and before she had the opportunity to gather her wits about her, I deposited the plate in her hand without even waiting for an answer, while pulling Sarah from the settee with my other hand.

"Of course, a piece of lemon cake would be lovely, thank you, Lady Stewart," Mary replied, with a rather puzzled look on her face.

"Please excuse us," I sweetly offered as I turned my back to her.

Sarah and I locked arms as she gave me a squeeze of gratitude, and a knowing sideways glance that required no words. We headed for the terrace doors that had been left open, allowing the spring air to flood in. We didn't even glance back.

"Fresh, glorious air!" Sarah remarked, throwing her arms skyward and filling her lungs with as much air as one could while wearing a corset.

Sarah was petite, almost childlike in stature with a beautiful heart-shaped face, and long eyelashes framing incredibly blue eyes. She wore her blond hair, that reminded me of corn silk glistening in the sun, without powder. The curls piled high upon her head, tied with satin ribbons to match her elegant, pale blue, satin gown.

Standing next to Sarah always made me feel awkward. Where she was petite and elegant, I was tall and robust and at least a full head taller than her. Sarah's body was so thin and slender that gowns tended to dwarf her with all those layers of material and large hoops underneath.

In comparison, I was voluptuous and well developed like my mother. I never liked the tradition of wearing corsets all the time. I found them too restrictive, not allowing for an active lifestyle, or even the ability to eat or breathe. No, I did not enjoy wearing corsets at all, but would conform when necessary.

My vibrant auburn locks could be unruly at times, slipping from the confines of their pins and tumbling down at all the wrong times. My mouth and lips were too large, like the permanent pout of a petulant child. My eyes were my one feature I did like—large almond-shaped emerald green, fringed with long dark lashes.

"I was ready to open a vein with a dull knife," I proclaimed as I walked to the edge of the upper terrace that looked out upon the manicured garden of the estate. "If I have to listen to one more simpering girl carry on about how she simply can't wait to marry and start a family, I will surely have to throw myself from the nearest tall balcony."

"And leave me to drudge on with the new season and no one to align myself with when things get ugly? You wouldn't be so cruel to me, your dearest friend in the world, I know you and you are not that thoughtless," she stated with derision and mockery in her voice.

"Of course, you are right as always. It would have caused such a scene right there in the middle of tea. Mother would be mortified, and that wouldn't be good for me," I said with my hand over my heart very dramatically. "I am positive Lady Ashton is sorry to have missed such a dramatic public display," I said.

"Whatever will she talk about with the ladies at tea tomorrow?" Sarah asked.

I rolled my eyes, feigning dramatic exasperation as I crumbled in a heap against the railing with my hand over my eyes.

"So how shall we celebrate your impending nineteenth birthday this year?" Sarah questioned, then continued as if I weren't there. "Shall we have a large soiree or, better yet, a garden party when we open up the houses in London? Oh yes, that is perfect," Sarah said with such glee and excitement.

"Why do I feel you don't really need an excuse for a party or a need to celebrate my birthday? Any reason will do, let's have a party for the sake of having a party. I really don't want to draw attention to the numbers adding up. Someone might start throwing words around like old maid, then tongues will wag and somehow, it will get back to Father that I need to be married or something crazy like that," I stated.

"But don't you want to ever get married?" Sarah asked.

"Honestly, Sarah, how long have we been friends? I don't wish to be owned like a piece of land, at some man's beck and call. No, thank you! Life is good right now. I have freedoms that I wouldn't have if I were someone's wife. For me to agree to marry, the man needs to be of superior make, and I need to be in love. And seeing how I have never been in love, or even close to swooning over some sad excuse for a man, I answer your query with a resounding *no*! I don't wish to wed, *ever*!" Turning to face her, I continued my rant. "I don't think that it is in my nature, Sarah. Some young ladies fawn all over the opposite gender, going all dewy eyed and stupid at the sight of a man. I can't see myself doing anything like that."

"All right, I will never bring it up again. In fact, I will erase the entire idea of you being happily wed with thirteen children to keep you company in your old age from my mind completely."

"Well, if that isn't a ghastly thought. Me, all soft in the middle and in the head over some man and, to add insult to injury, the very thought of me subjecting myself to thirteen children. Have you completely lost your mind? If all men were like my father or brother Jonathan, I might be in love with the male species as a whole. But in my dealings with them, they are arrogant, boorish creatures, completely in love with themselves. There is no way I am going to saddle myself with that."

"Someday you might change your mind," Sarah said while lifting her delicate little eyebrows and smiling at me.

"Not in this lifetime!"

"Crazier things have happened," Sarah said, with an impish gleam in her eye.

"Yes, me being struck by lightning. Now that might actually happen. As for me falling in love, I want to state for the record once again that it will not happen in this lifetime!"

With a shrug of Sarah's slender shoulders, "Never say never," she added before heading back to the tea party through the elegant french doors without looking back at me.

Smiling to myself, I decided to stroll through our garden. I was definitely not feeling up to anymore conversation with ignorant young ladies.

I walked down the steps to the garden below and wandered in and out of the perfectly shaped hedges toward the richly-colored roses. Brilliant red and white buds popping out to greet the warm rays of light, raining down on their lovely heads, I wandered past the fountain spouting streams of water in the freshly stocked water lily and koi pond and made my way to my favorite spot in the garden—a beautiful quiet place with a bench and trellis completely covered with fragrant purple wisteria.

In years past, Jonathan and I came out here to run, play and hideout in our secret spot, far from the prying eyes of the grownups. We sat on the bench or lay in the grass and talked and laughed as innocent children do. We could find so much to occupy us for hours.

Some might not understand the close bond between Jonathan and I, but those closest to the family did.

As I sat on my secret bench, my thoughts were drawn back to that fateful night so long ago. Mother recounted the story so often that I could see every scene in my mind's eye.

Jonathan Edward Allen Stewart II and Charles Albert Harry Stewart were twins. Jonathan came first with a head of raven-black hair like our father. His lungs were so strong; cook said she could hear his first cries of life all the way down the backstairs and into the kitchen.

Charles came into this world ten minutes later with a shock of red hair like Mother's. But he made his way into the world with less pomp and circumstance. My mother said that he opened his eyes and looked straight into her soul and greeted her with a proper christening of his own when he proceeded to wet on her.

Jonathan and Charlie were inseparable. Their nannies wanted to put them in separate cradles, but all they did was cry and fuss until they were placed together. Either side by side or snuggled like two spoons in a drawer always touching, never apart, two halves of the same coin.

I came into their world five years later in the spring. Mother had had two miscarriages and was grateful when I was born robust and healthy. I was born with a head full of auburn hair. It wasn't red or black but somewhere in the middle. Mother was so happy to have a daughter after two beautiful sons. I was christened Angelina Marguerite Amelia Stewart. But Mother just called me Angel.

That year, winter had lasted through the spring with the relentless rain and biting winds. Many of the young children and a few of the elderly had come down with a mysterious fever. Our house was not spared, and both Jonathan and Charlie were very ill with it.

Mother, in desperation, sent for a physician and Father, who had left on business, was not due back for a week and a half.

My brothers had been ill for two weeks by then, and Mother was beside herself with fear. Many had died, and her fear of losing another child was unfathomable. Facing such a dire situation with a new baby and no husband at home was nearly too much for her to bear.

Three days after sending for Father, Charlie passed in the night, much the same way he came into the world, without pomp or circumstance. Mother softly wept at his bedside, while Jonathan simply closed his eyes and went to sleep, refusing to open them again, as if he was willing himself to let go and pass to the next world with Charlie.

Mother tried reading to him from his favorite storybooks to no avail. Jonathan refused to open his eyes and take the broth Mother had prepared for him.

Her despair became palpable, and she was at her wit's end.

Finally, by early evening, Mother had come to a decision. Lady Clarissa Emerson Stewart had never given up before, and quitting now was not an option. She sent the nannies and nurses away. Taking me in her loving arms, she carried me down the long hallway to the boy's room.

As she quietly closed the door behind us, Jonathan's small emaciated body was bathed in the warm glow of the firelight as he lay in his now-enormous bed.

Mother opened his little arms and snuggled me next to his chest, folding his arm around me ever so gently. Then she climbed into bed on the other side, folding herself around us both. Speaking soft words to Jonathan and saying a prayer, pleading to the heavens above for a small miracle, she lay there waiting.

As if on cue, I began to stir from my slumber and, making small noises that babies will, a miracle happened. Jonathan opened his eyes. His small frail arms tightened around my small form, drawing me nearer as if his very life depended on it.

First, one tear fell and then another from those enormous hollowed eyes. As if a dam had broken loose, his hurt and anger came flooding out from his small anguished soul. And once the floodgates were opened, they didn't stop for over an hour.

When Jonathan had cried all the tears he could, it left him exhausted. With his last remaining strength, he clung to me as if I were air. Then he fell into a deep dreamless sleep, and Mother took her first deep breath in days, instinctively knowing that Jonathan would live. He had been given a reason to live, and Mother slept for the first time in a week, clinging to us both.

Mother awoke in the early hour just before dawn's light broke the morning sky to find her husband asleep in a chair, his head rested on the bed, and his hand holding tightly to hers.

Mother said that it was at that moment she knew that she couldn't love anyone more than she did Father. He begged her forgiveness for not being there and leaving her alone. His anguish over the loss of Charlie was evident in his eyes, only second to the thought of losing her.

After that I was Jonathan's shadow and constant companion. When he took lessons, I sat in his lap, absorbing knowledge like a sponge. He learned to ride horses. I followed on my pony. Where he went, I went. Always together, never apart.

He teased, and I pretended to pout, but we never truly fought, because one of us always catered to the other. We never had any need to disagree or bicker like other siblings.

Father too had changed for the better. He hired a foreman to run things at the textile mill so that he could be home with us more. He and his two brothers, Nicholas and James, were very successful businessmen. They had opened one of the first cotton processing plants in England. Then they started a textile plant and an import-export company together. They exported their cotton fabrics and other English textiles and goods.

Returning from other countries like Italy, Greece, and Spain, with silks and sumptuous fabrics and aromatic spices that couldn't be found in our region, our company sold to merchants and shop owners all over London, and our families thrived.

Mother miscarried two more times and gave birth to a stillborn child before they decided that their little family was perfectly complete just as it was.

Father loved Mother so very much, and he loved his children to a state of indulgence some might say. But he never cared about convention, and we were happy. To Lord Jonathan Edward Allan Stewart, that was all that mattered.

2

HE GLORIOUS DAY OF MY nineteenth birthday dawned like any other day. Anna woke me and helped me to dress in a morning gown before breakfast. Then off I went to the dining room.

Both Mother and Father greeted me with a cheery good morning as I joined them for breakfast.

"How did you sleep, my little angel?" Mother inquired sincerely.

"Very well, thank you for asking," I sweetly said, with the joy one feels when it is their birthday, and you just know something is up.

"I hope you didn't make any big plans today," Father asked with a bit of a smile, as if he had some grand secret he was keeping.

"No, Father, not really. I did tell Sarah I would meet her for lunch today. It seems she has something quite extraordinary she wants to tell me about. Why do you ask?" I stated while studying him with an inkling of suspicion now starting to creep in.

"Oh, no reason, darling, just interested. Say, would you like to accompany me to the wharf today, around ten thirty? I have something I wish to show you."

Mother and Father were being mysterious and cryptic that morning, so I decided to play along.

"Yes! Oh yes! That sounds like fun." Looking at the clock behind Father, I suddenly realized I would have to hurry. Swallowing my last mouthful of toast with a gulp of juice, I stood up and kissed them both on the cheek. "I have to get ready," I called over my shoulder as I ran from the room.

Anna was waiting for me with a hot bath, as if she knew that I was in a hurry.

"Happy birthday to you, my lady, and how are we feeling this day?" she said with her usual pleasantness and good cheer.

"Thank you so much, Anna, you are a lifesaver. What do you know about this mysterious thing Father wants to show me?" I inquired of her with no real expectation of learning anything.

"I don't have any idea, my lady." She attempted to avoid my eyes while busying herself. Anna was such a wonderful handmaiden, but more than that, she was a good friend. She was not scandalized by the fact that I preferred to bathe quite often and, without the traditional chemise worn for bathing, instead opting to bathe naked. It just felt better to me without a piece of clothing between me and my glorious hot bath.

Anna washed my hair and handed me my favorite sandalwood-scented soap. Afterward, I sat by the fire and dried myself as she readied my gown and sundries.

My suspicions were further fueled by the gown Anna pulled out of my dressing room—a lovely traveling gown made of light wool, pale green and heather gray.

I knew that it was useless to question Anna further, she wouldn't spill the surprise Father had planned, but I knew she was in on it. I could see it in her eyes.

Combing out my hair until it was dry, and shone of rich copper, Anna then fashioned my hair up with green satin ribbons woven throughout. I was getting more excited by the minute. What could it be this mysterious surprise? Two years ago, Father had gifted me with my own horse, a Friesian stallion I named Dante. He was black as coal, large of frame and every inch of him was magnificent!

I couldn't imagine Father ever topping that birthday surprise, and my mind could imagine all kinds of things. But for the life of me, I was stumped.

After one last look in the mirror, with a critical eye, I kissed Anna on the cheek and gave her a big squeeze and headed for the bedroom door.

"Wait!" Anna called out as my hand was on the doorknob. I turned as she rushed toward me holding out my wrap.

"Just in case you get cold," she offered, placing it in my hand.

"Thank you," I said. "Truly, for all that you do for me every day. I am so grateful that we are friends," I said, emotion getting the better of me. "I don't know what is wrong with me today." Tears welled up in my eyes.

"Me too. Now off with you before you make everyone late and your father has my hide," she said. Then turning around, she headed off to the dressing room as if she had something important to do. Running down the stairs, a strange feeling washed over me—a premonition, if you believe in that sort of thing. I stopped midway down and caught hold of the railing to steady myself. I felt the most distinct impression that something was about to change and that nothing would ever be the same again.

Taking a deep breath and then another to steady my racing heart, I opened my eyes and started down the steps once again, just a little more cautiously this time.

The London Wharf was teeming with activity and excitement, like so many worker bees in a hive striving for the common good. I don't think that I'd ever realized just how much activity took place at the wharf, with the loading and unloading of ships that would soon be off to exotic ports of call, all in the name of commerce.

While sitting in Father's carriage waiting his return, another carriage pulled up next to me blocking my view. A few short moments later, the carriage door opened, and Uncle Jamie hopped in and sat across from me.

I was left speechless. All I could do was screech and throw myself into his open arms.

Father jerked the carriage door open as if he would strangle the first person he could get his hands on. Jamie and I turned in surprise to see Father standing there, his face beet red, looking like he would murder someone. We of course found it very funny and started to laugh.

"Oh, Father, you should see your face," I said through the tears streaming down my cheeks. Then, of course, Jamie started to laugh again, and Father thought the whole scene was ridiculous as he stepped into the carriage and shut the door.

"Have you told her yet?" Jamie asked of his older brother.

"No, I was on my way back to the carriage when I saw the carriage jumping around like a carnival show and heard Angelina scream. I thought one of those wharf rats had accosted her."

"So can I tell her? Please, I really want to be the one," Jamie asked with a twinkle of excitement in his eyes.

"All right, if you—" Father was cut off in midsentence by Jamie's jubilance and excitement.

"We are going to take the *Lady Clarisse* on a voyage to Italy. And by *we*, I mean you and me." Jamie gestured with his hands, pointing back and forth between us. "Doesn't that sound like fun?" Jamie blurted out with exuberance.

Turning to Father with disbelief, I said, "Really, Father? Why, this has got to be one of the best birthday surprises yet!" and I launched myself into his arms. My squeals of delight were not very refined or ladylike. But I didn't care.

Uncle Jamie was better known as Lord Stewart, the youngest brother to Jonathan and Nicholas Stewart. He was as tall and handsome as his older brothers, but instead of jet-black hair, Uncle Jamie had a hint of red in his dark locks. He had been married to Evelyn Marie Jones for two years before he lost her and the boy to complications during childbirth. Uncle Jamie never recovered from the tragic blow, and he never remarried.

Thirty-eight years old with a bit of a reputation with the ladies, some might even say he was a rake. But as far as I was concerned, he was the fun uncle, and I loved the idea of going with him to buy and trade for the family business.

Thirty minutes later, we were out of the carriage and boarding the *Lady Clarisse*, an eighty-five-foot caravel sailing ship fitted with square masts and freshly cleaned decks.

The smell of salt air and the breeze coming up from the east that day could not be more perfect for a trip to the coast of Italy. Father had never allowed me to accompany Uncle Jamie or Uncle Nicholas anywhere, let alone all the way to Italy. So the thought of being on the open ocean seeing different cities was a thrill of a lifetime for me. Oh, what a glorious day this had turned out to be, indeed.

Kissing Father farewell and promising to stick close to Uncle Jamie every step of the way, we were off. The tide was headed out and Captain Kinkaid barked, "Weigh anchor and hoist the main sail." Our journey was under way.

I had been so grateful that Anna handed me a wrap on the way out the door because the breeze had picked up slightly. Since I couldn't bear the thought of leaving the deck before Father was out of sight, and London was no longer in view, the wrap came in handy.

Captain Kincaid barked out orders, and deckhands scurried about securing the rigging, hoisting sails, and getting our ship underway. Uncle Jamie and I stood at the railing, breathing in the glorious sea air. Yes, life was headed in a grand direction, and I couldn't wait to see just where it would take me.

3

JUDE DEVERAUX, CAPTAIN OF A group of French privateers, walked the decks of his newest acquisition, an English Brigantine ship loaded down with goods from the American colonies. The privateers would lure an unsuspecting ship near their eighty-five-foot schooner by appearing to be stranded in the middle of the North Atlantic Ocean near the Bay of Biscay.

The English schooner named *Lady Frances* flew the English colors and a distress flag. A few men were positioned on deck in English clothing and the rest of the crew were out of sight. The ship had also been fitted with hidden cannons in case they were needed. The whole maneuver could normally be managed without a shot being fired. At least that was Captain Deveraux's plan. After all, what good was a ship with a hole in her side or resting at the bottom of the ocean?

Captain Jude Deveraux was a tall and formidable figure of a man. Taller than most of his countrymen, he stood six feet three inches tall, with broad shoulders and well-shaped narrow hips. He had raven-black hair worn long and pulled back in a ponytail most days. But sometimes he liked to leave it wild. It was more for dramatic effect. If one was going to play the part of a bloodthirsty pirate, one must dress the part.

Rumor was that his looks had never been a deterrent when it came to women. And once he set his piercing blue eyes on his victim, all hopes of resistance were lost. At the age of twenty-six, Jude had learned to use those assets to his full advantage. And he always left them wanting more.

Jude had made the mistake of falling in love once at the tender age of nineteen. He had been young and naive and Juliette Moreau had not. She took one look at Jude Deveraux and knew that she had to have him. He fell hard for Juliette who had her eyes set on a bigger prize, the Marquis of Bourbon.

The Marquis of Bourbon was a refined man of advancing years and girth, who came with status, prestige, and wealth. The only things truly important to Juliette Moreau were pedigree, a title, and money!

This unfortunate situation left Jude brokenhearted and vowing to never let a gold-digging woman get the better of him again.

While in the service of King Louis XV during the Seven Years' War, Jude saved the life of the king's favorite cousin, Jean Luc Bernard II. For this he was handsomely rewarded with a ship and a letter of Marque, giving him license to pillage and plunder to his heart's content without fear of prosecution.

His parents also benefited from Jude's heroics. They were given land and titles and appointed to the royal court. His father was made prime minister of France, making him Count Philippe Gerard Deveraux of Bordeaux, a diplomat to the French Crown. And Jude's mother was named Countess Genevieve Sophia Deveraux of Bordeaux. She traveled with her husband everywhere and loved her only child Jude very much.

Jude was made captain of his own ship and given the title Duke of Bayonne, which came with land as well. His estates lay along the coastline of France. The properties were side by side and conveniently situated along the Bay of Biscay, which turned out to be Jude's favorite place to return to.

Captain Jude Deveraux walked the decks of the impressive 110 foot Brigantine that was loaded to the gills with colonial goods headed for London by way of Portugal.

The prior captain had made the fateful mistake of getting caught in a severe gale that damaged the main mast. He put into Portugal for repairs and subsequently loaded his ship down with extra supplies making the ship sit dangerously low in the water. The ship carried a crew of only seventy-five men due to natural attrition of an ocean voyage. Fifteen men had been tossed overboard during a fierce gale—and the subsequent illness that followed. The captain of the *Miranda* further jeopardized his ship by coming upon a seemingly vulnerable schooner, the *Lady Frances* at dusk. The majority of the *Miranda* crew was below deck resting before their shift change, leaving the ship vulnerable to attack.

Upon capturing the *Miranda*, Captain Deveraux's men disarmed the crew, blindfolded them, and placed them below deck of the schooner *Lady Frances*. A skeleton crew sailed them to nearby landfall and freed the men on neutral ground (never being able to identify their abductors, for they never saw their faces).

4

I AWOKE THAT MORNING, A FEELING of foreboding in the pit of my stomach. I dressed in a simple, dark blue, cotton dress, pulling my hair back and up with a couple of pins.

In my attempts to stay busy, I had been helping Cook each day in the galley. I didn't care if I stirred porridge in the mornings and peeled potatoes in the afternoon. It felt great to be of some use. I enjoyed getting to know the crew by name.

Sailors by nature are a ruckus and rough sort, but I found them to be refreshingly honest. Their language could be a bit colorful, but they cleaned it up some in my presence.

Afterward I enjoyed walking along the decks in the ocean breeze or reading a book from Captain Kincaid's library. It all helped to make the time pass quickly.

"Good morning to you, Mr. Jones," I said to Cook as I put my apron on attempting to sound extra cheerful that morning.

Cook was as round as he was tall with a receding hairline and a pleasant disposition. He had a bit of an Irish brogue, and he loved to hum as he cooked. He reminded me of a little leprechaun. The only thing missing was a shillelagh and a pot of gold.

"Top of the morn to ya, lassie, I trust you slept well," he called over his shoulder as he busily prepared the biscuits.

"Like a baby gently rocked by her momma. How can I help this morning?"

"The porridge could use a bit of water and a little loving care, if you know what I'm a sayin'." He gestured toward the pot of thick porridge with his head.

"I'll get straight to it," I said as I retrieved the pitcher of water and looked around for the other pitcher that held the fresh milk.

"I did wake up this morning with a strange feeling. Like something different is coming, and I can't quite shake the feeling," I casually said, trying to make conversation while stirring the large pot of glop.

"So you got a wee bit of the sight in ya, now don't you, lassie?" he said as he turned and gave me a grin and a wink.

"What do you mean, 'a wee bit of the sight in me'?" I said, mimicking his brogue.

"My ma and her ma always knew when things were about to be changing or when things were just a wee bit off. My ma said it was like a tingle that touched her deep. Like someone reached in and touched her soul, and she always knew something was about to change," he said with a reverent hush.

"Oh, don't be daft, as if I could tell the future." I tried to laugh it off.

"Now don't go tempting the gods, little lassie. They don't like being made a fool. You best be paying attention now." And with that, he turned to preparing the meal while humming an Irish tune. I pondered his words in silence.

The rest of the morning passed without incident, and I enjoyed my stroll on deck. The skies were turning a dark gray, and one of the deck hands said there was a storm blowing in. He had a bad knee that always let him know that rain was coming.

The man in the crow's nest called out, "Ship to port, Captain, dead in the water. She is flying English colors and a distress flag, sir."

Captain Kincaid called out, "Bring her about, boys, and somebody bring me my looking glass."

The men started a shanty while they worked to change the rigging. It helped them to stay in sync.

"Up aloft this yard must go," one man would call out, and a group would respond while pulling ropes in unison.

"Way hay and up you go."
"Up aloft from down below."
"Way hay and up you go."
"Up you go to see the crows flying."
"Way hay and up you go."
"A top the nest from down below."
"Way hay and up you go."
"I can see land a yo ho ho."
"Way hay and up you go."
"I can stay here all day long."
"Way hay and up you go."
"I can kiss the girls from way up here."
"Way hay and up you go."
"They come to me when I touch the stars."
"Way hay and up you go."

"Proceed with caution, boys, keep a sharp eye out," the captain called.

Uncle Jamie had been below deck playing cards with some of the men to pass the time and had wandered around deck for fresh air.

"What seems to be the matter?" Jamie asked, standing close to me while putting a protective arm around my shoulder.

"I'm not quite sure, but it seems there is an English ship flying a distress flag. The captain wants to check it out."

"Well, this could be a bit of excitement. One can only play so many hands of cards before the old backside gets stiff," he said as he put his hands to his lower back and stretched some to relieve his stiffness.

As we came about, the ship was off to our port side. We could see a dozen men standing at the rail waving to us. They were dressed in full English military uniforms and greeted us with cheers.

When we were a mere fifteen feet apart, Captain Kincaid called out to them, "What seems to be the problem, boys, and how can we be of service today?"

The man from the other ship called back, gesturing to the other crewmen, "Our captain, first mate, and most of the crew have fallen ill. All we have left is what you see. Could we get some provisions from you?" the man asked sincerely.

"We can spare a barrel of water, and some oats, but I don't want your sickness to spread to my crew," the captain stated firmly.

"We would be grateful for anything you could spare, sir," the other man said with a little too much emphasis on the word *spare*. Suddenly, the whole ship came alive with men and grappling hooks.

The men who had been dressed in military uniforms reached into their pockets pulling out scarves tying them around their faces. The rest of the crew came out from hiding, and with ear splitting yells, they boarded our ship with firearms and swords.

Before our captain and crew could fully react to defend themselves, the ship had been boarded and taken over by the band of pirates.

While everyone was distracted, Jamie had pushed me behind him and was backing up toward a long boat turned over on deck. He pushed me down and said, "Don't come out for anything." Then he stepped away.

A scream caught in my throat as panic and fear combined to keep me frozen. I couldn't breathe, and my brain went numb. I could barely comprehend what was happening.

I wanted to run after Uncle Jamie and pull him under the boat with me. Then out of the chaos and noise, there came a hush on the deck. I wanted to sneak a look, but sheer panic kept me frozen to the spot.

"We are privateers, and we are seizing the contents of this ship. If you cooperate, no one will be hurt. We don't wish to make anyone's wife a widow today, so follow orders, and everyone will make it out alive," the man said in perfect English with a hint of a foreign accent.

"Is everyone accounted for? We wouldn't want anyone to miss out on all the fun now, would we, boys?" The man asked boldly as he walked about my family's ship.

"Come on now, speak up. You there, in the fancy clothes with your fancy boots, step forward," he ordered. "What is your name?" the leader said, pointing to Uncle Jamie.

"James Stewart, my good man, what can I do for you today?" Jamie said, stepping forward, trying to sound jovial and upbeat for someone whose ship had just been boarded by pirates.

"Are there any others who might be hiding about this ship? Be quick about it, man, or it will cost you your life," he taunted with an undertone of a threat lacing his words. The sound of his boots hitting the boards of the deck grated on my raw nerves as he passed several times by the overturned boat I was hiding under. My pulse quickened even more, and I was like a trapped rabbit with nowhere to run.

As Jamie stammered for an answer, the boat I was hiding under was suddenly gone. I looked up to see a hulk of a man lifting the small craft with one hand and reaching down to take hold of my arm with the other. He yanked me upright and to my feet as I screamed in surprise.

Dropping the boat and pulling me against him, he pinned my one arm behind my back. I feared my legs would give out as I started to see stars. Everything moved in slow motion, including my brain.

Standing, I took several deep breaths to calm my racing heart and clear my head. I mustered the will to be strong and face this beast dressed as a man. Turning my face upward, I squared my shoulders and willed myself not to flinch or look away.

With my best defiant stare, I put my free hand against his chest and gave a little rebellious shove against his chest. "Good, sir, if you would please unhand me, I would greatly appreciate it," I said as my voice shook only slightly, trying not to give away my total disdain for him.

Releasing my trapped arm and stepping back a bit, he gave me a polite bow and said in a mocking voice, "Forgive me, my lady, if I did offend."

He wore well-made black boots that hugged his calves and came just above his knees. His breaches were tan in color and formed around his muscular thighs. His crisp white shirt, which hung open at the neck, was belted at his waist.

My eyes made their way with effort to his bearded face, for he was taller than most. Our eyes connected, and I felt a slight moment of trepidation as the hair on the nape of my neck stood on end.

I was staring into the bluest eyes I had ever seen. They were the color of sapphires as they burned a hole straight through me.

His hair was completely covered by a red scarf, but I could tell it was black and very long, and he wore another scarf across his face.

We stood there for a moment assessing each other without a word. It was as if time had momentarily stopped.

"Throw him overboard," he ordered, pointing his finger at Jamie while still holding my gaze.

"No. Stop! I beg you don't hurt him," I screamed as panic rose in my throat.

"So you wish to save your lover," the man scoffed, sarcasm dripping from his lips.

I suddenly began to laugh. I don't know why I did it, but I did. Maybe it was stress getting the better of me. Maybe my circumstance was too bizarre.

I was trapped on a ship in the middle of the ocean by a man who had held me so tightly I could smell the soap he used to bathe with that day. The thought of a pirate taking a bath before raiding a ship was, well, funny to me.

Then he subtly raised an eyebrow as he grabbed me again and gave me a little shake. Maybe he thought I had suddenly lost my faculties and gone stark raving mad.

Copper-colored hair spilled loose from its constraint and tumbled down my shoulders and back as I suddenly came to my senses. After all, I was surrounded by pirates.

Uncle Jamie stepped forward. "Stop that and unhand her," he demanded, trying to pull me free from the pirate, for which he was rewarded with a kick to the back of the knees dropping him down on all fours. Then another pirate knocked him out with a punch to the face.

I screamed, pulling my arm from his grasp and ran toward Uncle Jamie. Two more pirates impeded my progress. With angry tears in my eyes, I turned back to the leader. My blood boiling now, I did not care what happened to me, but I would protect my family at all cost.

"He is my uncle, and this is our family's ship. It carries nothing more exciting than some textiles we make in our factory," I screamed. My anger barely contained as I spat the words at him, pulling my arms free from the two men and making my way back to where he stood.

"I hardly think you will get rich off of the haul you take from us today, but you are welcome to it," I finished saying, as I now stood toe to toe with him, defiance reflected in my eyes.

Reaching out, he grabbed my arm, twisting it behind my back as he pulled me up against his taut body.

"You speak boldly, my lady, and yet I can feel your heart racing," he stated while holding tightly to my wrist, wrenching it even higher than before.

"I have never come face-to-face with a real pirate before. So you will forgive me if I don't know how to react," I said sarcastically.

"A privateer!" he corrected while still staring uncomfortably into my eyes.

"Pirate or privateer, whatever name you give yourself, you are still cut from the same cloth. The only difference between the two careers is one has a license to pillage, plunder, and murder and the other one doesn't," I stated, all the while staring straight into his deep blue eyes, trying to gauge how my words had been received.

First his eyes seemed to cloud up, and I was sure a storm was coming my way, but I didn't care. Tossing my head back in defiance, I dared him to do his worst, and then he startled me when suddenly he turned loose my arm and began to laugh.

I stood in complete shock, not quite sure what had just happened. I fully expected to be murdered right there on the deck of the family ship.

"Get these men secured below deck," he barked at his crew.

Jumping into action, they obeyed, his crew moved the prisoners in one direction like sheep to the slaughter.

A rough hand took hold of my arm as I turned to see what was happening. I was being pulled in the opposite direction of everyone else. A question formed on my lips but was silenced by a muscular arm grabbing me by the waist like a vise. I struggled to free myself while looking over the pirate's shoulder for Uncle Jamie who was being carried along by the crew of the *Lady Clarisse*.

Turning in time to see the pirate captain take hold of a rope with his other hand and leaping from the deck of the ship, I screamed and scrambled to take hold of something by wrapping my arms tightly about his neck, squeezing my eyes closed.

Mere seconds later, he landed on the deck of the pirate ship with a loud thud and yet I kept my grip tight and my eyes shut. He shifted my weight, and I could feel his suppressed amusement by the reverberation through his stone-hard chest. But I didn't care. I couldn't swim, and I was genuinely scared.

He continued to carry me across the deck, down a few steps, and through a doorway. He kicked the door shut with his booted foot, and it slammed with a resounding bang.

Depositing me unceremoniously on the bed, he turned and walked across the room to retrieve two glasses and a carafe. Setting them down on the large table, he removed his hat and scarves, tossing them down on the table.

Coming to my senses, I scrambled from the large bed, but wasn't sure how I would escape this viper's nest.

Looking down, I noticed that my top buttons had come undone in my attempts to free myself, and I was providing him a wonderful view of my overflowing assets.

I felt the heat rising to my cheeks, and yet I refused to let him see the panic threatening to overtake me. I willed my hands not to shake as I buttoned my gown and smoothed my skirts. Then, with great effort, I swept back the stray hairs that had tumbled into my face. With one last deep breath, I straightened my spine, squared my shoulders and looked him directly in the eyes.

"Well, that was terribly fun, can we do it again?" I said with great sarcasm, for which he rewarded me with another rich, deep laugh.

Tipping the chair back on two legs, he put his boots on the table. "Drink?" he offered, holding a cup up to me from his seated position at the table.

"Yes, thank you, I've had a bloody dreadful day." Attempting to sound calm, while moving as far away from his bed as possible, I took the cup and drank long and deep. Immediately, realizing my mistake when the heat rose to my cheeks, I began to gasp for air as the contents burned my throat.

"What the bloody hell did you give me? Poison?" I said through my gasps for air, followed by a fit of coughing.

"That's some of the best whisky that can be had, straight from the American colonies," he said with just a hint of amusement in his voice. "We commandeered it from an Irish ship just yesterday."

"Water," was all I could manage between my clenched teeth as I fixed him with a murderous stare.

"Of course, where are my manners?" Going to the cupboard, he retrieved a different carafe and poured the water in a glass and brought it to me.

Feeling suspicious of his motives, I first smelled the contents of the glass. Finding it to be water, I drank as if I had been lost in the desert for a week.

"So what shall I call you, mademoiselle?" He feigned genteel politeness as he helped me into a chair across the table.

"Lady Angelina Marguerite Amelia Stewart," I stated boldly, lifting my chin just a bit for emphasis, all the while looking directly at him.

"My, that is a mouthful. I think I will address you as Lady Stewart just to show you my manners."

"And what do you like to be called?" I asked, attempting to ascertain with whom I was dealing. I maintained eye contact to hide the fact that my legs were shaking so uncontrollably that my knees were knocking together.

"You, madam, may address me as Captain or Sir," he answered back, all the while looking directly back at me. "You stare, madam, do you like what you see? Or perhaps you simply find me handsome?" he asked with bold directness.

"No! Ah . . . heavens, no," I stammered unsure what game he was playing now.

Taking a better look at him now, I decided to change tactics. "What I meant to say is, I don't know. Your hair, it is long. You wear it wildly tossed about, and please excuse my frankness, but what is with the braids?" I stated, picking him apart piece by piece deciding that he was obviously too full of himself. "And this beard, it is long and wild as well. It hides your features. So I dare say I could not tell you if I find you handsome or not. You could be physically appealing to a certain type of woman, but you hide behind anonymity with your beard and hair." I gestured with my hand, tilting my head from one side to the other, trying to see beyond the scruff of all that hair. "As for my staring at you, good sir, I do apologize for the rudeness, but I am having difficulty reconciling your demeanor with your speech. You are a pirate who speaks like a gentleman," I said in a tone that bordered on insolence.

"Privateer!" he corrected, irritation building in his tone.

"Yes, yes, so you keep saying. My uncle and the other men, they won't be harmed then? Since a pirate and a privateer, according to you have entirely different sets, of standards," I finished with a biting tone of cynicism.

"We aren't barbarians! Your men will be well taken care of," he said as he stood and walked to the large glass window that stood open to the ocean breeze. "You puzzle me, madam."

"Oh? How so, if I may be so bold in my asking?" I countered.

"You swear like a sailor and dress like a lowly maid, but you speak like a high born. Tell me what exactly are they teaching young ladies in finishing school these days?" His words were meant as a barb to my character.

His reproach stung, and again, I could feel the color climbing to my face and decided to change the subject.

"So why did you bring me here, and for what purpose, dare I ask?" I cautiously inquired as I also walked to the window to gaze at the ocean below. I decided to attempt to make some kind of connection between us in the hope that I could save my family's ship and crew.

"I like your boldness and feel I might enjoy your company for a time. Perhaps we could speak as equals," he commented while staring out to sea. "You don't cower and shrink from me. I find that most refreshing," he concluded, turning toward me to study my face.

I found his stare penetrating like a thunderstorm with lightning. The hair on my neck stood on end as he took a step closer to me.

A knock on the door interrupted him, and he turned to address the intruder.

"Enter and state your business," the captain called out.

"Sir, Cook asks if there will be one or two for dinner, and if you would like it brought up soon?" the young crewman asked while looking at the captain directly.

"Tell Cook that he may ready supper for two and leave it at the door. We will dine at the usual time. Thank you, boy. That will be all."

"Yes, sir." And with that, the cabin boy walked out and shut the door.

Walking over to a tall cabinet in the corner of the room, he opened it and rummaged through, looking for something in particular.

Removing a dress from the cabinet, he shut the door, depositing a lovely, navy blue, satin gown on the bed, then turned and fixed me with a look that sent a shiver up my spine.

"If you would indulge me, my lady, I think you will find this garment most suitable. Will you require my assistance to put it on?" he asked, fixing me with a rakish smile. "I am very good with buttons and hooks," he informed me.

A blush crept up my chest once again, and I turned toward the window to find my composure. "No, thank you. I believe I can manage," I said over my shoulder, praying all the while that he would leave me to change in peace and not stay to watch.

"As you wish, mademoiselle." And with that, I heard the door close quietly behind me and then silence.

Sweet precious silence, I thought to myself, breathing in a deep cleansing breath of the ocean air.

Taking notice of the darkened skies, I breathed deeply again. It smelled like a storm was coming. I guess the man with the bad leg was right.

An hour later, there came a knock on the door, then a pause.

"Come in," I called out.

The door opened cautiously, and the young man from earlier entered. He hung several lit lanterns, then set about lighting the sconces that hung around the cabin and the candles on the table.

The room, taking on an intimate atmosphere of glowing candle light, did not help quiet my apprehensions and misgivings about eating alone with a pirate.

My frayed nerves were raw as I stood at the window in my borrowed gown, watching the last bit of light fade from the dusky sky.

The young man exited the room without a word and, as if on cue, the captain entered.

He had changed into formal evening attire. His jacket was green and brown brocade with gold threading throughout. He wore a freshly laundered white shirt tucked into his dark brown trousers. The boots were of fine Italian leather, black on the bottom with a cuff of brown along the top. He was the picture of French nobility except for the long beard and hair. He had taken the braids out of his hair, pulling it back he had plaited it, which only added to his rakishly masculine good looks.

Carrying in a large tray, which he placed in the middle of the table, he greeted me with a most gracious smile, as if we were merely long-time acquaintances sitting down to a friendly meal.

"I see you fared well with the gown. And might I add how lovely that color is on you," he said with a display of courtly graciousness that also added to the discomfort of my situation.

The gown was fashionable but very low cut and swept just off the shoulders. The skirt of the gown opened in the front to reveal my delicate petticoats in a slightly more provocative way than I would have liked. The only real problem with the gown was my inability to fasten all the hooks and buttons down the back. So there I stood in my state of undress.

"I have only one complaint with your dress, sir. You see, try as I may, I am not a contortionist, and I am unable to fasten the gown. Would you mind?" I asked as I stood still casting my eyes to the ground.

Slowly walking over to me, stopping only inches from me for a full minute before tipping my head slowly up, forcing my eyes to meet his gaze, he leaned down close to my ear. "I know I told you I was an expert at buttons and hooks, but what I neglected to tell you was that I am more prone to undoing them," he purred seductively in my ear.

Before my right hand could land a slap a crossed his face, he grabbed it in anticipation of my reaction, spun me around in one fluid motion and pinned me against the wall with his body. Turning loose of my arm, I used them both to brace against the wall, terrified to move and enrage him further.

He stood so close to me I could feel his breath on the back of my neck as he mocked me with a derisive laugh. His hands were large and his touch burned my skin through the thin cloth as he fastened the gown.

My knees had begun to shake, and I feared I might fall to the ground if not for the fact that I was pinned against the wall by his solid body. Taking one large breath and letting it out slowly and then another attempting to clear my head, I could still feel his hot breath on my neck as he worked to fasten the last few buttons.

When he had finished, he turned me back around and placed my hand over his arm in a gentlemanly fashion as he led me to the table. Pulling out a chair and seeing me properly seated before stepping around the table, he took the seat across from mine.

"Now what shall we talk about tonight?" he asked, rubbing his hands together as if he couldn't wait for the fun to begin. "Let's see, do you read much?"

Finding my voice once again, I said, "How are my uncle and crew doing, Captain? May I see them soon?" I asked as I noticed the joy leave his face, replaced with a mask of politeness.

"I told you that they are fine, but how they fare is dependent upon you." I seemed to understand his thinly-veiled threat.

He suddenly seemed angry. Standing to retrieve the tray of food, I noticed him taking several deep breaths to gain control of his frustration.

"Wine?" he asked. As he turned back around, he had miraculously become the doting host once again.

"Yes, please," I replied.

"Now I hope you don't turn out to be like every other woman I know. Appearances can be so deceiving. They are lovely on the outside and no true substance on the inside," he said mockingly.

He poured me a glass of wine, then handed it to me as he placed a plate of cheese and bread before me, and waited for my reaction.

Gauging that I would get nowhere with him using the direct approach, I decided that I would play along and beat him at his own game.

"I quite know what you mean. All the women I know haven't a care in the world beyond marriage, children, and a healthy wallet to sponsor their lifestyle. It is simply abhorrent to me the emptiness of their heads, and the way they maneuver for the best matches," I said, lifting my wine to my mouth and sipping while I studied him over the rim of my glass.

"What of you? Doesn't your father have someone lined up for you to marry? You have to be what, eighteen or nineteen? Isn't there someone you are pining for?" he asked.

"No!" I said with a credulous look on my face, while wagging my finger to and fro in the air. "My father has not lined someone up for me as if I am his property to do with as he will. Nor am I a bargaining chip to furthering his place in society. Our family is different, and as such, I was brought up differently. The choice will be mine if the time ever comes that I would choose to get married. But it will never happen, so there is no need to discuss the matter further."

"What do you mean it will never happen? Is there something wrong with you?

"On the contrary," I corrected him. "I am completely in my right mind and healthy as a horse."

"But I thought every woman dreamed of being married," he said, completely confused.

"I would agree with you to a point. But I see marriage as a life sentence. Men want to rule over them and abuse them, and it's just not for me," I said, placing some cheese in my mouth.

"Is that how your father treats your mother? Where did you come up with this thought process of yours?" he asked with real interest.

Nearly choking on my cheese, I coughed a minute, taking a sip of wine to clear my throat.

"My father treats my mother like a queen, but all men are not like my father, and I have seen and heard of too many bad tales of men marrying for fortune, taking a mistress, spending his wife's entire fortune, then leaving her and the children destitute or worse: a wife living in fear of her husband's return home because she knows when he does finally leave his mistress he will beat her and torment the children. And I ask you what recourse does that woman have? None! No, thank you. That is not the life for me," I finished dramatically, putting my empty glass down on the table.

"How did one so young become so cynical?" he asked, staring at me intently.

"I don't know if it is cynicism or just being aware of what is really happening in the world. Young ladies are cloistered away as if they are a fine China doll. Then they are handed over to the highest bidder for money or title, dreaming of their happily ever after, and what do they really get in the end?" I asked, shaking my index finger at him while looking directly into his eyes as if he were the offending man.

"What do they get besides a nice home and children from the bargain?" he said with a slight air of indignation leaning over the table to fill my glass.

"A gilded cage if they are lucky. A coffin six feet under if they are not," I stated matter-of-factly.

"I am just surprised by your attitude, that is all."

"Did I shock you?" I asked as I stood with the intent to close the window. The breeze had picked up, and I was getting cold.

"You have expressed your opinion of marriage and women. How do you feel about Voltaire?"

"I like him. Voltaire wrote, 'It is better to risk saving a guilty person —'"

"Than to condemn an innocent one," he finished my sentence with excitement, like a child who just received a new toy. Walking over to me, he placed the filled glass of wine in my hand, as he continued. "Have you read any of Rousseau?"

"Of course. Would you like to speak of his latest writings, *The Social Contract*?" I said as I held my wine with one hand trying to close the window with the other.

"Yes, that very one," he continued. "Here let me," he said. Touching my hand as he moved close to me to close the window, a spark nearly popped between us, causing me to jump in surprise.

Taking another sip of wine, I pretended to study something through the window in the distance.

"Did you hear me? I asked if you enjoyed Rousseau's writings," he asked again.

"Of course. He is brilliant, but I prefer Montesquieu, *The Spirit of the Laws*. And I quote, 'Liberty consists of being able to do what you want to do, and not being forced to do what you do not want to do.' It just might be the most perfect definition of *liberty* that I have ever read," I said reverently.

"And is this what they are teaching young ladies for curriculum at modern finishing schools?" he asked with a playful smile.

"No, I am afraid not. I like to borrow my brother's books and dig for treasures in Father's library. It's fascinating what one can find if you bother to look."

"Most extraordinary," he said, turning toward me and fixing me with his penetrating eyes. "You truly are most extraordinary."

As I stood staring into the fathomless depths of his eyes, I found my emotions confused. Never before had I desired to be kissed by any man, as I stood in front of this man being drawn to him like a flower to the sun. What would it feel like? Would I run screaming from the room, or would I never want it to stop?

A knock on the door temporarily broke the spell as he called out to the unwelcomed intruder. "It better damn well be important," he bellowed while still fixing me with his intense stare. Then turning toward the door as it opened, the young man cautiously entered.

Stammering for just a second, the boy cleared his throat and found his spine. "Ah yes, sir, I was told to inform you that there is a storm coming, and inquire what do you want to do about the two ships still being tied together?" he inquired, diverting his eyes downward.

"Take the sails down on both ships and cut us loose. Tell the first mate to stay close and head for the cove. We will meet up at our regular rendezvous when it blows over," he ordered with the ease and comfort of one used to being in complete control.

With that the young man closed the door quietly and the captain turned to me again trying to read my face.

"So what does that mean for me? And what about the crew trapped below on the other ship, will they be all right?" I asked concerned for my uncle and the entire crew.

"You will stay here with me tonight, and we will see what we see in the morning," he informed me with a confident smile playing across his mouth.

Walking to my chair, he again pulled it out and stood waiting for me to take my seat. I finished the glass of wine I was holding and then took my seat. I felt slightly intoxicated, and it had nothing to do with the wine.

"Perhaps you would like some supper now before the seas get too rough," he said with a slight lift of one eyebrow, as if his statement had a dual meaning.

I swallowed hard. "Yes, I think that might be wise." I needed time to think, and right now my brain was betraying me. All I could think about was what his gloriously full lips might feel like pressed against mine.

Dinner consisted of fish seasoned and poached with a wine and mushroom sauce, served with steamed carrots, crusty bread, and soft cheese.

After supper, we enjoyed a plate of dried figs and apricots. The topic of conversation ranged from philosophy to the state of the economy in England as opposed to France. And somewhere between the main course and dessert the seas became rougher, and the rain began to fall.

We extinguished the candles on the table, fearing they might tip over. We moved to the window to enjoy the light show displayed by the storm.

The remaining lighting in the room threw off a most intimate glow, when it happened.

Leaning over to put his empty glass down, the ship pitched suddenly, causing me to lose my balance. Grabbing hold of me with one arm, he steadied himself against the wall with the other. Placing his back to the wall, he pulled me around, crushing me to his chest.

His mouth hovered above mine for just a moment before his lip came down on mine ever so tender. Then one hand came up and wrapped around my neck, and his kiss became demanding. Like a starving man finely served a meal, his lips devoured mine as his tongue hungrily sought for more.

My mind was screaming in protest, but my senses were reeling. All at once, I couldn't breathe, and I didn't care. Nothing in my imaginings had prepared me for the sensation of this. Momentarily lost in the sensation, I let him kiss me deeper as I reciprocated.

His lips left mine as he moved to my throat and then to my shoulders. An entirely new sensation assaulted my mind, and a moan escaped from my throat, and the very core of me began to melt. I pushed hard against his chest with all my might and attempted to voice my protest as his hands reached for the buttons of my gown. I couldn't tell if the ship was pitching or if I had lost all sense of up from down.

Lifting his head to look into my eyes, I could see the war that raged behind his storm-filled orbs.

Shrugging out of his coat, he simply dropped it to the ground. Lifting me in his muscular arms, he headed for the bed. Tenderly placing me on the bed and weaving his fingers through my hair, he began to kiss me so desperately and deeply, that I could hardly have told you my name let alone what day it was.

I scarcely knew what was happening when my gown fell from my shoulders and onto the floor as I stood there in my thin white slip.

Lifting me up once again, as if I weighed a mere few ounces, he gently laid me across his bed. In one fluid motion, he untied his white linen shirt and pulled it over his head.

Curiosity causing my eyes to wonder every magnificent inch of his muscular, scar-filled chest. My wanton desire turning my limbs to liquid unable to stop what would be coming next and not even sure I wanted to try.

Kneeling in the middle of the bed, he reached down and took my hand, pulling me up to face him. Lightning flashed just outside, lighting the interior of the cabin for only a moment, yet the unbridled passion that reflected back at me sent a lurid sensation up my spine.

Reaching for him as if in need of sustenance, I ran my fingers through his hair and pulled his mouth to mine. Every nerve was raw, and I desired what I did not have words for yet.

My breathing had become sporadic, and my mind wasn't working. This wasn't me. I was not that kind of woman. I scoffed at promiscuous women.

I had never before thought that such sensual desire was possible and yet here I was, aching for his touch.

The storm outside raged on, but the only fear I had was being completely consumed by his passion, leaving behind nothing more of me than a burnt pile of ashes.

I barely noticed the pounding at the door and the man, yelling, "Captain, come quick!"

I could not tell you if the groan of anguish came from my throat or his, but slowly, he stood. Torn between duty and desire, he bent to retrieve his shirt and put it on before going to the door. Opening the door, he stepped into the hall to speak to his crew member.

Suddenly, a chill came over me, and I realized what had nearly happened. I could not say for sure if I was angry at myself or disappointed that we were interrupted.

Propriety started to seep into my numb brain. Crawling beneath the quilt, I turned to face the wall. A flush of shame washed over me, and I began to shake. The sting of tears welled in my eyes, but I refused to let them fall. How could I have so quickly become a fallen unchaste woman? What magic did he used to cast his wicked spell over me? And what would come next?

Quietly entering the room, I heard him rummaging around in the cabinet, his boots hit the ground with a terse clunk one after the other. I wanted him to say something, anything, but instead, he changed his clothes and started toward the bed, stopping just a few feet from where I lay.

If only I knew what he was thinking! Did he think me a strumpet, or a woman of easy virtue?

Turning without a word, he extinguished all the sconces, but one. Then made his way to the cupboard and removed the carafe of whiskey. Pouring a glass, he swallowed it all down at once.

Without a word, he opened the cabin door and walked out, slamming the door behind him.

The raging storm blowing outside was no match for the storm that raged inside of me. Tears flowed hot and free, as my shame scalded and tormented my very core.

Hours passed, and the storm continued, becoming stronger and more agitated, like my mood. My pitiable disposition turned to anger, as my resolve hardened. I pulled back the covers and placed my feet on the floor and was immediately thrown back into bed by a sudden pitching of the ship. My stomach began to feel like the frenzied ocean beating against the ship. Jumping from the bed, I made a frantic search of the cabin for an acceptable receptacle for my stomach's contents. Finding an empty bowl, I relieved myself of the evening's victuals. Feeling spent, I went in search of my clothes.

Finding three more evening gowns of varying sizes in the cabinet, the only alternative was the previously worn evening gown, discarded on the floor next to the bed along with my dignity.

I felt my staunch resolve begin to fade. The memory of his touch burned anew, and the taste of his mouth on mine was more than I could stand.

He smelled of masculinity and salty ocean breezes. His lips were soft, warm, tender and demanding, all at the same time.

I found myself unable to put the dress back on again without reliving every shameful moment of the evening. I pulled a quilt off the end of the bed and headed for the large high-backed chair positioned by the window. Wrapping the blanket around me, I curled up in the chair to await the captain's return.

Coming out of a fitful dream, hours later, my eyes and mind had difficulty adjusting to the dim predawn light that filled the room. Recollections awakened in me like the rising sun as I stood and straightened my leg, and my cramped neck.

Feeling my way over to the bed because the cabin was still awash in darkness, I decided that I was in dire need of a comfortable bed. The cold room combined with the uncomfortable chair left my limbs stiff and sore.

Climbing into bed, I snuggled deep into the blankets before I realizing my mistake.

Sometime in the dark, while I slept, the captain had come in from the storm soaked to the skin from the rain. Stripping off his wet clothing, he had climbed into bed and fallen asleep.

Fearing that I would awaken him by moving too fast, I attempted to move slowly. I had moved no more than an inch or two when a large hand snaked out and snagged me by the waist, pulling me closer to his unadorned body and trapping my legs under his.

"I see you finally decided to bless me with your presence," he purred in my ear as he began to come awake.

Attempting to remove myself from his viselike grip, my squirming only made matters worse. "Honestly, I didn't know you had returned or that you were asleep," I cried as panic was setting in.

"So you wished to find me awake. Well, give me a minute and I will see what I can do about that." A tired smile began to form on his rakish lips.

"No, wait. There has been a mistake." I pushed at his hand as it started its exploration of my breasts.

"The only mistake was my leaving you alone last night to go up on deck," he said in a gravelly, passion-filled voice that was like quicksand to my senses.

My protests were lost as he wrapped his large hands through my hair and around my neck, pulling me to his sensuous lips, kissing me so passionately that all hope of escape was lost in an instant, along with my words of protest.

Leaning up on his elbow, he laid me back on the pillow as my eyes searched his face.

I began to explore more completely the contours of his scars. I touched him tentatively at first then more boldly as my confidence grew.

The feel of his solid form as his muscles moved under my hands sent a thrilling sensation through me. I knew it was wrong, but something about him made it impossible for me to resist. The sudden quickening of desire was foreign, and I was unable to fathom to what end it would all lead. The only thing I knew for sure was my mind had given up thinking for the moment.

"Angelina, you are an angel," he whispered feverishly against my throat as he trailed impassioned kisses downward, unhooking the bodice of my slip and slipping his hand beneath the thin material to retrieve his prize.

My breathing now coming in ragged pants as I fought to find my sanity that was slipping away as I was consumed by him.

His lips worked their magic while his mouth ravaged my flesh. I moaned deep in my throat, wrapping my fingers through his hair, encouraging him on.

Looking up I found his tempest-filled eyes penetrating me to my marrow as he studied my face. "I beg you release me from the spell you have cast over me," I rasped while trying to catch my breath.

Groaning as if he were in pain, he raked his hand through his raven hair. "Oh, Angel, how you make me burn with desire for you, and I fear that it is not I who has cast the spell, but you have bewitched me with some dark magic you possess," he rasped as his French accent became thicker.

I turned my head slightly to the side to hide the tears stinging my eyes as distress and humiliation began to set in again. Disentangling myself from his grasp, I sat up and moved away, turning my back to him to hide my disgrace. Quickly working to right my disheveled appearance, I fastened my bodice and walked to the window. The chill in the room helped to cool the hot flush that had crept its way to my face.

"I was unable to find the gown I was wearing yesterday," I said over my shoulder while trying to keep my voice level and impassionate. Wrapping my arms about myself to stop the shaking that had begun, I waited for his reply.

I had not heard him get up, but when I turned to see why he didn't answer, he was standing behind me with a quilt in hand. Wrapping the quilt around my shoulders, he turned me around and tilted my chin up to meet his gaze. We stood like that for a few minutes not speaking. Not moving, just looking at one another; then leaning down slowly, he kissed my cheek so gently. Then he brushed a stray hair from my face with the back of his hand.

"*Ma belle Ange.* My beautiful angel," he said with such tenderness before turning to walk across the room, unashamed of his nudity as he opened the cabin door.

"Boy, bring me the lady's clothes!" he bellowed out the door. Shutting it behind him with a bang, he walked to the cabinet and pulled out a pair of black trousers and slipped them on. I marveled at the ease with which he moved about unashamed of his nakedness. Then he reached in again to retrieve a shirt, slipping it over his head.

A knock on the door interrupted my curious voyeuristic view, and I turned as he walked to the door to retrieve my dress. I heard him saying something to the young man, but my mind was somewhere else, and I had no idea what they discussed.

Laying my dress over a chair and returning to finish dressing in silence, the tension was palpable. He headed for the door but turned back around a moment as if he meant to tell me something and then thought better of it. Opening the door, he stepped out slowly and closed it almost reverently.

Sometime later, I heard a knock on the door and I called out, "Come in." The young cabin boy came in bearing a tray with porridge, toast and tea on it. Setting it on the table, he turned to leave, but I stopped him.

"Please, could you be so kind as to tell me if the captain will be joining me?" I asked while standing at the window.

"No, my lady, he is on deck and will be there awhile," he said, never making eye contact. Turning, he left, shutting the door behind him. I heard a click like the tumbles of a door being locked, but that couldn't be right.

Running to the door, I tried to open it only to realize I had been locked in. I thought to myself that it was curious, but decided that I would attempt to enjoy breakfast and make myself busy while waiting for the captain's return.

I finished my meal, made the bed, washed my face, straightened the room, and still no captain. The sun was now high in the sky, and I was getting more frustrated with each passing hour. Frustration soon turned to anger as the day wore on.

I had paced the floor for another twenty minutes or so when real anger struck. Going to the door, I called out. "Boy, can you hear me? I need to see the captain. Please let me out." I attempted to sound calm and reserved.

Not getting a response, and not caring if I made a fool of myself, I began to pound on the door now, screaming at the door and kicking it at the same time. "Let me out of here right now, you wharf rat! You bunch of cowards! Answer me, you little duffer! I am warning you to unlock this door this instant or I will bloody well make someone pay!" Still I got no response from the other side.

Looking around for inanimate objects I could get my hands on, candle sticks and pitchers were all hurled at the locked door. I imagined the captain's face. Running out of things that were readily at hand, I started pulling cabinets open.

"Ha-ha, this would do," I said to myself as I came across the captain's coveted Irish whiskey.

I was winding up, preparing to throw it when the door suddenly opened, and the true target of my discontent entered. A primal scream of anger and frustration came from my mouth as I hurled the bottle straight at his head.

Scrambling to get out of the way of the flying object, the captain dodged to his right. Unfortunately for him, I had better aim than he anticipated, and the bottle grazed his shoulder, crashing into the doorjamb and shattered into a million shards raining liquid everywhere.

Dissatisfied with my aim, I turned to locate another object to throw. Finding the washbasin, I had used earlier, I dumped the water on the floor just as his strong arm clamped around my waist. Lifting me off the ground in one fluid motion, he plucked the bowl from my hand, setting it safely out of reach.

He began cursing in his native tongue. Fortunately for him, I didn't understand it all. My French was somewhat rusty, but I got the gist of his anger.

Throwing me roughly down on the bed, he glowered at me with eyes ablaze with anger, now void of any amusement. Still muttering curses at me in French, he pulled his fingers through his windblown hair.

"Have you lost your mind? What is the meaning of all this, you little hellion?" he growled at me through clenched teeth while attempting to get his anger under control.

"I warned the little duffer there would be hell to pay if he didn't unlock the door," I screamed at him.

"What did you say?" he asked, glaring at me with an unspoken threat between us.

"You heard what I said. I didn't stutter," I said with my eyes blazing and my tone just as threatening.

He began pacing again, muttering under his breath.

"Why have I been locked in this room all day? I demand you let me out of here to see my uncle!" I yelled at him, coming up on my knees.

Scoffing at me, he lunged toward me, coming short of my face by a mere six inches.

"What makes you think you give the orders around here?" he said, pinning me with his storm-filled eyes.

Coming even closer to his face, I stopped within an inch from his nose. "What in my demeanor makes you think I am afraid of you?" I said with bravado.

Attempting to stare me down for what felt like an eternity, he suddenly pulled back, walked to the door and opened it. "Boy, get in here and clean up this mess," he roared. Then turning back to me his anger broiling, he clenched and unclenched his hand. Tension hung in the air.

As he paced back and forth for a few minutes I could almost see his mind at work as he walked to the window and staring out to sea. "Are you a gambler, Miss Stewart?"

"What are you talking about?" I asked in total confusion.

"It's a simple question, *Lady Stewart*. Are you a gambler? Do you believe in games of chance to determine your future?" he said as he turned from the window and stood in front of me. His startling blue eyes piercing through me. I could not make sense of what he was asking of me.

"I have never been a gambler before, and I am not sure just what a game of chance has to do with my future," I said with an incredulous tone.

"I have a proposition for you, Lady Stewart," he said in a tone that would suggest a friendly alliance being made.

"What say we play a little game of chance? If you are the winner, you and your crew are free to sail away without harm. You also get to keep your cargo and ship."

"And if I lose?" I asked, the question hanging in the air.

"If I should win this little game of chance, your crew is safely put to shore and I get the ship, the cargo, and you," he said with a hint of a dare in his voice as a devilish smile played on his lips.

Now I began to pace back and forth weighing my options.

"Well?" he challenged, raising an eyebrow brashly.

That damnable eyebrow, I thought to myself.

"The decision cannot be that hard to make. So what do you say? Do we have ourselves a little wager?" he taunted, pressing me for an answer while rubbing his hands together. "I will even let you choose. We could play a game of piquet or simply cut cards aces high. Best five out of seven draws wins. So, what do you say?"

"Just give me a minute. It's a big decision with inherent pitfalls as far as I can see." Now feeling somewhat uncomfortable under the scrutiny of his intense stare, I began to chew on the corner of my bottom lip.

What's the worst that could happen? I asked myself. *Well, I could end up the companion of a pirate for the rest of my natural-born life, that's what. Or, I could be off on my merry way with ship in tow and my somewhat spotless virtue intact. What to do, what to do?* Again, pacing, I felt like a caged animal my mind was whirling, and I was unsure of which option to pick.

"I have to speak with my uncle," I said, hoping that he could advise me of my chances.

"I am afraid that the decision is yours alone to make. Your uncle can be of no help now," he said as he took a seat in the chair closest to the window and watched me deliberate with myself.

I used to play cards with my brother Jonathan, but I was never any good at piquet. He tried teaching me the subtleties of the game, but it required so much memory and strategizing it often gave me a headache. Chances are, he has the game down pat, and I would lose. If I were to take him up on it, my only chance would be to draw the best cards.

Another fifteen minutes went by as I weighed the pros and cons of this game of chance.

"Fine, I'll do it. But what is to keep you from cheating or going back on your word if I win?" I challenged.

"You severely wound me with your mistrust, Lady Stewart," he said, dramatically bringing his hand to his chest as if I pierced him to his very heart, black as it may be.

"It is a legitimate question. After all, I have a lot to lose should I be on the wrong end of this deal," I told him in all seriousness.

"I guess it is all a matter of perspective, my dear," he said as he gave me a wolfish smile that alluded to the pleasures that could be had for the taking.

A blush touched my cheeks and resolve stiffened my spine as I made my decision.

"Fine, you are on! Best five out of seven, aces high, and I will shuffle first." I was feeling lucky today. At least I prayed the gods were on my side.

Retrieving cards from a drawer, he handed them to me, and I examined them. Determining that they were fairly new, I began to shuffle. An expression of appreciation played across his face. I had learned from Jonathan how to shuffle like the dealers at the London parlors.

Placing the deck in the middle of the table, I allowed him to go first. Reaching over he cut the deck and lifted his card up. He drew a queen. I went next and drew a three of clubs.

I kept telling myself that it was only the first match. Placing my card back down, he proceeded to pick up the deck and show me how shuffling was really done. My stomach sunk, and I felt sick. His skills far exceeded mine in that respect. Now it was my turn to draw. Cutting the deck, I pulled out a ten of hearts. Then he drew out a five of diamonds. Now we were even with five more draws to go.

Next, the pirate captain drew an ace of hearts, and I drew a queen of spades. I shuffled again and drew out a king of diamonds, and he drew a nine card. I breathed a sigh of relief, even again.

I shuffled again. This time he drew first pulling a two of clubs, and I drew a jack of hearts, and I was up by one.

The tension grew as I drew a card close to the bottom. I turned the card over to reveal a seven of spades, and my heart dropped because I just knew I would lose this one.

Reaching for the deck of cards, he never broke eye contact with me. Picking a card from the middle, he lifted it to show me without looking at it himself. He had drawn the six of hearts and my breath caught in my chest as I could hardly believe that I was up by two now.

"Yes!" I blurted out, and I couldn't help but smile.

The official count was now four to two, and all I needed was one more win, and I would be free.

My deal, which I hoped would be the last. Shuffling the deck, I felt apprehensively confident. Laying the cards in the middle of the table between us, he cut the deck and pulled out a king of diamonds, and my confidence vanished.

Holding my hands together under the table to stop the shaking, I breathed deeply to steady my nerves. Reaching out to cut the deck, I hesitated and said a little prayer to heaven above. I couldn't breathe, and my head felt dizzy now. Rolling my hand over to reveal the card I had drawn, breath escaped from my lungs in one enormous gasp as my card was the king of hearts, making this round a tie.

I wanted to cry out in frustration but refused to let him see my feelings.

Taking the deck, he shuffled with precision and confidence, this time placing the cards down in the middle of the table. I reached for the pile of cards and rested my hand on the deck. I looked at him for a few seconds trying to read him, but he had masked his emotions. I drew from the middle, turning my hand over to reveal the eight of diamonds. Feeling the full force of disappointment, I was sure it was written all over my face as I placed my card back on the deck.

I noticed that he was studying me intently. I could not read his eyes for they held a look I had not seen before. Peering at me intently, he reached over to cut the deck as his eyes never left mine. Lifting up the cards so that I would be the one to see his card first, I had to look twice because I could not believe my eyes. He had drawn the six of clubs.

I looked at his face. His expression never changed. Not waiting for me to say anything, he simply placed the deck back on top of the pile as if he knew that it was a losing draw. "Congratulations," he said.

Slightly confused by his reaction, I wondered what would happen next.

"When can I see my uncle?" I asked with a mixture of joy and something else that I couldn't quite put my finger on. It wasn't that I had not enjoyed my time aboard the pirate ship. It's that I was not cut out to be someone's prisoner and did not enjoy the confinement and loss of my free will.

He walked out the door and secured it behind him without saying a word. I sat there for a minute, wondering exactly what just happened. If I had just won, why did he lock me in again?

I should have known I couldn't trust a pirate.

I walked to the door and tried to pull it open to no avail. Then I gave it a good swift kick out of sheer frustration and immediately started hopping about on one foot which I had hurt on the solid wood door.

I was about to start screaming insults at the door again when it suddenly swung open.

"We are ready now," he announced.

"Ready for what?" I asked while holding my injured foot.

Grabbing my hand, he proceeded to pull me behind him as I hopped on one foot yelling for him to slow down.

Standing on the deck of the privateers ship near the railing I could see the *Lady Clarisse*. She had fared well through the storm, and the two ships had rendezvoused just as the captain had instructed.

Looking about the ship for the first time, I noticed all the pirates had their faces covered and their backs turned to me.

I thought it strange but didn't have long to ponder it.

Only one pirate remained aboard the *Lady Clarisse*.

As we stepped closer to the railing, I could see two ropes that connected the ships together.

Realization dawned like a bad dream, and I instantly knew exactly how I was to get back to my ship.

Trying to break free of his strong grip, he had anticipated my reluctance and accurately gauged my fear. Taking hold of my shoulders, he forced me to look at him.

"I never took you for a hysterical female, so I need you to take a breath and calm down," he said while placing his face only a few inches from mine.

"I never learned to swim, and I am not going across that cavernous gap on that little rope," I anxiously said while pointing to the rope.

"Well, I am afraid that is the only way to get there," he said, indicating the other ship with his one hand. "Of course, we could forget the deal we struck, and I could cut your ship loose if you would prefer," he informed me in a tone that suggested something more as he smiled provocatively.

"Where exactly do I hold on?" I retorted with a sober expression.

Leading me to the railing, he stepped up and onto a board that had been secured and extended out. Taking hold of the rope, he turned and offered me a hand. I hesitated for an instant, then finding my backbone, I reached out and took his hand. He pulled me up and led me out onto the board as I lost my balance and screamed.

Clamping his strong arm around my waist, he lifted me up. I grabbed his neck so tightly that he momentarily gasped for breath.

"Madam, if you wish for us both to arrive at our destination and not in the drink, might I suggest you allow me to breathe," he rasped.

Unable to speak, I loosened my death grip and dared a peek. I tightly closed my eyes again and buried my head in his neck as I felt all the color drain from my face.

I shook every paralyzing second it took us to swing through the air from one ship to the other, landing on the deck with a thud. The sour taste in my mouth made me nearly throw up.

My legs felt like wet noodles as they gave out. His hand reached out to steady me. Taking several deep breaths to stop the buzzing between my ears and calm my rapidly beating heart, I tried to give a reassuring smile.

"I think I will be fine now," I said formally.

"Last chance to change your mind and become a privateer," he said, looking at my face and attempting to judge whether or not I was going to faint.

"I thank you, sir, for my safe return in one piece and for keeping your word. And as much as I abhor the crush of societal demands, I do not believe I could live confined to a cabin below decks for the rest of my life," I said as my confidence returned along with the color to my face.

"In that case, Ma belle Ange, I will bid you adieu and be off," he said as he gave me a courtly bow and backed away. "It's really a shame."

"What is?" I inquired.

"You would have made a wonderful pirate," he answered with a wink.

"Privateer," I corrected.

Then turning with a hearty laugh, he walked to the railing. The other man waiting for him released a rope that held the two ships together. They both grabbed hold of a rope and swung across in unison with grace and ease to the other ship.

Immediately barking orders to his crew, each man turned around, and they all moved like the gears of a well-oiled machine, moving as one. The sails were hoisted and the wind caught hold as the ship pulled away at a good clip.

The captain and his first mate stood together near the wheel on the upper deck. Shoulder to shoulder, they watched the distance grow between our two ships.

As I stood on the deserted deck of the *Lady Clarisse*, melancholy began to set in. I was not exactly sure why the tears sprang to my eyes as my mind wandered. I didn't leave the deck until the other ship was a mere speck on the horizon.

The wind had picked up, and a shiver went up my spine. Pulling my wrap tighter around my shoulders, I turned toward the crew's quarters below deck. Reality had hit me like a cold bath, and I sobered up suddenly having the desire to see Uncle Jamie and make sure everyone was alive and well.

The darkness below deck was palpable and the stench of chamber pots left too long assaulted my senses. But I would not be deterred.

I searched for something to light my way. Finding a lantern that had been left burning, I looked for others that I could light.

Hanging two lanterns up, I carried a third one with me as I called for Uncle Jamie. The men had been tied by their wrists to the supporting poles, and blindfolds covered their eyes. They did not look any worse for wear. I untied the first two men I came across as I made my way through the darkened chamber.

"Is anyone hurt?" I called out.

"No, miss, they didn't harm us," answered one man.

"You untie the others, and I will find Captain Kincaid and my uncle"

"James Stewart, you answer me! Where are you?" I called out, feeling a bit disconcerted not hearing him call back to me.

"Lassie, over here, could you be helping an old feller out just a bit?" came the voice of Mr. Jones, the cook. Running to his side, I quickly removed his restraints and helping him up. "Oh, how grateful I am to be sure, seeing a lovely sight such as yourself, lassie," he crowed, finally free from his ties.

"Have you seen my uncle or the captain? I don't see them and Uncle Jamie isn't calling out. Is he still alive?" I cried as I looked around with one of the lanterns held high above my head trying to peer into the darkness.

"To be sure, little lassie, he's fine. Heard one of those packs of thieves say something about taken them to the captain's quarters. You have nothing to worry about," Cook replied as he worked to free someone else.

"Thank you so much, Mr. Jones." And with that, I handed him my lantern and headed for the captain's quarters.

Throwing the door open, I found Uncle Jamie and the captain blind-folded and tied to chairs. Relief washed over me, and I ran to Jamie and wrapped my arms around him so tightly that I nearly choked him.

"Angelina, is that you? Are you harmed, child? Did that pirate touch you? Untie me so I can kill the bloody beast. He calls himself a man. I am going to —" Uncle Jamie muttered as I untied his hands.

"Lord Stewart, there is a lady present, sir," the captain said, not allowing Jamie to finish that sentence.

"Sorry, old chap. I apologize to you, Angelina," he said as his hands came free, and he could see me for the first time since our capture.

Looking between Uncle Jamie and Captain Kincaid, all I could do was wrap my arms around them and laugh, then cry, then laugh again. Jamie had sustained a black eye and his limbs were stiff from being in one position for so long, but the two were unharmed. They had a mil-lion questions, some of which I didn't wish to answer with complete truthfulness, so I lied. May I be forgiven for my sins, but I couldn't be completely honest. The scandal would be social suicide, there would be endless questions, and my reputation would be destroyed, not to men-tion the family's good name being raked over the coals and through the mud. No, we couldn't have that.

So my story went something like this: I was taken aboard the pi-rate ship and blindfolded like everyone else. The captain was a perfect gentleman, and he never laid a hand on me. For this part of the story, I had to turn to the side because a flush came to my cheeks every time I thought of the pirate captain.

I stayed in the captain's cabin since he was on deck all night dealing with the storm. The next day, the captain and I played a little game of chance, which I won, securing the safe return of the ship, its cargo, and crew. End of story, nothing more to tell. I figured if my story were simple, the easier it would be to keep it all straight.

My uncle and Captain Kinkaid seemed to believe my version, which made the long trip home easier. And what a story the men of the *Lady Clarisse* would have to tell of their harrowing encounter with real pirates on the open seas.

"SO WHAT WAS THAT ALL ABOUT?" Honore Lacroix asked of his best friend and captain as they stood shoulder to shoulder on the deck of the *Miranda*.

"I don't know what you are talking about," Jude said to the man he had not only grown up with but had fought beside in many battles.

"Oh, my friend, why do you insist in lying to me, unsuccessfully I might add? I know you better than you know yourself. So you might as well come clean with it. Why are we still standing here on this deck when there is so much to do? And why do we not have a new ship to call ours?" he asked, pointing to the *Lady Clarisse*. He had been with Jude when that witch Juliette Moreau had destroyed him.

"I do not think that you can comprehend what I see in her," Jude told him still, staring at the other ship, his gaze never leaving the figure of Angelina standing alone on the deck of the *Lady Clarisse*.

"Why don't you humor me then?" Honore insisted.

"Well, I could explain it to you, but it would require charts and graphs," Jude replied, trying to make a joke of it, but his emotions were a tangled knot in the pit of his stomach.

"Have you fallen for the little enchantress, Jude? I think she has put a spell on you, and you had better snap out of it and soon," his friend and first mate advised in all seriousness.

"Look, Honore, she is different! She is passion and fire, refinement and elegance all rolled into one exquisite, dare I say extraordinary form. Did I mention she is intelligent too?"

"But you will never see this one again. There she goes, never to be seen by you in this lifetime," Honore pointed out. "And might I just say good riddance. Women, as a whole, are nothing but trouble."

"Not so fast, my dear friend. I know exactly where to find her. You did not think that I would let her go so easily if I didn't have a plan?" Jude informed his skeptical friend with the confidence of a man holding a winning hand. "And might I just add that if that is trouble, I wish to be in it up to my head all the time," Jude said, soberly pointing at Angelina, then turning to look at Honore. "All the time, my dear friend." His smile speaking volumes to his oldest friend.

5

HE VOYAGE HOME HAD GONE relatively smooth barring a small storm or two but uneventful nonetheless. The men's nerves were raw, and who could blame them? My nerves had been on edge as well but for a far different reason than the crew's.

I could still smell him in the sea air, and his scent clung to my dress and wrap that I refused to wash. I couldn't get away from him, even in my dreams and, to tell the truth, I wasn't sure that I wanted to.

Upon arriving home, the wild stories started circulating almost the instant the ship docked. I was made out to be some kind of heroine, though I tried to tell everyone that I hadn't done half the things they were hearing. It didn't matter what I said. The stories got bigger and more outrageous as the season wore on.

One account of the story actually had me sword fighting with a one-eyed grizzly pirate who would rather eat the crew's livers for supper than look at you. But there was no stopping insanity, so I just went along with it and hoped that it would all blow over soon, like a fast-moving rainstorm.

When things got too crazy, I took Dante out for a strenuous ride to give my nerves and muscles a good workout. It tended to clear my head and help me forget the rakish pirate that haunted my days and nights.

People didn't say too much about my independent demeanor after that, or about the fact that I preferred to ride astride my horse instead of sidesaddle. People gave me plenty of leeway because, after all, I had stared down a treacherous, unscrupulous, one-eyed pirate and lived to tell the tale with my virtue intact.

Today was a good day. The sun was out, the rain had ceased, and I was enjoying my midmorning ride through the park when Darcy Montgomery rode up alongside me in his carriage.

Darcy was an interesting enough fellow of average height. In fact, he and I could stand side by side, and he would be at eye level. But that would be the only time Mr. Montgomery and I would see things eye to eye. I didn't particularly like his politics, nor did I appreciate his views on women and where they belonged. He had always been polite to me, sometimes overly so. The man had never done anything to truly offend me, except sharing his views of the woman's role in society; however, I always got this strange feeling when he was around. He made my skin crawl!

An attractive man with blond hair, handsome brown eyes that were large in size, his features were slightly feminine in my opinion, but some women liked that about him.

He came from a prominent family that had been well managed while his father was alive, but I heard Darcy liked to gamble in the gentlemen's clubs at night and that he was neither a very good gambler nor a gracious loser.

I didn't particularly like the way his eyes shifted when he was talking to me or how he talked to me as if I didn't have a brain in my head.

"Good day to you, Lady Stewart," Darcy said in his best gentlemanly fashion.

"Good day to you, Mr. Montgomery," I replied politely while giving him a passing glance in hopes that he would move on.

"Lovely weather we are having, don't you think?" he continued in his effort to strike up a conversation.

"Yes, Mr. Montgomery, very lovely weather," I replied again.

"Are you planning to go to Lord and Lady Burgess's gathering this evening?" he asked while trying to hold eye contact with me.

"I had intended to, Mr. Montgomery. Thank you for inquiring," I said even more politely than before.

"Please, call me Darcy. We have known each other for two years now. I think we should be on a first-name basis, don't you?" he said, trying to be cordial.

"I am not sure that I am completely comfortable with that, Mr. Montgomery," I replied, rebuffing him.

"Oh, I mean no impropriety in my suggestion of it?" he simpered.

"Of course, but I will have to take your suggestion under advisement and get back with you." Turning my head to look him straight in the eyes, I fixed him with my best aristocratic stare. "Now, if you will excuse me, Mr. Montgomery, my ride is over, and I am headed home." I tried to politely excuse myself from further conversation and dismiss him with my statement, but I guess some people just can't take a hint.

"I would be happy to accompany you safely home," he said, trying to insert himself into my day.

"Thank you, but no, I will be perfectly fine. If I can handle a band of pirates, I think I will be fine riding home on my own," I said in an attempt to make him as uncomfortable as he was making me at that moment.

And with that, I turned Dante to the left and down a path leaving Darcy Montgomery and his driver with no choice but to continue in the direction he had been traveling.

Dante was a beautiful Friesian stallion my father had given me two years ago as a birthday present. From the moment I set eyes on his magnificent frame and ebony coat it was love. Granted, he could be a handful from time to time, and Mother was very concerned over Father's gift, but I wouldn't trade him for all the gold in London.

On those long rainy days that Dante and I couldn't go out for a ride I still found my way to the stables to brush him or bring him a treat or two. I even found myself having one-sided conversations with him.

My mind had been wandering as I rounded the corner to the stables when my eye caught sight of several horses tied up and saddled next to the stable doors.

It only took a split second for recognition to dawn, and I kicked Dante into a full run. Yelling like a madwoman, I pulled Dante up short as Jonathan walked through the stable doors.

I leaped at him from the back of my horse as he caught me in his arms and spun me around, hooting and carrying on like when we were children. He was finally home, and I felt whole again.

"Am I dreaming, are you really here?" I said between my gasps of excitement. I held his face in my hands. "I don't believe it, why didn't you tell me? Did Mother know you were coming?"

"Well, if you will be quiet a moment and let me talk." He laughed as he placed me back on the ground while giving me the once over twirling me around to get a better look. "Did you get even more beautiful while I was gone?" he said.

"Oh, how I have missed you and your teasing!" I said through my tears of joy.

"No, I am serious, I think you grew six inches, and before I forget, I brought you something in case you run into any more pirates." Pulling a package out of his coat pocket, he handed it to me.

"Oh, Jonathan, you don't believe all of those crazy stories going around, do you?" I scolded, while removing the ribbon from my present.

I opened the box and discovered a beautiful six-inch dagger with a jewel incrusted handle. "Jonathan, it is lovely, but what am I supposed to do with this?" I asked with confusion distorting my face.

"Keep it in the pocket of your gowns. It's just the right size, in case you ever run into any more pirates," he told me in all seriousness.

"Oh, Jonathan, you are always so thoughtful," I teased as I punched his arm.

Just then a man cleared his throat, and two gentlemen stepped out from behind Jonathan.

I had some difficulty seeing them clearly because the sun was in my eyes. Using my hand to shade my eyes, I had to look up.

Jonathan turned as if he just remembered that we were not alone and that he had brought home two companions. Gesturing to the first man, he said, "Allow me to introduce you to my friends, Lord Honore Lacroix and Jude Deveraux, Duke of Bayonne," he said in his best French accent.

"We went to school together two years ago. I ran into them at the tavern in town on my way home yesterday. What are the odds?" Jonathan said.

Offering my hand to Lord Lacroix in greeting, I gave him a shallow curtsy. He had handsome features with shoulder-length hair that curled up on the ends. His eyes were brown and held a look of complete amusement as if someone just told a good joke. He was tall for a French man, standing even with Jonathan and four inches taller than myself.

"A pleasure to meet you, Lord Lacroix. Please forgive our ridiculous behavior," I pleaded with him.

"Think nothing of it. It does my heart good to see such love between brother and sister," he replied with a polite chuckle that did not mock me.

Turning to the Duke of Bayonne, I bobbed a polite curtsy and offered him my hand. When his fingers touched mine it was as if an electrical current traveled through his fingers to mine.

Looking up, my breath caught in my throat. He was the most handsome man I had ever laid eyes on. Taller than the other two by nearly two inches; his shoulders were remarkably broad, his glossy raven-black hair had been neatly plaited and tied in the back, and his face was cleanly shaven; however, his most remarkable feature had to be his eyes.

They were blue, but not just any blue. They were like the clear crisp blue of the most magnificent ocean. It was as if for a moment time stood still, or maybe it was my heart skipping a beat.

Maintaining eye contact for longer than was polite, I tried to pull away. He simply increased the pressure of his grip as he bent over and placed his lips on the top of my hand.

"Mademoiselle, please call me Jude," was all he said, and I knew, without a doubt, as I looked into his eyes that I was face-to-face with my pirate captain again.

My knees went weak, and I couldn't breathe as I felt the color leave my face.

Jonathan grabbed my arm as I felt my legs go out from under me. The next conscious recollections I had was the sensation of being carried by two strong arms while the sound of chaos assaulted my brain. Was I dreaming? My senses were sluggish. I took a deep breath to clear my head. What was happening?

Then I remembered! Opening my eyes, I felt a jolt go through me like a hot poker.

No, this most definitely was not a dream! But how could that be? It didn't make sense. Those were his eyes and that was his smell. Oh, that intoxicating, unforgettable smell.

"Sir, I am not an invalid to be carried around to and fro. Please put me down," I whispered, feeling slightly ridiculous.

"I am afraid I cannot do that, Lady Angelina Stewart. You obviously overexerted yourself riding that beast you call a horse. Your brother instructed me to take you upstairs and deposit you in your chambers. He went to find your mother," Jude said as he continued up the stairs.

"I just had a shock, that is all, nothing more. You caught me by surprise, sir," I replied while pushing against his chest attempting to free myself from his vicelike grip.

"I didn't realize I had such an effect on the female persuasion, or perhaps it is only you," he stated with a satisfied grin on his face.

"You know exactly of what I speak, sir. You are the very pirate that took me captive last month," I said with slight malice in my tone.

"I assure you, Lady Stewart, that I have no idea of what you are speaking. Although Jonathan did spin some wild tale yesterday about you besting a treacherous pirate and his entire crew at sea," he said with a wry grin and a slight chuckle.

"I would know you anywhere! You are the very same notorious pirate of which we speak, and you know it. Do not pretend as if I have lost my faculties," I said between clenched teeth.

"If you would be so kind, point me in the direction of the room in which you normally reside," he asked matter-of-factly.

He acted as if we had never met before, and I almost believed him. Maybe I was losing my mind. Could my mind be playing tricks on me? This refined and highly educated man could not be my pirate. He went to school with Jonathan and grew up with privilege. Extending my hand, I pointed to the door just across from where he stood.

Opening the door and walking in, he took a minute to admire the interior and headed for the bed. Gently laying me down on the quilt, he brought the back of his hand to my forehead as if feeling for fever. The act was very proper and disconcerting, all at the same time.

Opening his mouth as if he were about to say something to me, he was stopped when Anna came rushing in followed by Mother and Jonathan.

"I am so sorry, I wasn't here when you were brought up, miss." Anna rushed in with fresh water and a cloth as she immediately began fussing over me. Turning to look at Jude, she gave him a questioning stare before turning her full attention back to me.

"Angel, what happened?" Mother didn't even notice that I had a strange man in my room, or if she did, she didn't acknowledge him. "I told your father that horse was too much for you. He is going to kill you one of these days," Mother said frantically.

"Would you both stop fussing! I didn't eat much this morning and overdid it on my ride, that is all. I am fine now," I demanded getting slightly irritated with all the attention. I looked past Mother and Anna trying to see Lord Deveraux, but he had slipped out of the room during all the commotion. I felt a little disappointed and tried to get out of bed, but Mother and Anna wouldn't hear of it.

Something heavy bumped against my leg. Reaching into my pocket, I discovered the jeweled incrusted dagger that Jonathan had given me. For the life of me, I couldn't remember putting it in my pocket, but there it was. The metal felt warm and heavy in my hand, and somehow comforting.

I was not completely convinced that Jude Deveraux and the pirate captain were not one and the same man. It walked like a pirate and smelled like a pirate, it even sounded like a pirate. Who knows, maybe I was seeing scary things in the shadows, or in this case, a perfectly handsome, well-bred duke.

Reaching into my pocket again to feel the comfort of the knife once more, it did feel good in my hand. Yes, Captain, until we meet again.

6

EVENING OF APRIL 12, 1763;
SEEING SARAH AGAIN

WAS EXCITED TO ATTEND THE Burgess's party because I had not had time to see Sarah since I left on my voyage in March. By the time I returned, Sarah had left with her mother and father on a trip of their own. Not much had been said, and I was terribly curious since I had not found out what it was that Sarah had wanted to tell me.

Mother and Anna had fussed over me all afternoon, which almost drove me crazy. Cloistered in my room like an invalid, while all I wanted to do was find out more about Jonathan's guests. By the time I had secured my escape, all three of them had left with Father to conduct business in town.

The added bonus for Anna was that she didn't have to chase me down in her attempt to get me ready in less than an hour for the evening. She had the whole day to style my hair and make me look presentable.

My hair had been freshly washed, curled, and fashioned on my head with enough pins and ribbons to assure that there would be no embarrassing mishaps.

My gown was new and had been picked up from the dress shop only two days prior. It was of rich blue satin and modestly cut low in the front for the standard. Material grazed just off my shoulders with three-quarter-length sleeves and delicate hand made four-inch lace around the cuffs. The skirt was bustled for dancing and would not hamper me by someone accidentally stepping on the hem. With intricate silver stitching of vines and flowers throughout the bodice front and hem of the gown, the effect was simply breathtaking as Anna cinched me into the gown.

We argued for twenty minutes about how tightly the corset really needed to be, and in the end we reached a compromise. She loosened the corset a little so that I could actually breathe and take in nourishment, and I promised not to pass out on her.

Our carriage had arrived promptly at eight-thirty, and the house was already abuzz with guests mingling about and talking.

"Lord Jonathan Edward Allen Stewart, Lady Clarisse Emerson Stewart, and Lady Angelina Marguerite Amelia Stewart." Our names were announced as we entered the main room just outside of the dining hall. The loud boisterous noise of so many people talking ceased as heads turned, and the buzz of hushed whispers began.

Lord and Lady Burgess immediately came over to welcome us, and the talking resumed. Mother and Lady Katrina had been good friends for years and never missed an opportunity to visit with one another. Father and Lord John loved to talk politics and business, and I went in search of my dear friend, Sarah, excited to find out what she had been doing all these weeks.

Running into a few of the young ladies I knew from our social circle, I asked after Sarah, but nobody had seen her.

Puzzled by Sarah's absence, I found my way back to Mother and Lady Burgess.

"Lady Burgess, is Sarah coming down soon?" I inquired, feeling some concern.

"Don't fuss so, child. She will be along," Lady Burgess informed me. Something in her tone and look led me to believe that there was something more to it.

Excusing myself from the ladies as they continued their riveting conversation about the intricate workings of our social circle, I decided to again go in search of Sarah. This time I took the backstairs to her room to see for myself what was really going on.

Bypassing certain guests and maneuvering around the Wheatly's, I headed for the hallway that leads to the servants' quarters near the kitchen.

Sarah and I had loved running through these halls as children, and we had always given the servants a run for their money when it came to hide-and-seek. I knew these halls better than most of the servants who had been living there for years. Just a quick left at the door, and I would be home free. Sneaking past the kitchen made me feel like a kid again, just like when Sarah and I would—

"Excuse me, miss, but this part of the house is off-limits to guests," I heard a rich, deep male voice behind me say.

Turning around slowly, I saw an older gentleman that I instantly recognized.

"Oh hello, Mr. Buckley. It is so good to see you again," I said, trying to be nonchalant. Mr. Buckley was Lord Burgess's personal valet and head servant.

"Is that you, Lady Angelina?" he said as he squinted to get a better look at me.

"Yes, sir, it is. I'm going to find Sarah. She isn't down yet, and it is almost time to sit down to supper." I crossed my fingers hoping that Mr. Buckley wasn't going to be a stickler for protocol and that he would take into consideration all the years I spent running through these halls.

"If anyone asks you, we never saw each other tonight," he said with a wink and a smile.

"Your name will not cross these lips." Winking back at him, off I went up the stairs and down the hall to the third door on the right.

I knocked and called out to Sarah as I put my hand on the doorknob to open it. The door suddenly opened in my hand, and I was left staring at an unfamiliar face.

"Oh, you're not Sarah," I said with slight shock registering all over my face.

"No, miss, I am Mrs. Lawrence. May I help you?" she stated matter-of-factly, daring me to get past her.

"What happened to Mary?" I inquired of this stone-faced woman blocking my way.

"I am not at liberty to say, miss. Now if you will be so kind and return to the guests downstairs, Lady Sarah will be down shortly," the old bat said as she began to close the door on me.

"That will be Lady Angelina Stewart to you, and I do mind. Please be so kind and move aside, or I will be forced to move you," I said with an air of authority as I pushed my way past Mrs. Lawrence and into the room.

"I will have to get Mr. Buckley and have you removed if you don't leave right now," she said with bravado this time.

"Do you have any idea who I am, madam? Never mind. Please go and fetch Mr. Buckley and shut the door on your way out!" I said, turning my back to her as I looked around the room for Sarah.

Waiting for the old hag to leave the room, I turned and locked the door so that Sarah and I wouldn't be disturbed by Mrs. Lawrence.

"Sarah, talk to me. What is going on? And where is Mary?" I asked in a rush of words as I walked over to my best friend and found her sitting at her mirror, not moving. "Why is that woman standing guard at your door?" I demanded, standing in front of her now looking down at her beautiful face.

I was shocked by what I saw. The normally lovely complexion that radiated health and joy was replaced with someone who was pale and gaunt.

"What the hell is going on, Sarah? You will forgive my shock, but it has only been six weeks since I saw you last, but I hardly recognize you." I took her small frame in my arms and just held her.

"Oh, Angelina, I have missed you so much. You are like a breath of fresh air. Don't you ever leave me alone again," she whispered into my neck as she put her head on my shoulder, like a little child searching for comfort.

"I won't, Sarah, I promise." Tears ran down my cheeks as I rocked her back and forth. We sat in silence for the longest time as I held her small frame in my arms rocking her, trying to take her pain away. I didn't know what had happened, and it didn't matter at the moment. I just knew that she needed me, and I would never leave her alone again. When the time was right, she would tell me everything.

Twenty minutes later, Mrs. Lawrence had returned with reinforcements, was now pounding on the door and demanding to be let in. Walking to the door, I opened it, irritated by this annoying woman. Mrs. Lawrence was short in stature, standing only five feet four inches tall, so it was easy to look down my nose at her. Mr. Buckley and another servant I didn't recognize stood behind her.

"My lady, you will remove yourself from these quarters immediately," Mrs. Lawrence said with a sullen tone attempting to assert her authority.

"We were just going down to supper, Mrs. Lawrence. And in the future, you might remember your place. Lady Stewart is not only my best friend but your superior. I hope that we never have to speak of this again," Sarah said from behind me with more strength than I would have believed her to have a mere five minutes before. Taking hold of my right arm, she gave Mrs. Lawrence a snub as we passed.

"Mr. Buckley, Tom," Sarah acknowledged the other two servants in the hall blessing them with a gracious smile as I winked and nodded to Mr. Buckley when we passed. We headed down the stairs like old times, arm in arm. Sarah's mother was very happy to see us coming down together.

Soon after, the announcement was made inviting all the guests to dinner and they began to gather near the doors.

Sarah said something to one of the servants dressed in his evening finery, and he disappeared behind the closed doors.

Lord and Lady Burgess were the first through the doors followed by visiting dignitaries and then everyone else, according to their social ranking.

Sarah and I escorted each other into the dining room and found our seats. To my great surprise, we were seated beside each other and somewhere around the middle of the table. This gave greater access to the goings-on and made for wonderful entertainment during lulls in conversations with the dinner guests on either side of us.

To my left sat Lord Bute. He had just been elected prime minister of Parliament and stirred up a lot of controversy during the signing of the Treaty of Paris. Controversy because it was his belief that Great Brittan would not be able to protect all of the territories captured during the Seven Years' War. So on the tenth of February in the year of our Lord one thousand seven hundred and sixty-three, the Treaty of Paris was signed, giving those territories back to France and Spain.

Seated strategically down the table, and on the other side of John Wilkes, was a tremendously interesting figure in his own right. John hated Lord Bute with a passion for several reasons, but the most outstanding reason was his origin of birth. Lord Bute had the misfortune of being born a Scotsman, and John Wilkes despised the Scottish people in general, and especially Lord Bute, because he was a Scotsman with power.

John Wilkes owned a magazine and used it to his full advantage when he had something on his mind. He was, after all, a very opinionated man. Some would say that the things printed and published were libelous and inflammatory at best.

John Wilkes was elected to the House of Parliament, and the icing on the cake was when his cronies elevated him to the rank of prime minister because he then became immune from being prosecuted for libel.

However, that was not what stood out about him to me. John Wilkes was easily the ugliest man in England with his stubby features, squinty eyes, and balding head. Yet he had a reputation as a notorious womanizer. I guess there is no accounting for taste.

Next to Sarah on her right sat my brother Jonathan, who always had a bit of a crush on her, and I believe she reciprocated. Across from

Jonathan sat Honore Lacroix. To his right, Mary Taylor, and next to her and directly across from me Jude Deveraux, Duke of Bayonne.

Tipping his glass and fixing me with a cordial but piercing stare, he studied my face for a moment as if he were thinking of something else. Then dismissively turning to his left, he began speaking with Mary Taylor. Slightly disturbed by his subtle assessment and dismissal of me, I decided to play his game.

Turning my attention to Lord Bute, we began to discuss the benefits of fostering good relations with France and Spain by returning certain territories to them, and the impact it might have on the English economy.

As the plates were being removed after the first course and the second course was being served, I felt a prickling on the back of my neck. Turning, I noticed Jude Deveraux had obviously gotten bored with his dinner companion and her stimulating wit and was once again studying me. Turning slightly from my provocative conversation with Lord Bute, I intended to stimulate the duke in a different way and pull him into our new topic.

"Tell me, Mr. Deveraux, where do you stand on the policy of foreign countries giving out Letters of Marque to pirates and giving them permission to plunder helpless ships and kill good men at will?" I asked with a spark of interest shining in my eyes as I fixed him with a piercing gaze of my own. *Oh yes, Jude Deveraux or pirate captain, I will draw you out and make you show your true colors.*

"To tell you the truth, Lady Stewart, I have no real opinion on the matter. I don't like the sea that much. In fact, I find it lovely to look at, but you wouldn't catch me out on the open ocean unless I had to be. I never really learned to swim," he replied while crinkling up his nose as if he found the thought of an ocean voyage distasteful.

"Surely, you have some opinion one way or the other on the matter regardless of your distaste for ocean voyages, good sir. The sheer act of piracy, and the taking of innocent lives, then calling it all well and good with a letter of decree from their government protecting them from prosecution is a travesty," Lord Bute pushed him with an impassioned plea to stop sitting on the fence regarding such an important matter.

Pushing matters just a little further, I looked across from me and noticed Honore had an amused smile on his face and was attempting not to laugh at his friend who was being sucked into a conversation with so many potential pitfalls.

"Tell me, Lord Lacroix, where do you stand on the matter of piracy for hire?" I asked, fixing my big jade eyes on him in an attempt to lure him in as well.

"Please, call me Honore. We are all friends here, Lady Stewart." He was applying me with his smooth French accent in an attempt to distract me from the question at hand and lighten the mood.

"Please, call me Angelina. Honore, let me pose the question another way. Where do you stand on the matter of bloodthirsty cutthroats being hired by their own governments and, when caught, given immunity?" I sweetly asked, fixing him with my most beguiling smile and innocent look.

"And why does one so beautiful and lovely want to speak of such unpleasantness during dinner?" Honore stated, fixing me with his most stunning smile that would melt any young woman causing her to lose her train of thought. I have no doubt that his tactics had worked on other woman in the past, but I had a point to make and a mystery to uncover, and I was not ready to let it go.

"I don't think that I have ever met two men in my life so devoid of an opinion before. Have you, Sarah?" I said, looking at Sarah now as she was about to put a bite of food in her mouth.

Placing her fork on her plate, Sarah turned to me and fixed me with her large pale blue eyes.

"Sometimes, Angelina, I honestly don't know what comes over you. These gentlemen are trying to enjoy their dinner, and you want to talk about the most ridiculous things. Could we please change the subject? I am still upset every time I think about your life being in danger. Honestly, it is simply morbid of you to speak on the matter further." Sarah scolded. Her eyes sparkled with tears and unspent emotion as she turned to her plate and took a bite.

I had to give in to her. Sarah always knew how to put me in my place, and with that, the subject was changed.

Reaching under the table, I found Sarah's delicate hand and gave it a squeeze — our sign for "I am sorry." As she squeezed back, I decided to keep the conversation light and easy for the remainder of the meal. But all bets were off when I had Jude Deveraux all to myself.

The main course was served, and I felt unable to eat any more than three small bites due to the constriction of my corset.

The beautifully prepared pheasant dish with spring onions and baby carrots smelled delicious, and I wanted to take the plate home with me for later when I found myself free of my restraint.

I turned my attention down the table. Sarah and I often amused ourselves by observing the fashionably dressed, or should I say the outrageously attired men and women of the upper social class.

Leaning over to whisper near my ear, Sarah directed my attention to our left five seats on the opposite side of the table.

"Do you think Sir James Thornhill has bathed yet this season?" she asked, lifting a delicate eye brow in that direction.

Casually looking down the table, I could see Elizabeth Caldredge fanning herself vigorously and attempting to lean as far to her right as possible while drinking her wine.

"Maybe if she drinks enough, the smell won't be that bad," I whispered back.

Using my fan to hide behind, I directed her gaze toward Darcy Montgomery seated four seats down. He and Georgina Cavendish had their heads together deep in conversation.

"I will lay money down that Mr. Montgomery is cultivating his next move for an easy income and an invitation to join the family. Just look at the way he is plying Georgina with his attentions," I said with the slightest bit of derision to my tone.

Sarah never even looked down the table to her right, and I could see her visibly straighten up in her seat. Tears glistened in those soft blue eyes again, and I knew somehow I had hit a raw nerve, but I didn't know why.

Jonathan noticed something was wrong and looked at me with wise and loving eyes. "Sometimes these dinners go on forever, and all I need to do is stretch my legs. Sarah, would you do me the honor of saving the first dance this evening? It has been so long since we have all been together it almost feels like old times," he said to break the tension that was building in the sudden silence.

"I would very much enjoy that, thank you, Jonathan," Sarah replied, trying her best not to cry.

After signaling a footman, Sarah whispered in his ear, and I noticed him walk directly to Lord Burgess and lean down to say something.

Then the footman walked out of the dining room, and Lord Burgess waited five minutes before announcing dinner was over and dancing would be in the ballroom shortly.

I, for one, was relieved. If I had to remain seated for one more minute, I think my head would have exploded. My bottom was numb as were my legs.

Jonathan helped Sarah from her seat, and I was attempting to restore the feeling to my legs when I felt a tug at my seat. Figuring it had to be Jonathan coming to my rescue and help me from my seat, I offered him my hand.

I immediately realized my mistake as my hand was engulfed by a far larger one than Jonathan's. I tried pulling away, but my effort to extract my appendage was useless as Jude held tight and pulled me out of my chair. I had no choice but to smile graciously as he escorted me from the room.

"I couldn't help notice that you and Lord Bute were having a very lively conversation in regards to the peace treaty between our two countries," Jude said while patting my hand he draped over his very muscular forearm.

"And I couldn't help noticing that you and the lovely Miss Taylor ran out of things to say to one another after the first course," I replied with a slight tone of sarcasm.

"Well, you are wrong on both accounts," he answered with a slight chuckle.

"Oh, and how is that?" I inquired, slightly intrigued by his statement.

"Miss Taylor is neither lovely nor entertaining. I lost interest before the first course was over," he stated matter-of-factly, as he guided me toward the open doors to the balcony.

"Is that why you were so interested in my conversation with Lord Bute?"

"No, not really," was all he said as he guided me toward the railing to the left and away from the other couples milling around in the cool night air.

"So tell me, Mr. Deveraux, what do you do with yourself when you are not being the Duke of Bayonne?" I asked, trying to make conversation and unearth another piece to the puzzle that was Jude Deveraux.

"What more is there? I serve at the pleasure of the king. What do you imagine dukes do with their time?" he said, turning the question back around.

"Well, I would imagine they ride horses and read books, take care of stately matters and perhaps hunt with other dukes, lords, and kings. So, are you on assignment from your king?" I asked.

"No, not really. My parents are here on assignment from the king," he informed me.

"Oh, and who are your parents?" I asked, feeling the warmth coming off his body when he moved closer to me as if we were about to share a secret.

"My father is the prime minister of France, Count Philippe Gerard Deveraux, and my mother is Countess Genevieve Sophia

Deveraux of Bordeaux. They are here to smooth things over with your king and improve personal relations between the two countries. I am here accompanying them as I am their only living son and heir," he stated, in all seriousness while piercing me with his intense blue stare.

Momentarily speechless, I stood inches from his face deciding how to proceed. I had not just been given a piece of the puzzle. I had been given a glimpse inside Lord Deveraux.

His nearness was a culmination of disconcertion and thrill all at once, and my head felt like it was packed with cotton. If only he would stop looking at me that way. He smelled of lavender soap and leather, which was terribly distracting, and I shivered slightly.

"Lord Deveraux, the dancing is ready to start. Won't you join us?" Sarah announced from behind us.

"Of course, Lady Burgess, we were just about to head in. It seems Lady Stewart is chilled and forgot her wrap inside," he answered as his eyes never straying from mine as another shiver went up my spine that had nothing to do with cold air.

Jude turned to address Jonathan and Sarah now as he guided me toward the open doors.

"Have you seen Mr. Lacroix?" Jude asked as we walked all together.

"I think I saw him talking to several young eligible maidens in the ballroom," Jonathan answered.

"That sounds like Honore. He will have danced with half of them by night's end and secured promises from the rest to meet him tomorrow at the opera house," Jude said rather dryly.

"I don't know how he does it. All the endless chattering he has to listen to with that many young ladies. I wouldn't do it," Jonathan stated while escorting Sarah.

"He isn't into it for the endless chatter," Jude said, a knowing look traveling between the two men.

I rolled my eyes, and Sarah pretended not to hear.

"Would anyone like refreshments before the dancing begins?" Jonathon cordially asked while patting Sarah's hand resting delicately on his arm.

"No, thank you. I am afraid I couldn't get one more ounce down my throat," I said as I looked at Sarah. "But I could use a minute with Sarah, if you don't mind?" I took her by the hand and led her to the powder room.

"Sarah, is everything all right? You look a little pale," I said while taking her face in my hand to force her to look at me. "I will take you upstairs right now if you need to go."

"No, I am fine. I think that cow Mrs. Lawrence synched me in too tightly. I can hardly breathe," Sarah indicated her lower waist. I locked the door to prevent anyone walking in on us.

"Turn around. Let me look," I said as I spun her and unlacing her gown in one fluid motion. When I got to her corset I noticed marks on her back where the corset had been digging into her flesh.

"Oh, Sarah," I gasped. "Don't ever let that witch do this to you again. Your back is all bruised. How did you even make it through dinner?" I had to bite my lip to keep from crying.

"Why are you even wearing a corset? You are so thin. You don't need this thing" I insisted, letting my breath out. "Please let's just take it off."

"NO! No, it's fine, just lace me back up." Almost a desperate cry as she looked at me through the mirror. I couldn't tell if it was fear, sorrow, or anger that I saw in her eyes. "It will remind me," was all she said.

"Remind you of what, Sarah? Sarah! What is this pain supposed to remind you of?" Putting her head down for a few minutes then when she looked at me again, she had replaced the raw emotion with a mask of societal propriety.

"It will be fine. Just make it looser." And there it was. Her well-practiced smile was back, like too much makeup one wears to hide behind. And against my better judgment, I did as she asked.

Jonathan and Jude had ambushed Honore, and the three of them were discussing something when Sarah and I returned.

"Please don't let us interrupt you, gentlemen." I was hoping they would continue as if we were not even there, still interested in delving into the mind of Monsieur Deveraux.

"I wouldn't hear of it. We are with the two most beautiful ladies at the ball. No more talk of business tonight. Agreed?" Honore said with his usual flare. His boisterous and jovial behavior caught the attention of a group of young ladies off to his right that he had been eyeing for some time. "If you would be so kind as to excuse me for a moment, my dear friends." And with that, he was off on his next pursuit.

"Well, I think that we have lost Honore for the evening," Jonathan said with a chuckle.

"I would have to agree," Jude said as he watched his good friend saunter over to the other group.

I had been pondering my exchange with Sarah as I watched her play the part of a perfectly happy young woman of society. And not really paying attention to the others.

"May I have this dance, Lady Stewart?" I turned to see Jude's outstretched hand as recognition brought me back to reality. Placing my hand in his, I allowed him to lead me onto the dance floor.

"So where did you go back there?" Jude asked in my ear.

"I just took Sarah to the powder room," I answered without really thinking.

"No, I mean when we were all standing around talking. Your mind was somewhere else. What were you thinking about?" He asked again as we waltzed around the room. His eyes searched my face as if trying to see straight into my soul.

"You are very bold, Mr. Deveraux. We only met this morning and already you wish to know my thoughts," I rebuked him, trying to change the subject.

"Would you prefer to speak on the lovely weather?" he said with just a touch of sarcastic undertones. "Or perhaps what you might wear to the opera tomorrow evening?"

Looking up now to search his eyes, my breath caught for a second. I knew those eyes and the feel of his firm hands on my back, so intimate and assured as if it had been there before. I almost missed a step if not for him pulling me along, nearly lifting me off the ground as if I were a doll.

"Do you still claim that you and I have never met before?" I asked as I studied his reaction.

"Madam, you wound me. You have insisted on two separate occasions that I am this bloodthirsty pirate captain that you encountered some weeks back. And yet here I stand before you a gentleman and not a pirate."

"And yet you do not deny it but dance around my direct question as easily as you twirl me about this dance floor."

"How can you reconcile the idea of me the man who stands before you of being a pirate?" He craftily worded his statement in a way to make the entire idea sound ridiculous.

"And yet your eyes, your hands, and even the timber of your voice are just too familiar to me," I added with determination in my voice.

"Surely you cannot believe that I am the only person alive to have eyes of this color?" He emphasized the question with a lift of his one brow.

"There! What you just did right there. He did that," I said, indicating the one brow that went up in the very same manner as the pirate captain.

"And again that cannot be enough evidence to charge a mere man such as myself with piracy."

Again, he had a point. And yet the feeling still nagged at the back of my mind.

"Please forgive me. My mind has been playing tricks on me lately. I hope you don't think me a complete loon," I lied.

"Of course not. You have been through quite an ordeal. Your brother related some of the story yesterday. It must have been ghastly. How did you survive?" he said with an expression of genuine concern.

"Could we change the subject? I don't really like to talk about it. In fact, I am hoping the whole thing will blow over soon, and everyone will have another scandal to talk about before long." I put my head down and turned to the side slightly, trying to hide the flush that inevitably came to my cheeks every time I thought of my pirate.

He didn't say anything for the longest time. The dance ended, and he tipped my head back gently, forcing me to look at him.

"Was your ordeal truly that horrible?" he asked, searching deep into my eyes. "You truly do have the greenest eyes I have ever seen."

His compliment made me smile and the unanswered question laid between us as we left the dance floor in search of refreshments.

7

TEN DAYS IN A ROW I presented my calling card to the Burgess's butler and stood in their grand entry hall waiting.

I had not heard from or seen Sarah since saying good night to her the night of her family's ball. And every day, after my morning ride on Dante through the park, I had stopped by the Burgess's home and presented myself to the staff. And for ten days, I had been told that Sarah was unavailable for visitors.

I had begun to imagine all sorts of terrible and tragic fates befalling my dear friend. Today I would not be turned away. I was, if nothing else, persistent and I had decided today was the day. I was not leaving without seeing Sarah today!

"I am terribly sorry, miss."

"I get it, she is unavailable," I said, cutting poor, faithful George off. "And I am terribly sorry, George, but I am not leaving without speaking to Sarah or Lady Burgess, so you might want to go back and tell them. Otherwise, I will show myself up the stairs and go through this house room by room!"

"I truly am sorry, Lady Stewart," George said obediently following orders.

"George, you know me, you have always addressed me as Lady Angelina. Lady Stewart is my mother. What is going on here? And where is Sarah?" Taking the direct approach, I tried to appeal to his humanity.

"It's all right, George, I will handle this," came Sarah's voice from the morning room as she walked toward me.

Waiting for George to leave, I held my tongue as she walked up to me and took my arm.

"Let's walk in the garden, shall we?" Sarah pulled me in that direction as we walked in silence.

"I have called on you for ten days, and I have been turned away like a common beggar. If I didn't value you as a true friend I might be insulted," I said to her once we were outside.

"And if you were not such a good friend you wouldn't have been so persistent. I really love that about you," Sarah answered, turning her brilliant blue eyes on me.

"Well?" I left the question hanging in the air as I stopped walking to look at her.

Taking my arm again and leading me through the rose garden in silence, she touched the petals with their brilliant colors popping brightly in the morning sun.

"I am serious. What is going on? I didn't see you for six weeks. Then I see you at your family party and you are thin and bruised. You avoid me for ten days. Why won't you talk to me?" I pleaded with her. "You are my best friend, talk to me, please."

"I can't! Something truly terrible happened and I just can't," Sarah cried, turning away from me.

"Sarah! Sarah, look at me." I was desperately trying to make eye contact with her as I sat down on the garden bench.

"You will judge me, and I just can't bear the disgrace," she finally said with a sob in her throat.

"Sarah, you know me better than that. I would never judge you. We practically grew up together. You are like the sister I never had. I would die first before I betrayed you. I swear it!" I cried as I sat there next to her taking her hand in mine.

"If it is a matter of trust, I will tell you a secret first. One that I never revealed to anyone else, and you better take it to your grave as well, or I will have to kill you myself." The tone in my voice revealed to Sarah that I was about to share a truly great secret.

Sarah sat looking at me with her large, crystal-blue eyes sparkling with unshed tears. "I swear, Angelina, I would never reveal your secret." The sincerity in her voice and on her face made me confident.

"When our ship was captured and the pirate captain took me to his ship. I was alone with him. He kissed me."

"Oh, dear Lord, Angelina did he, well, you know, did he hurt you?" she said wide eyed and unblinking as she took my hand in hers offering comfort.

"No, he didn't hurt me. I kissed him back. He wasn't what I expected. He was intelligent and brilliantly smart for a pirate. He talked to me like I was a human being with a brain. We talked about politics and books and worldly matters. It was exhilarating. And then he kissed me and I kissed him back. And I liked it!"

"Angelina, how truly scandalous of you," she said as a spark of my old friend surfaced.

"No, you don't understand. He didn't just kiss my lips. That's why no one can ever know. I think he has ruined me for any other man," I told her.

"What do you mean, Angelina? Ruined you? Did he violate you?" she asked, concerned.

"Not in that way. I just mean he was the most wonderful kisser. Not like that time Thomas Mortly tried awkwardly to steal a kiss from me when we were sixteen. Do you remember that?" I asked her.

"Absolutely horrifying if I recall," Sarah said with a laugh.

"I don't think I could ever let anyone touch me like that again. It was so passionate and intimate all at the same time. I just don't think that it would be the same."

"Oh, Angie." Her words came out as she began to sob. She turned her head to hide her face and the tears that spilled from her eyes.

"Sarah, talk to me. What is the matter? You can tell me." Turning her face around gently with my hand and looking into her tear streaked face. "Please talk to me."

"Oh, Angelina, I have made such a mess of it," she cried.

"Made a mess of what? Sarah, what have you made such a mess of?" pulling a hanky from my pocket and handing it to her.

"I let someone touch me in an intimate way." Sarah started crying anew.

"Sarah, it's going to be all right. Just tell me what happened. Is that what you were going to tell me about before I left?" I asked.

"Yes. I mean no. I mean, oh, Angelina." Putting her head on my shoulder, she took a deep breath, trying to gain control of her emotions.

"Sarah, just say it. You are safe with me." Tipping her face up to mine, I looked at her, again trying to reassure her.

"Darcy Montgomery and I were going to have a child. I wanted to tell you and then I was going to tell him that I was with child."

"Well, what happened next?" I eagerly prodded like someone halfway through a good book, impatient to get to the end.

"I went to find him in the park at our usual spot and saw him with Agnes Newton," she said, grief laced with irony.

"What do you mean you saw them together in the park?"

"They were kissing and then his hand was all over her breast," Sarah revealed her pain with words of derision dripping from her lips.

"What did you do?" I asked, impatiently.

"I went home, and when he called on me later that day, I had George turn him away. And I refused to see him again." With the words out, Sarah was finally freed from her isolation that had confined her for so many weeks.

"Well? Go on, what happened next?" I pushed for more details.

"I cried and refused to eat, and Mother finally asked me what was wrong and I told her."

"You didn't!" Shock hung heavily in my words.

"I had to. You were gone, and I was all alone. I didn't know what else to do." More unshed tears sparkled in her eyes as she recalled how helpless she had felt.

"Mother insisted that we travel to a spa in Ireland. She didn't even tell Father the reason. She just said we were going. She fired Mary before we left. I was sad, but Mother said it was for the best.

"While I was at the spa, they made me drink some awful tea, and they put me in really hot water. Three days later, I lost the baby." The pain and guilt she still bore reflected in her eyes as she grabbed herself about the middle as if she were reliving the pain of that day.

"I am so sorry, Sarah, that I wasn't here for you. But why did you hide this from me? You know that I will never betray your confidence. Never!" I stood and started pacing.

"I always knew Darcy Montgomery was a snake. The plundering, despoiling lout. Why, I could skin him alive, leave his bloody carcass on display in a public place as a reminder to all the other snakes slithering about on their bellies in society!"

"Oh, Angelina, you will never know just how much I have missed you." Her eyes sparkled again." I am so terribly glad you and I are friends, but did I ever tell you that you truly are bloodthirsty and more than a little strange?" Sarah teased, allowing a smile to creep in. "Of course, I say this to you with nothing but love."

"Maybe once or twice." Walking back to her and taking her hand to help her from the bench. "No more talk of snakes or lusty pirates," I told her with a laugh. "Oh, did I tell you that my pirate had incredibly deep blue eyes? I could have dove into them and not cared that I was drowning." As I joked with her to lighten the mood, we continued to walk and talk our way through the garden for an hour.

8

 XCITEMENT HAD BEEN BUILDING FOR weeks in anticipation of one of the biggest parties of the season—King George III's Annual Venetian Breakfast held every year. I really don't know why they call it a Venetian Breakfast, it always starts in the afternoon, lasting well into the evening.

It was an excuse to dress outlandishly, consume fine wines in excess and eat exquisite foods to one's full content.

There are jugglers, acrobats, contortionists, musicians, and singers from all over London. Some of the entertainment are brought in from foreign countries to enliven and astound the guests, as well as the king. The atmosphere is lively with just a touch of debauchery, and everyone wants to be there.

King George married Princess Charlotte of Mecklenburg-Strelitz on September 8, 1761, in Chapel Royal, St. James Palace. The first heir to the throne was born eleven months later on the twelfth of August and christened George IV.

This year the royal couple was expecting their second child later in the summer, but Charlotte refused to miss out on the festivities.

King George purchased Buckingham House last year and spent the year renovating the house and gardens into a family retreat. He was determined to turn it into a show place for his lavish affairs.

Everyone lucky enough to receive an invitation planned their wardrobe with care. Dress shops were busy around the clock designing one of a kind gowns so over the top that the parade of scantily clad women vying for attention was truly entertainment in itself.

Elaborate shoes were designed and made to match the gowns and tiny little quirky hats fashioned to sit on top of the ladies wigs or hair that had been greased, powdered and piled high on their heads. Extravagant fans and delicately designed parasols were provided to guests courtesy of the king for protection from too much sun and intimate moments.

It really was a spectacle to behold. The who's who of London's town would be in attendance.

I opted to be more conservative than most, choosing a satin gown dyed in the brown to burnt amber tones that would change hues as I walked, giving it an exquisite texture. A delicate design of vines and flowers stitched around the collar twisted down the bodice and along the cuff of the low cut dress in gold thread with tiny pearl beads sown throughout. The skirt of the gown opened as I walked revealing a delicate petticoat underneath of ivory with emerald green and gold stitching with tiny pearls beading to match the top. A corset was called for with ample layers beneath the skirts to give the illusion of poof.

I chose to wear a wig instead of greasing and powdering my hair. It was always so difficult to wash the grease completely out, and it would leave a dull sheen to my hair for a week. A wig was securely in place adorned with strings of pearls. The stage had been set, and all the players had arrived.

Let the orchestrated chaos begin.

Sarah and I had agreed to arrive about two o'clock and meet at the nearest fountain upon entering the garden. We knew that it was a safe bet that there would be multiple fountains so the importance of being specific would prove a significant detail.

Mother, Father, Jonathan, and I arrived at ten minutes after two; and I was very excited. The line of carriages was long as people arrived and were helped out, one by one, then escorted to the entrance to have their names announced. After that, we greeted our host, the king and his immediate party as they stood in a procession line.

There was art on display in the main hall as the line slowly moved through and the artists themselves in attendance answered questions or obtained commissions for future work or portraits from the very wealthy.

One portrait caught my eye as I stopped to study it further. It was of a little boy that appeared to be about five years of age. He was dressed in a beautiful royal blue outfit with lace on the cuffs. He was looking for his puppy as it hid under a chair from him.

My question was, how did the artist capture this scene when clearly neither the boy nor the puppy would stay still for any length of time?

"How very lovely you look today, Lady Angelina. That gown sets off your coloring most desirably," the simpering voice came from behind me.

"Mr. Montgomery, I do not recall giving you leave to address me by my given name." I fixed Darcy with my best high and mighty societal stare.

"Please forgive me, Lady Stewart, I was under the impression that you and I could be friends." As he attempted to look properly rebuffed, an air of insincerity lingered in his words.

"I didn't realize they started letting the masses attend the king's parties!" I scoffed, rebuffing Darcy Montgomery in hopes that he would get the point and avoid me at all costs. Unfortunately, he wasn't that bright.

"Madam, you cut me to the quick, and my only desire is to be amicable." His whine grated me to my very marrow and I wished for him to disappear.

"Sir, we are neither comrades nor equals in my eyes. I do not understand why you insist on playing the simpleton?" The shock on his face told me that I had hit my mark as I continued to press the point. "And in the future, I would be appreciative if you would refrain from approaching me in public or private since I neither intend to befriend you nor bring merit to your social climb. I would be more inclined to assist you in your social descent, Mr. Montgomery." The acidic tone dripped from my lips as I punctuated each word, then turning my back on him to further emphasize my point. "Good day to you."

He stepped close behind me so anyone who might observe us would think that we were having an intimate conversation. "You have always been an uppity bitch, and you will get yours one day. I will see to it personally! Mark my words, Lady Stewart. Mark my words," Darcy said with real malice in his voice as he dared to touch my neck with his finger. His malodorous fragrance and foul breath on the back of my neck turned my stomach as he leaned in for emphasis.

My shaking hand rested on the dagger in my pocket. The weight of the blade felt like a balm to my nerves. I closed my eyes and visualized the dagger sinking deep into his chest. Taking two deep breaths to steady my hands I opened my eyes to find him gone. A wave of relief washed over me as I sought out the security of my family near the head of the line.

Jonathan sat with me by the fountain as I waited for Sarah to arrive. If I didn't know better, I would wager my brother was smitten with my best friend. Jonathan had simply smiled sweetly at me when I had suggested it.

From our vantage point we had a clear view of everyone entering the garden area in their outlandish attire.

Lady Carvon and Lord Baltimore came through together, even though they were not a couple officially. Lady Carvon had lost her husband three years prior and Lord Baltimore had lost his wife four and a half years ago. Neither one of them had remarried, but the rumor was they spent a lot of time together.

Lady Charlotte Edwin was very entertaining with her dress that revealed more than any of us wished to see. The bodice was made of white Norwich crepe that was almost see through, cut low off the shoulder with the bodice plunging even lower still. She didn't even have the decency to place a lace hanky in her décolletage. One's imagination certainly didn't have to work hard at all. The skirt opened in front to reveal delicate pale pink petticoats so thin I thought I saw the outline of her legs.

Prince Edward, Duke of York was in attendance along with his wife, Princess Mary of Albany. Their attire was somewhat conservative and yet the debauchery that took place in the hedges later that evening I hear was completely scandalous and observed by more than a few guests.

Lady Sarah Lennox and Lord Lennox had on coordinating attire and were by far the best dressed couple in attendance. Their garments were made with ivory brocades, with gold and green leaf pattern stitched around the cuffs. The pattern was mimicked on her bodice and sleeve as well as his jacket and breeches worn with white stockings and gold shoes.

Sarah Burgess came floating across the lawn in her elegant white silk gown trimmed in rose pink threading and satin bows. Her hair was fashioned high on her head with a sweet little hat with delicate pink and white flowers throughout. She was a picture of gentility and grace.

The color had returned to her face, and she had gained a couple of pounds due to my daily hounding and threat to force feed her if she wouldn't eat. Our bond of friendship was stronger than ever.

"Dear Jonathan, how wonderful it is to see you," Sarah said as she offered my brother her hand.

"You are truly a vision of perfection today, Lady Sarah," Jonathan said, planting a kiss on her delicate hand.

"Why, Lord Stewart, you do know how to turn a phrase and a lady's head." Then turning to me she greeted me with a wide smile and hug. "Angelina, what an incredible gown you are wearing."

"I am afraid I pale in comparison to your elegant beauty, dear friend," I said, taking her by the arm as we started walking toward the festivities. "Jonathan, you had planned on joining us?" Looking back I gave him the eye that said, *you better hurry along if you are coming.*

"Yes, of course." Jonathan had to take large steps to catch up.

Leaning over, I whispered in her ear. "I have to warn you that Darcy is here, and he and I had a most unpleasant exchange earlier. I dare say I left him in a rather foul mood, so stay close to Jonathan or myself." The color completely drained from Sarah's face. "Sarah, keep it together. One mistake cannot define us, so hold your head up and don't stop smiling. We are here to have fun today. Take hold of Jonathan's arm and let's have fun."

We stopped to watch a band of jugglers immediately followed by trained dogs dressed in little outfits that walked on their back legs. Everywhere we looked there was entertainment surrounding us.

There were strategically placed tables with food and fruit over- flowing.

Servants wandered through the crowd passing out glasses of refreshments. Everything one could desire was simply at your fingertips. The entire day was perfect except for the looming presence of Darcy Montgomery.

"Jonathan, are those your friends Lords Lacroix and Deveraux?" Sarah asked.

Jonathan and I turned to see the other party just a few feet away.

"My good friends, how pleasant to see you here. Please come and join us." Jonathan extended his hand in friendship to them both, as a woman I had never met before draped herself all over the two men.

Coming face-to-face with Jude Deveraux in his entire refined splendor was breathtaking. His three-piece suit charcoal gray silk was trimmed in black velvet with silver and green stitching of vines, leaves, and pheasants which lined the front of his coat and cuffs. The richly elegant attire combined with his height and regal stature caused woman to swoon at his feet. Even dressed as a dandy he radiated masculinity and vitality. I didn't think that it was possible for his shoulders to look broader, but they did.

"Allow me to introduce you to Lady Elyse Barrett," Jude said, while staring directly at me, gestured to his right.

The woman standing next to him was slightly shorter than me with her hand resting possessively on Jude's arm. I could tell her hair was dark but she had it greased, powdered and piled high on her head. The decollate of her dress was more than revealing as her abundant assets spilled out from the top. Her face was also powdered in the old style with a small black heart drawn on her right cheek bone, and her lips and eyebrows had been painted. I could tell she had once been very pretty, but the years had taken their toll. The powder caked on her face showing fine lines made her look somewhat comical.

Jude had been studying my face intently as I looked Lady Elyse Barrett up and down. When our eyes met, he lifted his one eyebrow in that familiar way. I could not tell if he was asking a question or throwing down a gauntlet of challenge, but either way, I would not take the bait. Biting my tongue while stemming the laundry list of insults that begged to be released from my mouth, I chose instead to go a different way.

"What a lovely gown, Lady Barrett. That shade of yellow plays well with your eyes." I tried to sound as sincere as possible without choking on my lie. Truth is, the color of her gown only added to her already yellowed complexion.

"Thank you so very much, Lady Stewart. You are too kind," she said as she kept touching Jude's arm possessively. "Jude has been so kind introducing me around to all of his friends."

My eyes meeting his as she spoke, her voice—a culmination of a whine and nasal—grated on my nerves. I made note of his placid demeanor and wondered at the root cause of it.

"And how long have you known the Duke, Lady Barrett?" I asked with curiosity burning inside of me. Or was it something else that had me seeing red? The simpering pawing creature and her whiny irritating voice drove me to distraction.

"My husband, the late Lord Barrett and Jude's parents were very old friends," she said.

I bet they were, I thought to myself.

"We spent many a holidays with the Deveraux's on their estate in France. Jude has always been such a delight to be around," she cooed, turning to look at him and press her breasts against his arm as she squealed like a young girl.

If you ask me, she was trying too hard and I, for one, was getting ill standing this close to her.

"It was a pleasure meeting you, Lady Barrett. So nice to see you again, Honore, Lord Deveraux, but if you would excuse us now Sarah was just saying how terribly famished she was," I announced, slightly rushed as I smiled brilliantly at Honore and avoided Jude's eyes all together. I couldn't stand watching Lady Barrett drape herself across Jude one moment longer. With that I took Sarah's arm and headed for the farthest refreshment table I could find.

I could hear Jonathan saying something to Jude and Honore behind me as I chanced a look back. Jude had a rakish smile on his face as those piercing blue eyes of his followed my retreat.

"What was that about, Angelina? I never said that I was hungry," Sarah inquired as I pulled her across the lawn headed for the other side and as far away from Jude's probing eyes.

"I think I have been in the sun too long without an umbrella. I am getting light headed and I need something to drink," I said in hopes that my veiled lie would do the trick.

"Your cheeks do look a bit flushed. Here, drink this." Handing me a glass of sparkling wine she took off the table as we passed by. "Let's get you inside and some food in your stomach," she said, fussing over me all the way to the main house.

Jonathan caught up to us as we entered the house through wide opened doors. "Angelina, what was that all about? Don't you think you were being a bit rude?" Jonathan asked as he lowered his voice next to my ear.

"Wait here while I get some food. Jonathan don't leave her alone, Angelina got too much sun and feels light headed," Sarah sweetly told me as she left the table to rest.

"I couldn't look at that woman's over abundance spilling out of her gown like a cheap tramp one second longer, Jonathan. Did you see her? Better yet did you hear that grating voice? I thought I would be ill," I nearly screamed at him between my teeth as I tried not to cause a scene.

"Was that the problem?" he said speculatively, "or was it that she was hanging all over Jude?" As his face lit up with a large grin I was transported back in time when I was eight years old again. Jonathan had always been a terrible tease and right now was not the time, nor was I in the mood.

"Did you not hear Sarah? I was getting light headed and slightly nauseous," I insisted. "Besides if I had to listen to Lady Barrett squeal again I might have slapped her."

"Someone has a jealous streak. I must say you have always worn green well, my dear." Jonathan laughed at me with enough distance between us that I couldn't punch his arm like I did when we were children.

"Stop teasing me so, Jonathan. It's unbecoming. I just need some food in my stomach. You really should be fussing over Sarah and leave me be for now," I sweetly said.

"I think I will go help Sarah with the food. Don't move and I will be right back." And with that, Jonathan was off to find Sarah.

Oh, thank heavens. I don't think that I could take anymore of his teasing just now. The quiet was nice and so was the parade of people passing by.

The hairs on the back of my neck stood on end and I felt a prickling feeling go up my spine as if someone was watching me. Turning my head slowly to the right then to the left, I couldn't see anyone leering sinisterly at me.

"I just needed to be sure that you were feeling all right," Jude's unmistakable voice said from behind me.

Visibly jumping from the start he gave me, I turned around to find Jude standing behind me and he was missing his lap dog. I had no way of knowing just how long he had been there. But there he stood.

"May I?" Jude asked gesturing with his hand toward the chair next to me. "I was concerned and wanted to see for myself that nothing was wrong. You looked a little flushed when you left so suddenly," he said, pulling out the chair next to mine.

"Yes, thank you for your concern, but I'm fine, just too much sun. I hope you didn't leave your special friend alone on my account," I said so innocently with sweetness dripping from my lips not daring to look at him.

"As delightful as Lady Barrett can be, I didn't come today to tarry with her."

Looking up to read his face and gauge his true meaning, my eyes strayed to his lips a moment too long before meeting his eyes. A slow grin played on his mouth and I felt my cheeks color slightly.

"What happened to Honore? Surely you didn't desert him to check on me," I said, trying to hide my embarrassment.

"I am sure Lady Barrett can find someone else to entertain her. As for Honore, he is always able to find companionship to entertain himself." Jude reached over taking my hand in his and checking my pulse. "You do feel a bit warm and your pulse is racing." Gauging my response as I suddenly looked down. I tried to pull my hand free of his grip as he tightened his grasp.

"I would ask you to please return my hand to me, sir." Trying to remain civil as my heart raced from his probing touch, I felt my face flush crimson.

Moving his chair closer, he maintained his grasp on my hand and his intense eye contact. "I only wish to gauge the severity of your heart, I mean your condition." He flashed me a wry half-smile, and narrowed his eyes as he leaned in closer. "I believe, my lady, that you are getting worse." Using his free hand, he reached up to touch my cheek and forehead.

I nibbled on my bottom lip to hide the pleasure that his touch brought as his fingers trailed across my cheek and his thumb played with my swollen lip where I had chewed it. Using my fan to cool the heat I felt, I prayed he would stop before I was completely undone by his touch.

Reaching hesitantly to take his hand from my face, I was fascinated by the long tapered fingers. They had been well groomed but were somehow still manly, not the hands of one who had never labored with them, but strong, masculine hands.

"You truly can return to your festivities without further concern over my welfare. I am in excellent hands," I said as breathing suddenly became difficult.

"Yes, madam, you are truly in good hands, of that I can assure you." I was pondering his meaning, which seemed to have more than just one implication, as Jonathan and Sarah returned with an assortment of delectable delights for us all to consume.

"So good of you to join us, old man," Jonathan exclaimed, reaching out his hand to Jude as he instructed the two gentlemen following him where to set down the trays of food and drinks. "What happened to Lady Barrett and Honore?" Jonathan asked as he attentively focused on Sarah.

"They found their own means of entertainment. I was worried about Lady Stewart and I thought I might come and check on her." Sitting back down, Jude turned his full attention back to me. "I found her in quite a state. It seems she got quite over heated," Jude stated, taking one of the glasses off the refreshment tray and handing it to me, which I took from him gratefully and drank deeply.

"Are we intending to talk all day and night of my condition, or is someone going to pass me some food?" I complained, finding my voice again. And yet the tingling of my lip where he had touched them lingered.

Sarah passed me a fork and knife as Jonathan passed a plate to me. The conversation flowed and the camaraderie was sincere as we ate and made merry. An hour later, I felt that strange sensation once again. The hair on the back of my neck stood on end, and I felt a prickling up my spine causing me to shiver slightly. I had a strong feeling that I was being watched as I looked around to see who it might be. But evening had begun to descend and the shadows held their own secrets.

"Are you cold, Lady Stewart? Do you want me to fetch your wrap?" Jude inquired as he leaned over, placing his hand on my arm.

"Please, I think we have moved beyond such formalities, call me Angelina. And I think I will be fine for now, maybe later," attempting what I hoped was a sincere smile while trying to push the eerie feeling aside.

The guests had begun to show their true colors as some had indulged far too much and fallen asleep on tables and benches, their makeup smeared and beauty marks no longer in their original placements. Others had to be helped to carriages and sent home.

Tables were cleared off of the huge veranda and the orchestra began to play. King George and Princess Charlotte danced the first waltz, and halfway through, lords, dukes and ladies alike joined in as the true essence of the Venetian Breakfast party began.

The four of us enjoyed ourselves as Honore and his latest conquest, a Miss Elizabeth Gray, joined us. She was very lovely dressed in a white gown trimmed in pale blue satin ribbons with a delicate floral design around the bodice and sleeves. She stood only three inches shorter than Honore who was very taken with Miss Gray at the moment. Her heart-shaped face turned upward as he whispered something to her which left a smile lingering on both of their lips.

"Honore seems to be very content at the moment," I said, turning to Jude, noting that he had been staring at me.

"He is until he isn't any longer," he replied very noncommittal.

"Would you say your friend is fickle?" I asked, trying to make conversation.

"Not fickle, particular would be a better word," Jude answered as he turned his eyes to his dear friend. "Honore says that he will know the right one when he meets her. But until then he must talk to as many lovely maidens as he can," Jude finished, then turned his full attention back to me.

"I see. So he feels inclined to sample from all the lovely cakes and pastries on display to find out which flavor suits him best," I stated.

"Yes, that would probably be right. And what of you, Lady Angelina, how would you go about conducting your affairs?" He asked directly while studying my reaction to his personal question.

"I suppose that would depend on what exactly is meant by conducting my affairs? I answered, turning the question back on him.

"I saw you earlier with Lord Darcy Montgomery and it looked very intimate."

"Things are not always as they seem. Sometimes one's eyes deceive them, Lord Deveraux," I quipped, as I could feel my blood beginning to boil when I recalled my earlier conversation with Darcy.

"Please call me Jude. As you pointed out earlier, we have moved beyond such formalities. So you don't know Lord Montgomery well?"

"Oh, but I do know Lord Montgomery well, sir, and I take exception to the sincerity of your questioning," I said as my agitations began to show.

"I see," Jude said pensively.

"No, I don't think you do see, and I would thank you to speak of someone else. Anyone else would do." Turning my head to look for Sarah and Jonathan on the dance floor as tears began to sparkle in my eyes. Tears of sadness for what Darcy had done to my friend. Tears of anger for what he had said to me earlier and the fear his words stirred in me. I dabbed at the corners of my eyes with a finger.

"Would you care to dance then?" Turning to face Jude with my mask of society firmly in place, he was standing by my chair offering me his hand. Placing my hand in his, I let him lead me to the dance floor as a new waltz began to play.

The tension was thick between us as we began to dance.

"Lovely weather we are having, don't you think?" Jude commented, as we turned around the floor. Looking up slowly to see if I heard him correctly, a half smile played across his lips, so I figured I would play along.

"Yes. I was just telling the ladies at our last sewing circle how incredible the weather has been. Right after I told them about the latest needlepoint I had been working on. You forgot to compliment me on my dress, Mr. Deveraux," I said mockingly, trying not to laugh as the corners of his mouth turned up further.

"Angelina, my dear, do you truly think that any man gives a whit about a lady's gown and whether or not it was tailor made? It is not the stitch that turns the blood to boil." His eyes suddenly turning a deeper shade of blue as the full meaning of his words hit home. Suddenly I felt very warm and the tension between us was different.

Tightening his grip about my waist as he held me so close it was nearly scandalous. "Extraordinary," is all he said as we continued around the dance floor.

The song finally ended and I moved to leave the floor but was hindered by his hand still around my waist. Looking to his face for an answer, a shadow moved across it and his lips worked to form words that never were said out loud.

"Hello, son, your Poppy and I would be most pleased if you would introduce us to your friend," came the feminine voice behind Jude, as his mother placed the emphasis on "your friend."

Both of us turned around to find a very tall, elegantly dressed woman, with raven-black hair and eyes the color of sapphires, staring directly at me. She was holding the arm of a handsomely dressed older man who chose to give his wife free rein while he remained silent.

There was no doubt in my mind who she was, and by the tone in her voice I was about to face an inquisition or worse.

"Mama, Papa, it is so good to see you." Kissing his mother first on one cheek and then the other, and then repeating the whole thing with his father I stood frozen in place by the chill radiating from the woman's eyes.

"Please, where are my manners? Papa, Mama, may I present to you Lady Angelina Marguerite Amelia Stewart. Lady Stewart, if you please, this is my father, Prime Minister of France, Count Philippe Gerard Deveraux, and his beautiful and gracious wife, my mother, Countess Genevieve Sophia Deveraux of Bordeaux.

I dropped to a proper curtsy and bowed my head. "It is a pleasure to meet you both," I said with a pleasant smile pasted to my face.

"We noticed you both made a handsome couple dancing the waltz, so tall and striking," Jude's father said as his wife glared at him.

"How did you come to be introduced to my son, Miss Stewart?" Lady Deveraux asked.

"Lady Stewart, Mother," Jude corrected.

"Yes, of course, please forgive me."

"We met a few weeks ago at my family's home. Lord Deveraux and my brother attended school together," I answered, turning toward Jude.

"I do believe we were introduced to your parents earlier today. Your mother is a very lovely woman," Lady Deveraux said, trying to be polite.

"Your father is very knowledgeable in regards to importing and exporting. I enjoyed our talk," his father replied, giving his wife a look that I did not yet understand.

"Your father and I have been in London for five weeks now and still you have been by to visit me only two times. I will be expecting you to come by this week without fail," his mother said, giving him such a guilt-filled look he had no choice but to cater to her.

"Mama, you know that I am here on business and I have been busy. I promise that I will get by to see you and Poppy before the end of the week," he assured her. His words intended to placate his mother.

"Genevieve, darling, we must be going now. The night is still young, but we are not. I feel we have delayed these two from their fun long enough," Philippe said to his wife as he tried to lead her away. Looking up I could see unspoken words pass between Jude and his mother. A secret code passed between mother and son before she turned and walked away with her husband, glancing back one last time to give me the once over.

I turned on my heels and headed in the opposite direction passing our table. I just kept going. I needed some air, which was funny because the enormous dance floor was outdoors.

The gardens were alight with thousands of lanterns, and I needed distance. I headed toward the topiaries at the other end of the royal gardens and as far away from Jude as I could get. Anger mingled with humiliation fueled my escape. I could hear Jude behind me, but I didn't slow down.

Breathing hard at this point because I was nearly running and my tight corset restricted my ability to breathe deeply, I didn't even know exactly what it was that I was running from. I just knew I needed space.

When he grabbed my arm, I came to a sudden stop as I gasped for air. Jude grasped my shoulders, shaking me like a rag doll. My wig toppled to the ground and pins flew as copper strands tumbled down, spilling over my shoulders.

"Why didn't you stop? Didn't you hear me calling after you? What is wrong?" Jude's anger was mixed with frustration as he tried to make sense of his own feelings.

"Help me, please. I cannot breathe," my words came out in short gasps for air before I went limp.

Spinning me around while holding me against his left arm, he proceeded to unlace the top portion of my gown. Reaching into the pocket of my gown, he retrieved the dagger and cut the top laces of my corset. The air flooded into my lungs in one giant gasp as my knees gave out. Placing the dagger between his teeth, he picked me up in his arms, like one would a hurt child, and carried me toward a bench void of light. It was probably extinguished by the bench's previous occupants.

Shadows playing across his face made him look ruthless and savage. I had to blink twice for I thought my eyes deceived me.

Gently placing me on the bench he kneeled down. Retrieving the sheath from my pocket, he placed it on the end of the dagger and put it back into my pocket.

"You can really never tell when these things will come in handy." He patted the dagger that lay in my pocket against my leg. "Good thing you took your brother's advice."

"How did you know I had it on me?" Astonishment showing on my face.

"I felt it when we were dancing," he answered offhandedly.

"Is it often you hold a woman so closely while dancing that you know exactly what she carries in her dress pocket?" I asked slightly scandalized by his admission.

"You can lose the disapproving tone, if you please. It isn't often that I have the need to hold a woman so closely. They usually press in on me," he added, feeling rather full of himself.

"Hah . . . you have rather a high opinion of yourself." I found his attitude grating on my nerves. Abruptly standing to leave, I took three steps before remembering my dress was undone

"I heard no protests from you while we were dancing."

Whirling around, I fixed him with an angry scowl. "I couldn't protest since your arm was cutting off my circulation, you pompous toad." I turned around presenting my back to him and indicating my need by pointing to my dress where it gaped open. "Assistance, please."

"Toads don't have thumbs." Playing the fool, he held his hands up as if all his digits were stuck together.

I turned on him with hands on my hips. "You have some nerve, Jude Deveraux, or would Judas be a more appropriate name for you?"

I angrily said through clenched teeth so mad that I would swear steam escaped from my ears.

"You have so many moods it is difficult to pick just which one is my favorite." His arm snaked out ensnaring me tightly against his taut form. Tipping my head back with his free hand under my chin his kiss was tender and passionate at the same time. He tasted of red wine and sensuality and something so familiar. Then it hit me. Those gloriously full lips had kissed me before.

Opening my eyes and pulling back as my hands furiously worked to untie his cravat and open his shirt. "Slow down, my pet, I enjoy enthusiasm but there are limits to even my self-control," Jude said in his thick French accent which I discovered came out when he was amorous.

Reaching my hands beneath the collar of his crisp white linen shirt, I worked one hand over his chest as my other hand sought out his left shoulder. Every scar just as I had remembered them, but the left shoulder would be the tell.

"Ah hah! It was you all along, I knew it! And you tried to tell me I was mistaken." I pushed hard against his chest to free myself from our entanglement.

I paced back and forth in front of him, as I proceeded to berate his good name and parentage in the process. I turned to face him squarely now with hands on hips and eyes shooting daggers at him. "You lied to me. You tried to make me think that I had lost my mind because I said that the pirate captain and Jude Deveraux, the Duke of Bayonne, was one in the same. And yet here you are, and much to my surprise you are the very same! Care to explain yourself, Monsieur Deveraux?" My breathing labored heavily, so filled with anger I struggled to catch my breath.

"*Ma belle Ange*, you truly are an angel," Jude purred the words. "You now know my secret and the question that lies between us is what will you do with that knowledge?" He stood silently in front of me for a moment, then dropped to one knee. "My life is now in your hands, *ma amour.*"

My anger suddenly dissipating like steam off a lake. The very thought of never being with him or touching him again weighed heavy on my heart. My breathing came in short bursts now for a different reason. "No! Don't you start with your French and your sincere eyes. How could you?" A small scream mixed with a growl of frustration omitted from my throat as I clenched and unclenched my hands by my side, trying desperately to think.

Walking over to him, I placed my hands on his face, tilting it up to mine. "I have not breathed deeply since the day you left me on the deck of that ship, and sailed away." Tears springing to my eyes as one single tear escaped making a trail down my cheek. "I believed I would never see you again and my heart broke that day," I confessed, while tears freely spilled from my eyes as I spoke what was truly in my heart. "Then like a dream you came strolling up one day, unconstrained, giving me a shock only to deny the truth. My imprisoned heart cannot take any more lies. I implore you take my heart or lock it away forever, never to be used again."

And with that, Jude wrapped one arm around my waist as he gently caressed my face. "You truly are a remarkable woman." Our lips touched gently at first, as I reached up, releasing his hair from its tie and threading my fingers through it pulling him even closer still. My desire was igniting deep inside of me as a moan escaped from Jude's throat.

Lifting me in his arms, he began to look around as I rained kisses on his neck and face. I could tell we were moving but in what direction I did not care.

Coming to a stop on the lake docks, he placed me down on the deck of the boat tied there. "Sit down before you tip the bloody thing over," he ordered, and I obeyed.

Throwing the rope into the boat, he climbed aboard and pushed off from the dock. We were now afloat on Buckingham House's lake in one of the king's specially designed boats.

It conveniently came with pillows for comfort, a three-sided structure for added privacy and a blanket for warmth. What more could one ask for?

Taking up an oar, he paddled the boat to the middle of the lake as I continued to cling to him. I tormented him with vexing kisses on his neck and face while I reached my hands under his shirt frantically re-visiting every inch of him.

"You little vixen!" his words coming out between clenched teeth.

Giving up on the paddling for more rewarding endeavors, he shirked out of his coat and already unbuttoned waistcoat. Jude pulled my hands from their exploration of him, as I heard his sharp intake of breath. "Madam, if you don't want me to completely shred your gown and rep-utation in one move, I suggest you wait one moment."

I began to feel suddenly self-conscious at his words, not sure if I was doing it wrong, so casting my eyes down slightly I began chewing the corner of my lip.

Raking his hand through his hair he took several deep breaths to re-gain the control he was in danger of losing. An expression of frustration escaping his lips, Jude gently cupped my face with his hand as he pulled me closer. "My beautiful angel, you are like the devil himself come to tempt me into the grave. Look at me, please." Cautiously, I looked into his eyes. "I could not go one more day without you. *Ma Coeur*, how do you say, my heart." Removing his shirt, he reached behind me to unlace my gown. Slipping it over my head, he laid it gently on the other side of him. Next, he finished unlacing the ties of my corset and flung it into the lake before the words of protest could leave my lips.

We knelt across from each other on the deck of the boat, moonlight bathing us both with soft glow. My heart beat faster as I anticipated what was to come next. I know I should have been scandalized by his actions, but I wasn't.

He caressed my hair and then my face as my blood began to boil. He pulled on the tie of my delicate slip, allowing firm breasts to strain against the material of their confines begging to be released.

He kissed my swollen lips tenderly at first then greedily becoming more demanding. His hands searched my body leaving a scalding trail on my skin every place he touched. I shivered as my entire body tingled, demanding fulfillment.

Pulling my lips from his to look into his storm-filled eyes, I saw the desire and lust he was keeping bridled. Touching his lips with my fingertips, I leaned down kissing his chest and nipples licking and sucking until they constricted into tight balls and his breathing came in harsh ragged pants. I felt him shiver as goose bumps formed on his skin.

Taking hold of my shoulders he pulled me up, ravaging my lips with his mouth as if he were a starving man given but a small morsel of food. He worked his way down my neck and finally to my breasts, fondling my taut flesh as a cry fell from my lips. My breathing matched his harsh, gasps for air, sensations so foreign I scarcely believed them to be real.

"Tell me that you want me, Angelina." The smoldering passion of his words sent delicious tingling sensations over my skin and to my core.

"Yes, Jude, I desire you, I need you." My words came out as a desperate cry, a longing for release but from what I could not fathom.

His hand reached for the hem of my slip. The air was sucked from my lungs once again as he ran his hand along the inside of my thigh. My insides were aflame with quivering sensations that pooled near the lower portion of my belly, like liquid gold sitting over a flame.

His sinfully sensuous lips were on mine as he pushed me back on the pillows. I arched my back and thrust my breasts toward him in hopes that he would never stop what he was doing. Ever!

My entire body tingled as he raised the thin material higher and his hand continued to explore even deeper into my womanhood. Touching on one spot sent tiny explosions of pleasure to my brain so exquisite it hurt. Cries of ecstasy escaped my lips as he covered my mouth with his. Wave after wave swept through me. As I clung to him to keep from shattering into a million pieces' tears rolled down my cheeks. Not tears of sorrow or pain, but tears of unbelievable rapture that I never knew existed.

"Did I hurt you?" concern etching his voice, while he cradled me in his arms and brushed tears from my cheeks.

"No!" Is all I could get out at first as I clung to him. My breathing still erratic, as emotion kept me from speaking. "Please, I beg you to do it again, even if my heart stops beating from the sheer pleasure of it. Don't ever stop," I begged.

Squeezing me tightly to his chest, I could feel the pounding of his heart as he held me there secure and safe.

"Aye, *ma amour*, I will never stop loving you."

9

SUNDAY, MAY 1, 1763;
MORE THAN JUST A BAD DREAM

UDE HAD ARRANGED WITH HONORE to leave his carriage on the other side of the Buckingham property and to tell Jonathan that he would be taking me home after the party. This was the reason it had taken him so long to catch up to me when I had fled the dance floor.

After our little tryst on the king's boat Jude rowed us to the other side of the lake and docked the boat. I was thankful that I did not have to face the throngs of guests and his parents when leaving the party. With the state of my dress, not to mention my hair, I would have again been the talk of the season but for a very different reason.

Sneaking in the servant's entrance of the house carrying my shoes, I headed up the back staircase. Hearing the chimes on the clock announce three o'clock I said a little prayer that no one would be up and about to witness my unsightly circumstance.

Slowly turning the knob on my door, I expected the room to be dark but instead it was bathed in light. Anna had waited up for me but fallen asleep on the chase. Attempting to sneak past her less she saw my condition, I turned and blew out one of the lanterns.

I headed for the dressing room as I heard her voice behind me.

"Did you have a fun evening, miss?"

Turning around slowly I knew that I had been caught. I said with a sheepish smile pasted on my face, "Yes, thank you for inquiring. Why are you still up?"

Anna lifted her eyebrows, giving me a curious look but not commenting on the state of my dress or hair. "Shall we get you out of that dress then?" Walking over to me, she waited for me to present my back to her.

"I could have managed. You really didn't need to wait up, Anna."

"Would you like me to brush out your hair tonight or would you prefer in a few hours when I get you up? Oh, and don't forget I will need to start packing early if we are to leave for the country by noon," Anna said, reminding me about the move. After Easter each year, Parliament took a five-week holiday and so did London socialites.

"And what happened to the corset that you were wearing, Angelina? I also recall a wig being on your head when you left here yesterday," she said with a hint of scolding added to her tone.

"Now that is a bit of a story to tell, for sure, my wee lassie," I said as I attempted to lighten the mood by giving her my best impersonation of a leprechaun.

"To be sure and I'll be hearing all about it in the morn. Of that you can be sure," Anna teased as she mimicked an Irish brogue of her own.

"Aye, to be sure." Stepping out of my gown, I headed for the bed not wishing to explain anything more. "I think I will dispense with the nightgown tonight I just need some sleep, Anna. Good night," I called out over my shoulder as I retreated under the covers pulling them over me as Anna blew out the lamps and went to bed herself.

Tossing and turning all night, I relived over and over again the tantalizing memories from the boat as Jude invaded my dreams. His sapphire eyes penetrated every blood-boiling, toe-curling moment again and again.

One moment I was blissfully happy, then a more sinister feeling of dread crept into the dream. Jude's face was no longer his face but that of someone wearing a distorted mask. No longer experiencing pleasure, but instead, an overwhelming feeling of ominous foreboding reached into my imaginings grabbing me by the throat. I had the sensation of drowning over and over again. One moment I was being choked, then a knife was making small cuts to my neck and wrists. I couldn't breathe as I felt the terrifying sensation of being held under the water. The liquid filled my lung, and I gasped, fighting for a lung full of precious air.

I awakened suddenly, desperately gulping for air as Anna set the breakfast tray down loudly, dishes clanking together as she rushed to the bedside.

"Angelina, it's all right. You had a bad dream." She grabbed hold of me and cradled me in her arms as I shook uncontrollably, sweat clinging to me along with my slip from the night before. "It's all right. I'm here now, nothing can hurt you," she shushed away the remnants of the nightmare, like a protective mother while speaking comforting words. But her protective nature did nothing to relieve the looming darkness that was inching its way into the marrow of my bones. A sinister black cloud was setting in like a dense London fog ever looming as it fills one's lungs with its pungent thickness.

Oh, dear sweet Anna, this omen could not be "shushed" away so easily. I thought to myself.

An hour later, Anna ordered the tub to be brought up and filled with hot water, and William lit a fire to chase the chill from my room. These simple comforts did nothing to chase away the fears now living in the shadows of my nightmares. Nor did it stop the harbinger of doom that followed me throughout the day.

I had settled on the black riding habit for traveling since it fit my mood. I would ride Dante out to our country estate instead of in the carriage for one main reason. Mother would want to talk nonstop about the king's marvelous party the day before which would bring me back to the dream I had had that morning and that would never do. And for the second reason, I was restless and needed to stretch my legs and what better place than from atop one of the strongest beasts I knew, Dante.

Despite Mother's protests that it was too far to ride, in the end I got my way by sweet-talking Father.

The carriages were finally loaded with luggage and people and began to pull out one by one. I tried to be patient and wait for Jonathan as I grew irritated with every passing minute. He was supposed to ride with me and keep me company at Mother's insistence, but Jonathan was taking his sweet time and daylight was burning.

Cantering alongside the carriages for the longest time my eagerness got the best of me. The moment we reached the main road, I gave Dante his head and let him run. The exhilarating feeling of freedom flying down the road, leaving behind the darkness of doom with the wind blowing in my face and hair was glorious.

Dante and I had been galloping for some time when I rounded a corner of a narrow portion of road to discover a cart had turned over and the contents were spread across the road. Coming to a screeching halt as I nearly ran into the overturned cart and the person lying prone in front of it. Dante reared up nearly toppling me backward from my seat in his excitement.

Leaping from the saddle I ran to the man and rolled him over to see if I could help. As I did so a large burley man ran out from the bushes and the one on the ground grabbed hold of my wrist.

"Ha-ha, now lookie what we have us here. It's a high born come to help the poor peasant out," the first one said as he leered at me, grinning with his mouth full of blackened rotting teeth.

"Now ain't she a Good Samaritan? She is." The tall skinny one said in a strong cockney tongue as he held tightly to my wrist.

"Grab that horse before he takes off and someone discovers her missing before they are supposed to," the fat one yelled to his partner.

The skinny man jumped up, turning loose of my arm, then tried to grab Dante's reins as I yelled loudly, startling Dante, causing him to rear up, sending the smaller man stumbling backward and tumbling to the ground.

Dante pranced about a minute threatening to stomp on the fallen man until I shouted and smacked him on his rear flank, sending him running back in the direction from which we had come.

"Now why did ya go and do that?" My tormenter slapped me across the face, stunning me momentarily.

"He said she ain't to be harmed, Roy," the skinny man warned.

"Shut your trap before I shuts it for you," Roy threatened the thin man.

Catching Roy by surprise, I stomped on his foot with my boot and clocked him in the face with my free elbow. Breaking free I ran from them, gathering produce from the fallen cart as I went, then launching the fruit and vegetables at them. I watched as they tried to dodge the flying rotten produce but were unsuccessful. Running out of ammunition, I pulled the dagger from my pocket ready to do them both harm if they touched me again.

"I will kill the first one who lays a hand on me. I swear it, you filthy gutter snipes!" I screamed at them as I danced around dodging their lame attempts to trap me in between them.

"Get around her, Tommy, you useless wanker," Roy yelled at Tommy, trying to distract me so he could move in and grab me.

His biggest mistake was coming at me in the first place. His second mistake was thinking that I carried a dagger merely for show.

"What a pretty little sticker you got there, girly," Roy taunted as he reached for my wrist.

Slashing his hand, I laid it open from the top of his wrist to the first knuckle.

"Ouch! You little tramp. She cut me, Tommy," Roy cried out as he quickly withdrew his hand, blood squirting out from a vein.

"Come on, Tommy, give it a try, you may not be so lucky," I taunted. "I have an older brother who should be along any minute now. If you think I'm tough, just wait till he gets here," I yelled, trying to buy time.

Roy made a noise close to me as he came in again. I whirled around, clocking him with the palm of my hand. I heard a gruesome snapping noise as I smashed his face, then I swiftly stuck my dagger hilt deep into his soft belly. Pulling it out, I turned to Tommy who had used the opportunity to come up behind me, grabbed me around the waist and trapping my arms to my side. I could hear the pounding of horse hooves approaching, but I was unsure if they were coming to rescue me or assist Tommy and Roy. My mind went wild. I was not going to be taken hostage by a couple of gutter rats.

Pretending that I had fainted I became dead weight in Tommy's arms. When he shifted to pick me up, I lashed out at him, slashing him across the face. He screamed in surprise as I swung again getting his upper arm. Blood now dripping down his face as he grabbed his arm, retreating from what must have been his worst nightmare come true.

Instead of running from him, I advanced on him, my dagger held high and a murderous gleam in my eye. "I am going to kill you slowly, so I hope the horses I hear coming are my people and not yours," I said with real malice.

Tommy tripped over a branch as he backed away from me. Falling to the ground, he curled up into a ball, covering his head with his arms.

There I stood over Tommy, the would-be kidnapper with my chest heaving legs spread apart, dagger in hand, covered in blood when Jonathan, Jude, and Honore sped in on their horses to rescue me.

Jonathan leaped from his horse and ran to me first, his hands searching me head to toe.

"Angelina, are you hurt?" he asked, looking for the source of the blood. "Look at me, speak to me." I could hear the concern evident in his voice. But I couldn't speak. Not yet.

Honore had reached Roy as he lay on the ground dying from the blood loss and writhing in pain.

Jude simply walked up to me taking the dagger from my hand and handed it to Jonathan. Picking me up in his arms, he cradled me gently, his breathing was calm and steady as he carried me to his horse. Honore was there in an instant as Jude handed me off to him.

Jude climbed into his saddle, reaching his arms out to retrieve me from his friend as the two moved as one. Safely seated in front of him I clung to his neck as reality struck, and hot tears of pain and relief began to flow.

"Honore, you know what to do with the one still breathing." Honore moved to retrieve his charge and be off. "Jonathan, I am taking Angelina to the nearest inn. Go back and tell your parents that she is safe and get her horse. I'll meet you there. Don't concern yourself with him," gesturing to the man on the ground curled into a ball, Honore will see to him." With that, Jude kicked his horse into action and we were off.

Spent from the fear of fending off two would be attackers, shock set in as I lay silently in his arms, comforted by the steady beating of his heart, lulled by the clopping of his horse's pace.

Feeling my movement against him, Jude shifted to look down at me as I reached up to touch his face.

"Why is your face so beautiful to me?" I asked softly. "Right now you look like a carved statue so strong and stern."

"I thought you had been thrown from your beast of a horse and lay dead on the side of the road. Imagine my surprise when I came upon you standing over that cowering man covered in blood," Jude said, his words filled with pent-up emotion. "Did you really kill the one and go after the other yourself?"

"I don't know exactly what came over me, I just went crazy for a minute. If the other one hadn't let go of me, he probably would be dead now as well."

"Most likely they are highway men and you were in the wrong place at the wrong time," Jude replied, attempting to comfort me.

"No! I heard one of them tell the other that I was to be delivered unharmed, but I didn't have time to ask any questions."

"Don't worry, Honore is the best man for the job. He will ask all the pertinent questions. For now, you are safely in my arms where you belong," he lovingly pulled me closer, wrapping his arm tightly about me as I snuggled in for the ride.

Jude found an inn, two and a half hours ride from where we began. Exhaustion overtook me and I drifted in and out of sleep a few times, knowing that I was safe.

He secured a room once we reached our destination and ordered a tub and hot water to be brought up to the room while I waited in the stables. Then sneaking me in, with his coat wrapped around me, Jude kept his arm draped protectively around me.

I sat at the window staring at nothing in particular, shock still burdening my mind. Nothing made sense. Who would want to kidnap me?

Jude arranged for a clean gown and linens to be brought up, as he paid the young man filling the tub a few extra coins for his discretion.

Hesitant at first, I let Jude lead me to the tub and helped me from my gown. He soaped up a cloth and scrubbed the blood from my face and hands as I sat emotionless. My eyes filling with tears, but I simply refused to let them spill.

Helping me to stand, he gently wrapped me in a clean linen, then carried me over to the turned down bed when I stood frozen in place. Pulling the covers over me, he smoothed back the stray hair that fell across my face, before leaning over to place a kiss on my forehead and eyes.

"Sleep now, I will only be a moment," he said, turning he walked to the door and waited for me to obediently close my eyes before closing the door.

I fell into a deep fitful sleep, awakening with a start and screaming at the top of my lungs.

"Wake up, Angelina. I'm here with you." Jude shook me gently by my shoulders, his face showed distress. We must get you dressed now." I could hear the urgency in his tone. He helped me into a clean dress then slipped my riding boots on and laced them for me like I was a helpless child.

"What has happened, Jude? Tell me why we are rushing?" I asked, searching his face for answers.

"I went down to get a pint of ale and the entire room is abuzz with talk of the murder."

"What murder? Who was murdered, Jude?" I asked feeling darkness engulfing me. Somehow I already knew what he was going to tell me before the words passed from his lips.

"There was a murder at the king's party last night. They say a girl was violated, cut several times and drowned." Jude kept looking at me as if I would suddenly fall to pieces.

"There's more isn't there? Tell me the rest, Jude. I need to know it all." My nightmare came back to me in vivid detail.

"Yes, my love, but you're not going to like it," he added, concern for my well-being written on his face.

"Please, Jude." Taking a hold of him for strength as we locked eyes.

"She was wearing nothing but a slip, a corset and a wig with pearl strands laced through it." Each word was like a punch to my gut.

"Tell me the rest. I know that isn't all. I see it in your eyes, Jude," My voice cracked with strain as tension gripped my chest.

"She was found on a boat tied to the docks on the south side of the lake. The same boat we made love on Angelina. They are saying that she wasn't a guest from the party. They said she was from the gas lamp district and she had red hair. Darling, I think she was wearing your corset and wig." Fear etched in his voice.

I felt the blood draining from my face and the room began to spin.

"Stay with me, my love," was the last thing I heard Jude say as I surrendered to the darkness.

Sweet blissful darkness swallowed me whole.

10

MONDAY, MAY 4, 1763;
THE GREAT AWAKENING

AWOKE IN THE EARLY MORNING hours just before the sky took on the dusky hues of the sun rising over the ridge.

My room was dark except for a single lamp still lit at the bed side. Jonathan was keeping vigil asleep in a chair next to my bed.

"Could I have a glass of water?" I managed to choke out, my throat bone dry and tasting of so much waste left behind. Getting no response, I went to move the covers and felt damp from head to toe.

"Jonathan, wake up. Why are you in my room at this hour?" I questioned, indignation tainting my tone.

Stirring in his chair, Jonathan opened his eyes slowly to see me looking at him.

"I'm sorry, did you just say something?" he asked, wiping the sleep from his eyes.

"Yes, I asked why you are in my room at this hour. And could you please pour me some water? My mouth is terribly dry," I admonished, trying to sit up.

A huge smile broke out on his face as he jumped from his chair to do my bidding. Helping me sit up in bed, Jonathan handed me a glass of water, then ran to fetch Anna and Mother.

Before I knew it my room was abuzz with activity before the sun had come up, and Jonathan was eagerly filling me in.

I had gone unconscious after hearing the shocking news of the murder. Jude had carried me from the inn to the waiting carriage.

When I developed a fever, the doctor was called. He had wanted to bleed me, but Mother told him he was crazy and sent him away vowing never to recommend such an incompetent physician again.

I had been in a state of unconsciousness for nearly three days, restlessly tossing and talking in my sleep.

Jonathan told me that Jude had been vigilantly by my bedside for two and half days without sleep, only agreeing to get some rest four hours ago. Jonathan didn't have the heart to wake him just yet.

Sarah had been by every day sitting at my bedside talking to me and wiping my fevered forehead with cool cloths.

Honore had returned early yesterday. Tommy, the surviving would-be-kidnapper, didn't know who had hired them. He went on to say that Roy had been the one to secure the job. The only thing he did know for sure was the man must be rich because he had paid them well. They were given a one-pound note each which was six months wages to them, for their efforts making it an impossible opportunity to pass up. Afterward Honore turned the man over to the constable and filed a report.

"I, for one, have had enough rest and would like a bath and something to eat. I am positively famished," I announced to the room.

Anna jumped into action, ordering a fire and bath immediately, and Mother went down to the kitchen to get toast and tea.

Jonathan dutifully helped me from the bed, slipping me into a robe when Jude came through the door.

"You look simply awful," I quipped. Jude's eyes were bloodshot while his shirt and trousers were a wrinkled mess. A three day growth of beard replaced his normally smooth-shaven face.

"Thank you, kind woman, but I am not the concern here, you are." He took over for Jonathan, as he tied my robe closed and helped me to the lounge.

"So what exactly happened? One minute you were talking to me, the next you were gone," Jude asked, concerned.

"I really can't talk about it because I really don't know what happened," I lied. If I told them that I dreamed the murder, I would be committed to the nearest asylum. What's more I was having a hard time understanding the whole thing myself. No, it was best for me to remain quiet. After all, it was merely a freak occurrence, a phenomenon and it would never happen again. And I, for one, was thankful.

"I have to say you really scared me when I couldn't wake you at the inn. After all that talk in the pub about the murdered woman, I carried you down the stairs unconscious. Why, I thought the folks were going to string me up. I had to do a lot of fast talking. Then Jonathan came through the door while I was explaining and vouched for me."

"Fortunately, I might add for you both," Jonathan concluded.

"They really stopped you from carrying me out?" I asked in shock.

"The owners of that fine establishment, along with everyone who was downstairs eating in the pub." His expression was very animated as he related the story. "I think someone even called for a rope," he added, bugging out his eyes while sticking his tongue out, he tilted his head to one side like someone just hung.

The crazy animation and storytelling made me laugh and for a moment, I forgot all about the bad dream and the last three days. Anna had the tub set as Mother returned with tea and toast.

Anna, who was in protective mode, started shooing everyone out the door. Mother passed me toast while Anna scrubbed my hair, and I was grateful for the distraction. It gave me less time to think about anything else.

11

TOP IT, JONATHAN! I MEAN it. You are no longer funny," I said, giving my brother the stern eye as he continued teasing me.

"Or what?" Jonathan challenged. "Do you think to make short work of me too just like those thugs you singlehandedly subdued?" he teased, prancing around Dante with his equally powerful stallion Galahad.

Jonathan and I had been to Sarah's visiting for the afternoon.

"Don't ever doubt my abilities, big brother. My handiwork is proof enough," I teased back and kicked Dante in the side as my horse shot forward. And the race for home was on.

I was constantly surrounded by body guards everywhere I went now, namely Jonathan, Jude or Honore. Father had feared the attempted kidnapping was not an isolated incident and therefore, being overly protective, decided I was not to leave the house without an escort.

I had not had any recurring dreams, and life was getting back to normal. Jude and Honore were staying at the estate at the request of Father to watch over Mother and me while he was away on business with Uncle Jamie.

Uncle Nicholas was holding down the family business while his two brothers were gone. Nicholas's wife and kids were visiting with us. Aunt Victoria, and my cousins — Albert, sixteen, Andrew, fourteen, and Emma, age ten — were a lively bunch. Our house was filled to capacity with bodies and noise, so finding a quiet moment alone with Jude had proven to be more than a small challenge.

Taking matters into my own hands, I arranged for Anna to make ready the hunting lodge for me in case an opportunity presented itself. All that was left for me to do now was wait patiently, and patience was never my strong suit.

I was having delicious thoughts of Jude and what I intended to do to him next time I had him alone when Dante's powerful legs stampeded down the road and through the gates of our estate. I pulled Dante up short to prevent running over my two cousins Albert and Andrew as I raced for the official finish line with Jonathan.

I had Jonathan beat. Breathing deeply of victory I tasted the sweetness of besting my brother again.

"Hey, watch out, get out of the way," I yelled as I tried to stop in time.

Albert shoved his younger brother Andrew out of the way and barely managed to avoid being trampled by Dante's enormous hooves.

"I am so terribly sorry," I cried as I jumped from my horse to help Albert up. "Are you all right? Albert speak to me!"

"Have you lost your mind, Angelina?" a very indignant Albert said as he dusted himself off and walked over to Andrew pulling him from the pile of dung he landed in.

"I do believe you have landed in it this time, my dear Andrew," Jonathan said, stating the obvious as he dismounted from his horse and chuckled under his breath.

"You really aren't helping, Jonathan," I said derisively, as I fixed him with my most stern look.

"Poor Andrew would not be in this predicament if you didn't feel the need to always win at any cost, you know," Jonathan taunted me again.

"Jonathan Edward Allan Stewart, I am warning you! Tread lightly less you go too far!" My face no longer that of comportment, I attempted to console Andrew and make amends. Storm clouds formed over my head. I was in no mood for anymore teasing.

"Honestly, how careless must one be to nearly kill a pair of hapless young men minding their own business?"

"That tears it. Jonathan Edward the Third, enjoy your last full breath of air because it is about to be your last!" Suddenly, the clouds burst and thunder and lightning exploded. I took off running after Jonathan, my intent clear — I was going to do him harm.

Jonathan took one look at my face and realized too late that he had taken his joke a step too far. Turning around he headed down the drive laughing and yelling in terror at the same time.

Stopping momentarily to pick up a large stick with the intent to beat the stuffing out of him, I chased after him.

Two men on horseback came through the gates and witnessed the entire incident. I was consumed with blind rage and had not noticed them because my focus was on the fool running from me.

"Do something! I truly think she intends to harm me this time," Jonathan screamed as he ran past them.

Next thing I knew my immediate path was blocked by a horse. I stopped, then looked up and saw a very amused Honore motioning for me to turn around.

My first mistake was getting distracted by Honore and my second was turning my back on that shiftless rogue.

Before I knew what was up Jude had a hold of my arms as Honore was lifting me up to him.

"I will take that, thank you Mademoiselle," Honore said as he removed the branch from my hand. "Best of luck, my good friend," saluting us both as his laughter rang in my ears.

"Honore, I thought we were friends," I added, my disappointment apparent.

"You might want to go after him before we find him in the next county still running for his life," gesturing toward Jonathan's departing figure with a twitch of his head. "This might take a while, so tell the cook not to hold supper for us." Jude turned his horse around and headed for the woods.

"He really doesn't know when to stop," I said to Jude, trying my best to look guileless. "You know, I wasn't really going to hurt him," I added under my breath, "not much anyway." A pout forming on my lips as I crossed my arms defiantly, and settled in against his hardened chest.

"What did he say to get you so worked up, my love?" A small chuckle escaping as he cleared his throat trying to cover up the fact that he was laughing at me.

"He has been pushing the boundaries for two days now. Don't ask me what made me snap because I can't really define it. I have felt on edge for days now and I don't know why."

"I think I might have the cure. If it doesn't work, I may have to throw you in the cold lake," Jude declared.

"Don't joke about it, Jude. You know I don't like the water," I said, a shiver running down my spine.

Stopping his horse, he tilted my face up to his.

"I truly didn't mean it that way. I would never hurt you. Do you trust me?" His eyes sober as they looked at me.

"Yes, of course. I believe you. Just don't talk about water now. It terrifies me," I answered begrudgingly, looking down at my hands.

We rode for a little while in silence. I didn't pay attention to where we were headed, lost in my own thoughts.

Finally he broke the silence. "Anna was telling me about this place in the woods and she conveniently gave me a key and told me that I might have need of a quiet place, seeing how the manor house is so full at the moment."

"I can't believe she really told you about this place." My head snapped up, realizing just where we were. "Jude Deveraux, are you trying to seduce me?" I asked as a decadent smile formed.

"Unless you have any objections, *ma amour*, consider this fair warning." His French accent suddenly becoming more pronounced.

A devilish smile played on his lips as the promise of what was to come lingered between us.

Sliding down the leather saddle into Jude's waiting arms, anticipation sent goose bumps throughout my body. Wrapping my arms around his neck, I touched his lips with my finger outlining every sensuous curve of them as he stood there holding me.

I was mesmerized by him as he captured my mouth with his, my breath catching in my throat. A sigh of desire mixed with his groan of longing.

"I have been waiting all week to do that," Jude whispered close to my ear as he carried me toward the door. I kissed his neck and nibbling his ear, as I felt him shiver. "I will never get this door opened if you keep that up," he scolded. But I refused to stop.

"Is it your intent that I take you right here on this porch?" Jude asked as he put me down on the ground so he could use both hands on the lock.

I started to pull his shirt from his breaches, but he secured my hands behind my back with one swift move, while still working the key in the lock.

Kicking the door open he picked me up, shutting the door behind him with the heel of his boot. My eyes searched his face, intense determination etched on it. He was of one mind and he would not be deterred.

The light in the small hunting lodge was dim from surrounding trees blocking the daylight.

"Stay right there just a minute," he said as he searched about the room for something to light the lanterns.

Finding the flint, he lit the lanterns by the bedside and then the fireplace. Soft flames cast a dim light about the room and set a very seductive atmosphere.

"Why did you light the lanterns?" I asked feeling a bit shy about the brightness of the room.

"I need to see you. Nay, I desire to see your face," he answered with passion in his tone. "I must see all of you when I make love to you."

His eyes shone with intensity when he crossed the room to where I stood, quivering with anticipation, his words eliciting emotions in me. "I need to feel you and see you. I wish to remember every inch of you as I bring you into womanhood," His words touched a chord inside of me so tense and taut I thought I would snap. "*Ma belle Ange.*" The word spoken so tenderly, his seductive voice made me ache for his touch.

He ran his hands through my hair as he removed the pins, letting them drop to the floor one by one. My hair tumbled down about my shoulders. Reaching out I shoved his coat from his arms, letting it fall to the floor, my need building with each passionate kiss he rained on my face and mouth.

"There is no need to rush, *ma petite minette.*" His words meant to sooth and calm me had the opposite affect.

I loved it when he spoke French, but his words neither soothed nor calmed me. *Oh, contraire mon coeur, my heart.* His words only drove me wild, igniting a fire deep inside of me that burned for every wanton touch, smell and taste of him.

He sat me on the bed, removed first one shoe and then the other. Reaching up my thigh, while looking intently into my eyes he pulled my stockings off slowly. The sensation of his hands sliding along my inner thigh caused tiny ripples of pleasure. Closing my eyes, I drank in each new sensation. I felt him pull me to my feet then turn me around. Slipping my riding jacket from my back, he tossed it to the floor. Then moving my hair to one side, he began nibbling my neck while his hands worked to undo the buttons of my riding habit.

It was pure torture not being able to touch him. I tried to turn around but each time he would push me back to the same position.

"Why do you torture me so?" My desire was evident in the husky tone of my voice.

"I am teaching you patience, my love," his words steady and strong while he slowly and deliberately finished with his task. Pushing the outfit from my shoulders, it fell to the floor in a pool of material.

He caressed and kissed the nape of my neck and shoulders from behind. Each touch was sweet, agonizing bliss as I closed my eyes and leaned my head back. My breathing coming in short shallow intakes of air as he finally turned me around to face him.

Staring up into his eyes as he pulled the shirt over his head, I felt a thrill shoot through my entire being, mesmerized by his magnificent muscles, taut and firm. Each line was enhanced and defined by the shadow cast by the lantern's light. All the while we made eye contact, which only heightened the intimacy we shared.

Untying the strings of my slip, he reached his hand under the thin material to cup the round fullness of my breast. He teased my nipples with his thumb as I stared longingly into his eyes.

I unfastened his breeches as his manhood strained against the material. Pushing them off his hips, I ran my hands over his muscular hips pulling him up against me as I marveled at the size of it.

"I need you to trust me, my love. Can you do that?" Cupping my face in his hands, I looked deep into his limpid sapphire orbs. I could feel my heart pounding in my throat.

"I trust you completely, *mon amour*," I said boldly.

My slip hit the floor and I stood before him bathed in the soft glow of the lanterns, unashamed and eager for whatever came next. I desired him with every breath I took.

Lifting me in his arms, he lay me across the bed, his nakedness straddling mine.

I ran my fingers through his hair while his mouth captured my breasts, sucking and licking till they tingled. The sensation of his mouth so intimate and warm on my body caused tiny moans of pleasure to escape. Rippling sensations started to pool in my stomach.

His mouth rained tiny kisses down my stomach as his hand rubbed my inner thigh. Arching my back instinctively, I called out to him as my breathing became even more shallow.

Inching his way back up to capture my lips passionately then nuzzling my ear. "Open your legs to me," he whispered hovering over me as I obeyed. "I want to see all of you," his words were filled with such passion.

I felt his lips kissing my inner thigh and I stiffened. "*Ma chere*, I would not hurt you. I only wish to bring you pleasure. Do not deny me this."

His fingers working the inner depths of my valley as glorious warmth began to spread. His mouth kissing me in so intimate a way, and yet I did not feel horror or shame. Instead I felt my body writhing from the unbelievable sensations he was eliciting, like lightning bolts shooting all through my body. I had never felt more alive than I did at that very moment. Tiny cries of ecstasy escaped my lips my breath ragged and harsh. "Please," was all I could say.

My entire body felt taut as I arched my back and thrust my hips. I wanted to scream, but I couldn't.

He was now hovering over me, the marvelous smell of his body driving me wild. My hands now searched out the object that would release me from my torture. Desire making me bolder now I locked eyes with Jude as I instinctively guided him to me. Lifting my hips to meet his, I saw caution in his eyes.

"There is no going back from here," his words grave as he fought to keep control.

"I don't care. I need you now!" I cried urgently.

"You are a she devil," caution now gone from his eyes, replaced instead with a burning passion that matched my own, his lips finding mine kissing me more passionately than before. His hunger was intoxicating as our harsh breathing matched.

A small cry of momentary pain escaping from me and I felt his entire body stiffen and freeze instantly. Reaching up to pull his mouth to mine, I hungrily kissed him as a burning of a different kind took over.

I was sure I couldn't take any more pleasure, yet I knew something more was just on the other side of one more thrust of his hips.

Deeper and more intense waves of passion began to build inside of me. I could feel him looking at me but I did not care. It felt too good to stop.

His hand brushed hair from my face as I cried out. And then the waves came more intense than I could have ever imagined. Again and again as I cried out his name, our hips working in unison. I felt my thighs bathed in warmth and my body convulsed in the ecstasy of glorious release.

Our sweat-drenched bodies lay entangled, melting into each other, every breath, every touch heightened.

Rolling to his side, he pulled me with him. Our legs entwined together my head resting on his chest, exhausted yet exhilarated at the same time.

"Is it always like that?" I asked.

"Like what?" Jude answered, looking at me through heavy lids.

"You know. So incredible. I didn't know it could be like that."

"No, my love. I have never experienced what we just did before." Then he got a funny look on his face. "What I mean to say is I have had sex before. That was not sex. I just made love to you. We just made love to each other. There is a difference."

"Well then, explain it to me because I don't understand." I propped my head on my hands as I looked down at him.

"I can try but I don't know if it is easy to explain," he said, placing his arms behind his head so he could look at me. "The French have a term. *Fou d 'amour* or *le grand amour*. Madly in love or the grand love, either way its meaning is true love. The one great love of your life. To express your true emotions for someone through something as intimate as what we just did is making love. To call what we did sex only cheapens it. Sex is something you have with a stranger to feel some kind of pleasure," he explained cocking an eyebrow at me. "You see?"

"I am not sure." Puzzled more now than before.

"I will explain it to you later. Right now my mind is in a fog and my eyes won't stay open." He turned on his side tucking me into his arm, then kissed my forehead and both eyes before he drifted off to sleep.

I lay awake pondering his words. Was he saying that he loved me? Most women would be thrilled and elated, but I felt ambiguous. Certainly, I had never expected to experience anything like this in my wildest dream. And I truly enjoyed his presence. He was intelligent, adventurous, and very handsome to look at. He didn't treat me as a lesser class of human being because I was not privileged to be born a man. I had to hand it to him, he had a lot going in his favor.

And yet I still pondered the age old question. Is he really that perfect? Would he change if I committed myself to him? And what part of myself would I be required to give up to have him in my life?

The hard questions began to make my head pound. No, I would not think of such things now. I simply wished to bask in the simple joy of being. I did truly feel elated and relaxed. So instead of pondering the hard questions, I inhaled his scent deeply, sighing contentedly as I always did when I thought of the way he kissed me. I closed my eyes and drifted off to slumber, safely tucked in his arms as he tightened them about my waist. I would ponder later. Now was too perfect a moment to worry.

Waking with a start, I had a feeling of foreboding again in the pit of my stomach. Frantically, I searched about for Jude but he wasn't there. Was it all a dream? The sleep induced fog slowly lifting from my mind, I began to get my bearings.

My habit and slip neatly lay at the foot of the bed, but Jude was nowhere to be found. Placing the slip over my head, I attempted to comb my fingers through my hair. All the while, the feeling of dread hung in the air.

Jude opened the door and I jumped.

"It's only me, my love. Why do you look as if you've just seen a spirit?" Jude asked, coming over to where I stood. "You're shaking, my angel." Concern laced his words, as he wrapped his arms about me.

"I'm fine, really the room is just chilly, nothing more," I said, trying to convince myself.

"Then we must get you dressed, although I prefer what you wore earlier," he said with a devilish glint. Leaning down he slanted his head, kissing my lips long and passionately.

"Jude Deveraux, you will completely corrupt me if I let you," I said, looking at him as I tried to sound stern. "We had better get back to the house before a search party is sent out to look for us."

"Your stallion awaits, my lady, and your hand maiden is here."

"You sent for Anna?" I questioned with fear in my voice as I looked around him.

"No, my love, I meant me, I will help you dress. Not as much fun as taking them off but it can have its benefits." He rakishly smiled while reaching for my riding habit.

"How are you with hair?" I asked, smiling back.

An hour later, we were ready to leave, one last look back to make sure all was in order. The lanterns extinguished, the bed hastily made and my hairpins back in place. Yes, everything was in order. So why was my stomach still tied up in knots?

Stepping out onto the porch I locked the door and placed the key into my pocket. The hair on the back of my neck was standing on end. I was overcome by an eerie feeling that someone was watching every move I made.

I turned to find the tree line filled with shadowy figures. The sun was down, and I couldn't see beyond the clearing, but I could feel him.

Patting the dagger in my pocket that I always carried with me brought some small comfort as I forced myself to put one foot in front of the other.

Jude helped me up and climbed into the saddle behind me. "Ready?" he asked as he leaned down to kiss my ear tenderly.

Smiling up at him, a shiver crawled up my spine. But it wasn't from his kiss.

12

ATHER AND UNCLE JAMIE HAD returned from a very profitable exporting expedition. Uncle Nicholas was back at home in the evenings now, so Aunt Victoria had returned home to London with Albert, Andrew, and Emma in tow.

I would be making the long trip to London comfortably seated in the carriage next to Mother and my best friend, Sarah. Everything was packed. The carriages were loaded and Dante was secured to the back for the trip.

Sarah had been staying with us for the last week because her parents needed to return to the city early for the opening of parliament. I was happy for the distraction to keep my mind occupied. The feeling of looming foreboding woke with me each morning and lasted all day.

Honore and Jude had left for Manchester four days ago after receiving a letter delivered by horseman from his father. No other explanation was given except that it was urgent and I had not heard a word from him since. I was a mess and needed routine along with calm, tranquil surroundings.

The arduous preparation for a trip to London, while waiting for the other shoe to drop, was neither calming nor tranquil.

Father hired a guard detail of ten well-armed men to accompany us to London. Depending on their performance, Father was considering keeping the men round the clock until he deemed it safe. The leader of the group was an older, but well-formed muscular man of refinement.

"Ladies, my name is General Moore. You may address me as General or Sir. I am here to inform you of a few guidelines that will make the trip safer for everyone. First we will make one and only one stop on our journey to London unless there is an emergency," he said informatively, as he paced back and forth in front of us like the general that he was, addressing his troops.

"We will be taking one of three possible routes and the only one who knows that route is yours truly," he pointed to himself with his riding crop. "Not even Lord Stewart knows which way we will be traveling."

"I will thank you to stay in the carriage at all times until we open the door for you. And if possible you will need to keep the curtains closed." Finishing this sentence, he stopped looking at us pointedly. "If you have need of one of us at any time during the trip, you will simply hang this red strip of material from the window and we will assist you," he said, presenting a large strip of red cotton material to Mother.

"If there are any problems along the way the drivers have been instructed to drive like Satan himself were on their tails and head for the nearest inn. Are there any questions, ladies?" Looking at each of us and seeing no objections, he gestured toward the carriage door.

"Very good, then we will be on our way, ladies, if you would please." Assisting each of us into the rig, he saluted us before closing the door. Then giving a distinct rap on the carriage he signaled the driver to pull out.

Three hours into our leisurely carriage ride my bottom had fallen asleep and I was in need of facilities. Mother signaled out the window with her red cloth and the general was gracious enough to acquiesce to our requests for mercy.

Three armed men went ahead to check out the inn before we arrived. As the line of carriages pulled up, we were informed that there was no danger present and that we were free to go in.

General Moore personally opened the carriage door and assisted us down the step, and another young man flanked each of us as we entered the inn doors.

One of the men sent ahead secured a table in the corner strategically situated for full view of the front door. Mother, Sarah, and I took a seat as four of the men stood at attention on each corner of the table. One man was posted just inside the door, and the remaining men were posted outside.

If I had not been so anxious about my feelings of impending doom, I might have laughed about the zealousness of our traveling companions.

Tea was ordered and a light tray of cheeses, breads and fruit were brought to the table after passing inspection first. I was not very talkative thus far, and Sarah was beginning to notice.

"Is everything all right with you, Angelina? You have been so quiet for days," Mother finally asked.

"It's nothing. I'm just tired lately. I haven't been sleeping well," I said, trying to smile pleasantly. "I really need to visit the privy. Excuse me, Mother." Standing, I headed for the facilities provided for the customers near the back of the inn.

"Oh, me too! Wait for me." Sarah stood and followed rushing to catch up.

One young man followed us while the other three men lined up across the hallway preventing anyone else from entering the corridor leading to the privies.

"I truly think the detail to the privy is a bit excessive, if anyone were to inquire of my opinion," I called over my shoulder as I closed the door.

"Really, Angelina, you do like to stir the pot," Sarah added, as she used the pot first.

"A ten-man detail and people following me to the bathroom, honestly it is too much!"

"Are you not scared after your ordeal just a few weeks ago?" Sarah asked, her eyes large and wide.

"I can take care of myself, Sarah." With a glint of self-assurance, I patted my side where the dagger rested.

"Well, I am scared enough for us both," Sarah said as she finished up.

"I will not live my life fearing shadows and things in the night." That was a complete lie. I was afraid of things I could not see or touch, and I had an overwhelming feeling that it was coming for me.

"Surely there must be something you are afraid of," she asked.

"Yes, of course, I am afraid of something. I just haven't come across it yet," I said with bravado. But, truth be told, I was afraid. The evening Jude and I left the hunting lodge the hair on my neck stood up on end most of the way home. The one constant, my solid ground was gone, and I had this secret I could not tell anyone, not even my best friend.

We left the privy, heading back down the hall as the men lined up, escorting us as if we were royalty. I felt silly and a bit conspicuous.

Mother had called one of the young men over. "Would you please ask General Moore how much longer until we reach the city?"

"Yes, Lady Stewart. When we leave the inn that will be possible. But right now, I can't leave my post," the young man informed her.

"Well, they are certainly thorough," Mother said, looking at me.

The general walked in, saying something to the man at the door. I saw him nod as General Moore walked over to our table.

"I trust you ladies have had a nice stretch, but we really do need to get back on the road now," he said in his usual air of formality.

Waiting for Mother to stand, the general escorted her as Sarah and I followed behind, giggling like schoolgirls. He then helped us climb into the carriage as one of the young men walked up to the general and spoke into his ear.

"Ladies, I need you to settle in and hang on, it is going to be a bumpy ride," he informed us, trying to keep his tone light.

"What has happened, General?" Mother asked, concern straining her voice.

"One of my men is reporting some sort of disturbance down the road. Nothing to worry about, my lady, but we are going to move swiftly the rest of the way," he advised, trying to be as vague as possible.

Three men rode far ahead of the party while four men surrounded the carriage. One man rode directly in front of our party and the last two hung back some to make sure we didn't have anyone trying to sneak up from behind.

When the general told us to hold on, he wasn't exaggerating. The three of us bounced around like coins in a gentleman's pouch.

We had traveled about three miles when I happened to peek out the window to see three of the guards detailed, standing over three men on the ground. Two of the men on the ground appeared to be dead from injuries sustained in a sword fight, and one man was lying face down with a guard's foot in the middle of his back, his sword discarded.

By the time we made London, none of us wanted to see the inside of a carriage for a very long time. I had bruises in places that should never bruise. Sarah stepped down from the rig and lost her afternoon meal. Mother, the consummate gracious lady, climbed down from the carriage and promptly thanked the general for delivering us safely. She then proceeded to invite all ten men to supper that night. All I wanted was a quiet night and a very soft bed.

Father arrived home a few hours later just before dinner. After our dinner had been served and every men had eaten their fill, Father invited them into the study for a scotch, a smoke and a full report of the day's occurrences.

I used this opportunity to slip away, using the excuse of extreme exhaustion. Slipping upstairs and away from the chaos, I retired to my room.

"Anna, I am in dire need, nay, in desperate need of a hot soak for my bruised posterior area," I called out as I entered my room.

"I have anticipated your need and lit a fire," she added, coming out of the dressing area.

"When was the last time I told you I really truly loved you?" I asked as I pulled pins from my hair and Anna unlaced my gown.

"Do you think you can fix me one of your sleeping tonics tonight?" I pleaded with my eyes.

"I will get it for you as soon as you are safely in the bath."

"You are truly an angel from above the way you take such good care of me. Promise you will never leave me," I said as I brought her hand to my cheek.

"Oh, go on now. You do carry on so." Anna's cheeks turned red as she blushed and took the gown into the other room.

Climbing into the tub I sunk completely down till my hair was under the water. Holding my breath I just wanted to see how long I could stand it before panic set in; twenty seconds then thirty eight seconds.

Sitting up sputtering water from my mouth and nose I took in a couple of deep breaths of air trying to slow my racing heart. At some point, I know that I will get over my fear of being under the water.

"Have you received any word from Lord Deveraux?" Anna inquired as she came out of the dressing room causing me to jump, sloshing water from the tub.

"My goodness, you certainly have been jumpy these past few days," Anna said as she came over to wash my hair.

"You just caught me by surprise, that's all. I really should put a bell about your neck, sneaking up on me like that," I teased. "To answer your question, no I have not heard from him.

"Let me get your hair washed and I will get that sleeping tonic for you. That will do the trick." That was my Anna. Nothing ruffled her feathers, always so cheery. I sometimes wish I could be more like that.

"I think that would be splendid, thank you, Anna. I will just sit here and soak until I get cold." *And I will obsess over why I haven't heard from Jude and where he might be. And think and think and think.*

Sinking low in the bath to ensure the hot water would get all my bruised and battered parts, I placed a hot cloth over my eyes as I lay my head against the rim.

I heard a clinking noise like something hitting the balcony door, but that just couldn't be. My mind must be playing tricks on me again. Then I heard it again. Stepping from the tub, I wrapped a clean sheet about me and went to see what it could be.

I opened the drapes then cautiously unlatched the door that led onto my balcony. Curiosity got the better of me as I ventured further out onto the balcony to see what that noise might have been. Stepping to the ivy covered railing, I looked as far as I dared without actually leaning over the edge.

"Is someone there?" I quietly called, still afraid of what might be lurking in those shadows. Nobody called back, and I figured it must have been my mind playing tricks on me again.

I turned away just as a hand reached over the ledge, grabbing ahold of my wrist. I screamed and jumped back, fear gripping me by the throat. I would have made it to the door except my feet got tangled up in the sheet and I tripped.

Paralyzed with fear I was unable to call out. Frantically trying to untangle myself and stand proved to be difficult. I was frozen with terror as someone climbed over the balcony ledge, landing in front of me with a thud.

Covering my face with my hands, I cowered beneath my thin sheet. Two strong hands picked me up, and I began flailing my fist against my attacker, guttural growls coming from my throat.

"Don't touch me, you filthy pig! Unhand me," I demanded pushing against his chest whilst holding tightly to my sheet.

"What a little spit fire you are, my love," Jude purred the words at me.

Relief rushed through me like a waterfall. "Damn you, Jude. You scared ten years off my life," I said, snatching my sheet up. "Leave my sheet alone. What do you think you are doing?" I hissed, slapping his hand away as he tugged at the top of it. "Anna will be back any minute now. She cannot see you."

"Send her away. I have been on the road for days and I need you, *ma amour*." Jude smiled slyly down at me.

"A fine invitation, *mon amour*. But I have bruises in places that shouldn't bruise and I ache all over. Your sweet talk won't work on me," I said, looking at him placidly. His beard had started to grow and he looked ruggedly handsome. My resolve would melt away if he kept looking at me that way much longer.

"I would be happy to kiss away every bruise of yours, my love," Jude said, his eyes pleading his case. "You know you want me to stay." Smiling down at me, he tenderly kissed my lips as his hunger began to build.

Putting me down Jude turned me about, giving me a slight push toward the open doorway. Once I was through the threshold, he pulled the drapery closed and partially closed the door.

I sat down by the fire to dry my hair when Anna came back with my tonic.

"Here you go, drink this down while I brush out your hair," Anna said, handing me the glass.

"I am really tired, Anna. Could we brush out my hair in the morning?" I asked.

"It will only take me a minute, Angelina." Taking the brush from my hand Anna began. I could tell by the look in her eye she would not take no for an answer.

Anna finished my hair, and I finished my tonic and handed the glass back to her.

"Thank you, Anna, I am so very tired now. I won't need you anymore tonight," I said while still sitting in front of the fire.

"Would you like me to get you a night gown or a slip?" she asked.

"If you want to leave me a slip and robe at the foot of the bed I would be thankful. And I might want to sleep in late tomorrow, so please don't wake me," I said, looking at her hoping she didn't see through my ploy.

Coming back into the room with a slip and robe she lay them out.

"I feel a breeze just let me close that door for you."

"No! It's fine, Anna. I opened it because I was warm. I promise to close it before I go to sleep." Trying to appear nonchalant and keep my breathing normal. I could feel my heart racing in anticipation of Jude's kisses.

"If you are sure you don't need anything else?" Anna asked one last time as she walked to the door.

"I will call for you in the morning when I get up. Thank you, Anna, that will do." I listened for the door to close. Getting up, I nearly ran to the door flipping the lock as I released the breath I had been holding.

Taking the left corner of my sheet, I twisted it bringing it across my chest then around my neck. Next, I twisted the right corner of the sheet, tying it to the left forming a kind of Grecian look.

Turning around I found Jude standing just inside of the drapes watching me, and my heart skipped a beat. Oh, how I had missed him.

Gathering the sheet up from the bottom, I ran across the room throwing myself into his arms. "I have missed you," his words filled with emotion and passion as he kissed my lips ravenously.

"I can't believe your boldness, sir. Scaling walls and scaring the life out of me." I tried to sound stern, but I was so happy to see him. The evidence was written all over my face as his wandering hand began its exploration of my sheet.

Patting his riding coat, a cloud of dust flew from it. "You, sir, need a bath first. Now unhand me." This time my voice was stern.

He put me down, then gave me a courtly bow. "As the lady orders I am obligated to obey," he said. Removing his riding coat, he placed it on the back of the nearest chair. Then taking a seat, he removed his boots and socks.

I went to retrieve a fresh bath sheet and soap from the cabinet in the dressing room, returning to find him in nothing but a white linen shirt. What an appealing sight he made. My breath caught in my lungs, and my pulse quickened as a sly smile played on his lips.

"It was very fortuitous of you to order me a bath," he loudly whispered as he boldly looked me up and down dressed in my stylish sheet.

"Yes, good sir, how fortuitous indeed," I replied and curtsied with my hands full of bath supplies.

Removing his shirt, his eyes boldly assessed me as I slowly looked him up and down. "Will you join me?" His hand held out in invitation.

"I am afraid I will forgo another bath as I have already had mine. But please enjoy yours," I quipped playfully.

Stepping into the tub, he gave a shiver from the coolness of the water as he sat down. "Good mistress, this water has gone cold." His face showed dissatisfaction for the condition of his bath water.

"Then you won't tarry long," I said, pouring water over his head to wet his hair.

"Not if you wish me to perform this night." He shivered again as I doused him with the cold water.

"I do believe you gain pleasure from your duties," he said, reaching around to capture my hand that was busy soaping his hair.

"Yes, pleasure indeed, good sir," I whispered in his ear while soaping a rag. Scrubbing the dirt from his neck and ears I pushed him forward so I could reach his back.

"Now I am the one enjoying your duties, madam," he quietly said, relaxing from his long ride.

Soaping the rag again, I pulled him back against the tub. Boldly looking at him, I began scrubbing his chest and arms as he leaned his head back against the tub's rim. I slowly moved my rag farther down as his eyes slowly opened, a look of surprise on his face at my sheer boldness.

"I truly missed you while I was away." Jude's sincere words were evident by his hushed tone.

"And I you," I replied as I leaned down to kiss his lips. "Tell me what happened with your father? What was so urgent?" I asked as I retrieved the water warming by the fire to rinse him with.

"Honore and I arrived in Manchester and went to meet Father at the Greyhound Inn as instructed. When we arrived, there were six thugs waiting instead."

"Did you get hurt?" I said as I almost dropping the bucket of water I was carrying.

"No, they were untrained thugs, not really committed to the task. We dispensed with them rather quickly. I was just worried that something had happened to my parents so I had to check in on them before returning. They were fine and the whole thing was a ruse."

"Who would do such a thing? What would someone have to gain by luring you into a trap?" I asked, wondering more to myself than actually expecting an answer, also considering if that could have been the reason for the knot in my stomach. Or was something else coming for me?

"What is it? You have a funny look on your face," he said, puzzled.

"It's nothing really. I have had a knot in my stomach for days. And now that you are here it is gone," as I continued with the pail in hand. Lifting it over his head, I rinsed the soap from his hair and chest.

"*Ma amour*, that is wonderful." He sighed with satisfaction as the warm water slid down his body.

I was lost in thought, pondering who would want to hurt him and why. I put the pail on the floor and retrieved the sheet to dry Jude as he climbed out of the tub.

"I thought we could share this one, no need to soil a second sheet." He snatched my makeshift dress before I could turn around.

"You, sir, are simply scandalous," I teased as I found myself pulled up against his front while his nimble fingers worked at the knot I had tied.

Before I could blink twice, my sheet was on the floor and he had lifted me into his wet arms.

"Jude you are still wet," I protested, trying to push against his solid chest.

"Don't worry, love, I won't be for long," his bold words whispered in my ear as he carried me to the bed.

"You cad!" I retorted as he tossed me unceremoniously onto the bed causing me to squeal in surprise.

"Don't forget the other names I am called by," he said as he crawled across the bed on all fours like a leopard stocking prey.

"And pray tell what name would that be?" I replied with a seductive tone as his bold look made my blood boil.

"Bloodthirsty pirate captain." Each word punctuated with a kiss on my body as he crawled his way to my mouth.

"I find breathing a difficult task when you are around, my blood-thirsty pirate captain," I said with a sigh as I lay in his arms content.

13

Y MIND KEPT TELLING ME that it wasn't real, that this was just a dream. But I could feel every agonizing moment. Sheer terror gripped my throat as I tried to scream, but I was paralyzed.

My brain felt like it was in a fog, unable to think. I could see my surroundings, yet I couldn't move a muscle. The trees were large and old with gnarled branches that only added to the eeriness.

Tears trailed down, pooling in my ears, as my silent sobs lodged in my throat. I lay on a cold stone altar. There was something heavy resting on my chest but moving to get a look at it was impossible. Why wouldn't my body respond? Why couldn't I move?

Dread and fear made my heart pound until I thought it would explode. Who was doing this to me, and why couldn't I see his face? I heard words being spoken but they didn't make any sense. What was he saying? My eyes kept coming back to the quarter moon looming through the branches of the old oak tree.

I heard other people chanting, repeating his words, and they were getting louder, more frantic. It all smacked of a pagan ritual, but it didn't make sense. They had been outlawed.

The man was now standing over me. He wore a red hat and jacket to match. But what was on his face? It looked strange, somehow distorted. What was he holding in his hands?

I was now surrounded by men dressed in white, all standing around me also with distorted faces. They lifted the large slab that had been holding me down and still I could not move. I felt a scream escape my lips, yet nobody moved to help me. They just kept chanting their strange words.

He had a dagger in his hand and some kind of symbol drawn on his left wrist, but I couldn't make it out clearly. Stark terror permeated me now. Somehow, I knew what was going to happen but was powerless to do anything about it.

I was going to die. A pagan ritual was being performed and I was the sacrifice. I wanted to turn away, close my eyes, anything but watch it unfold before me.

I couldn't breathe. I felt myself shaking all over as the man in red raised the blade over my chest, his eyes looking into mine. Those evil sadistic eyes chilled me to my very marrow. The blade was coming down. This was it. I was finished. This I knew with certainty.

Sitting straight up in bed, gripping my chest, my screams of sheer terror were caught halfway in my throat and tears soaked my face. My chest heaved as I struggled to breathe.

Jude's frightened face hovered over my own, terror-struck face.

I couldn't distinguish between the two realities as confusion fogged my thoughts. Jude tried to console me but I cowered from him in fear, trying to get away. But Jude held on tight. His soothing words and calming tone finally got through my fog-riddled mind, pacifying the panic coursing through me. Jude held me in his arms, rocking me back and forth while stroking my hair.

"Shush, *ma belle Ange*, shush now. It was all a bad dream, my love. I'm here with you now. Shush, *ma amour.*"

Tears rolled down my cheeks, the dream still fresh in my mind. I tried to understand what had happened. Just like the other dream, it was so vivid, as if I was the one actually experiencing every agonizing painful moment.

My chest still felt tender where the dagger in my dream, had been driven into it. My tears subsided and Jude tipped my chin up as I held my hands to my chest. Breathing hurt and I winced in pain.

"What is it, Angelina?" his frightened eyes desperately searching my own.

"It was a very bad dream, that's all. I will be fine in a minute." I turned my head to avoid his penetrating stare.

Crawling from the bed, I slipped my robe on, tying it at the waist. Walking to the basin, I poured water and splashed my face.

"As much as I enjoy your company, my love, I am afraid the entire household was probably awakened by my screams and will soon be descending on my room," I said, looking over my shoulder.

Climbing from the bed he slipped a shirt over his head then pulled his breaches on, tucking in the shirt. I watched him dress, slipping his boots on over his socks.

The sun had not yet crested the hills as the rooster crowed on the gate.

"I do not like sneaking about like a bandit stealing the family silver," Jude said, watching me from the chair.

I turned from the window to look at him in all his rugged finery covered in dust. Closing the distance between us, I stood before him searching his face for what he was really trying to say to me.

"Jude, I love being with you, what more is there?" I asked.

"We could wed," he said, his voice taking on a seriousness I had not known from him before.

Jude took my hands in his as he brought my palms to his lips, kissing them then pulling me onto his lap.

"You know how I feel about the bonds of marriage. We have discussed it at length. Remember?" I said, looking into his face searchingly.

"Surely you can see that what we share between us could never be a prison," he said, pleading his case.

"I am not sure, I need time to think," I answered, kissing him lightly on the lips as a way to end this line of discussion. I had hoped he would leave before the entire house became aware of our transgression.

"I will not be dismissed so easily, Angelina," Jude said. I could tell he was becoming frustrated by my negative attitude on the matter.

"Can we discuss it further another time when I am not in fear of being discovered? Please, Jude?" I said, pleading with my eyes.

"I know when I am not wanted," he joked, breaking the tension.

Standing, we walked to the balcony door. "Before I forget, Mother is having a dinner party and would like for you to attend."

"Oh, Jude, surely not your mother, she scares me. Besides I didn't get the feeling she approves of me the last time we met," I pleaded, wanting to do anything other than sit at a table with his mother and make intelligent conversation.

"Lady Angelina Marguerite Amelia Stewart, are you trying to tell me the woman who stood toe to toe with a ruthless bloodthirsty pirate is afraid of my mother?" He laughed under his breath. "Tell me it isn't so." Lifting his eyebrow as if to challenge my pride.

"It isn't funny. She truly frightens me, Jude. You are going to have to tell her I can't make it. She will take one look at me and see everything written all over my face," I said somberly.

"I am afraid I can't do that. She was very insistent when I went to visit." The evidence of his amusement laced in his words.

"Honestly, Jude Deveraux, I curse you with a pox," I said, stomping my foot.

"I could stand here discussing it further or you could agree that I will pick you up Wednesday afternoon at four and we will spend time with my folks." A rakish half-smile lit his face.

"Only on one condition," I asserted.

"And what is that, may I inquire?" he asked, satisfied that he had won.

"Sarah and Jonathan accompany us so that I may have reinforcements to support me,"

"I will be there to support you," he assured me.

"I mean someone that is on my side, not blackmailing me on his way out the door," I said, narrowing my eyes at him.

"Darling, your words wound me to the quick," feigning a mortal wound to his heart.

"Good! You may leave now. I am through with you," I pretended to be indifferent to his charms.

Grabbing me as I turned to walk away, he kissed my lips roughly, demanding my attention before he left. He wanted to prove that I could never be indifferent to his touch. My skin was scorched where his hands had grasped my shoulders. I moaned with pleasure.

Pulling away he silently climbed down the trellis. I stood with swollen lips from his passionate kiss, and my skin still tingled from his touch.

I heard knocking at my bedroom door and Anna calling me. "Lady Angelina, are you all right. Someone said they heard a scream." Running through the room, I unlatched the bedroom door to a frantic Anna.

"I'm fine, Anna, I just had another bad dream, that's all. I will be fine," I said, reassuring her.

Stepping into the room she put the tray down on the table. "Well, even I can see that. Look at you. You look as if you had been tossed about all night. You are lucky that it was me come to your room and not your mother or your brother," Anna scolded me in her subtle way.

"What are you talking about, Anna?" I played coy, trying to avoid eye contact as I poured myself some tea.

"So that is the way you wish to play this then. You think I don't know what it is to be young. Your secret is safe with me," she said, her knowing eyes searched the room as she picked things up off the floor as she went. "So I take it that Lord Deveraux has communicated with you and that you are no longer worried for his well-being," Anna continued while giving me a wry smile.

"Yes, I have heard from him directly and he is well and kicking. His mother has requested my presence Wednesday for a dinner party," I told her glumly.

"And what can be wrong with that?" she asked, stopping her chores to look at me.

"Last time, I met her I got the distinct impression that she didn't like me," I whined.

"What is there not to like? You hold your head high and be yourself. She cannot help but fall in love with you."

"Did I tell you how much I love you today?" I asked as I turned to her.

14

I AWOKE FEELING RESTLESS. THE VESTIGES of yesterday's dream had hung with me. I couldn't shake it. The eerie feelings and visions kept coming to my mind. The pain still lingering in my chest as I struggled to make sense of the whole thing.

I had decided that a brisk ride would clear my head and help chase away the feeling of unease. Checking my image in the mirror one last time on the way out the door, I had my hand on the knob.

"And exactly where do you think you are going, Angelina?" Father's voice bellowed from the doorway of his office.

"I thought that I would stretch Dante's legs and get some fresh air," I answered not quite sure what the problem was.

"I can see that. My real question is, why are you going out alone?" he said, leaning against the door jam.

"Jonathan isn't up yet. He stayed late at the Burgess's last night, and you look like you are headed out. What would you suggest I do, Father, become a prisoner in my own home?" feeling more than a bit frustrated.

"I have retained the services of General Moore's outfit. There will be three men on guard at all times. Stop by the kitchen on your way out; you should be able to find one of them in there," his tone suggesting complete cooperation.

"Of course, Father." Turning around to head back down the hall, I kissed him on the cheek as I passed by.

"And before I forget, Lord Deveraux stopped by my office yesterday with Jonathan. We had a nice long chat." A smile played across his lips, as if he just remembered a funny joke.

Stopping in my tracks, I came back around to face him. "Oh, and what exactly did the two of you chat about, Father?" Feeling somewhat apprehensive about my father and my lover having an in-depth conversation about me.

"You, my dear, we talked about you. I gave him my full blessing to call on you," he said with a chuckle then headed back to his office.

"What is so funny, Father?" I followed him into the office, indignation sitting on the tip of my tongue.

"It's just that he understands you so well," he said, now standing on the other side of his desk.

"What exactly does that mean, Father? He knows me so well," I prickled, trying to keep the panic from my voice.

"I find him intelligent and I think he is a very nice young man, and I approve. That is all you need to know." If he only knew the half of it! I wonder if he would approve of Jude Deveraux then. Color rising in my cheeks, I was unable to decide whether I was mortified over the fact that my father and Jude obviously shared a secret between them regarding me, or angry that Jude had gone to my father behind my back.

"Thank you, Father." I tried to sound normal as I walked towards the door. "Well, if that isn't the kiss of death," I murmured under my breath as I got to the door.

"Excuse me, dear, did you say something?" Father smiled.

Shaking my head, "no, Father, just making an observation," I smiled back.

I went in search of one of the three body guards on duty because I desperately needed to ride now, returning three hours later exhausted with one body guard trailing behind.

"Lady Stewart, if you would be so kind and slow down!" Young Thomas yelled to me as he tried to catch up. I proceeded to the stables as if I didn't hear him, a large smile of satisfaction sat on my lips.

Spying Sarah's carriage in the courtyard, I handed Dante off to one of the stable boys and rushed into the house to greet her.

"Mary, have you seen Sarah?" I asked, poking my head into the kitchen.

"Yes, Lady Angelina, she was in the garden with your brother," she answered with a flick of her head.

"Thanks, Mary, you just saved me a lot of searching." I flashed her a brilliant smile. Pouring myself a glass of water, I drank it down, and promptly left to find Sarah and Jonathan.

"Sarah, Jonathan!" I called out when I was unable to find them.

"Over here, Angelina," Sarah called back, now standing and waving to me. They had been sitting in the Wisteria arbor secluded from sight.

"What are the two of you doing way over here, cloistered away?" I questioned, noticing a flush to her normally pale skin. Sarah blushed as Jonathan attempted to smooth things over.

"So I understand that you would like the two of us to accompany you and Lord Deveraux to his family's dinner party. I hear you are in need of some reinforcements," he said, stepping forward, attempting to distract me from what was really going on.

Giving him a knowing smile, I decided to ply him with his own tactics.

"Distract and conquer, dear brother. Yes, I am in need of reinforcements tomorrow evening, thank you for being so understanding. I am assuming that you are both willing to accompany us." Smiling innocently at them both, I moved in between them, taking Sarah by the arm.

"Do you mind if I steal Sarah away for just a little bit? It has been so long since we had time together, seeing how the two of you spent so much time together as of late," I said, leading Sarah away from him.

"But we were still talking, Angelina," he stammered somewhat uncertain, not sure if he should follow after us.

"I promise to return her, Jonathan," I called over my shoulder, then looked back to make sure he didn't follow.

"What game are you playing at, Angie?" Sarah asked, looking over her shoulder, giving Jonathan a reassuring smile to let him know all was well.

"Why, whatever do you mean?" I queried innocently. "I am simply in need of my best friend in the world and her advice, that is all." Squeezing her arm, I looked in to her eyes. "Besides, Jonathan can survive an hour without you, I may not."

Sarah now giving me her full attention. "What is it, Angie?" Concern was etched in her voice.

"I'm not completely sure, that's why I need your advice," I said, not meaning to be cryptic. "I have been afraid of saying anything to anyone. It's a little crazy."

"Well? Go on, don't keep me in suspense," she encouraged me to say more as we walked.

"Remember when I was unconscious for three days?"

"After you took those two highway men on all by yourself? Who could forget? I was sure you had knocked your head or something," she recalled, her eyes reflecting the fear she had had for me.

"I had dreamed the murder of that woman at the king's party. The red head found assaulted and drowned in the boat," my voice cracking as emotion seeped in.

"What do you mean you dreamed the murder?" Shock registering on Sarah's face.

"I mean I woke that morning having experienced every agonizing detail of her murder. From the man cutting her to the moment she was held under the water and drowned. That's what I mean."

"But how is that possible, Angie?" Skepticism was written all over her delicate face.

"I don't know, Sarah, that's the problem," I replied as she pulled away from me.

"There is more to this story, isn't there?" She studied my face then took my arm again. "If you want my help, you are going to have to tell me the whole thing."

"She was dressed in my wig and corset from that night," I said. I could feel my face color from the admission.

"Well?" was all she said. Then the long pause came as I decided just how much I would confess.

"What I am about to reveal to you goes to your grave. Not even Jonathan can know and you will understand when I tell you the whole thing," giving Sarah a severe look.

"I swear!" Sarah said, holding her right hand over her heart.

"I mean it, Sarah, not even Jonathan!" I said, steering her toward a bench.

"Now you have me worried," she said.

"Swear, Sarah, and truly mean it! A man's life depends upon it." The gravity of my words began to sink in.

"I swear it, Angie, on my life I will never reveal what you are about to tell me. Not even to Jonathan." Sarah sat down next to me on the bench with quiet reverence. Taking my hands in hers, she waited for me to get the courage to tell her everything.

"Jude Deveraux is in fact the pirate captain that captured my ship in March. I discovered his secret that night when he kissed me." The shadow of disbelief and shock played across Sarah's face. "There is more. Do you need a minute?" I asked, waiting for the astounding news to sink in before continuing.

"And?" she prodded.

"He made love to me on the boat that night. Well, sort of. We didn't go all the way, but in the process, my corset was removed. It was the very same boat the murdered prostitute was found on, wearing my corset and wig," I said solemnly as she gasped. "Have I completely scandalized you now?" I asked, concerned about what she must be thinking.

"It is just that . . . well, it's a lot to absorb all at once," she said, giving me a puzzled look.

"Then you are really going to have a hard time with the rest of it." I was beginning to wonder if it was a good idea to confide in her.

"The rest of it? You mean there's still more?" Surprise registered on Sarah's face.

"I had another dream just before dawn, Monday," I said, looking away as tears formed in my eyes.

"Well, how do you know this dream means that another girl has been murdered, like the last one?" Sarah asked, turning my face to hers.

"Because they are just different, that's how," I answered, wiping at a stray tear rolling down my face.

"Different how, Angie?" I hesitated a moment trying to think of a way to word the entire thing that didn't make me sound completely crazy. "Don't keep me in suspense, Angie. How are these dreams different?" Sarah's attitude changed from shock to curiosity.

"Because when I dream it I also experienced every terrifying moment. I felt her pain. I mean physically feel everything." I unconsciously grabbed my chest as the remnants of the last dream came flooding back.

"How awful!" She sat pondering what I had just revealed to her a moment, chewing on her finger nail. "You said you had another dream yesterday. Why haven't we heard about the murder yet?" she added, standing to pace in front of the bench.

"I don't know. All I do know for sure is she was part of a pagan ceremonial ritual, and I think they cut her heart out while she was still alive, because I felt this terrible pain throbbing in my chest."

Sarah stopped her pacing and turned to me, her face going pale as she gasped for a second time. "How could they have done such a thing? Didn't she struggle and scream out?"

"I think she was drugged because she could see everything going on, but she couldn't move or stop them," I said as I related some of the dream to her. "But just before she was stabbed in the chest she managed to scream out. Everyone was wearing strange masks and no one tried to stop it or help her."

"You have to tell someone," Sarah said, suddenly very serious.

"I can't, Sarah. They will think me crazy and lock me up in the nearest asylum." Fear gripped me by the throat. "That is why I am telling you. I have been feeling like someone is watching me and I think they are coming for me."

"Now *that* is crazy. Why would someone be after you?" she asked, pacing back and forth again.

"But I get this strange feeling every so often, like this entire mess leads back to me somehow. Like everything that has been happening lately was not just coincidence. And yes, I know it sounds crazy, but I feel it getting closer," my words trailed off. Saying it out loud sounded crazier than when I said it in my head.

"What is this '*it*' you speak of?" Worry distorted her face.

"I don't know. I never see a face. I just have a feeling and it is terrifying." A shiver crawled up my spine.

"Now I am terrified for you." Coming back to sit beside me, Sarah took me in her little arms to offer comfort.

"I don't know what to do." Tears rolled freely down my face. "You can't tell anyone, Sarah, you swore," I said sternly through my tears.

"I will take it to my grave, Angie, I swear it," she assured, patting my back as she began to rock me back and forth in her arms.

15

J ONATHAN HAD PICKED SARAH UP earlier in the day and brought her back to our home so we could all leave from here by four o'clock for dinner with Jude's family. It was now four thirty, and I had just slipped into my dress. Anna fastened the last of the buttons.

I realized I was being childish over the matter of Jude and my father discussing me as if I were a piece of property. And somehow, the two of them felt it all right to work out the details of my purchase between them. But for some reason, I was not of the same attitude.

My dress was especially stunning for the evening's festivities. I wore an emerald green Italian silk gown cut low in the front, coming to a point just between my breasts. A delicate white lace hanky slipped into my décolletage preventing any accidental viewing of breasts with the slightest hint of rounding mounds peaking over the top. This gave the gown a provocative feel. I realized at the time that I was playing with fire, but I did not care. The collar grazed my shoulders, showing off plenty of creamy skin, with tiny crystal beads sown along the edge. I was assured this would drive Jude crazy only being able to look but not touch. The skirt of my gown opened in the front as I walked showing the petticoat beneath made from delicate white crepe.

Anna had piled my hair high on my head with small delicate curls cascading down the back. She had allowed small pieces to escape at the sides, creating an alluring affect.

A thin ribbon tied at my throat with small crystal drops dangling caught the light as I moved, completing the outfit. One last look in the mirror and I was ready to go. Kissing Anna on the cheek as she handed me a black velvet wrap, I headed for the stairs. Yes, by the night's end Jude Deveraux would know the true meaning of patience.

Descending the stairs as the clock chimed forty-five minutes past the hour, I smiled sweetly to Father standing at the bottom.

"Might I remind you that there is something known as fashionably late, and then there is just rude," he said quietly between his teeth, offering his arm guiding me into the parlor where everyone waited.

"Heavens, Father, one might think that you are the one being inconvenienced." I innocently smiled up at him.

"And I thought your mother and I raised you better than that," Father said, as he gave a jovial laugh as we entered the room. "Well, here she is everyone, and isn't she a vision," he announced. "One might even say well worth the wait, wouldn't you say Lord Deveraux?" Walking me over to Jude, he placed my hand into his.

"Well worth the wait," Jude said with a smile that didn't quite make it all the way to his eyes. "I believe our carriage is ready." Taking my arm, he moved toward the door.

I glanced over my shoulder to see Jonathan and Sarah just standing there as Jude hurried me through the doorway into the hallway and out the front door. Looking up at him, I noticed his face was set.

"What game are you playing, Madam?" He finally broke the silence as we reached the carriage.

"Whatever do you mean, good sir?" Playing coy, I smiled, looking into his stormy eyes.

"I told you we would be leaving by four but now it is nearly five and you glide into the room as if you have all the time in the world," he said with indignation in his voice. "And not even a word of apology for your tardiness," he said. Palpable anger hung in the air.

"Father informs me that you and he had a meeting the other day."

"Is that what this is about?" he asked, stopping me midway up. "I asked your father's permission to court you." Understanding dawned on him. "So you have made us late because you are displeased that I talked to your father?"

Sheepishly looking at him through my eyelashes, I suddenly felt ashamed and foolish. "I am sorry, Jude. I was being ridiculous."

"Next time you are displeased might I suggest you simply tell me instead of manipulating the situation." His anger began to dissipate. "You certainly know how to provoke me."

"Yes, and again, I am sorry, Jude. Sometimes I can be a handful, but I never wish to be any man's property, Jude," I said thoughtfully while studying his face.

"And I do not see you as such. But speaking to your father of my intent is only proper." Bringing my hand to his lips, he gently placed a chaste kiss in my palm.

"If you were angry at me, perhaps you should not have worn that particular gown this evening, Mademoiselle," he said, looking up at me with hooded eyes, as Jonathan and Sarah arrived.

I smiled provocatively at him and climbed in the waiting carriage. Sarah climbed in and sat across from me, lifting her eyebrows, as if to say what happened? A half smile played on my lips letting her know that I would tell her everything later.

The ride to Jude's parent's home took us nearly an hour. They had been provided with lovely accommodations near the Buckingham house, where the king resided for the season. We were led to the parlor as beautiful music drifted into the hall. A pianist and harpist played a duet as a young woman sang. We slipped into empty seats in the back row so we didn't disturb the private concert.

Jude's mother, Countess Genevieve Deveraux, turned her head and looked at us as we took our seats. I said a little prayer for the floor to open up and swallow me whole.

My father's words came back to me like a slap in the face. "There is fashionably late and then there is just rude." I believe I had made us the latter.

The music ended twenty minutes later, and we all stood and clapped for the performers. People began to mingle about and the staff provided refreshments before dinner. Jude took me by the arm as Sarah and Jonathan followed us to greet the hosts.

"Momma, Poppy, so sorry for our tardiness, but it really couldn't be helped. The carriage I ordered up broke down, and I had to wait for a new one to arrive."

I squeezed his arm grateful for the lie as I curtsied to his parents. "What a pleasure it is to see you both again," I said as I came up, making eye contact with each in turn.

The count was gracious as he greeted me taking my hand in his. "The pleasure is truly all mine," he said, grasping my hand and placing his other hand over top, his sincerity evident in his warm smile.

Jude kissed his mother on both cheeks and I offered my hand to her in greeting. "How lovely it is to see you again, my dear. You simply look stunning in that color. I don't think I noticed your lovely green eyes before." she said warmly, taking me by the hand. "I have to introduce you to some people." Wrapping her arm around my waist, she guided me toward a large group standing off to the side. I felt somewhat astounded by her sudden warmth and familiarity toward me.

"Please allow me to introduce you to Eli Collins, Inspector General of Scotland Yard. And this is Charles Keats and his wife, Louisa. Charles is the head inspector of the local magistrates."

"It is a pleasure to make your acquaintance," I said, bobbing my head to the group as Jude came up on my left with Honore.

"Jude, you remember Juliette Maureau Walters, the Marquise of Bourbon, don't you?" Lady Deveraux asked.

"Lady Walters, I was so sorry to hear of your husband's passing," Jude said as Honore cursed in French under his breath.

"I'm sorry, Honore, I didn't quite catch that. Would you care to repeat yourself?" Lady Walters said with sarcastic undertones and a piercing stare.

"My apologies, Lady Walters, I meant no disrespect to your late husband," Honore countered with a mocking bow. "If you will excuse me, I see some acquaintances." Walking away, he picked up a glass of wine and downed it with a toss of his head.

Jude took a hold of my arm in a show of possession. "Momma, I promised to introduce Lady Stewart to some friends, if you will excuse us, please." Not waiting for an answer, he led me to the balcony terrace.

"So, would you care to elaborate about what just took place?" I asked when we were alone.

"Would you care to explain this dress that I am unable to tear my eyes from?" Jude countered, attempting to guide me away from my line of questioning.

"Are you trying to distract me, Jude Deveraux?" Suspicious of his motives.

Reaching up he ran his thumb along my jaw line as he stepped closer to whisper in my ear. "Have I told you how enchanting you look tonight?" sending a tingle up my spine and causing me to shiver.

"You are trying to distract me, but I don't care," I said as I reached up to pull his mouth to mine.

"We had better go in before I change my mind about staying for dinner." Jude's words, meant as a warning as his smoldering eyes caused me to shiver again.

"Here you, two are, I have been looking for you," Lady Deveraux said as she came out on to the terrace. "We are just going in for dinner."

Jude turned slowly to look at his mother and their eyes met. A cryptic message was passing between them, but I didn't know how to read it. "We were just coming in, it seems that Lady Stewart is feeling rather chilled." He rakishly smiled at her then down at me.

Wrapping my arm over his, we followed his mother to the dining room. Jude seated me in my assigned place at the table and then escorted his mother to her chair at one end. I noticed he bent over to say something in her ear and she got a stricken look on her face. Moments later, she looked up again and stared straight at me as he left to find his own seat.

I was seated next to Lady Juliette Maureau Walter, the Marquise of Bourbon on my right and Mr. Eli Collins on my left. Sarah had been seated to the left of Inspector Collins and his friend, Magistrate Charles Keats sat across from Sarah. To the left of Mr. Keats sat Honore, Mrs. Keats, Jude and finally Jonathan.

I was thankful that I had allies around me and prayed the evening would pass quickly. I was feeling a bit put out as Lady Deveraux's eyes seems determined to bore a hole into my skull.

Mr. Collins leaned over and started the conversation rolling. "I hear you are the same Lady Stewart who defeated a pirate ship full of blood-thirsty men all by yourself," he stated, sounding proud that he had such a good memory.

"Well now, Mr. Collins, that would depend upon your definition of bloodthirsty pirates," I dramatically added, leaning over giving him a wink in hopes that he would drop the subject and move on to a new topic of conversation.

"Word is you took on a one-eyed shiftless lout to win the freedom of yourself and crew as well as retaining your family ship and cargo," he said in awe.

"Is that true, Lady Stewart?" Mrs. Keats asked from across the table.

Looking at Jude and wondering how far I could take my wild tale before he and Honore started to squirm in their seats. Smiling mischievously at Jude and winking at Honore I began my wild tale with a lie.

"To tell you the truth, Mr. Collins, the pirate captain and his first mate were not much of a challenge. It is true they were a shiftless lot, but there was barely a brain to split between the two of them." Chancing a look at Jude, who was smirking, I knew he was enjoying my wild tale. Honore, on the other hand, was rolling his eyes, so I relished the telling of the rest of my story, all the more.

"I made a bargain with the pirate captain and I never had to lift a blade. So you see, outsmarting them and liberating the ship and crew was not much of a challenge."

"You are either very brave or extremely lucky, Lady Stewart," Lady Walters commented, leaning in towards me.

"It isn't a matter of luck, Lady Walters, I assure you. Lady Stewart is one of the bravest individuals I have ever had the privilege to meet." Jude's words carried an undertone of pride.

"Is that so, Lord Deveraux?" Lady Walters inquired, raising her eyebrows as a show of skepticism.

"It is true. Lady Stewart took on two highway men singlehandedly, killing one and leaving the other one on the ground cowering in fear," Honore interceded, his dislike of Lady Walters apparent by the look on his face.

"Weren't you afraid, Lady Stewart, when you faced the highwaymen not the dimwitted pirates, I mean?" Mrs. Keats asked, sitting on the edge of her seat.

"Yes. Of course, I was afraid. But the choice was clear," I said, just a little surprised by her question.

"What do you mean your choice was clear?" Lady Walters asked sarcastically, her tone derisive as she scoffed, looking directly at Jude. I looked at him staring at Lady Walters, his eyes narrowed in anger.

"The very definition of courage is not the absence of fear but the acknowledgment of it, with the will to go on. We all have fears, Lady Walters, whether we are afraid of growing older or of things that lurk in the shadows of our dreams," I said. "It is how we choose to face those fears that shape our character, and who we are lies not just on the surface but deep down to our moral fiber."

"Here, here, Lady Stewart," Mr. Collins said, encouraging me on.

"Well, aren't you a cheeky one!" Lady Walters said, looking around the table for support from anyone.

"I could not have put it better myself, Lady Stewart. My son was right, you are extraordinary," Philippe Deveraux said from the other end of the table, his voice booming through the room. "I wish to make a toast." Standing, he raised his glass high as he looked down the table directly at his wife and then at me. "May we all have courage to face life as it comes. Never flinching from what we fear the most. And if the Devil himself comes knocking upon your door may you have the fortitude to spit in his eye."

A round of "Here, here" could be heard echoing around the table as they all raised their glasses, that is, except for Lady Walters, who seemed to be brooding as she brought her fan out and was using it to stem the color now staining her face.

I looked down the table to Lady Genevieve who was looking at her husband with her glass raised high. She nodded her head then sipped her wine. Her eyes turned thoughtfully to her son as he looked intently at me.

Finally, my eyes settled on Jude's beautiful face. The way he studied me caused my cheeks to blush. I had seen that look in his eyes before. I smiled, unable to help myself, as he raised his glass to toast me with the promise of much to come later smoldering in his eyes.

The first course was served. We enjoyed a lovely tomato bisque soup and crusty bread with amiable banter from Mr. Collins and Mr. Keats as they discussed several cases they had collaborated on.

Sarah was especially animated that evening as she and Mrs. Keats carried on conversations with Honore and the two inspectors.

My evening was not dampened by the soured disposition of the dinner companion to my right, Mrs. Walters. She simply turned to her right and engaged the gentleman in conversation, as well as others at that end of the table.

Jude and I carried on our own conversation from time to time with flirtatious glances and alluring smiles over our wine glasses. I found him so distracting that I barely noticed the main course.

Dinner finally concluded as Philippe Deveraux announced that coffee, tea and pastries would be served in the parlor. Inspector Collins and I were just concluding our conversation on the economy and the affect it had on crime when I felt a tug at the back of my seat. Looking up, I found Jude waiting impatiently to assist me up from my chair.

"If you would be so kind and excuse us, Father has requested an audience," Jude informed me as he took my hand, leading me to the study.

Philippe Deveraux was holding court in his private study. On entering, I was introduced to Lord Alexander Grayson and Lord Victor Whitehead both members of Parliament, one from the House of Lords and the other House of Commons.

"It is a pleasure to meet you both." I curtsied first, reaching my hand out to Lord Whitehead and then Lord Alexander Grayson. When my hand touched Lord Grayson's, the hairs on the back of my neck stood on end.

"Have we met before, Lord Grayson?" I inquired looking at him more closely, curious as to why I had such a reaction.

"I am afraid not, miss. I would have remembered such a meeting, I assure you," he said, holding my hand longer than he should have. I tried pulling away but he held on tighter. Then bending deliberately slowly he placed a kiss on the back of my hand.

My entire body wanted to shake, as if someone had just walked over my grave, but I managed to maintain my composure. Making a mental note to research his background later, I continued to smile politely at him.

"If you gentlemen will excuse me now, I would like to talk with Lady Stewart for a moment," Philippe announced to everyone in the room, while making a sweeping motion with his hands toward the door.

Jude and I walked over to the davenport in the center of the room and sat down.

"I meant you too, son, out with you," his father said, waiting for Jude to comply with his request. "And please, shut the door on your way out."

Pouring two drinks from his personal bar, he walked over to offer me a glass.

"Thank you, but I think I have had enough this evening," I said apprehensively, watching Jude walk out the door.

He placed the glass on the table in front of me, "In case you change your mind, my dear."

"So, Lord Deveraux, to what do I owe the privilege of this private audience with you?" I asked directly.

"You are a bold thing," he laughed, surprised by my question.

"You sound surprised, Lord Deveraux," I said, feeling less apprehensive now.

"Please, call me Philippe. I feel as if I know you already. My son has gone on and on about you." He was gesturing with his hands as he spoke.

"If we are to be on a first name basis then I insist you call me Angelina. Please enlighten me. What exactly has your son gone on and on about where I am concerned? He has told me virtually nothing of you or your lovely wife, and I am feeling at a disadvantage," I said, looking directly at him.

"Just that he found you to be intelligent and fascinating. My son is very intrigued by you, to say the least. I only wish to get to know the woman who captured my son's attention so profoundly." He narrowed his eyes at me, as if trying to determine the best approach.

"Then, Philippe, you and I must make a deal. I will answer all of your questions and you will answer any and all of my questions honestly." I narrowed my eyes as I studied his reaction to my brash bargain. I could tell he was weighing his options.

"My son truly is a lucky man. You have yourself a deal!" He stood to offer his hand to me in a gentleman's agreement. Chuckling he sat back down in his chair. Taking a cigar out of his pocket, he held it up to me.

"Do you mind if I smoke? It is one of the last pleasures a man my age can enjoy."

"I am merely a guest, sir, please feel free." Standing, I walked over to a window, opened it then turned toward Philippe. "I think I will go first," I said pointedly. "What is the nature of the relationship between Lady Walters and Jude?" Walking back to my seat I paused to read his face before sitting.

Taking his cigar deliberately to his mouth and slowly blowing the smoke from his lips gave him plenty of time to ponder just how he intended to answer that loaded question. "My son was infatuated with her many years ago. Juliette had plans of her own. She married an older man by the name of Lord Albert Walters, the Marquis of Bourbon. She never bore him any children and he has been dead three years past now." Philippe watched my reaction to his words closely.

"If this is true, why would you have invited Lady Walters to your private dinner gathering and why seat her next to me?" I asked.

"Now, if this is going to be fair, it would be my turn to ask a question," he said, holding up his hand.

"Of course, where are my manners? My life is an open book," I quipped.

"Is it true that you carry a six-inch dagger with you at all times?" his tone fascinated by the prospect.

"Is that the question you have been dying to ask me all night?" I asked, my tone slightly skeptical.

"Yes, I really wish to know," he said, taking another drag from his cigar.

Patting the side pocket of my gown with my right hand, I replied, "Yes, I have it with me at all times."

"Well, let's see it!" Putting his cigar in the ashtray, he put his hand out.

Reaching into my pocket to retrieve the blade, I handed it to him.

"Marvelous." Turning the dagger over in his hand, he then removing the sheath from the blade.

"Please be careful, it is very sharp," I cautioned him as he ran his finger down the blade.

Placing the sheath on the blade again he handed it back to me. "I couldn't believe the story when my son told it to me. But now I see it with my own eyes," he said, sitting down and picking up his drink. "Did you really stab that man and leave the other cowering on the ground?"

"In short, yes, and in my defense, I did warn him. It seems it is back to my question," I challenged, placing the dagger back into my pocket. "Now back to the matter of Lady Juliette Maureau Walters. Why would you invite her to dinner and sit her next to me?" I inquired, looking directly at him.

"If it had been left up to me, she would not be let back into this house, let alone placed anywhere near you. But these things are left up to my wife," he said, very matter of factly.

"Of course, which would beg the question, what have I done to offend your wife, Lady Deveraux?" Standing, I pensively walked back to the window to get some air. His cigar had started to affect me, and I was feeling queasy.

"My wife is a different sort," he said, trying to be diplomatic. "Very protective of her only child, you see. So when she saw you and Jude together, she felt the need to test the waters, so to speak." Jude's father walked over to where I stood. "She will come around, just give her time."

Taking several deep breaths to stave off the sick feeling starting in my stomach, I continued. "And you sir, how do you feel about the matter of Jude and me?" I turned from the window to look him directly in the eye.

"Are you all right, my dear, you look pale?" Concern etched his voice.

"I think it is the smoke. I am feeling a little ill," I said, looking at the offensive cigar.

Stubbing out his cigar, he took me by the arm, leading me to the nearest chair and fetched a glass of water.

"To answer your question, Lady Angelina, I am fascinated by you." Handing me the glass of water he poured. "Most young ladies your age are preening, self-indulged little twits. You are nothing I would have expected and everything I could have hoped for my son. My wife will come around once she sees your qualities," he finished.

"I believe I will be fine now." Taking a couple more deep breaths, I stood as he walked over to take my arm.

Opening the door, we walked out together arm and arm to find Jude had been pacing the hallway.

"Why, Jude Deveraux, were you worried about me?" I asked when I saw the look on his face. "I was perfectly fine in your father's capable hands."

"It wasn't you I was worried about," he said looking at his father with feigned concern. He leaned down to place a kiss on my cheek. "I am in need of a word in private with my father."

"I will just amuse myself and find Sarah and Jonathan. Don't be long," I added, walking down the hall.

Still feeling a little ill, I looked for the door to the powder room. Turning down the hall to my left, I found the door. Not bothering to lock the door behind me, I bent down and scooped up water in my hands, splashing it onto my face several times. The cool refreshing water revived me as I felt around for the towel I had left next to me.

"Here, allow me," Lady Walters said, handing me the towel.

"I'm sorry, I didn't hear you come in," I said, patting my face dry.

"You know that you are simply a dalliance of Jude's and that I will be winning him back," she said coldly.

"Is that so? And how do you figure, Lady Walters?" I asked, feeling angry color staining my cheeks.

"He always comes back to me," she said, preening herself in the mirror.

"And exactly how many times has he come back to you?" The words nearly stuck in my throat.

"We were together right after I married Lord Walters and then again after his death. I know what he needs and no simpering little bint such as you will come between us." Her biting words were like a dagger to my heart.

Tears I refused to shed welled up in the back of my eyes. She would never know the effect her words had on me. Turning the knob on the door, I paused for a moment. "I hope the two of you are truly happy together." The words coming from me so quietly I was not sure she heard me. Chancing a glance back at her reflection in the mirror, I knew that she had. Then I quietly shut the door behind me.

Stepping to the door of the parlor downstairs, I stood in the doorway, looking around the room for Sarah and Jonathan. I spotted them standing next to Honore, Eli Collins, Mr. and Mrs. Keats and Lady Deveraux. I slipped into the group next to Honore and Sarah as the two inspectors were recounting some of their more recent cases together.

Sarah giving me a questioning look as I joined the group. "Where have you been? I was getting worried," she whispered in my ear, taking hold of my hand.

"Private audience with Lord Deveraux," I whispered back.

"Junior or senior?" she prodded as she gave me a scandalous look.

"Senior. What are we discussing?" I asked, trying to figure out what I had missed.

"They have been regaling us with gruesome tales of their cases together. They said they would tell us about the latest one. If you are feeling squeamish, you might want to leave. Some of them have been simply gory," she said in a giddy tone, like a child witnessing something she shouldn't.

"Maybe I will take my leave. I'm not feeling well right now," I said, squeezing her hand.

"She was found tied to an old oak tree. The thing must have been a hundred years old at least, the tree not the girl," Mr. Collins said, realizing the way he described the scene could be misinterpreted.

His words stopping me in my tracks as I grasped Honore's arm to steady myself as my entire body began to tingle.

Mr. Keats cut in, finishing the story. "Not only was she tied to this gnarled old oak tree but her heart had been cut out of her chest," he finished with a whisper, looking around to make sure people outside of the circle didn't hear him.

Sarah gasped and grabbed my arm. I could feel the color leave my face and my peripheral view went gray. I felt like the air had been sucked from my chest.

Lady Deveraux noticed me first and quickly took charge. "Honore, help her to the next room. Lord Stewart, fetch a glass of water for your sister."

I didn't remember walking to the next room but I must have made it on my own feet. The next thing I remember I was sitting in a chair and taking the glass of water Jonathan offered me. Sarah stood over me giving me that look, that secret code that longtime friends develop between them that make words unnecessary.

"Maria, have the staff prepare the rooms upstairs for guests," Lady Deveraux instructed as Jude and his father came into the room followed by Honore.

"I truly don't think that will be necessary, Lady Deveraux. I am sure I will be fine now," I said, handing the glass back to Jonathan. Taking a deep breath, I tried to stand, grabbing hold of Sarah's arm to steady myself.

My knees buckled as Jude grabbed hold of me by the waist scooping me into his arms. "This is no time to be stubborn, Angelina." He carried me through the doors at the opposite end of the room and up the back staircase as Sarah, Jonathan, and his mother followed behind.

"Jude, I am fine. Inspector Keats story took me by surprise, that is all." My eyes were pleading with Sarah, over Jude's shoulder, to do something. Sarah's face was a mix of confusion and disbelief as she struggled to keep up with Jude's long strides.

Stepping inside a room, Jude ordered the staff to leave. "Everyone out, now!" he barked, taking control of the situation like the pirate captain that he was.

The upstairs maids rushed to comply with his orders as I stared up at his face.

The maids had no more than run from the room when Jude turned, blocking the door. Sarah, Jonathan, and Lady Deveraux stopped where they stood. "Honore, no one is to enter this room unless I open this door and invite them in. Is that understood?" The stone hard look in Jude's eyes left no room for insubordination. Honore nodded his head and took up his post in front of the door.

"Mother, you still have guests to attend to. Please assure anyone who might have questions about Lady Stewart that she is fine. Tell them it was just a case of the vapors." He stood waiting for Lady Deveraux to comply with his wishes. When she hesitated, he lifted his eyebrows at her then looked to his father to take charge. Lord Deveraux, taking his wife by the arm, escorted her down the hall as the sound of her displeasure could be heard all the way down the back staircase.

"Jonathan, Sarah, please rejoin the party. Angelina will be fine. I will send for you if your services are needed." With that he turned, shutting the door with the heel of his boot.

"You truly are magnificent when you do that," I said, looking up at him while he carried me across the room.

"When I do what, my love?" he asked while gently placing me on the bed.

"Take charge like that. I stand in awe of the way you command attention and absolute obedience," I answered, feeling secure and safe like nothing could hurt me.

"What happened? Is your corset too tight again?" he asked, reaching for the buttons of my gown.

"No. Really, I am fine. My corset is fine," I assured him, slapping his hand away.

"Then what is the matter? Father said you got ill while you and he were talking," he stated, very concerned, running his hand through his hair.

"Your father's cigar smoke got to me, that is all. Maybe I ate too much and my corset cut off my air a little. I don't know, but I am fine, please don't worry," I said, taking his face in my hands to place a kiss on his cheek.

"But I do worry. I can't help but worry. If something happened to you . . ." His words trailed off. Looking deep into my eyes his hand wrapping around my neck, he pulled my lips to his, kissing me passionately.

"Darling, I find that I can't go another day without you bound to me," he said into my ear, his passion evident in his voice.

"What are you saying, Jude? I am devoted to you. There could be no other man for me," I said, pulling back from him slightly. "I could never let someone else touch me like you do, my love. I swear it."

"Then marry me, Angelina," his words hit me like a punch to the stomach. Shock slowly registered all over my face.

Rolling to the other side of the bed, I sat there dangling my feet off the bed then looking back at him. "Let me consider your captivating proposal." Pausing to think a minute with my finger to my mouth. "There, I've considered it. No!" Climbing off the bed, I turned to face him as he sat there puzzled by my reaction.

"Jude Deveraux, you know how I feel about marriage. I will not be owned! Not even by one as alluring as yourself," my last words coming out in a whisper as I walked to the window.

"I am saying this all wrong, or maybe you do not understand me. Please look at me," he pleaded, walking around the bed to stand by me at the window. Turning me to face him as he took my hands into his large stronger ones, he bent to one knee forcing me to look down into his eyes.

"I feel this force that inexplicably connects the two of us that cannot be severed without causing irreparable damage to my heart." Something in his tone began a stirring deep inside of me. "As if we are directly linked and your breath is my breath without which I could not survive each day."

Placing my fingers over his lips to stem his passionate words, tears filled my eyes.

"Do you think me without a heart or soul unmoved by your words because I am of the feminine persuasion, like a machine that moves without feelings? I speak to you from my soul to yours, as an individual human being with a will and mind that works independent and of its own. I beg you burden me no further with your impassioned words of persuasion to bid me marry you because I do not believe it is in my makeup to resist you further. I fear I am not that strong," I pleaded with him as my tears threatening to spill over.

"Then hear me out." His eyes pleaded with me. "Keep your free will and desire to be your own person. I seek to take nothing from you. My only desire is to give to you all that I have and all that I am. I offer you my heart that is true and faithful, full of love, desiring only you. I give to you freely my soul that we may walk all the days of our lives together as equals, one never ruling over the other. If there should be a Here and After, may we be entwined still, for I fear a lifetime with you could never be enough to satisfy me." Reaching into his pocket, he pulled out a small blue box. "I ask you, no, I beg you with impassioned pleadings, to walk through this life by my side as my equal. For it is your soul that I desire to come to me freely, consenting to be my wife." Jude opened the small blue box to reveal a hidden treasure nestled in blue velvet. A large square-cut sapphire engagement ring surrounded with tiny diamonds set in a white gold band. The ring was simply breath taking.

Tears freely rolled down my cheeks as I held his face in my hands. "Jude Deveraux, you have made me a wanton woman with no will of my own. The devil himself could not break my resolve with his lovely words or pretty trinkets, but I find my resolutions dissolve into dust when it comes to you." Bending to kiss him, my tears bathed his face.

Slipping the ring on my left hand, Jude placed the box back into his pocket and stood. "Come with me," he said, pulling me behind him to the door.

Jude pulled open the door as Honore turned. "Honore, you are the first to know. There is to be a wedding. How would you like to be my best man?" Jude asked as surprise registered on Honore's face.

"Congratulations, my friend. I would be honored to be your best man," he said, shaking Jude's hand. "If you will forgive me but it is our custom." Smiling, Honore took hold of my shoulders and kissed me on both cheeks. "Congratulations, Lady Stewart."

"Please . . . this practically makes us family, call me Angelina," I said.

"Angelina it is then," Honore said.

"Let us go open some champagne. Father promised to put some on ice," Jude said enthusiastically, pulling me down the hall toward the stairs.

"How did you know I would say yes?" I asked, pulling him to a stop, narrowing my eyes at him.

"I didn't, that is why they are only on ice and not already opened." He kissed me as he grinned from ear to ear. "Let's not keep them waiting any longer."

Jude stopped halfway down the hall poking his head in a room. "You there, Mary, isn't it?"

"Yes, sir," the young maid curtsied and bobbed her head.

"Run downstairs and tell my father, 'she said yes.' He will know what it means," Jude ordered. "And be quick about it."

"Jude, slow down, we haven't even told my father," I insisted, pulling on his arm. "This is moving too fast."

"But I did ask your father Monday, and he gave his blessing. So you see it is all very proper and I wish to make the announcement before you change your mind." He looked down at me as I hesitated. "Honore, will you excuse us a moment?"

"Certainly, my friend." I watched Honore walk away wondering what I had gotten myself into this time. Had I been too rash? Had I answered this all important question too quickly?

"*Ma amour. Bella Ange.* Forgive my enthusiasm, but I wish to shout my love for you from the tallest mountain. You have made me a very happy man this day, and I wish to share the good news. Smile for I truly do love you and only you. *Ma petite tresor.* Come we will do this together." His persuasive words and tender looks alleviated my fears. How could I say no?

We descended the staircase arm and arm. Philippe and Genevieve met us near the bottom landing.

"Excuse me. May I have your attention, please. My son Lord Deveraux, the Duke of Bayonne would like to make an announcement." Philippe proclaimed loudly to his dinner guests as champagne glasses were passed around.

"After much compelling inducement liberally applied, I have convinced Lady Stewart to consent to wed. So please raise your glasses with me and toast my beautiful bride to be, Lady Stewart."

Shortly after the toast we made our way around the room to accept the well wishes offered, I noticed that Lady Walter was nowhere to be found after our announcement.

Sarah was simply giddy with excitement and talked relentlessly about wedding preparations on the ride home. She was nearly heartbroken when I insisted that we drop her off on our way. She was however consoled by the promise to meet on Friday to further discuss wedding preparations.

Mother and Father had waited up for us and were happily surprised that I had accepted Jude's proposal. One might have thought me an old maid of which my parents were relieved to unburden themselves.

Looking back on that night it felt like a beautiful dream I wished I would never awaken from. Like everything else, all good things eventually come to an end.

16

SATURDAY, JULY 15, 1763;
NIGHTMARES DO COME TRUE

ITH MY IMPENDING WEDDING DATE only three weeks away, I was feeling slightly on edge. To make matters worse I still had an eerie feeling that I was being watched everywhere I went. I could not shake the overwhelming sensation that seemed to follow me.

Jude promised that he would be home by the fourteenth or fifteenth of the month at the latest and I had been anxiously awaiting word from him.

Jude and Honore had left on business to "tie up loose ends" as he had put it right after our engagement was announced, but not before he proclaimed the date of our wedding would be Saturday August the fifth. Realizing that it was uncustomary to set a date so close to the engagement, Jude's excuse was that he needed to return to Bayonne and that sea travel could be treacherous in the winter.

Sarah and I were on our way to the dress shop in London for what I hoped would be the last fitting for my wedding gown.

I had grown accustomed to the presence of bodyguards and learned each of them by name. Today Gordon, Emerson and Carlyle accompanied us to the fitting.

When we were out and about, Mr. Gordon was the superior officer and gave the orders. He was also the one to open the carriage door and send Emerson or Carlyle ahead to the shop to secure the premises.

"Thank you, Mr. Gordon," I said genuinely to him, as Sarah and I entered the shop through the door Gordon held for us.

"My pleasure, Lady Stewart and Lady Burgess." He gave us a gallant sweep of his hand then preceded us into the shop. "I will take my usual seat if you need me. Emerson, far wall and Carlyle, you have the door," Mr. Gordon ordered.

"Lady Stewart, how wonderful to see you today. I have a room ready for you, and Lara will help you try on your gown," Prudence Wheatly graciously greeted us.

"Mrs. Wheatly, you are always so prompt," I said as Sarah and I followed her to a room.

"Good morning, Lara, how are you doing today?" Sarah asked as Lara assisted me out of my gown.

"Very well, Lady Burgess, and you, Lady Stewart, are you excited for the impending wedding?" she asked, making pleasant conversation.

"Of course, now that the preparations are nearly complete," I said as I stepped out of my gown. "I am hoping this is the last fitting."

"I have finished the stitching and the gown is just beautiful," Lara assured me.

Retrieving the wedding gown from the other side of the room, she carefully carried it over to us, presenting the beautiful gown as if it were the crowned jewels. Made from cream Mantua silk with patterned Spitafields silk, the gown was magnificent. A modest square neckline, fitted three quarter sleeves with gold scroll embroidery at the elbow and around the bodice. Delicate three-inch cream lace dangled from the sleeves. The gold embroidery continued in a scalloped pattern at the edge of the skirt.

"It seems the bodice is a little tight, Lara. Is there anything you can do about that?" I mentioned as I tugged at the bodice.

"I don't understand. The gown fit perfectly last time," she said, completely puzzled by the fit. "I will let it out here and here, it will be fine. It will require one more fitting," Lara indicated, pointing to a couple of spots.

"Thank you so much, Lara. What you do with a needle and thread is magical," I gushed, slipping out of the gown.

Sarah helped me back into my gown giving me a questioning look as I turned to present my back to her.

"Have you been eating lately? Not that you look bad. It's just that I have noticed you looking extra busty as of late," Sarah asked as soon as Lara had left the room with my wedding gown.

"Sarah, you are simply scandalous." Feeling somewhat indignant as my cheeks colored, I looked around to make sure no one had overheard her.

"I am just saying being in love seems to agree with you, that is all."

"I could use some tea before we head back," I said, changing the subject.

"I thought you would never ask," Sarah said enthusiastically, while walking to the door. "Shall we be off then?"

"Mr. Gordon, we are going to tea," Sarah said, assuming control of the situation.

"Very good, Lady Burgess," he replied, giving his men a signal.

"Lady Stewart, what a fortuitous happenstance running into you here today," a voice said from the corner.

I turned slowly to identify the familiar voice. "Lady Walter, I did not see you standing there in the corner, how lovely to see you again," I said, lying through my teeth.

"Might I have a private word with you, Lady Stewart?" she asked, making it sound more like a demand than a question.

"I am afraid we were just on our way out to tea," I said, trying to avoid being alone with the detestable woman.

"This will just take a minute. I won't bite," she said, moving closer to me. I hesitated a moment then decided that I was curious to hear her out.

"Mr. Gordon, if you will take Sarah to the carriage, please. I will be along shortly," I said, looking at him helplessly.

"Emerson will take Lady Burgess to the carriage, Carlyle and I will be just outside the door. I won't hear any arguments, Lady Stewart," Mr. Gordon added with authority when I gave him a look.

"If you think it best, Mr. Gordon. Thank you. This should only take a minute."

I turned my attention back to Juliette Walters. "Now, Lady Walters, what is it that I may help you with?"

"I just wanted to pass on a warning to you," she said after Mr. Gordon and Carlyle stepped outside.

"What would you need to warn me about, Madam?" I asked feeling suspicion prickle at the back of my neck.

"If you truly love Jude, you won't marry him." She narrowed her eyes, taking a step closer to me than necessary.

"Why in the world would you say such a thing?" confusion clouded my mind.

"Because he is mine and he will always be mine." Acid tainted her words.

"You have lost your faculties and I don't have to listen to this," I said, indignation and anger rising up I turned to leave.

"I know his secret, and if you don't walk away, I cannot be responsible for what happens to him," Lady Walters said, sounding like a petulant child. "There are those in authority that would take considerable umbrage to Lord Deveraux's past undertakings." Her words stopping me where I stood as a chill ran up my spine.

"What is your true agenda, Lady Walters?" I asked turning on her. "Clearly you don't really love him or you would never have married someone else." The frosty words rolling off my tongue like icicles as I advanced on her. "So what is it you wish to accomplish by keeping us apart?" I screamed at her with a murderous glint in my eyes causing her to flinch in surprise.

"I married that fat old pig so that I would be in a position to better our status. And I was winning him back until you came along," she hissed through her teeth.

"You did what you did for the advancement of no one else but yourself, Lady Walters. You had no thought of Jude in your master plan.

Now that he is of higher ranking you wish to better your status once again. You are no better than a common bint," I hissed back at her.

"I will not warn you again, Lady Angelina Stewart." Her face turned so red with anger I thought she might strike me, even as I dared her to.

"Is everything all right, ladies?" Mrs. Wheatly asked hesitantly, as she cautiously entered the room.

"Yes, of course, Mrs. Wheatly. Lady Walters was just a bit confused. I am hoping she has it all straight in her mind now, for her sake." Directing my words at Juliette, I turned my back to her and walked toward the door. I could feel Lady Walters' piercing stare follow me.

Mr. Gordon saw me coming and immediately opened the door. He escorted me to the carriage giving me a hand up. "Is everything all right, Lady Stewart?" he asked, concern showing in his eyes as he turned and looked toward the shop.

"Yes, yes, everything is fine," I reassured him as my words sounded flat to me.

He paused for a minute then looked back at the shop, then back at me before he shut the door.

"Angie, what happened?" Sarah asked, sensing something had changed.

"I have a headache, and I just need to lie down before the masked ball in the park tonight. Do you mind if we forgo tea today?" I said, trying to sound cheerful and avoid direct eye contact with Sarah. She could always tell when I was lying. I really just needed to see Jude again. He would know what to do.

"Of course I would not mind, whatever you want," she said, patting my hands as she studied my face. "Mr. Gordon, we are not feeling up to tea today. I think we will simply go home," Sarah informed Mr. Gordon out the carriage window.

"Your wish is our command," Mr. Gordon said gallantly, giving the signal to the other men to head for home.

I opened the curtain and stared out the window. That familiar feeling of dread had returned, and it sat in the pit of my stomach, like a meal that won't digest.

"Sarah, will you send word to Lara that I would be grateful if she could come around to the house with the dress when she is finished with the alterations." My words were spoken absentmindedly as I continued to stare out the window.

"Yes, I would be happy to, Angie. Is there anything else I could do for you?" Juliette's words were still ringing in my ears. Pulling my eyes from the window, I just stared at her for a minute. "You look really pale, Angie, are you sure you are feeling all right?

"Yes, of course, it's just this nagging headache. I will be better once I lay down. Don't look so worried, Sarah," I said to her, hoping my words rang truer in her ears than they did in mine.

17

EST AND QUIET DID LITTLE to ease the tension that was building inside of me. The feeling of impending disaster continued as I prepared for the ball.

Black and white was the theme colors of this year's masquerade ball being held in Vauxhall Gardens. I had picked out a black-on-black brocade gown with loose fitting three quarter length sleeves and a full skirt. I had donned a white powdered wig with a black and gold mask.

"Why do women's fashions have to be so abominably uncomfortable?" I mused as Anna tightened my corset. "Honestly you will have to leave me some room to breathe, Anna," I complained.

"Sorry, Lady Angelina, but the top . . ." her words trailed off.

"Now that really hurts, Anna," I said, giving her the eye. "I can't imagine what the problem is. Just leave the top looser and don't tighten it anymore or you will choke the very life from me."

"Lady Angelina." Her tone caused me to stop what I was doing.

"What is it, Anna?" Something in her voice made me turn to look at her.

"Is there any possibility that you could be with child?" Her tentative question caught me off guard as Anna fidgeted with her hands. "The only reason I question is you are late this month and your breasts have gotten larger and they seem to be tender."

Realization dawned as I sat down in the nearest chair. Why hadn't I seen that small little fact myself? It all made sense. Being on edge, not feeling exactly myself, of course, I was with child. What did I expect?

"Anna, you are to tell no one about this!" I said, standing up. "Let's finish getting ready, I have a ball to attend." Now I had another secret to keep.

I was getting worried that I had not heard from Jude but decided he had probably been delayed somewhere along his travels and that I would attend the ball with Jonathan and Sarah.

Our detail consisted of Mr. Burns, nicknamed Burney, Jones, Smithy, and Duncan. Burney was the senior member and therefore in charge.

Mother and Father decided to take a carriage with Lord and Lady Burgess, meeting up with us at the park.

Sarah was so excited about the ball she hardly noticed my pensive mood, but Jonathan did. He reached over giving my hand a squeeze.

"Angelina, you simply look ravishing tonight. Too bad, Lord Deveraux, isn't here," Jonathan said without thinking.

Sarah poked him in the ribs with her elbow. "Jonathan! What a thing to say." Sarah cried.

"Well, it is true. I think it a crime that so much beauty should be left to one man," Jonathan protested, smoothing it all out with a compliment directed at Sarah and me. I smiled and Sarah melted.

I could almost guarantee the two of them would be getting engaged before the season was through. What a lovely pair they made. Sarah and Jonathan had both gone with white brocade trimmed in gold and truly made a stunning pair.

On arriving at the park, Burney sent Jones and Smithy ahead to secure the entrance and make sure the path was safe.

Burney opened the carriage door, assisting Sarah and me down, as Duncan ran point.

The park was well lit with torches and lanterns lining the paths. Large swaths of black and white fabrics had been hung, lending an air of jubilation and grandeur to Vauxhall Park.

A stage for dancing had been built along with an orchestra stage above it. No expense had been spared. The atmosphere was lively and the air felt magical.

People entering the park presented their invitation, and a special ribbon was tied to their wrist. Anyone found without a ribbon on their wrist would be escorted from the park.

Lively music could be heard through the park and the festivities were well underway by the time we arrived at nine-thirty.

I was thankful that Anna had thought ahead and prepared me a small repast to eat before I had left. My stomach had been acting up, and I didn't know what would agree with me until I smelled it first.

A few ejected patrons trying to crash the ball had been forcibly removed and were complaining loudly as we entered the gates. If I had to guess I would say they had already imbibed a bit too much.

Jonathan had one of us on each arm and seemed to be strutting. One might even call it a swagger. I looked at Sarah and winked. She just giggled.

I was disappointed Jude wasn't there with me, but I was determined to make the best of it.

A large table was reserved for our group replete with refreshments and fresh fruit. We were located next to the dance floor, so even though I would not be dancing much, I could enjoy watching everyone whirl by. Burney and Jones stood by the table while Smithy and Duncan were strategically placed always behind the table.

Sarah and Jonathan left for the dance floor while I waited for the arrival of the rest of our party.

I was enjoyed watching the dancers doing a minuet when a strange sensation struck me. My neck hairs stood on edge and my arms got all goose bumpy. Someone was watching me.

I tried looking around but didn't notice anyone paying particular attention to me.

"Mr. Burns, do you happen to see anyone staring in my direction?" I asked casually, attempting to stay calm as I shivered.

"No, Lady Stewart. Is something wrong?" he asked somewhat puzzled.

"Just a feeling, I'm sure it's nothing. Sorry to bother you," I replied, feeling a bit stupid now.

"Jones, is anyone suspicious looking toward me, from where you stand?" Burney asked.

"No, sir," Jones answered.

"Keep an extra sharp eye out, Jones, you're not looking hard enough," Burney ordered. Then he turned to me and winked. He always knew how to make me smile. I went back to eating my fruit, but I could not shake the feeling.

Mother and Father showed up with the Burgesses shortly after. I was happy to have the distraction. Eventually, Sarah and Jonathan returned from dancing to join us. That is when the real party began.

"Come on, Sis, won't you dance at least one dance with me?" Jonathan's eyes pleading with me to join him. I was sure Sarah had put him up to it.

"I would be honored to dance with you, Jonathan. Thank you for asking." It was to be a group dance where you join hands and circle around each other, bow or curtsy, depending on your gender, then move down the line to repeat the steps with the person to your right, and so on, until you eventually end up with your original partner.

Jonathan and I found a spot on the dance floor as the music begun. I curtsied then joined hands and continued down the line. The music was wonderful. As I got caught up in the rhythm I let it sweep me away. I was on to my third partner when my blood ran cold.

"What a delight it is to see you out and about, Lady Stewart," the man said, with an undertone of menace.

"Lord Montgomery, what a delight." Sarcasm dripped from each word I spoke.

"I see you haven't lost any of your sweetness. One might wonder why Lord Deveraux is so often absent since the announcement of your impending nuptials." Darcy meant for his words to be cutting but two could play at that.

"Derision and ridicule are guaranteed to repel mediocrity masquerading as conventional wisdom, Lord Montgomery," I sweetly answered him on the upbeat.

"Perhaps we will have more time later to discuss the follies of your mind set, Lady Stewart." His ominous words left me feeling disjointed and a little cold as I moved on.

The dance seemed to go on forever after my exchange with Darcy Montgomery. I kept recalling our previous unfortunate exchange when he promised to make me sorry for them. The man gave me the willies, and I just wanted to be away from him.

Just one more person and I would be back with Jonathan.

As I came around instead of Jonathan reaching out to take my hand a much larger one was there in its stead. Grasping my hand, he spun me around and my heart stopped. I had to blink twice to be sure my eyes weren't playing tricks on me.

There he stood before me in all his splendor, Jude Deveraux. He was replete in black brocade, and black mask. But I would know those eyes anywhere. They sparkled like sapphires glowing in the light. The flame I saw reflecting back made me forget everything else. It was as if we were the only two people in the world. No words were necessary as his piercing eyes made inappropriate contact. The music ended as he pulled me to him.

Playing coy, I turned my face to the side. After all, I had not heard from him in weeks and then he simply showed up.

"Not exactly the welcome home I was expecting. Isn't distance supposed to make the heart grow fonder?" he teased, tipping my head up with his thumb.

"You, sir, have left me to fend off the slings and arrows of many on the flimsy excuse of tying up loose ends," I informed him, my sullen tone alerting him to my mood. I turned to leave the dance floor but his hand on my wrist stopped me.

"I made a request to the orchestra and they promised to play it immediately." His telling smile alerted me that he was up to something.

The music started and I was unsure what it meant. The dance was *La Volta*, a very intimate, seductive dance introduced in the courts of Elizabeth, not well known outside the courts for reasons that are self-explanatory.

One normally began with a galliard then transitioned to a closed position. The man is supposed to take one hand placing it below the woman's waist and his other hand he would place on her back above the far hip. It is a series of steps and lifts with his knee behind the upper thighs.

Instead of coming back around to an open position with a series of hops, twirls and a lively step, Jude decided to change things up just a bit. Standing side by side, he kissed the side of his right hand then presented it to me. I followed suit. Kissing my hand on the side of my left hand, I took his hand.

He pulled me in to a closed position our eyes never strayed from each other. Then, while facing one another, we walked in a circle as dancers maneuvered around us. Coming back to a side-by-side position with his arm behind and in front of me, we again took steps around in a circle.

Coming back into a closed position his hands were on either side of my waist as he lifted me high above him slowly lowering me close to his body as he walked in a circle. Our faces came conspicuously close to one another's as I slid down the front of his body.

"Are you attempting to seduce me on this dance floor, Lord Deveraux?" I questioned as our lips nearly touched.

"Well, I suppose that would depend, Lady Stewart." The deep rugged tones of his voice mingled with the music.

"Depend on what, pray tell?" I asked, looking at him seductively.

"Whether or not it is working." He laughed, lifting me in the air again.

This time I tenderly kissed his lips as he lowered me slowly down to the ground. I had never truly cared much for convention as I am certain we scandalized more than a few people with our display of affection for one another. At that moment I only saw him, and he was all that mattered to me in that brief minute of time.

We continued to dance till the end of the song, then we walked off the dance floor and headed for a path we both knew well.

"We have two interlopers intent on interrupting our interlude," Jude said as he pointed to Smithy and Duncan sent by Burney. They followed a respective four feet behind us but followed us nonetheless. This made me laugh because his wording was terribly clever.

"It is useless to attempt to send them away. They will only take orders from Burney. I have no real authority here."

"We could always try to lose them," he said, raising his eyebrow, which only made me laugh again.

"I have missed you, Jude. You can't leave me like that again." All the emotions of the last few days broiled up to the surface in my voice as tears filled my eyes. "I nearly died all these weeks without you." Tightening his arm about my shoulders he gave me a squeeze.

"Jude Deveraux, what could possibly have been so important that you had to be gone from me so long? Where did you go and why are you being so secretive?" I asked, looking up into his face searching for answers as we walked. I could tell that he wanted to say something to me, but he didn't.

"Jude, answer me please," I pleaded, and still he kept silent. I stopped in the middle of the path refusing to move, causing people to walk around us.

"Darling, I will explain, but not here, not now." Something in his words gave me cause to pause. I allowed him to lead me down the path and to the left, which led to a secluded spot surrounded by tall hedges.

"Smithy, Duncan, it has been a long few weeks and we need to discuss a few matters, privately," I said, turning to the two bodyguards trailing us.

"If we take our eyes off you, Lady Stewart, Burney will have our heads," Duncan informed me as his voice betrayed his fear.

"Then I propose a compromise. One of you go to this end of the path that leads into the hedges and the other at the other end of the hedges where the trail ends. Lord Deveraux and I will be somewhere in the middle having a private conversation," I said very matter-of-factly. "How is that?"

Smithy and Duncan looked at each other trying to decide what to do next.

"It is settled," I announced. Taking hold of Jude's arm, I pulled him deeper into the hedges. "If I need you, I will give you a shout."

"Start talking, Jude." My words sounded harsh even to my ears.

"Is it an explanation you really want, *ma amour*?" he asked, taking hold of my wrist to pull me close.

"Jude Deveraux, I am wise to your tactics and will not be played. Now answer the question." Frustrated by his stalling, I removed my mask.

"There is time to answer all of your questions but right this moment, I require proper motivation." His hand reaching out taking me by the back of my neck, he drew me closer until our faces nearly touched. "It has been a long journey, and I have dreamed of nothing else but the very moment I could hold you close, tasting of your soft sweet lips." His lips so close to mine caused a ripple of delight. I shivered with anticipation as the mere thought of his sinfully tempting lips against mine caused a thrill to shoot through me.

"But of course. If it is answers you wish instead of a reunion, I will be obligated to comply," he said, suddenly pulling away from me. A devilish smile played on his sumptuous lips as my heart skipped a beat.

"You truly are without scruples," I whispered.

He removed his mask while I wrapped my fingers through his hair. He drew my lips to his. Weeks of pent-up longing and need came flooding back all at once. I didn't care that we were in the middle of a park with men standing guard just feet away. I needed him.

The taste of his lips and the smell of his skin drove me crazy. His hands wrapped around my waist lifting me up. I wrapped my arms around his neck. The taste of him was enough to make me lose all concept of propriety. My moan of pleasure seemed to ignite his passion even more as his lips trailed down my throat.

"I have dreamed of holding you in my arms every night since I left." Jude's passion-filled words making me feel dizzy with desire.

One arm was wrapped around my waist as the other hand found its way under my skirts.

"Jude, we have to talk about something," I said breathlessly between passionate kisses.

"Yes, yes, of course, *ma chere*." Capturing my mouth with his again, he answered without really hearing what I had said.

"I need to tell you something, my love," I whispered near his ear.

Looking around I spotted a bench and pointed. A wicked grin came to his face as he carried me in that direction. Sliding me down to the ground, I could feel his need solid and bold.

"What I have to say is important, Jude, but you might want to take a seat first," I said as I began to worry how he would take the news of our impending arrival. I chewed at my lip as I paced in front of him wondering how I was going to tell him.

"This is serious, Jude," I said, feeling desperate.

He finally took hold of my hand in his as I paced in front of him.

"Come now, it can't be that bad, my love," he said, pulling me into his lap. He lifted my head so that my eyes were looking into his.

Taking a deep breath, I summoned my courage to say what I needed to say. "I am carrying your child," I said quietly while looking directly at him. His reaction was difficult to gauge. So many emotions seemed to cross his face all at once.

"Say something, Jude." I mistook his silence for disappointment.

Climbing from his lap, I walked a couple of feet away with my back to him. "You are angry, aren't you?" My words vibrated as I tried to hold the tears back.

Coming up behind me, he wrapped his arms around me. "No, I am not angry or disappointed." Turning me around in his arms to face him, he wiped a tear from my face. "I am thrilled, darling. We are not the first to marry after we have conceived, and we will not be the last," he said, placing his hand on my stomach. He bent to kiss my lips again.

His tempest-filled eyes sparkled clear and dark in the moonlight. Kissing my mouth and eyes, his ardent passion only seemed to lay momentarily dormant, as if any sudden movement would ignite him once again.

"I have never known such desire with anyone as I have for you, *ma amour*," he rasped trying to catch his breath. "*Fou d'amour*, I am madly in love with you." Taking my face in his hands, he forced me to look directly into his eyes. "I will love you until the day I die and when we both reach heaven, I will love you there too." Raw emotion filled his words as tears welled up in my eyes. "I cherish you with all my heart, *mon le grand amour*, my one true love." My heart was so full in that moment I felt that it would burst.

Suddenly out of nowhere, I felt someone grab me from behind. As Jude reached for me, he crumpled to the ground like a rag doll. Two men dressed completely in black stood behind him, their faces hidden by masks. I tried to scream, but a large hand covered my mouth as an arm lifted me off the ground by the waist. My attempts to kick and claw at my assailant resulted in a tightening of the arm around my waist until I couldn't breathe. I feared I would pass out.

My heart was beating so fast, I imagined it would give out any second. Terror filled my veins. My mind could not process what was happening. Jude's lifeless body lay before me on the ground. Was he dead? I couldn't tell. The only thing I knew for sure was he didn't move.

I caught movement out of the corner of my right eye, and I prayed it would be Smithy or Duncan coming to help. But instead, it was another man dressed head to toe in black with a gold and black mask covering his face.

"Lady Stewart, we meet again. How lovely you look by moonlight. I am terribly sorry to interfere with your little tryst with Lord Deveraux, especially at such a touching moment," Lord Montgomery said, his words sugary sweet as he gestured to Jude's crumpled lifeless form on the ground. Dramatically, he stepped over Jude's listless form. "It appears that he isn't feeling well at the moment." Darcy removed his mask. A sympathetic look plastered on his face as he looked at Jude and pretended to be sad. Just as suddenly, his face changed.

Darcy's menacing smile made him appear slightly unhinged. "My associate is going to remove his hand from your mouth now. But if you scream I will be forced to slit the throat of your beloved fiancé." He pulled a knife from his waistband for emphasis.

"I don't understand why you have done this." My confusion seemed to bring amusement to him as he chuckled sardonically.

"It really is quite simple, Angelina. Oh, you don't mind me using your given name, do you?" chuckling again, finding the entire situation amusing. "Of course you don't. As I was saying, it really is simple, Angelina. I have long admired your loveliness, but you have rebuffed and disrespected me publicly. I simply cannot abide with such deceitful behavior from a woman," he said, bringing his face only inches from mine. "So you will be dealt with."

"What does that mean?" My voice shook as I spoke.

"I intend to teach you your place in the great plan of all things, Angelina." The putrid smell of his breath in my face caused me to gag and turn away.

Grabbing my cheeks between his thumb and fingers he turned my face back so that he could leer at me. "You will learn how to treat a man with respect, Lady Stewart, or I am afraid your future won't be very bright," he snarled at me. Bringing his other hand up, he covered my face with a rag that smelled nauseatingly sweet and pungent.

I began to struggle with real earnest, but my muscles went slack and my head began to spin. I couldn't breathe. I tried to voice my protests as the bitter sweetness of dark enveloped me in her folds and I went limp.

Then nothing.

18

 HAT WAS THAT AWFUL NOISE? And why couldn't I see anything?

Palpable darkness so cold, damp and eerie it filled my lungs. These were my first recollections and thoughts.

Then realization hit me like a brick wall. That awful sound I was hearing was coming from me. "Hello?!" I cried, then lay still in the damp cold dark, moaning and shivering. Silence greeted me, except for the sound of tiny scurries of rodents. "Help!"

I tried to clear my head and remember how I got here but my head felt dull and fuzzy. I couldn't remember what happened. Squeezing my eyes tightly shut, forcing down the rising panic, I tried to slow my panicked breathing. I swallowed several times to keep the bile down as nausea overwhelmed me.

I struggled to remember. Where was I? Things started coming back to me in bits and pieces. Jude had been on the ground, beside me, his lifeless body crumpled. Was he dead? Hot tears of anger flowed at the sudden recollection of Jude's distorted form unmoving on the ground.

I will kill Darcy Montgomery when I get my hands on him. The narcissistic man would pay. He thinks he will show me my place in the world. Hah!

My eyes slowly began to focus in the darkness. My hands had been tied together above my head with a rough rope that was biting into my skin. I was lying on a mattress but, beyond that, I couldn't really see much past the foot of the bed.

Calling out again, "Hello? Is anyone there? Help me!" The words tore at my dry throat. I felt a hitch of pain in my tight chest cleared my throat and called out again. "Is anyone there! Hello!?"

Three tiny dots of light lined a wall that led to what looked like a tunnel. My head ached and my eyes were blurry. I could hear footsteps and then lantern lights. Four blurry figures made their way toward me.

"I am glad to see that you are no worse for wear, Angelina. Could I offer you a drink of water? Chloroform and ether can leave your mouth so dry, don't you think?"

"Yes, please." My words came out in a whisper because my throat had completely gone dry.

"I see we have learned some manners already," Darcy said as his sugary sweet words held an undertone of menace.

He snapped his fingers and the young woman who accompanied him ran to do his bidding. Putting the lantern and pitcher of water down on a small table next to the bed, she poured a cup of water, supported my head and poured a small amount of water into my mouth.

I swallowed, then began to choke, coughing and sputtering water everywhere.

"You imbecile, are you trying to kill her?" Darcy screamed at the woman, cuffing her in the back of the head.

"I'm sorry, sir," she said, ducking as she cowered from his abuse.

"It wasn't her fault, I just swallowed wrong. Please don't hurt her." I croaked through the spasms of coughs.

Throwing a glass of water in my face, he caught me by surprise. "When I wish to hear your opinion, I will let you know. Since you are new here, allow me to give you your first lesson." Darcy motioned to the two men who had accompanied him.

The bigger of the two men untied my wrists as the other one took hold of my arm. Together they dragged me from the mattress, pushing me into a kneeling position in front of the bed.

Glancing over my shoulder, fear began to take root deep inside. The perverse smile on Darcy's face caused my blood to run cold. I tried to get up, but the two men held me down.

"Don't fight it, my dear, it only excites me more," he said next to my ear as he untied the back of my gown. A shiver of revulsion crawled up my spine as he pushed the gown off my shoulders. "Hand me the cane, woman," Darcy demanded.

Searing pain ripped through my body as the cane struck me across my shoulder blades. He raised the cane high above his head striking me again. This time the pain was so severe I screamed out. His sadistic laugh ringing in my ears. Darcy struck me three more times before I collapsed, my body going limp as blood caused my slip to stick to my back.

"I think that will conclude our lesson for today," he cheerfully announced as if we were discussing how lovely the weather was. "Treat her wounds, woman. I would hate for that to scar. Tie her back up when you are done," Darcy ordered the woman. "You supervise," he said, pointing to the larger man.

Walking away, he whistled a happy tune all the way down the corridor.

The woman peeled my slip down, placing some sort of salve on my wounds. Then she gently helped me dress in a fresh gown and pressed a cup of hot broth with some bread in my hands.

"Do you need to use the pot before he ties you back up?" she quietly asked, avoiding eye contact.

"Please tell me your name," I whispered, trying to make a bond. "My name is Angelina Stewart."

"I know who you are." Her eyes darted back to the man standing guard at the end of the bed.

"You have to get a message out to Lord Deveraux or my father, Lord Stewart," I said, grabbing her hand when she turned to leave.

She slipped her hand away. "She's ready."

"Please, could I at least have a blanket?" I cried, my eyes pleading with her. "Please!"

She removed the shawl from her shoulders placing it around mine before she turned her back to me. My hands were once again bound to the bed. The man picked up his lantern, waiting for the woman to catch up.

She left behind a lantern on the table when she departed. "I am sorry," was all she whispered to me as she turned to go.

I couldn't tell you how long I lay there fading in and out of consciousness. It could have been hours or days. I had no way of gauging the passage of time in the dark. The lantern had run out of fuel while I slept, leaving me in total darkness with nothing but my own thoughts to keep me company.

The bed I was tied to was an old iron bed that was badly rusted. I tried pulling on it to see if there was any give at all, but I felt weak and sick to my stomach most of the time, so I tried to sleep and conserve my energy.

I maintained my sanity by recounting the passages from books I had read. Sometimes I sang to pass the time. When the truly dark moments overtook me, I thought of how many ways I would kill Darcy Montgomery. Those were the moments that brought me the most comfort.

Sometime later, I heard footsteps coming down the tunnel before I saw the lantern lights as Darcy and the woman came with a tray of food.

"Oh good, you are awake. I was hoping that you would be in a much more cooperative mood after our little lesson," he said, coming closer to me with the light. "Is that light hurting your eyes?" What is that look for?" His words implied sympathy as I glared at him. "Are you feeling sad?" Darcy asked sarcastically, his words cutting me to the quick. I turned away just as tears sprang to my eyes. "Maybe you are thinking of someone you will never see again. Let me guess, is it your mother? No, your father?" He was getting such perverse enjoyment from taunting me he nearly crowed. Crawling up the length of the bed, he straddled my body. Leering at me, he crept inch by inch by inch, smelling me as he went. "Or could it be your fiancé, Lord Deveraux?" he said, licking my neck and then my cheek.

"Did you kill him?" I asked, not sure I really wanted to know the truth. Liquid tears flooded my ears as I told myself to not cry. I took a deep breath to gain control over my emotions and stem off the nausea I felt.

"No. He just had a very bad headache. I figured killing him would be too merciful an act." His finger traced along my jaw line, down my neck and between my breasts. "And if there is one thing I am not, that is merciful. No, his true pain will come from never finding you again and knowing for the rest of his natural born days that he was at fault." His sadistic laugh echoed through the cavernous walls. I began to breathe in and out through my mouth because his stench made me physically ill.

"Oh, darling Angelina, just put him out of your mind, because you are never going to make it out of here alive," he began to laugh again, while he untied me. "Maggie has provided you with something over in the corner to relieve yourself in. Then we will have a meal together. I am sorry if the accommodations are not up to your standards, but we do the best we can. Now hurry along. I hate to be kept waiting."

I tried to stand and would have fallen to the floor if it had not been for Maggie slipping an arm around my waist. She assisted me to the pot in the corner and even stood in front of me, providing a small amount of privacy. "Thank you for your kindness, Maggie," I said as I stood up, grabbing hold of her arm for support.

She walked me back to the table where Darcy had pulled out a chair for me.

"That will be all for now, Maggie, you can wait for me back at the house," he said in a dismissive tone.

"Yes, sir." Maggie bobbed a curtsy and scurried down the passage way.

"Now, my dear, it looks like it is just you and me." His sinister grin churned my stomach. The food smelled delicious and I was starving. My empty stomach gurgled.

"It sounds to me like someone is hungry," he said while removing the covers from the two plates. "I took the liberty of requesting finger foods. I hope you don't mind." He snickered with delight. "Your reputation with a knife precedes you." He laughed to himself as if he told a funny joke. "My associates may not have been terribly bright, but did you really have to kill Roy?" he said, pausing a moment for his words to sink in.

"You sent those men to attack me on the road?" I was stunned by his admission. I could not believe what I was hearing.

"Yes. The two of them bungled the entire thing so badly. Too bad I had to finish the job for you. I couldn't very well have Tommy talking to the authorities now, could I?" He smiled with satisfaction when I gasped.

"You killed Tommy?" I cried, unable to hide my distaste and disbelief.

"You dare doubt my word?" Darcy's rapidly changing mood indicating to me an unstable nature.

"No! Of course not, it's just that I didn't know he was dead." Quickly backtracking, I decided to appeal to his vanity. "I'm sorry. I didn't realize how powerful you were, that's all. I'm impressed." Taking some cheese and bread from the tray, I ate a piece and slipped a few pieces under the table and into my pocket while he spooned soup into his mouth.

"What are you doing?" he asked, noticing my hands under the table.

"I was just massaging my wrists. The rope is so rough it has cut into my skin. See?" I said, bringing my hands up to show him. "And it doesn't help that my hands are tied above my head. I have been trying to get feeling back so that I might be able to grip the spoon."

"Well, you won't be uncomfortable for much longer, Angelina." An evil smile formed on his lips. "It is almost a full moon."

"What happens when the moon is full?" I asked, swallowing hard.

"We will be having a little ceremony, and you will be our guest of honor." His words filling me with dread as he laughed to himself.

I had to figure a way out of this. No one knew where I was. I didn't even know where I was or what day it was. What I did know was, Darcy was insanely deranged and meant to kill me.

"You just might want to keep me around for a while," I said, feigning sweetness.

"Oh, and why is that?" he asked skeptically.

"Because I know what you like." I looked at him through my eyelashes as I spooned some soup into my mouth.

"Oh, you do now, and what is that?" He seemed amused by our little game as it made him smile.

"I could make you feel good. That is what you want, isn't it?" I said, trying to sound seductive. "You know I have only been playing hard to get because you like a good game." I smiled suggestively.

"Don't try to play me for a fool, Angelina." He suddenly turned serious as I plied him with sweet womanly wiles to get his interest.

"No! No, I wouldn't do that. I know how much you hate it. You are much too smart for that," I said, placating his ego.

"Sounds like this might have just turned interesting for me," he said, grinning widely, like a cat playing with a mouse. "I hope you have finished your dinner, my dear." Taking me by the arm, he pulled me back to the bed.

I pleaded, "Wouldn't you like a chance to clean up just a bit? We just finished our meal and maybe you would allow me to wash myself. I have been lying here for I don't even know how many days. Surely you can understand that I want to be fresh for you." My words rushed out as I tried to keep the panic out of my voice.

"Of course, I understand, my dear. I will send Maggie back to get you ready for me. But for now, I am afraid I will have to tie you to the bed again." His behavior was solicitous now as he gently tied me to the bed.

"But how can I ready myself if I am tied up?" My childish pout meant to catch him off guard.

"It is only for a short while, just until I return." He leaned down and kissed my lips. I tried desperately not to flinch or shudder from the profound revulsion I was feeling. Instead, I smiled seductively at him when he pulled away. "Don't be long," I sweetly said. "I am already lonely for you," I called to him as he walked away.

Waiting a minute until I was sure he was out of earshot, I desperately began yanking at the bar I was tied to. I thought I had felt it give way earlier, but now my life depended on it. I could feel the slightest give as the rough rope dug into my skin, but I didn't care. I had to get free. The very thought of him touching me in an intimate way made me sick.

A few minutes later, Maggie came into the large room so quietly that I jumped when I looked up and saw her.

"What are you doing?" she timidly asked.

"I have to get free. Help me." Desperation underlining every word I spoke.

"I can't. He will kill me," she said, looking back at the entrance hall. I could see the fear on her face.

"Not if I kill him first," I said to her as I continued to yank on the bar.

"You don't know him like I do. He is a brick short of a full load." Maggie looked over her shoulder again while putting the bowl of warm water down on the table.

"Maybe so, but he is a man, and he bleeds just like the rest of them. Now untie me and help me find a weapon," I told her. "I will die either way. If he touches me, the truth will be revealed. I am not that good of an actor. My total revulsion of the man will come out, and he will kill me. Please, Maggie, I will take you with me. I just need your help to get free," I frantically pleaded with her.

My pleads for help went unanswered. Maggie began to clean and ready me for Lord Montgomery.

"Maggie, if you won't help me, leave me alone. I beg you."

"I am sorry. I fear him and what he will do to me if I help you," her words spoken so quietly I almost missed them.

"I had a dagger in my pocket when Lord Montgomery captured me. Do you know what happened to it?"

"The gold one with jewels on the handle?" Maggie asked.

"Yes, that's the one," I said with a glimmer of hope in my voice.

"He has been wearing it in his waistband."

"I didn't see it tonight," I replied.

"He is afraid of what you might do to him if you get your hands on any knife, let alone your dagger," Maggie said with awe as she looked at me now. "He said no one could have a weapon on them around you."

"Is this what you were looking for?" Darcy's voice startling us both as he brandished my dagger in his hand.

Maggie instantly gazed downward and shrunk back in fear.

"Thank you, Maggie. That will be all. I will deal with you later." Darcy's sinister message registering with Maggie instantly as her entire demeanor changed.

"Run, Maggie, and don't stop," I whispered to her.

I could see her mind racing as her breathing came in small gasps like a mouse trapped by a cat. She scurried away with the bowl and rag, ducking her head as she went. At least she could leave. I was tied to this bed with nothing to defend myself.

Desperation gripped my throat as my mind began to race. Pulling on the ropes, now tied to the metal headboard, the bar giving just enough to cause a glimmer of hope but not enough to free me, I felt my heart sink.

"I was suspicious of your motives when I left and now I see my suspicions were warranted." Darcy's crooked smile spoke volumes as he came to stand by the bed, looming over me.

I could feel my heart beating in my throat as fear made my head light and my entire body began to tingle. I tried to slow my breathing down in hopes that he wouldn't realize just how scared I was of him.

"You know, I think I like it when you struggle." He chuckled. Climbing on to the bed, he straddled my legs. Darcy trailed the dagger down the side of my throat and between my breasts

"So what else do you like?" I asked, trying to buy time while I continued to struggle with the bar.

"I like the fear I see in your eyes, knowing I hold your life in my hands," pricking my chest with the dagger, which made me cry out in surprise. I glared at him defiantly. "But mostly, I like it when you get angry and fight back."

Rage caused my eyes to tear up because all I could think about was how many ways I wanted to kill him.

"Oh, did I hurt you, my dear?" Darcy said, feigning sympathy as he slid his finger along the trail of blood dripping from the cut he inflicted and slowly placed it in his mouth. Then closing his eyes, he savored it like it was dessert. A morbid moan of ecstasy escaped his throat.

"You truly are sweet to the taste and I now see your appeal," he said in a perverse, sadistic tone.

"You are a cruel, ruthless beast," I screamed at him as feelings of sheer rage broiled inside of me.

"Is that the best you can do, my dear? I have heard worse," Darcy taunted, grabbing my face with his hand. "So tell me how you really feel," he said, leaning in closer. The stench of him made me want to puke when he brutally kissed my lips.

Struggling to break free of his contact, I began to scream and struggle. Breaking free of his kiss, I spat in disgust. "Why don't you take these ropes off and find out exactly how I feel about you?" I challenged, glaring boldly at him.

"Now why would I want to do that when I have you exactly where I want you?" Darcy answered, a lecherous half smile playing across his mouth. Brutally slapping my face, he snarled at me. "You are a lying, manipulative bitch, and you will die by my hands just like the others." He leaped from the bed to glare down at me.

I wasn't sure I heard him correctly because of the ringing in my ears. Turning to look at him, I spat the blood out of my mouth. "Did you just say *others*? As in you murdered others?" I asked with a deliberate tone of disbelief.

"Yes, I did. And tomorrow night you will join them." His laugh sounding especially loud as it echoed off the walls.

My skin crawled as I looked into his evil eyes. "What others?" I asked, trying to hide the revulsion I felt toward him.

"The night of the king's party when you and I had our little disagreement, I followed you around that night. I saw your little tryst with Lord Deveraux in the boat. How you begged him to take you just like the little whore that you are," he spat the words out as if they left a bad taste in his mouth.

The very thought of him watching us made me shiver with repugnance. "*You* killed that girl?" The shock on my face made him smile again.

"I didn't just kill her, I made love to her first. Then I cut her here, here, and here." He pointed to spots on my body with the dagger. "Then I held her under the water till she stopped moving. It was glorious." Darcy crowed like a rooster. "I retrieved your corset from the water and placed your wig upon her head. I thought myself very creative," he said, preening like a peacock. His deranged laughter caused me to shrink back in fear. "Then I posed her so she would experience the ultimate humiliation of being found in that way."

"You are a monster!" My words were barely audible as I fought the panic rising in my chest.

"Let's not forget the woman I sacrificed. I cut her heart out while she still lived. It was so invigorating, holding her heart in my hands as her warm blood pumped through my fingers," he said, his eyes turned perversely psychotic. "The sheer terror I saw in her eyes at that very moment I drove the knife into her chest was rejuvenating." Darcy's voice sounded giddy as he described in detail his horrific act of murder, a demonic cackle coming from his mouth.

His gruesome recounting caused memories to flood back to me of the dream I had. I leaned over the side of the bed purging myself of my stomach's contents.

"Does the preview of what is to come upset you, darling Angelina?" His sarcasm and total disdain for the sanctity of life angered me anew.

I began pulling on the bed frame again, this time with fierce determination. I could feel the rope bite into my flesh. I was going to kill him or die trying. Turning so that I could kick the bar with my feet, I screamed like an animal. I kicked at him when he took a step toward me.

Something in my eyes frightened him because he jumped back even though he held my dagger in his hands. I felt the bar give. Just one more kick and the bar came off in my hands.

Jumping from the bed, I swung wildly at him with the bar still attached to the rope.

"I'm going to kill you, you psychotic, murderous demon!" I screamed, swinging again, this time hitting him hard across his arm and chest. Darcey dropped the dagger he held, cried out in pain and grabbed his right arm.

Stepping back from him, I put the bar between my legs, pulling it free of the rope. This made it easy to slip my hands free from the rope when it went slack. I grabbed for the bar again as he lunged at me.

"You are going to pay with your life for that," Darcy yelled, trying to startle me into dropping the bar. Swinging the bar again with more precise aim this time, I struck him in the back as he tried to dodge me.

"Your words are confusing, Lord Montgomery. I thought you told me I would die," I countered, playing with him now. But this time, I was the cat and he was the mouse.

"Not at all, Angelina, I am going to cut your heart out just like I did the other woman's, and I am going to drink your blood and relish every drop before I am done."

Running at him, I screamed, "You bloody bastard, we will see who dies tonight," while whacking at him with the bar.

He stepped back, tripping over his own feet. Astonishment registering across his face just before I struck him several times, rendering him unconscious. Standing back to assess his condition, I struck him two more times just to make sure he truly was unconscious before I retrieved my dagger and sheath.

Grabbing the lantern, my dagger and the metal bar, I headed down the tunnel. I had no idea what I would find at the end, but the unknown was better than staying still.

Several rooms with doors off the long corridor stood open, but I didn't stop to look inside. Fear propelled me forward. I needed to keep moving. Coming to the end of the tunnel, there was another long expanse of corridors to the left and one to the right. I didn't know which way to go.

Taking three steps to the right, I stopped and listened. Did I hear a noise back down the hall from where I had just come? I convinced myself that it was just the dark playing tricks on me and decided to go to my left. Running now, as fast as I could, with the dim glow of the lantern to guide me, I had gone about four hundred yards when I came upon another door. Putting my ear to the wood, I listened for any sign of life on the other side, but heard nothing.

Quietly lifting the lever, I pulled the heavy door open a few inches, just enough to peek inside the room. The opulently furnished room was aglow with light from lanterns and candles throughout. Not seeing anyone about, I opened the door wider and stepped inside.

Clearly it was a man's bedroom. I cautiously left the door behind me opened in case I needed a quick escape and inched my way silently toward the other door at the far end of the room.

Listening at the door again, and hearing nothing from the other side, I slowly opened the door and again strained to listen for movement of any kind. Warily I poked my head out the door to look left and then right. Seeing that the hallway was deserted, I stepped out of the room and went to my right and down a flight of stairs. Holding my breath, I hoped my luck would last.

On the main landing of what was obviously the servant's entrance. I breathed a sigh of relief. All I needed now was the door to open and I would make for the woods.

"Excuse me, miss, but may I help you?"

Jumping clear out of my skin, I whirled around to face a tall, well-built man in his mid-forties dressed in a butler's uniform.

"I seem to be lost. If you would be so kind as to show me to the door, I will be on my way," I said, hoping that my disheveled appearance wasn't too shocking and that the staff wasn't in on Lord Montgomery's extracurricular activities.

"Of course, if you will follow me. It is right this way," he said, his genuine manner putting me at ease as he led the way down the hall and around a corner.

"Would you care for a cup of tea before you depart, Madam?" he asked, stopping to address me directly before continuing around the corner.

"No, thank you, I think I will be happy to be on—"

Two of Darcy's large henchmen grabbed me by the arms as I rounded the corner. And who should be standing there in front of me with a nasty gash on his head, blood dripping down the side of his face, but Lord Montgomery himself.

"You really should have finished the job, my dear." His face was distorted with rage and blood as he clenched and unclenched his right hand.

"I am going to take immense pleasure in tomorrow's ceremonial sacrifice," he said through clenched teeth while walking menacingly toward me.

"But, sir, this is Lady Stewart," the young man to my right blurted out in surprise.

"I know who she is, you idiot!" Darcy's words delivered with a ferocious slap across the young man's face. "And if you ever interrupt me again, I will put you on the altar next to her." The man appeared shocked by Lord Montgomery's vicious attack on him. Immediately coming to attention, he tightened his grip on my arm.

I was paralyzed with shock and fear as disbelief sunk in. One minute I was on my way out the door; the next minute, I was right back into the frying pan.

"You won't get away with this, someone will find out," I said in desperation, then shrinking back from the crazed look in his eyes.

"I have and will continue to get away with it, Angelina. But now I think it is time you got your beauty rest. Tomorrow is a very big day, and I want you looking your best for our guests." Taking a handkerchief and bottle from the butler, he was about to pour the liquid into the handkerchief with a flourish of show.

I struggled kicking at Darcy and the two men with every ounce of strength I had left, causing Darcy to drop the bottle, shattering it on the floor. The contents spilled everywhere. I heard Darcy scream, "Don't breathe the fumes," but it was too late. I felt their grips give as I held my breath, placing my sleeve over my nose and mouth.

I didn't waste a second scrambling around the corner, retrieving my metal bar as I went. I ran through the hallway as fast as I could. My legs felt like rubber, and they didn't respond like they should, but I was not giving up. I could hear Darcy behind me cursing. So I kept running. I wasn't going down without a fight.

Finding the front door, I threw it open and ran directly into a large man standing guard. Brandishing my metal rod, I swung at him and missed. I tried to dodge around him, but he blocked my way.

"Get out of my way!" I demanded with authority, but he wouldn't budge, and I could hear Darcy coming.

Charging him, I swung with all my might but to no avail. The man easily dodged it and captured me, pinning my arms to my sides as if I were nothing more than a rag doll.

Darcy came through the door like a charging bull, angry and snorting until he saw me. Then his cruel smile returned as he once again had the upper hand.

"You really do know how to try a man's patience, my dear," his words hitting me like a bucket of cold water.

"The only reason you have me again is your servants. You can't even fight your own battles like a real man," I said, my words meant to deliberately insult him.

"A man with my particular proclivities requires very loyal subjects surrounding him. And now for you, Lady Stewart, what shall I do with you?" he said, putting his palms together as he studied me.

I could see him seething just beneath the surface. Suddenly, his hand snaked out brutally, slapping me across the face, rendering me momentarily dazed.

"It is easy to take cheap shots at a defenseless woman while your man servant holds her arms, isn't it, Lord Montgomery," I said as I tried to antagonize him into doing something stupid. I spat the blood from my mouth on the ground at his feet.

Balling his fist up again to hit me, he stepped in closer. In his rage, he swung his fist as I went limp in my captor's arms, causing him to jerk forward as I ducked. Darcy's fist hit the man squarely in the jaw, catching him by surprise. His grip loosening just at the precise moment I needed it to.

Swinging around with the bar still in my hand, I clubbed the man across the chest, then in his head. He dropped to the ground like so much dead weight. Whirling around with the bar, I swung wildly for Darcy, but he stepped back, avoiding being hit.

"Well, aren't you the clever girl?" His tone solicitous as his eyes slowly met mine.

"Touch me again, and I will show you just how clever I can be," I said threateningly, while I backed away from him.

Following me as I backed down the steps away from him, I still held the bar in my hand ready to use it in case he charged me again. He was biding his time waiting for an opportunity to pounce if I had a miss step.

"I just want to know something, Lord Montgomery. How did you plan to get away with it?" I asked while still backing away from him.

"Get away with what, Lady Stewart?" he replied amicably, like two friends out for a walk in the dark.

"All those murders, including mine? There had to be a lot of witnesses. Weren't you worried that someone would turn you in?" I stopped to see what he would do.

"They wouldn't break the code," he answered, stopping also.

"And what code would that be, if I might be so bold as to inquire?" I asked as my head started feeling a bit clearer now that I could breathe fresh air.

"It is a secret society. If I tell you about it, it will no long be secret." His sadistic half-smile visible in the dark. "*Faise ce que tu boudres*, do what thou wilt."

"Yes, I studied Latin too. So how does one identify this secret society of nefarious delinquents, and what exactly does one do at these meetings of your very secret society?" I asked as my curiosity piqued, and I began to back up again.

"We have no real distinguishing marks that you would notice except for this tiny mark on the inside of our left wrist," he said, holding out his wrist to me for examination. He had six small dots in a circular pattern, one inch above his hand. "As for what exactly goes on at these meetings, I am afraid, Lady Stewart, it would make even a woman such as yourself blush. It is a pervasive befouling of all that is holy," his eyes lighting up as he spoke, reminiscing to himself.

"That is close enough, Darcy Montgomery!" I yelled suddenly, frightened by the ruthless glint in his eyes and confident smile on his face.

"Oh contraire, Angelina, I plan to get a lot closer before the night is through." Lunging at me, he grabbed at the rod when I swung at him, taking it from my hands, then knocking me to the ground. Pouncing the moment my head hit the ground, he pinned my arms by my head while straddling my hips.

For a brief moment, I thought I felt the ground rumbling beneath me, but I couldn't be sure because of the ringing in my ears. What I did know for sure was that he had me trapped and meant to kill me.

"I think it's time for lesson number two," he said, his voice and demeanor dramatically changing from civil to deranged.

"And what exactly did you have in mind?" I stalled, trying to clear my head again. "It seems you are missing a couple of henchmen to do your dirty work, Lord Montgomery," I taunted, deliberately baiting him.

"Then I guess I will have to get my hands dirty, but first, you must be sanctified and cleansed," he said, grinning at me like a madman.

I fought with all my might, but the weight of him sitting on my hips prevented me from getting to my dagger. Tucking my right hand under his knee, he shifted his weight slightly. He tried to do the same with my left hand, but I fought back.

Finally, he grabbed me about the throat with his left hand and tightened his grip until I could barely breathe. "Stop struggling! You are only making this harder on yourself."

"You mean the part where you choke the life from my body?" I whispered between clenched teeth.

"I can be merciful and it will be quick, or I can take my time and choke you over and over again, my dear. Which would you prefer?" He asked, tilting his head to one side as he shifted his weight.

"I would prefer the part where you let me go and we call it even." Struggling to free my trapped hands, I could feel myself slipping away.

I looked up just before I passed out to see a startled look on Darcy's face. I felt his weight removed from my chest, and I could breathe again. I thought I must be dreaming. I heard Darcy screaming and perceived someone lifting me into their arms and then Jude's voice was calling to me. "No no no! Angelina, don't you die on me. Speak to me!" His frantic cries penetrating my darkness.

"Is she breathing?" Honore called to him.

Jude placed his head to my chest. "I hear a heartbeat."

Tears welled in my eyes before I even opened them. "You found me." My voice sounded strange to my ears. Opening my eyes to gaze into his magnificent face, the tears began to flow. I couldn't believe that I was alive.

Honore stood peering over Jude's shoulder. "We thought we had lost you."

"That makes two of us." I managed to choke out the words.

Lifting me in his arms, Jude passed me off to Honore. Then purposely marching over to where Darcy was standing held by Carlyle and Emerson who were flanked by Jones and Smithy, Jude balled up his fist and clobbered Darcy in the jaw. While Darcy's head was bobbing back, Jude landed two more brutal punches to his gut, causing Darcy to fold in half. Jude grabbed Darcy by the throat forcing him to look directly at him. "I could kill you as easily as snuffing out the flame of a candle, Montgomery. But death offers more peace than you truly deserve," he said with deadly intent." So I have decided to let you live. And each morning, when you open your miserable eyes and curse the day that you draw another breath, I want you to know your wretched existence continues because I will it," Jude continued as he squeezed Darcy's throat tighter, till he gasped for air."

Jude continued through gritted teeth, "And as you live out the rest of your pathetic wretched little life, rotting in a cold dank cell, know that you will never be anything but a pathetic excuse for human life." Spitting on the ground next to him, Jude released Darcy as if the very touch of his skin were caustic. "Take him away," Jude ordered.

I followed Jude with my eyes when he went to retrieve his horse, and for the first time, I saw Maggie sitting astride his steed.

"Maggie, you made it out. I was so worried about you," I cried through the pain in my throat. Pushing against Honore's chest, I forced him to put me down.

Throwing my arms around her neck when Jude had helped her from his horse, she buried her face in my hair and sobbed.

"I thought I would be too late to help you. I did what you told me to and ran." Her tearstained face stared into mine while her hands touched my cheeks to make sure I was real.

"You were very brave, Maggie, you saved me. I truly thought my time had run out," I whispered in her ear as I hugged her tightly. "You saved my life, Maggie, and for that I will be eternally grateful."

"I hate to break this up, but we need to get you home. I sent Duncan ahead to alert your parents that we knew where you were being held." Jude's words took a moment to sink in.

"How many days has it been?" I asked, looking up suddenly. "Mother must be sick with worry."

"Four days, and yes, both she and your father have been going crazy," he said, staring down at me. "Honore, can Maggie ride with you?"

"Of course, my friend."

Jude climbed onto his horse, then reached down to help me up with the aid of Honore. He seated me in front of him. As soon as Honore and Maggie were ready, we headed for home.

There certainly had been moments in the last four days when I thought I would never see my loved ones again. Relief washed over me as Jude cradled me in his arms.

"Are you cold, my angel?" he asked with concern, pulling me tighter against him.

"Not anymore," I sighed, staring up at the stars. "Promise me you won't leave my side again," I whispered to him as we rode for home in near silence except for the sound of the horse's hooves clip-clopping on the cobblestoned streets. Everyone seemed to be lost in their own thoughts.

"Never, my love," Jude assured, his eyes searched my face. I snuggled into him to stay warm. The feel of his solidness against me brought comfort to my weary mind. I breathed in his scent and touched his face then closed my eyes as emotions threatened to overwhelm me. I buried my face in his chest and wept softly. His strong arms tightened around me, and we rode that way most of the way home until I had no tears left.

As we rode into the courtyard of my home, every street light was lit and the house was awash in light. I could hear someone calling out, alerting the household that we had arrived.

Moments later the doors flew open as Mother, Father, and Jonathan came rushing out.

Jude climbed down then reached up to help me down. My feet had no more than touched the ground when Mother whirled me around to look at her. Tears of joy rolled down her face as she took me in her arms and buried her face in my neck. "I thought I would never see my angel again."

"Well, get her upstairs, man, she has to be freezing dressed like that," Father said as he looked directly at Jude.

"Where is the monster?" Jonathan asked with murder in his eyes.

"I had the men take him to the local constables to be locked up," Jude answered him.

"Mother, Father, this is Maggie. I would not be alive if it were not for her bravery. Will you take good care of my friend for me?" My words nearly lost in the commotion as Jude lifted me into his arms. He carried me into the house and up the stairs to my room with Anna leading the way.

"I have a bath ready and the fire is burning, so your room is warm," Anna babbled all the way up the stairs like a crazy person, tears welling up in her eyes.

"Anna, I am fine now. I really could walk, but Hercules here is afraid I might stub my toe," I said, tipping my head sideways to smile at Jude.

Entering my bedroom, Jude turned to address Anna. "Anna, could you give us a few minutes of privacy, please? And shut the door on your way out." Turning back around, he headed for my bed as I looked at Anna over his shoulder helplessly. "Thank you, Anna, I've got it from here," Jude said, dismissing her.

Anna walked to the door then hesitated a minute before closing it quietly behind her.

"What was that all about?" I asked.

"Well, let's see. You have been held by a madman for four days. I thought I would never see you alive again, and I have been sick with worry. Oh, and there is this little matter of you carrying my child," he finished by setting me down on the ground in front of the bath. "Turn around, I will undo your gown so you can get in the bath," he said with his left hand on his hip rotating his other hand in a circular motion over my head.

"Are you sure you wouldn't rather have this conversation after I got cleaned up? What if someone walks in?" I said, trying to stall him.

"Angelina, what is going on? Turn around and I will help you," he said with a hint of suspicion in his tone. Not waiting for me to turn on my own, he turned me and started to undo my gown.

I heard the intake of air as Jude saw the blood on my slip. Slipping my gown from my shoulders, I didn't even fight him as it hit the ground. His hand frantically searched for the tie in the front of my slip. Finding it, he pulled it and stripped the thin material from my back. I heard a second intake of air and an animalistic growl when he saw the marked flesh.

Dropping the slip to the ground, I stepped into the tub and sank beneath the water. Enjoying the feeling of being warm for the first time in days, I savored every second of it until I couldn't hold my breath any longer. Coming out of the water, I leaned my head on the edge of the tub.

Jude retrieved the special soap I had for my hair that smelled of lavender and lemongrass. He massaged it into my head until he had created a wonderful lather. Next, he soaped a cloth and began to scrub my neck and chest. Working his way down my arms, I heard another sharp intake of air when he reached my wrists.

Pulling my hand away, I held them under the water to soak the pain from the joints.

Jude fetched the pails of water being warmed by the fire to rinse the soap from my hair and body. I stood up, then he wrapped a clean sheet around me, and lifted me out of the bath. He carried me to a stool by the fire to keep me warm as he gently patted me dry.

"I'm going to have your mother send for the doctor to examine you," Jude finally said, his voice sounding concerned.

"Examine me for what exactly?"

"I just want to make sure that you and the baby are fine," he replied gently, touching my stomach.

"If you are asking me if I have lost the baby, I didn't. I just need rest and food. That reminds me, I am starving. Could you ask Anna to bring me some food?" Turning to him, I touched his face. He looked torn and guilt ridden. "Jude, it wasn't your fault." I placed my hands on either side of his face, directing him to face me. "Darcy Montgomery is a very disturbed man. He killed those women."

"What women?" he asked, confusion written on his face.

"The woman on the boat at the king's party. Darcy was watching me the entire night. He was angry because I had insulted him earlier that day and he wanted to teach me a lesson. Oh, and the other woman found with her heart cut out. Darcy was behind that murder too. He also told me he had arranged my kidnapping."

"But why those women and what does their murder have to do with you?" he asked, looking directly at me.

"He felt that I had disrespected him and he wanted to teach me a lesson. He said that he was going to show me how to treat a man. The man was truly deranged. Did you know that there is a secret society out there doing pagan rituals and human sacrifices?" I shuddered, then stepped into his embrace in search of comfort and distraction from those memories. "I can't do this now, too many bad memories. Just promise me he won't go free, Jude." Looking up at him, I pleaded with him. "Promise me," I whispered, then buried my face in his chest.

Anna knocked on the door, then poked her head into the room. "Is there anything I can get you?"

"Yes, Anna, we need some salve, bandages, and food for your lady. She claims that she is starving," Jude sweetly asked, looking at me.

"I will be right back," Anna said, closing the door behind her.

Leaning down, he kissed my forehead, then each eye, and finally capturing my mouth. His desire was clear, but he kept it in check.

"I truly feared I would never see you again, *ma amour.*" His words were laced with heavy emotion as his eyes misted over. "I don't know how I would have survived if anything had happened to you," he ended, unable to say anything more for the knot in his throat.

"I don't know if I can explain to you everything that happened to me right now. It was such a nightmare. I just don't want to go through it again." The panic I felt just talking about it caused me to shake all over.

"We don't have to talk about it now or ever if you don't want to. The only thing that matters is you are here with me now." Jude picked me up and carried me to the bed as Anna came in with the salve and bandages.

"Cook is fixing you a tray and will send it up when it is ready," Anna said as she brought the supplies over to Jude. "Can I help?"

"Yes. If you will treat her wrists, then wrap them loosely. I will work on her back," he instructed her as if I wasn't there.

Over my shoulder I looked at Jude when he pushed my wet hair over the other shoulder, then pulled the sheet down in the back, causing me to blush.

Anna started working on my wrists, keeping her head down, refusing to look at me, but I could see the unshed tears in her eyes.

"Ouch!" I cried, then shifted uncomfortably.

"Sorry," Jude said from behind me.

"*Ouch!*" Crying even louder this time, I glared at Jude over my shoulder.

"If you would hold still, I will be done in just a minute," Jude replied, then cussed in French under his breath.

Anna looked up into my face, and I just smiled while she wrapped my last wrist.

Reaching around me under the sheet, Jude grazed my breast. At first, I couldn't tell if it was an accident, but then he did it again, and I knew for sure that it was deliberate.

"Anna, would you be so kind and hand me a nightgown? The thin one, please. I don't think I could stand the thick one tonight," I sweetly begged.

Jude leaned forward to nibble my neck the minute Anna went to fetch the gown.

"You have lost your bloody mind," I scolded him at the same time I relished the feel of his lips on my skin.

"I, madam, find you irresistible under any circumstance," he murmured suggestively in my ear.

"And you, sir, are a flirtatious lecher tantalizing a hapless victim when she is most vulnerable," I teased seductively.

"Anna, how long did you say that tray of food would be?" Jude called out just as Anna stepped back in the room carrying my nightgown.

"I will check on that right now. Would you like me to inform the rest of the family that you are very tired and would like not to be disturbed until the morning, Lady Stewart?" she replied, slipping the gown over my head. Then she gave me a wink and rushed from the room.

"I think she is on to us, Lord Deveraux," I said beguilingly as I turned on my knees to face him.

Entwining his fingers through my hair, he pulled me to him this time, kissing me more passionately. My pent-up anxiety from the last four days was released as I straddled his legs. The hunger for nourishment had nothing to do with my belly.

"Is it safe?" he asked, pulling away from our embrace.

"Shut up and kiss me," I demanded, clawing at his shirt.

"Someone has to be the voice of reason here, my love." His words did not match the passion I saw smoldering in his eyes.

"If you think it best, I will acquiesce to your wishes, my lord," I said coyly while dismounting my position from his lap. "Food is not what I require just this minute," I said boldly.

"Regardless, Anna will return any minute now, and I do not wish to be caught in a compromising position." His rakish smile promised more than his words alone could.

"Then perhaps the sitting area would be a more appropriate place than the bed," I said somewhat disappointed with a slight pout as I resigned myself to the fact that he was right.

"In that case." Throwing me over his shoulder, he twirled us around like one would play with a child, making me squeal.

"Jude, have you lost your faculties? Put me down!" I demanded, trying to sound stern while I giggled.

"Your wish is my command, my love," he replied as he playfully but gently depositing me on the settee.

Anna knocked, waited a few seconds, giving me time to straighten my gown and Jude time to fix his hair. Then she entered with a tray of food.

"Thank you so very much, Anna. I thought I would expire if I had to go one minute more without nourishment," I said innocently, directing my words at Jude while I pulled faces at him behind Anna's back. Childish I know but sometimes he could be aggravatingly right.

"Do you want me to get you a robe, Lady Stewart?"

"Anna, you can drop the proper maid act. It's only Jude, and he will be the master of the house soon," I said to her. "You have called me Angelina for years now, and I don't intend on changing everything just because I am getting married," I said while looking directly at Jude.

"Please don't change things on my account. We both know I am anything but a proper gentleman." Directing his statement at me, as his words double meaning hit home.

"So then it is settled. Anna, you will continue to call me Angelina in private without fear of repercussions." I smiled genuinely at her as she looked between Jude and back at me, unsure exactly what to make of the entire situation.

"Very good then, can I get you anything else this evening?" she asked.

"It's getting late, Anna, or should I say early and you need some sleep. I will probably sleep late in the morning, so don't worry about getting me up. I will call for you if I need anything. And, Anna, thank you for everything," I said, giving her a hug and a wink.

"I believe that is my cue to leave." Walking to the door, she quietly closed it behind her.

Sitting back down on the settee next to Jude, I reached for the bowl of warmed soup cook had made for me: split pea with ham, my favorite. I savored every delicious mouthful with fresh sliced bread.

Jude stood up to tend the fire. "Do you want another log on or should I let it burn out?" he asked, looking over his shoulder at me.

"Let it burn out. I am feeling tired and full now," I replied, placing the bowl and spoon back on the tray. I stood and walked to him. "Will you hold me tonight? I don't want to be alone in the dark."

"Of course," he said, kneeling before me kissing my stomach before he stood up. "I will never leave you alone again, *ma bella ange.*" Taking me in his arms, he carried me to the bed and gently lay me down.

I watched as he walked to the chair and removed his boots and stockings, then his coat and vest before untucking his shirt. Coming back to bed still half-dressed, he saw the puzzled look on my face. "I will stay until you fall asleep. I can't have people talking badly about my future wife and the mother of my children."

"Since when have you concerned yourself with convention and what others think?" I questioned.

"Ever since I started putting my life in order. I wish to be viewed as a proper gentleman for myself and my house. Which will include you shortly," he quipped, giving me his best aristocratic gesture as he looked down his nose at me.

"Do tell," I queried, sitting up in bed a little taller like a child, waiting for their fairy tale story.

"Honore and I have officially retired from the privateer business," Jude proudly announced. "Your family business has expanded. Your father, uncles, and I have completed negotiations, and it will be official soon."

"Darling, that is incredible!" I said, thrilled at the prospect of Jude being connected to my family after we wed. I threw my arms around his neck and kissed his face. "I can't believe it. This is wonderful news. But how did all this come about?" I asked as my curiosity peeked.

"I went to your father awhile ago with an idea and proposal to join the family business, which would keep us all connected and provide income without putting my neck in a noose every time I went out to sea," he said very matter-of-factly. "Besides, if anything ever happened to me, Honore will see to the daily running of the business and that way you will always have a piece of your family's business just like your brother, Jonathan."

"Are you expecting something to happen to you?" I asked suddenly, concerned.

"No, my love, absolutely not," he reassured. "But should something happen to me in the future, you and our children will be well taken care of."

"Are you sure nothing is going to happen to you and there isn't anything you aren't telling me?" I asked, looking at him suspiciously.

Snuggling me into his arms, as he laid my head on a pillow, he laid his head next to mine. "I am positive, *ma chere*, nothing is going to happen to me. We will be married soon and then we will set sail for Bayonne where you will give me many strong healthy sons and everything will be fine."

"You promise?" I asked with a yawn as my eyes got heavier.

"I give you my word," he said reassuringly as I yawned again, snuggling in closer to him as he stroked my hair, lulling me to sleep.

The last thing I remembered was the cracking of the fire and Jude's hand cradling my head.

19

 BLOODCURDLING SCREAM RANG THROUGHOUT THE halls of the Stewart family home in the early hours of dawn for the third morning in a row.

Sheer panic ran through my veins like ice water, causing me to shake uncontrollably, unable to tell the difference between my nightmares and reality in those moments before consciousness.

The horror of being trapped by my subconscious glazed over in my eyes as Jude held me in his arms trying to awaken me. His reassuring words telling me that it was all a bad dream and that I was safe did nothing to stop the night terrors I experienced.

"Darling, please wake up. I'm here, and I won't let anything happen to you I promise. You are safe now." Jude's loving words finally penetrated my brain and my vision began to clear. I lay in his arms crying like a child. I was inconsolable.

"I will fetch some tea and toast," Anna said before leaving the room.

Father burst through the door like a wild bull. "I don't care what the staff says or whose tongue starts to wag, you have my permission to stay with her through the night, Jude. You seem to be the only one who calms her when she gets like this," Father announced to the entire room.

"Jon! Her reputation will be ruined," Mother protested.

"We never thought that she would agree to marry anyone, but here we are, and just days before the wedding. If we had given a damn about her reputation, we would have raised her differently. My main concern is her well-being," Father countered, and Mother looking directly into her eyes.

"Are you sure about this, darling?" Mother asked, slightly scandalized by Father's declaration.

"We have tried having Anna and Sarah stayed with her to no avail. The only person she recognizes when she is like this is Jude," he said gruffly.

"Father is right, Mother," Jonathan chimed in. "About the only thing we haven't tried yet is drugging her before she goes to bed like the doctor suggested."

"No!" I screamed. "Darcy drugged me and I will not be drugged again." Anger was apparent in my tone as my hand automatically went to my stomach. Jude recognized the protective gesture while everyone else was busy discussing what to do with me as if I weren't in the room.

"Angelina is right. She will experience night terrors until she no longer has them. Patience is the key here," Jude informed everyone. "I guess it is a good thing that I am a very patient man." This time his words were said directly to me as he gazed into my eyes and stroked my cheek.

I smiled up at him as he dried my tears. "I think I could use some fresh air this morning."

"Maybe we should wait until the sun is actually up, darling." Jude gestured toward the darkened window, causing everyone in the room to chuckle.

"Sarah and I will join you both, if you don't mind," Jonathan added. "We could make a day of it."

"That would be delightful," I replied.

Maggie brought me a robe and Anna brought in the tray of tea and toast. "Don't forget your final gown fitting is today at eleven," Anna reminded.

"Just have her drop it off. If there is a problem with the fit, you or Maggie can alter it. Besides nobody needs to see my wounds and spread any more lovely gossip about my kidnapping than necessary," I replied.

"I understand," Anna answered.

Maggie had been taken in as a member of the family. Father had offered her money for helping me to escape, but Maggie insisted that she just wanted a job that she could be proud of. Father gave her a job with very generous pay.

Maggie and Anna roomed together and the two of them became inseparable in no time, filling a spot in the other's life that had been missing for years. Anna took it on herself to properly train Maggie in the ways of a lady's handmaiden with the understanding that when I got married they would both accompany me to France.

Maggie was excited to leave the streets of London and bad memories of the last few years behind her. Anna, who had been orphaned when she was a toddler, relished the idea of an adventure in a foreign land.

Packing for the journey to France had begun, so I made myself as scarce as possible. Arrangements were being made for my horse, Dante's transport, and Jude had made me promise not to ride "the Beast" as he had affectionately nicknamed him until after the baby was born. But that did not prevent me from visiting Dante each day to brush his beautiful coat and bring him treats. I talked one of the brave stable hands into taking him out for exercise every day or he would have truly turned into a beast.

Jude and I were in the stables caring for Dante when Jonathan returned with the carriage and Sarah for our outing. I had not been out and about in public since my kidnapping and was delighted with the idea of a turn around the park in the warm sunlight. Afterward, we planned to stop in at the Gray Dove for tea and crumpets.

"Come along, most lovely sister, your carriage awaits," Jonathan said in a show of flourish, bowing to me as if I were the queen of England.

"And what is this, dear brother, gallantry?" I teased.

"I am simply grateful that I still have a sister to take on carriage rides through the park," he said, becoming serious as he helped me into the carriage.

I kissed his cheek as I climbed in. "Sarah, you simply look radiant in that gown," I said, sitting directly across from her.

Sarah wore a simple, pale blue, satin gown with a pearl necklace and matching earrings. "Thank you, Angie. Your dress is beautiful as well. Is it new?" Sarah inquired.

"Yes. I had it made a few weeks ago as part of my new wardrobe for the trip to France but decided that life is too short. Why not enjoy it now?" I answered, making room for Jude to sit next to me.

Jonathan signaled the driver as soon as he was seated, and we were on our way. The conversation was lively and light as we talked and laughed the day away.

"The two of you have been spending a lot of time together lately," I casually started out. "So spill it, Jonathan. You have been antsy the entire ride, and I have been your sister far too long not to notice when something is up," I said, staring at them both, just waiting for one of them to break.

Jonathan began to stammer and looked at Sarah who sat in her seat smiling at me.

"Well, which one of you is going to tell me?" I pressured while looking between the two of them.

"Give what up, darling?" Jude asked. I could see that he was completely baffled and confused by the entire conversation.

"Jonathan has been acting overly flamboyant and Sarah has been acting very coy. So I know by deductive reasoning that mischief is afoot," I finished my statement, then waited. "Well?"

"Jonathan, you have to tell her," Sarah said, looking into Jonathan's eyes.

"I don't know that this is the proper time. Besides, I haven't even told my parents yet," he replied, looking lovingly into Sarah's eyes.

"Ah ha! There is something going on here! I knew it!" I said, turning to Jude as if the evidence was obviously right there before his eyes.

"Be patient, darling, they will tell us in their own good time," Jude said, trying to keep me calm.

"You have caught us. I could never keep anything from your keen eyes, little sister." Jonathan turned to me while holding Sarah's hand possessively. "I have asked Sarah to marry me and she has agreed."

"That is marvelous news. Congratulations to you both," Jude said, holding out his hand to Jonathan.

Jonathan looked at me, sitting there in my seat stunned. "Well, Angelina, what do you have to say? I can see your mind turning. Just spit it out."

"Of course, I am happy for the two of you. This is marvelous news. But when are you planning to get married?" I asked, afraid that I would not be involved because of my own pending motherhood and trip to France.

"There is so much to be done," Sarah rushed on excitedly. "I need a dress made, and of course we have to secure the church and the reception will be at my parent's home, —"

"What my bride-to-be is trying to say is, we haven't picked a date yet, but we are both very excited." Jonathan said, placing a hand on Sarah's flustered cheek, ceasing her rambling.

"I am so happy you found each other. I always thought the two of you would be a perfect match. I just have to wonder why it took you so long to figure it out," I said, reaching for a handkerchief as my eyes welled up with tears. "Driver, I think that we are ready to eat." I sniffed, taking the handkerchief Jude pulled from his pocket. "I, for one, have worked up an appetite."

"Very good, madam, I will have you there in just a few minutes," the driver answered as he slowed down and made a right turn at the next block.

"Your wedding is going to be a perfect day, whichever day you two decide on." I couldn't help my exuberant joy. "So, is the ring under the glove?" I prodded.

"I thought I would burst if we had to keep it from you one more minute," Sarah gushed as she pulled her glove off to reveal her delicate hand with an exquisite, square-cut emerald set in a silver band. So plain and elegant on her little fingers. It was perfection.

"Sarah, that has to be one of the most beautiful engagement rings ever. Jonathan, you picked the most perfect ring," I declared.

"Thank you, Angelina, that is high praise coming from you." Jonathan's chest puffed up with pride.

"We have arrived," Jude announced, not waiting for the driver to disembark. Stepping down from the carriage, he held out his hand, helping me down the step and Jonathan in turn did the same for Sarah.

Stepping into the Gray Dove, we were immediately shown to a table next to the window. Some would say we had the best seats in the house. Not only could we watch the goings-on in the establishment but we could enjoy the display of people outside as well. The streets of London were never boring.

Street vendors sold their wares as wealthy and poor alike meandered along the avenue at this time of day. If you kept a sharp eye out, one could even witness the occasional unsuspecting victim having their pockets picked.

Our order was placed, and we were enjoying a lively retelling of Jonathan's encounter with Lord Burgess when he asked his permission to wed his daughter. I laughed so hard that tears rolled down my face.

"How ever did you get the words out, Jonathan?" I asked.

"I squared my shoulders and poked myself in the leg with a pin I had in my trouser pocket to stop the bloody thing from shaking. I was afraid I would fall down in front of Lord Burgess and humiliate myself," he said, making a face that had us all laughing again.

"You truly are a funny boob sometimes, Jonathan." The sobering thought of being far away from the two of them brought me up short. "I am truly going to miss this."

"Miss what, Angie?" Sarah questioned.

"This," I said, gesturing my hands to them. "All of us together laughing and sharing everything about our lives together." Jude took a hold of my hand to lend comfort.

"Do not be sad, *ma Ange*," he said with his thick accent.

"Angie, we will come to see you, I promise, and you can always come home when you get homesick," Sarah said, trying to be encouraging, which only made me sadder.

"But it will never be the same. We will both get busy with our lives and children, and before you know it, years will pass without seeing one another," I said as my fatalistic outcome brought the fun party to a resounding halt.

"What are you talking about, little sister? You already have us all getting older and with children. Get a hold of yourself," Jonathan plainly said in a matter-of-fact tone while lifting his eyebrows at me, which elicited a smile and brought me back to reality.

"I can always count on you to bring me around," I said, dramatically gesturing to both Jonathan and Sarah.

Our server returned with a tray of tea, finger sandwiches, and pastries. He set about placing cups, saucers, and plates held the tray of dishes in his right hand placing the dishes before us with his left hand. As he did so, I caught a glimpse of a circular pattern on his inner wrist. I could feel myself go pale as the air was sucked from my lungs. When he reached me, I tried not to stare, but I couldn't help myself.

"Darling, are you feeling all right? You look very pale," Jude asked, taking hold of my hand.

"Yes, I am just fine. I must be hungrier than I thought," I absently answered while my eyes never left our server's face.

"Excuse me, but I didn't catch your name. Are you new here?" I said to the server, as suspicion began prickling up the back of my neck.

"Yes, madam. I started two weeks ago. I do apologize to you. I thought I had introduced myself earlier. My name is John, John Lynch, madam. Would you like me to pour the tea?" he asked.

"Yes, please. Would you be so kind?" I sweetly replied, anxious to get another look at the markings on his wrist.

Jude gave my hand a squeeze, but my eyes never lifted from John Lynch or his left wrist as he proceeded to pour the tea. When John came around to me, his wrist was directly in front of my face.

Now I could see the markings clearly and my breath caught in my throat and my hand started to shake. I squeezed Jude's fingers so tightly I thought I might break them.

I could tell he was about to ask me a question until I gave him a look.

"Would you be a dear and pass me that lovely plate of sandwiches, darling," I sweetly asked, praying my voice wouldn't shake as well and give me away.

"Thank you, John, for your excellent service, that will be all for now," Jonathan informed him as he gave me a curious look. If nothing else, my brother had always been perceptive.

"Of course, sir, as you wish." And with that John Lynch, our very attentive server, left to attend to another table.

"What was that all about, Angelina?" Jude asked as soon as John was out of earshot. "You nearly broke my fingers."

"The markings on his left wrist, did you see them?" I asked, looking around the table at each one of them.

"I'm sorry, I don't understand what you are talking about," Sarah said, completely puzzled by my question.

"I don't understand the question either, Angelina. What markings are you talking about?" Jonathan asked, baffled by my reaction to our waiter.

"You have to admit that it is a strange question, darling," Jude added, turning around to check where John Lynch was. "I can only assume that you are talking about our server."

"Well, of course, I am speaking of our server. He has the same makings on his left wrist as Darcy Montgomery that identifies him as a member of the very same secret society," I said in a loud whisper, attempting to keep my hysteria at bay.

"What makes you so certain, Angie?" Sarah whispered back.

"I got a good look at it when he was serving us. There are certain things that will be forever burned into my brain and that marking is one of them."

"And you are positive that you're not just being paranoid?" Jonathan asked, bringing the cup of tea to his mouth.

"Stop!" I grabbed his arm before he got the cup to his mouth. "What if he poisoned the tea?"

"Oh, now I know you are being paranoid," Jonathan scolded, wiping the spilled tea with his napkin as he wore a sour look on his face.

"Am I? He started two weeks ago. He belongs to the same secret society as Montgomery who swore I would rue the day. What if he is orchestrating his revenge from his jail cell?" I said suspiciously as I looked at each one of them and spoke in a hushed tone. "Why don't you taste the tea and eat the sandwiches, and I for one will wait? Maybe you die on the spot or maybe it takes a while, but if you die, I will say I told you so as you draw your last breath."

"I have lost my appetite," Sarah announced while putting her napkin over her plate.

"Better safe than sorry," Jude added, placing his napkin over his plate as well.

"I think you are all being ridiculous." Jonathan tried to sound convincing, but even he seemed unsure of the situation as he followed suit, placing his napkin on his plate.

"Oh great, what else can go wrong?" Jude said as he watched Juliette Walters maneuver between the tables, making her way directly toward ours.

"What a lovely surprise running into you," Juliette purred as she looked directly at Jude and no one else.

"Juliette, you have a remarkable gift for making London seem so small." Jude's words were spoken offhanded as he snubbed Juliette by refusing to look directly at her or her companion Lord Alexander Grayson of parliament's House of Lords.

"Mr. Grayson, a pleasure to meet you, and if you both will forgive us, we were just about to leave," Jonathan informed the intruders.

"But it looks as if your food was just delivered," Juliette protested again looking at Jude.

"It was, but we have had a change of heart and have decided to eat someplace else. Now if you would be so kind as to excuse us?" Jude stood up, turning his back to them both.

"Of course, we are sorry to have bothered you," Lord Grayson graciously answered for the two of them as he led Juliette away, still shocked at Jude's rudeness.

"I'm sorry I ruined lunch for everyone," I said as soon as the couple was out of earshot, feeling badly and somewhat unsure now as I second guessed myself. "Do you think I am being paranoid, Jude?" I turned to him for reassurance.

"After what you have been through, it is better to travel the cautious path than the foolish one," Jude said, smiling down at me as he brought my hand gently to his lips. "I bet Mrs. Daniels has made something delicious at home. I will just settle our bill and meet everyone in the carriage," he replied, helping me from the chair.

Jonathan tried to protest, but Jude simply leaned over and whispered something in his ear. "All right, but I've got the next one," he said with a chuckle as he took hold of Sarah's arm and my hand and led us both outside to wait for Jude and our carriage.

Jude joined us a few minutes later, and we drove home with less-jovial spirits than when we had set out on our journey earlier. Jonathan and Sarah whispered back and forth until realization dawned and Jonathan tried to include us in their wedding excitement.

Jude joined in, but I was lost in thought as I kept going over in my head John Lynch, his markings, and how it all tied to Darcy Montgomery.

Was it all a strange coincidence or was there something more sinister at the heart of it all? Who was the true puppet master? Was it Darcy or was he merely a puppet at the mercy of the one pulling the strings?

My mind wouldn't turn off as I half-listened to Sarah, Jonathan, and Jude go on so innocently about wedding plans, as if they didn't have a care in the world.

The only thing that mattered to them at that moment was the culmination of careful planning and preparation for that one perfect day when our lives would be forever joined in union.

I envied them their innocent and trusting nature.

20

INSTEAD OF THE USUAL NIGHTMARE greeting me in the morning, I was awakened by the sensation of sensual lips assailing my person, sending tiny ripples of delight up my spine.

I was truly enjoying this kind of dream a lot more than the usual nightmares I had become accustomed to.

I heard myself softly moaning as the fog of sleep began to lift and realization dawned that I was not having a dream at all. Every glorious sensation was real.

"This is certainly a much more pleasant way to awake than the normal haunting nightmare," I whispered as his mouth engulfed mine, his tongue both impatient and demanding.

"You are truly a sorceress making me burn for you even while you slumber," his sensuous voice rasped. "I could not wait for you to awaken, my love," he said, raining passionate kisses along the side of my neck.

I was powerless to resist even if I had wanted to.

"Just promise me that you will wake me this way every morning," I said as I shuddered with delight at his touch. "What if Anna or someone else comes to wake us?" I asked, sitting straight up in bed terrified with the mere thought of someone walking in on us.

"Then we will have an audience," he simply replied with a half smile on his lips.

"Jude, I am serious," panic entering my voice as I looked toward the door.

"Not to fear, *ma bella Ange*, I told Anna that we would ring for her when we got up, and I also took the liberty of locking the door." A rakish smile playing across his mouth as he wrapped his hand around the back of my neck pulling me closer. He kissed me passionately.

The sky outside had just begun to lighten, and I could hear a rooster crowing as the dawn was breaking the crest.

It felt as if we were the only two people alive, all new again every time he touched me. My skin tingled, and I felt electrified somehow, more alive in his arms, like the sensation one has when caught outside in an electrical storm. Every nerve in my body was raw as the hairs on my arms stood on end with anticipation, waiting for the next lightning strike. Jude was my electrical storm.

Snuggled safely after in Jude's arms, I had fallen back into a peaceful slumber. Waking several hours later, I called for Anna. I bathed, then prepared with care for a leisurely day spent with Jude. We had agreed to meet in the sunroom by ten for breakfast to plan our day.

I arrived in the sunroom by five minutes past to find Jude and Honore enjoying a cup of tea while they waited for me.

"Good morning, Honore, what a pleasure to see you again. Where have you been keeping yourself as of late?" I asked pleasantly while pouring myself a cup of tea. When I turned around to join them, I could sense by the look on both of their faces that something was wrong.

"Darling, I need you to sit down." Concern laced Jude's words as he rose to take my arm and lead me to a chair.

"What is it?" I asked suddenly, feeling leery of the next words that would come out of his mouth.

"Honore just came from the local jail building," Jude's words were halted and measured.

I felt myself pale as blood rushed from my brain. I took several deep breaths to clear my head.

"Darcy Montgomery is no longer in custody," Honore blurted out impatiently. "I tried to talk with Inspector Keats, but I had to make an appointment. I thought as long as I had to wait until eleven thirty, I might as well come and get Jude," he finished.

My hand instinctively going to my stomach, and for a moment, I thought I would be sick. Jude's piercing blue eyes filled with worry and concern as he tried to gauge the full impact the news was having on me.

"I'm coming with you both," I boldly declared my tone, leaving no room for argument.

"But, Angelina, I don't think that would be advisable," Jude said as he looked to Honore for assistance.

"It really is a rough neighborhood, Angelina," Honore finally said in his attempt to dissuade me.

"I have complete confidence in your ability to keep me safe." I stood, then placed my teacup back on the cupboard. "Jude, would you be a love and fetch my shawl and parasol?" I asked sweetly, turning around to look at them both.

Jude turned to Honore. "Let's face it, old friend, eventually women turn every man into their errand boy." Then turning back to me, he said, "Does it matter which one I select, my love?" Jude playfully inquired, his sense of humor causing me to smile back.

"I think the white one with the lace trim, if you would be so kind. Maggie will know the one I want." I smiled sweetly at him before turning to prepare a piece of toast with jam. I was starving but dared not stop long enough for a proper breakfast and risk Honore and Jude leaving me behind. My mind was racing as it filled with questions.

"Jude and I could handle this matter if you would prefer. That way you could finish up the preparations for the wedding," Honore's words struck a chord in me and not a good one.

"Tell me, Honore, do you find all women feeble, weak minded, and frail, or just me?" my words delivered as I turned on him, my humor suddenly gone. "Because I can assure you that there is nothing weak, frail, or feeble about me," I said as I walked toward him. My tone was dead calm as I looked him in the eye even though my insides felt like they were turning over.

"I did not mean to imply that I thought you were not of sound mind, Angelina. I do offer my apology if I have insulted you." The helpless look on Honore's face made me feel bad for attacking him. Lately my emotions seemed to get the better of me.

"No, Honore, I am the one who should apologize to you. I don't know what has gotten into me."

"I just wanted to save you any further upset because of Darcy Montgomery. You don't need to relive the whole ordeal." The sincerity in his voice and the compassion in his eyes almost made me reconsider going with them.

"I relive the ordeal every night when I close my eyes. There is no way of undoing the harm that has already been done to me by that man. But knowing that he was behind bars where he belonged helped. Now you say he is gone and possibly out in society again." I wrapped my arms around my middle as I involuntarily shuttered. "The mere thought of that less-than-human beast doing horrible things to another woman, or worse, what if he comes after me again?" My voice shaking as I sat down, afraid that my legs would no longer hold me upright.

"I wouldn't let anything happen to you. You have my word on that," Honore declared, kneeling beside me and taking my hand in his. My vacant stare came around to look at him.

"We won't let anything happen to you," Jude asserted.

Honore, turning loose of my hand, stood and turned to face Jude. "My apologies, dear friend, I only meant to offer assurance that nothing would happen to Lady Stewart."

"No need to apologize, my friend," Jude said as he walked toward us. "I have retrieved your shawl and the proper parasol." Extending his hand to me, Jude gently pulled me to my feet and draped the shawl around my shoulders. "We should just have enough time to make our appointment."

Jude led me out the door and into the waiting carriage as Honore followed silently behind.

Forty minutes later, we found ourselves in the handsomely designed, but small, confined office of Inspector Charles Keats. He's the head inspector of the local magistrates and responsible for all cases that involve major crimes that take place in London.

"How may I be of assistance to you today?" the inspector said, leaning back in his chair, looking across his well-worn desk at us. "I understand that you had some questions about a case I have been working on." Attempting to appear calm and patient with us, but the deep furrow in his brows gave his true demeanor away.

"First of all, allow me to introduce myself in case you have forgotten that we have all met before. I am Jude Deveraux. I believe you know my parents." Then Jude gestured toward Honore with his hand. "Honore Lacroix."

"Yes yes, lovely people, your parents," he said, stepping around the desk to shake Jude's hand then Honore's. "We met at their dinner party," Inspector Keats continued, his tone changing as realization dawned in his eyes. "And how could I forget the lovely Lady Stewart."

The inspector took hold of my hand with both of his. "How have you been, my dear, since your horrific ordeal? You truly are very brave." Inspector Keats's eyes expressed real compassion.

"I am afraid that I have been having a rough go of it, sir," I said, looking directly into his eyes made ancient by all that he had seen over the years.

"I am terribly sorry to hear that." Inspector Keats let go of my hand. He walked over to retrieve a chair and pull it closer to me. "What can I do to ease your burden, Lady Stewart?"

"You could start by telling me if it is true that Darcy Montgomery is no longer in custody." My words were direct and to the point.

"It is true that we are having difficulty locating him at the moment, but I am fairly confident that he will be located." He never blinked or skipped a beat as if it had all been rehearsed.

"And how is that answer supposed to help me sleep at night, Inspector Keats?" I asked blandly.

"Well, I suppose it doesn't, but it is the only answer I have for you at the moment."

"But how can that be? I delivered the murderer to you myself." Honore's voice jumped, betraying his disbelief.

"One moment, please," the inspector said as he stood up and walked to the door calling to his secretary. "Williams, locate Collins for me. Tell him I need him in my office, now, if you don't mind!" Then shutting the door, he walked around his desk and sat back down. "It will just be a few minutes."

We all sat quietly for a few minutes before the inspector's door opened and in walked Eli Collins, the Inspector General of Scotland Yard. We had all been dinner companions at Jude's parents' gathering.

"How nice it is to see you again. I only wish it were under more favorable circumstances," Eli said as he handed Inspector Keats a file, then took the chair next to me. "I was distressed to hear that you had been caught up in the whole matter with Montgomery."

"Thank you, Inspector Collins, but I am more concerned about where Montgomery is right now and how he managed to escape the confines of his jail cell?" I said pointedly.

"We are still investigating the circumstances of his disappearance," Collins replied.

"I hear a lot of answers that don't really satisfy the questions." Jude stepped in.

"There are things that we cannot talk about because the investigation is ongoing," Keats interjected.

"Again, you didn't really answer the question. We came down here to get answers, and we are not leaving until we are satisfied that everything is being done to capture this monster and keep my bride-to-be safe." Jude's frustration began to show as he stood abruptly and began to pace.

"And I, for one, am not satisfied," Honore added.

"It is important that you remain calm, Lord Deveraux," Collins said.

"Calm? Calm? You want me to stay calm? I want answers, and by all that is holy in the heavens above, I will get them, is that clear, Inspector Collins?" Jude finished, his tirade rather loudly, then looked each man in the eye. "Now start talking, gentlemen, and give it to us without your double speak and pat answers that have been rehearsed a thousand times before."

A silent message passed between the two inspectors as if they thought with one mind, then Inspector Keats stood up and came around his desk.

"You want it straight, Lord Deveraux? I will give you what I can without jeopardizing the case. Darcy Montgomery was a member of a secret society called the Hell Fire Club. We haven't determined how they communicated those locations as of yet, but we know they identified one another by a small tattooed symbol on the inside of their left wrist." Holding up his wrist, he indicated the spot by drawing a circle with his right index finger."

"Yes, I know the symbol you speak of. I've seen it several times now," I interrupted. "Please go on."

Collins took over where Keats left off. "They move around to different location to prevent being too predictable. We still don't know how high up in the social circle this organization goes, but we suspect it is high. We also don't know who their appointed leader is. For a while we thought it might be Darcy, but we are beginning to have our doubts. We also know that Darcy's disappearance from jail was an inside job, we just don't know who broke him out yet. We have a short list of suspects and will be wrapping that up within the next few days," Collins finished.

"We also don't know why he was let out of jail. Was it because he knows too much and someone was afraid he would talk? Or is Montgomery somehow important to the organization? And if so, how will they deal with the present situation now that Darcy's particular proclivities have been discovered?" Keats concluded.

"I also have a few questions that need to be answered," I said, interrupting the men who seemed to have forgotten that I was even in the room. "If Darcy is out there somewhere, who is hiding him? He can't for obvious reasons return home. So where is he and what are you doing to track him down?" My questions seemed to momentarily catch the two inspectors off guard.

"We do have informants that are looking for him, and we also have people who have infiltrated the organization, but they are too low-down on the food chain to have any real relevant information to this case. But I want to assure you that we have made progress." Inspector Keats's words were carefully crafted to bring comfort to me, but somehow, they didn't.

"The nightmares that I have been forced to live with every time I close my eyes since my unfortunate kidnapping and subsequent imprisonment by that monster will not be alleviated by assurances and empty promises, Inspector." My voice began to shake. "I genuinely fear for my life. We went out to eat the other day, and the man serving us had the marking on his wrist. I wouldn't let anyone drink the tea or eat the sandwiches. I am becoming paranoid and constantly looking over my shoulder. I can't go on living like this," my voice escalating the longer my rant progressed. "And know I fear I won't sleep because Darcy Montgomery is on the loose, and the only way I heard about it was through Honore who decided to check in on your progress. Tell me, dear inspectors, when were you going to get around to informing me that Montgomery was no longer in your custody?" My somewhat calm bravado did not give away the real hysteria I was feeling inside as I looked at each of them dispassionately.

"We will post officers outside of your home to guard the perimeter," Collins jumped in.

"Isn't that like asking the fox to watch the henhouse, Inspector Collins?" I said dryly. Standing, I waited a moment to be sure that my legs wouldn't betray me by giving out. "I believe that we can provide our own security detail."

"I will expect frequent updates regarding this matter, gentlemen, and I want to know the second that Darcy Montgomery shows up." Jude's tone strongly suggesting that there'd be no arguments.

"We will keep you informed, Lord Deveraux. And again, may we express our most sincere apologies, Lady Stewart, for not informing you immediately when Darcy Montgomery turned up missing. In no way did we intend to cause you distress over the matter," Inspector Keats said, coming toward me to extend a hand to me.

"You can make it right with me, gentlemen, by catching the madman and putting him someplace from which he will never escape from. But mostly, I want him to pay for the wrongs he has done," I said, taking the arm Jude offered to me for support.

"That is our hope as well, Lady Stewart," Inspector Keats said as he stood with his hand on the doorknob. He shut the door behind us when we left.

Nobody spoke until we were outside on the street. Standing in front of the waiting carriage, Jude opened the door and helped me inside, then he turned to Honore.

"Honore, gather our men and get the ship ready to depart. Then stop by and inform General Moore that we will need a detail of at least eight to ten men for a few days if he can spare them. We will meet back at the house." Jude's words were spoken direct and concise as if he had this contingency plan all along.

"Of course, and I will order supplies for the ship while I am there. I will see you in a few hours." Honore tipped his hat to me as he turned to do Jude's bidding.

"What was that all about?" I questioned as soon as Jude closed the carriage door behind him.

"I am just trying to be prepared for anything," Jude said nonchalantly, as if this situation were an everyday occurrence.

"Well?" I asked, leaving the question open-ended.

"Well what, *ma Ange*?" Jude answered purposely, being evasive.

"Are you going to tell me the plan, or am I to be pleasantly surprised when the time comes?" I said dryly.

"I am still working out the details, but I will tell you when I have everything figured out." Taking my hand in his, he lifted my chin up with his free hand. "My only concern at this moment is your safety." Then Jude leaned down and gently kissed my lips.

Satisfied with his answer, I snuggled into the safety and comfort of his arms for the ride home, happy not to be forced to make any decisions for the moment.

Upon entering the house, Jude immediately sought out Anna who had been in the kitchen sipping some tea.

"Anna, your mistress is in need of food and rest. Could you assist her up the stairs and see that everything is taken care of?" Jude's solicitous request was quickly obeyed as he handed me off to her like a needy child. Not that I minded at the moment because I felt like a needy child.

"Come along, Lady Stewart. Mary, would you be a dear and fix a tray for Lady Stewart? Have Maggie bring it up when it's ready," Anna called over her shoulder as she took my arm and led me to the backstairs.

"Where are you going?" I asked Jude as he turned to leave, halting Anna's progress up the stairs.

"I have to find your father. I have a matter to discuss with him. I promise I will be back to fill you in on everything." And off he went before I could question him further.

I turned to Anna with a gracious smile on my face. "Well, I guess that answers that. Shall we proceed?" I said to Anna as we started up the stairs. "I am really hungry and tired and I can't for the life of me tell you which is more pressing at the moment."

"Then come along, my darling, and old Anna here will get you fixed up right as rain in no time." Anna's pleasant disposition and positive outlook on life was like a soothing balm to me.

"I think I am feeling better already, sweet Anna." I patted Anna's arm. "Now that I am in your capable hands do with me what you will."

"Then I think we will put your feet up, get you something in your stomach and see how you feel after that," Anna said as we walked down the hall together arm in arm.

"Have I told you today how much I love you?" I asked with the utmost sincerity.

"No, but I bet you are going to tell me," Anna laughed.

Due to the diligent and efficient care of Anna, I managed to relax enough after eating that I drifted off to sleep. I don't know how long I had slept as I drifted deeper and deeper into a peaceful unconscious slumber. Suddenly the calm quiet serenity of my dreams was invaded by cloudy skies over head.

But this was not a dream like the ones I experienced with Darcy Montgomery. No, the feeling was more insidious. Like a poisonous snake on a beautiful sunny day invading your garden, only to bite you on the ankle.

One moment I was laughing and smiling with loved ones filled with such joy, and the next I was experiencing a loss so great that I could scarcely comprehend.

I awoke with a start, realizing I had been crying as tears rolled down my face.

I sat in the dim room trying to recall what I had been dreaming about. It was such a blur to me, as if my mind refused to accept what it had seen because the pain inflicted was just too great for me to grasp.

"I was hoping to find you awake, my love." Jude's words interrupting my thoughts. "What is wrong?" Concern furrowed his brows as he sat on the bed next to me.

"I don't know," I answered, turning to look at him. "I woke up and I guess I had been dreaming."

"What was the dream about, *ma petite*?" he asked, brushing the remnants of stray hair from my face.

"I don't really remember exactly. I only remember how it made me feel," I said, while casting my eyes downward.

Placing his finger under my chin, Jude tipped my head up so that I was forced to look him in the eyes. "And how did the dream make you feel, my love?"

"The dream left me with a feeling of dread and apprehension." Fresh tears began to well up in my eyes. "Please don't think me crazy, but I think it is a premonition of something that will come to pass."

"I could never think you crazy, but don't you think that sometimes a dream can just be a dream?" Jude asked, tipping his head to one side and cocking his eyebrow up.

"Of course, I believe that a dream can just be a dream. But sometimes my dreams are more than just a dream." I touched his face as I tried desperately to make him comprehend.

"But I don't understand." His eyes searched mine.

"I know. I barely understand it myself." I turned my head and looked out the window as the light began to fade more. "Maybe you are right and it was just a dream," I said out loud, trying to convince myself.

Maggie entered the room with a lit hurricane lamp to light the sconces and candles.

"Do you want me to come back later, my lady?" Maggie dropped to a curtsy casting her eyes to the floor.

"Maggie, how many times do I have to tell you that it isn't necessary to look down here? You are like family and I won't have you acting like someone who is less than human," I scolded her, my frustration over the dream making me irritable.

"I'm sorry, my lady." I could see her hand start to shake. It always did when she got nervous.

Climbing from the bed I walked to where she stood. "No, Maggie, it is I who should apologize." I put my arms around her and gave her a hug. "You had the chance to live a life of comfort and you gave it up to serve me and my family." I tipped her head up to look at me. "It's just that I don't see you or Anna as servants and I want you to stop acting like one. Truth is, I consider you both more like close friends who help me out a lot and I want you to feel comfortable and happy. Can you try to do that for me, Maggie?"

"Yes, my lady, I will try," Maggie replied, giving me a smile which lit her face clear to her eyes.

"Thank you, Maggie. And to answer your earlier question, no — you do not need to come back later. Could you find Anna for me when you are done? I would like to start getting ready for dinner," I asked, giving her arm a gentle squeeze.

I turned my attention back to Jude who had settled into a chair by the window. Maggie slipping silently out of the room and quietly closing the door behind her.

"Now, where were we? Oh, yes, I remember what I wanted to ask you," I said as a smile settled on my lips. Sauntering over to him, I sat on his lap. "Why did you seek me out?"

"I wanted to discuss something with you," he replied with a suggestive smile on his face. Saying nothing more while he stared at my hair running the silken threads through his fingers then bringing it to his nose, he inhaled deeply.

"Well, are you going to sit there all day smelling my hair or are you going to tell me what you came here for?" I teased.

"I could get lost in you," Jude answered, his eyes searching my face as if he were trying to see into my soul. "I love you so deeply that the thought of not being with you hurts." Jude gently placed his hand over my stomach. "I never realized how empty my life had been before I met you. It was as if I merely existed," he chuckled to himself as he remembered something. "That day you stood up to me on the deck of that ship, so unafraid and ready to take me on, was the greatest day of my life, because it was the day you came into my life." His impassioned declaration of love touched me to my very soul.

Jude's crystal blue orbs and handsome face began to swim as my vision blurred, and tears of joy and love fell from my eyes. "And I, my beloved pirate captain, believed that a love such as ours only existed in fairy tales. The truth is the only thing that kept me sane after Darcy kidnapped me was the thought of seeing you again." I wiped the tears from my face with my hand. "If anything ever happened to you, I don't know if I could go on."

Jude reached up, touching my face with the back of his hand, his fingers entwining through my hair, slowly pulling me closer until our lips met. Never before had there been a more passionate kiss shared between two souls as his mouth expressed everything mere words could not.

When he had finished, I knew that my heart could never belong to anyone else other than Captain Jude Deveraux, the Duke of Bayonne. Not in this lifetime or the next.

21

TUESDAY, JULY 25, 1763;
GOING TO THE CHAPEL

HE CURTAINS WERE UNCEREMONIOUSLY OPENED, allowing the full extent of the summer's dawning sunlight to flood the room in all its glory.

"Get up, you sleepy head. Half the day is begun and you are going to be late if we don't get started," Anna announced as Maggie brought a breakfast tray in, the dishes clinking and rattling loudly as she set it on the table.

"What are you talking about Anna, late for what?" I asked in my sleep-induced stupor, rubbing sleep from my eyes and pushing stray hair from my face.

"What were you and Lord Deveraux talking about half the night if you weren't discussing the wedding?" Anna asked. Then she stopped fussing about to look at me. "Oh!" she said, giving me a sly look. "Never mind, I don't need the details. I can well imagine on my own."

"I still am not sure what we are talking about Anna." I sat up in bed, propping a pillow behind me as Maggie brought me a cup of tea.

"The wedding is today, miss," Maggie spoke up since Anna had disappeared into the closet.

"What wedding? I wasn't aware that anyone was getting married today," I said, setting the cup of tea on the nightstand so that I could climb out of bed.

Putting on the robe at the foot of the bed, I slipped on my slippers and followed Anna into the next room, tripping on a rug in my haste.

"I am talking about *your* wedding, Angelina," Anna answered, giving me a queer look as she stopped rustling through a cabinet. Satisfied that the matter was settled, she went back to her task.

"My wedding isn't until the fifth of August, Anna. Are you feeling all right?" I asked, puzzled and still groggy from sleep. I placed the back of my hand on her forehead to check for a fever.

"Maggie, let the boys know they can bring the hot water up for the bath now," Anna instructed. Then turning her full attention to me, she smiled patiently, "you are getting married today and I am to get you ready. Those are my orders, and I never argue with the head of the household. It would be bad for my continued employment."

"But why wasn't I told about this?" I stammered, trying to get my bearings straight.

"Lord Deveraux came up here last night to talk with you about it. I guess the two of you had better things to discuss." Again, Anna gave me a sly smile and continued preparing my bath as I followed her back into the main bedroom. "I was told that you were not to be disturbed unless I was called last night. I just assumed you were discussing it." Anna stopped and I nearly ran into her. Turning around to look at me, she smiled pleasantly. "Anything you would like to tell me about what you did discuss?" she asked.

I smiled remembering all the things we did discuss and it had nothing to do with wedding plans or today. "No, nothing comes to mind at the moment," I answered innocently.

"I didn't think so," Anna said as she placed towels and soap on the table next to the tub.

I stood watching as the young men came to fill the bath and Anna disappeared back into the other room.

I stepped out onto the balcony to breathe. Filling my lungs with the cool early morning air, it quickly cleared the cobwebs from my brain and steadied my nerves.

The day had dawned bright and beautiful with just a few fluffy clouds floating across the sky. The summer breeze was like a balm to my jangled emotions as I closed my eyes taking several deep breaths. The slight breeze that came up to cool the summer heat from the streets of London was like manna from heaven. The sound of bees buzzing nearby and the song of a meadowlark drifted up from the flower garden below. I could see two young ladies from the kitchen retrieving fresh herbs from the herb box next to the vegetable garden and men worked in the orchard.

Everyone was going about their day as normal, but today was anything but normal for me. Today was my wedding day and my life would be forever changed by it.

I came back into the room in time to see the door closing and Anna standing by the tub waiting patiently for me to appear.

"Maggie, make sure that the water sitting by the fire doesn't get too hot. It would never do to scald the bride on her wedding day," Anna instructed.

Taking a piece of toast from the table I bit into it, savoring the sweetness of the honey butter as I made my way to the waiting tub.

Stepping out of my slippers, I draped my robe over the back of the chair and dropped my gown to the floor.

I stepped into the tub promptly submerged myself in the water to wet my hair holding my breath for a count of forty then I sat up and gasped for air.

"For a second there I was afraid you intended to stay under the water," Anna teased while soaping my hair.

"Now why would I want to do that? It's my wedding day," I said, giving her my most brilliant smile. "Maggie, would you bring me the juice on the tray, please?" I sweetly asked.

"Oh yes, my lady, let me get that for you." Maggie rushed to bring the glass of orange juice. "Is there anything else I can get you?"

"Thank you, Maggie, you are most kind, but I think I am good for the moment," I said, fixing her with a radiant smile as well, trying to appear calm and collected on the outside even though I was a mass of raw nerves on the inside.

The rest of the morning progressed rather quickly. I moved through the hours in a daze as it all played out like a dream. I wanted to scream "pinch me" so that I could wake up and get on with my day as normal like everyone else. But then I would have to admit that nothing had been normal since the day my ship was seized by a pirate ship captained by a man with seductive blue eyes, who had turned my world upside down.

Let's face it, would I really go back to life as I knew it, before I met Captain Jude Deveraux? A safe little life based on pretense. Shielded, protected, and locked away in a gilded cage void of love, desire, and passion.

No! I would not trade one minute, one moment or one memory of my life now. Good or bad, each and every recollection is like a truth spoken clean and clear, falling from my mind as the dew drips from a leaf, pure and honest.

22

S WE STOOD THERE THAT day before family, friends and God to recite wedding vows in that tiny chapel conspicuously void of the pomp and circumstance normally afforded people of our station, I recall gazing up into Jude's handsome face memorizing every glorious curve and line that made him unique to me, tears of sheer joy springing to my eyes.

All the right answers recited on cue at the proper moments and, even though we were surrounded by people, I could see no one else but him. As if for that moment in time, no one and nothing but he and I existed.

"I present for all that are here to witness, husband and wife. You may kiss your bride," the priest announced.

Jude's hand reached out, touching my dampened cheek, brushing the tears aside. Then pulling me into his embrace, our lips touched softly at first as our kiss deepened to the point the priest was even blushing when we finished.

"I love you with my entire heart and soul," Jude declared in my ear.

"And I could love no other than you," I professed.

Turning to our family we received their hugs and best wishes.

"Welcome to the family, Angelina. I look forward to getting better acquainted on our journey home." Jude's mother, Genevieve said as she warmly embraced me. "I have been so lonely for female company."

"Let the girl breathe, my love," Philippe said as he joined in the hug, nearly squeezing the air from my lungs. "You will call me Father now that we are official," he insisted, smiling from ear to ear.

I laughed innocently as I got caught up in the moment, squeezing them both. "I will do my best not to forget."

"May I be the second to kiss the bride?" Jonathan broke in.

"Of course, where are our manners?" Philippe and Genevieve turned loose of me.

"You know that this is not farewell and that you and Sarah better come and visit me as soon as you have finished your honeymoon. I don't think I could do without my two best friends for long," I managed to say as my throat constricted.

"I have already been informed of that fact by my lovely bride-to-be. If I didn't know better, I would think that Jude and I were expendable as long as you and Sarah got to be together," Jonathan joked, leaning down to kiss my cheek. "Please be safe in the meantime. I would hate to become an only child," he said, his tone becoming serious.

"I will be fine and waiting for the two of you to come and visit for as long as you want to stay," I assured him.

"Is this a private moment, or can anyone get in on the tearful good-byes?" Sarah squeezed herself in between us.

"I really don't know how I am going to make it through my wedding day without my best friend by my side," Sarah declared with tears in her eyes.

"And I don't know how I am going to get on that ship knowing that I am going to be in another country when you do," I said as tears of sadness welled up in my eyes. Sarah and I clung to each other as if we would never see one another again.

"What have we here? I haven't seen such a display of caterwauling since the two of you were eight years old and found out that you would have to be apart for two months while we went on holiday to Spain," Jonathan Sr. interrupted.

"Oh, Father, I don't know if I can do this." I wrapped my arms around his neck and buried my face in his chest.

"There, there, my little angel, of course you can do this." Patting me on the back just like he did when I was small, Father reached into his suit pocket pulling out his handkerchief. "Now dry your eyes and put a smile on." Reaching under my chin to tilt my head up, he smiled. "Mother and I will come out for a visit in a few months. You know she wouldn't miss the birth of her first grandchild."

"You and mother know already?" I asked as my cheeks darkened.

"We know how these things work, Angelina. After all, how do you think you came into the world?" he replied, matter of fact. "Jonathan and Sarah will be on a ship headed your way in a few weeks and I promise your uncles will stop by when they are able. You will not be alone. I love you and have always felt blessed for being your father. I could not have asked for a better daughter than you."

"Oh, Father, you are going to make me break down and cry all over again," I said through the sobs.

"I just want you to know how much I have loved being your father." His eyes glistened with unshed tears.

"I am sorry to intrude on you both at this moment, but we have to get going soon," Jude said hesitantly. "Have you said goodbye to everyone?"

"Where is Mother?" I began to look frantically for her.

"Here I am," she called, rushing to my side.

"Oh, Mother, I will miss you so much. How will I get through everything without you?" I cried, throwing my arms around her.

"You will be just fine. Anna and Maggie will be with you until I can get there in a few months. I promise I won't let you go through this alone. You will be fine until then. You have a good strong man by your side. What more do you need?" Mother was trying to be strong as her words cracked and unshed tears welled in her eyes.

"You, Mother, I need you to help me. I don't know that I can do this now that the time has come to leave." Suddenly feeling very young and not so wise, I began to doubt myself.

Mother reached over and took a hold of Jude's hand. Placing my hand in his, she wrapped her hands around both of ours.

"You will be fine. The two of you are so strong together. Never let anything or anyone come between you," she said with conviction. "I am so happy that you have found someone to love, my little Angel." Hugging me tightly, Mother kissed my wet cheek then turned to Jude. "And I am so grateful that she found you. Now give us a hug then be off with you both before I start crying."

"Lady Stewart, you are a very wise woman," Jude said softly as he leaned down to give Mother a hug.

"I will have none of that. We are family now and I insist you call me Mother or Clarisse, for heaven's sake," Mother said, trying to sound stern. But I really think she was trying not to cry.

"Then Mother it is," Jude replied, flashing Mother his charming smile.

Tapping Jude on the shoulder, Honore interrupted. "Jones just informed me that the tide has turned and is now headed out. I have the two carriages waiting outside when you are ready." Honore leaned past Jude then touched my arm. "I just wanted to say congratulations to you both. Jude is a mighty lucky man."

"Thank you, Honore," I said as he leaned down to kiss me on both cheeks. "But I am the lucky one, today I married the man I love and got another brother to boot," I joked which caused everyone to laugh, breaking the somber mood. I kissed both of his cheeks in the traditional French greeting.

"Now it is official, we are one big happy family," Father's booming voice echoed in the chapel.

"Darling, we really must be going now," Jude said, taking my arm to lead me out the door.

"Wait!" My words coming out louder than I had intended as I turned to look back. I rushed to my mother and father to give them one last hug. "I am going to miss you both so much. Please don't wait too long to come and visit us," I whispered tearfully to them.

I turned to Sarah and Jonathan standing next to them and hugged them tightly to me. "You better hurry out to see me soon, or I will never forgive you," my words a mixture of tears and sniffles as I tried to be brave.

"Jude, you might be wise to take matters into your own hands before she has everyone bawling," Jonathan suggested as Jude came up behind me.

"*Ma amour*, we really have to leave now or we will miss the tide," Jude coaxed gently.

I couldn't say anything more as tears rolled down my cheeks. I turned, taking Jude's arm as Honore flanked me on the other side and my new in-laws followed behind. I refused to look back knowing that it would only make it harder to leave.

I wasn't moving down the street or even to the other side of London. I was leaving the country and moving away from the only home I had ever known. With each step I took my resolve became solidified and my courage became stronger. I would have a new home in a different country. So what if I didn't exactly know the language or their customs. I was a smart girl, and I could learn and adapt. How hard could it be, after all? I would have Jude by my side and Honore would be a familiar face.

I blew my nose in Father's hanky then wiped my tears. I even managed to smile when Jude offered his hand to help me into the carriage.

"Everything will be fine, my love. I promise," Jude's words encouraged me and bolstered my spirits.

"I know, *mon amour*," I replied, winning an appreciative smile from my husband.

He climbed into the carriage, shut the door, then rapped on the side, signaling the driver to proceed. Honore and Judes' parents took the second carriage, as we all headed for the wharf.

We held hands and rode the majority of the way in silence. Blowing my nose again as I looked out the window at the passing scenery, I wanted to remember the foliage of London in the summer.

"Just think, in a little over a week you will be settling into your new home," Jude commented absently to break the silence. "We could sleep late and have breakfast in bed. And if you don't feel like getting up, I would be happy to keep you company all day if you wish."

"And how will you feel about me when I turn into a round melon because I never get out of bed and eat all of my meals as well?" I queried, turning to face him with a wry smile on my face.

"Then I will simply tell you every morning that you are the most delectable melon I have ever seen before I devour you," he informed me as a lopsided smile formed and his eyebrows raised. Bringing my hand to his lips, he kissed the back then turned it over and placed another kiss in my palm. Seductively, his eyes met mine as he continued to my wrist. "I can do this all day."

My heart began to beat a little faster as my breath caught in my chest and suddenly thoughts of leaving home and everything I knew didn't matter any longer because I was looking into the eyes of the only one that truly mattered to me.

"I have another surprise for you," he said, as if he remembered something important, his face lighting up like a child on Christmas morning.

"I'm sure you have many surprises for me, my love, but all I really want right now is for you to kiss me," I answered as joy replaced my heavy heart.

By the time our carriage stopped at the wharf I had forgotten any talk of surprises.

"We are here, sir," the carriage driver called out.

Jude opened the door and stepped down, offering me a hand.

The smell of sea air and activity on the docks always made me feel alive, but I never felt more alive than I did at that moment. The wind had picked up and the noise of gulls fighting over discarded fish parts from a nearby fishing boats was exhilarating. Everything from that day is branded in my mind as if it were today.

I looked over and saw something different and remember thinking how strange it was that a royal carriage should be at the docks at this time of day. Then the thought was gone from my mind.

"What do you think of her?" I heard Jude say to me as I turned toward the port where all the ships were moored.

"What do I think of what, darling?" I asked, completely baffled by his question. Then I noticed the direction of his hand.

Before me stood a magnificent hundred and thirty-foot brigantine, fully rigged. The beauty of her took my breath away.

"Well, what do you think? Do you like her?" Jude eagerly waited for my answer.

"Where did this glorious ship come from, Jude?" I asked in a quiet, almost reverent tone.

"This magnificent beast of a ship belongs to us. If I am to be an exporter of goods I had to have the proper ship to do that with. So I purchased her last month and had the men busy cleaning her up," Jude announced with just a touch of pride in his voice.

"Well, they did a bang up job because I am just in awe and must see every inch of her," I was barely able to contain my excitement as we walked closer to take a better look. "I am speechless." I couldn't believe that it belonged to us.

Jude walked me from stem to stern on the docks so I could examine each plank of the ship.

The railings were polished until they glistened in the sunlight, and the sails appeared pristine and white. Every rope had been replaced and the lifeboats hanging from the side had recently been painted.

"What did you name her?" I asked in anticipation before we had reached the back of the ship.

"Patience is a virtue, my love." He laughed, giving me his half smile. Letting go of his hand, I quickened my pace because the suspense was too much for me.

"*Tempest*?" I stood on the docks puzzled with the unspoken question forming in my head.

"I chose the *Tempest* because no matter how bad the storm gets I will always find my way back to you," Jude spoke the words lovingly as he placed one arm around my shoulder and his other hand on my stomach, where our unborn child rested. I stood staring into the depths of his crystal blue eyes and my heart fell in love with him all over again that day. "Shall we explore the rest of your magnificent ship, my Angel?"

"Oh yes, please," I answered, unable to contain my excitement. I headed up the gangplank when suddenly a feeling of being watched stopped me in my tracks. Turning to look at the carriage with the royal insignia on the side still sitting in the same spot, I noticed a curtain had been opened, allowing it's occupant full view of the docks, but more specifically our ship.

The female occupying the carriage stayed in the shadow of the coach obscuring her face from view, but I knew with every fiber of my being that it was Juliette Maureau Walters, the Marquise of Bourbon. To this day, I still don't know how or why I knew it was her, but I could feel it in my bones.

The feeling of menacing foreboding crawled up my back, causing an involuntary shiver as the hairs at the back of my neck stood on end. I could sense myself slipping away into a dark place.

"Are you cold? Angelina, are you all right?" Jude touched my arm and like an anchor, his touch pulled me back to reality. His words of concern snapped me out of my trance.

"I'm sorry. What did you say?" I asked, stalling a moment to collect my thoughts and regain my composure.

"I asked if you were cold. I saw you shiver." His warm hand on my arm felt comforting.

"I just felt a chill. But I will be fine," I lied, not sure how I would explain an intangible feeling. Removing his morning coat, Jude draped it about my shoulders, then wrapped an arm protectively around me as we continued up the gangplank.

"Did you happen to notice the black carriage sitting over there?" I asked, glancing back over my shoulder only to find the space once occupied by the black coach now stood empty. I shivered once again.

"I hope you're not coming down with something," he said, pulling me tighter against his side.

Turning to look into his face, I smiled. "I will be fine once we leave port. How soon until we weigh anchor?" I asked as if one could outrun destiny with distance.

"As soon as we board, everyone else is already safely aboard, including your beast Dante," Jude answered, with a sardonic tone for my beloved horse.

"You will come to love my beast someday," I mocked, unable to hide my delight.

"So you keep insisting," Jude teased while trying to maintain a serious look, but a smile crept across his lips instead.

"Welcome aboard, Captain, Duchess," Honore greeted us, the first to use my new title. He gave a sweeping bow with his hat in one hand and a half-eaten apple in the other as he attempted to mock us and our high borne status.

"Thank you, my good man, I am starving." Jude snatched the apple from Honore's hand and began to eat it.

"Hey! Now see here, you're not a very good Governor, taking food from your peasants," Honore teased.

"You can have it back once I am done with it, if you like." Jude took another large bite from the apple then offered it to me. I relished taking a large bite from the apple just to play my part in the joke.

"I can't believe how much better stolen fruit tastes," I teased.

"There you go, my good man, I believe the Missus and I are finished with this." Placing the eaten apple back in Honore's hand, we continued on our way across the deck greeting Jude's parents, Philippe and Genevieve Deveraux who would be making the trip back to France with us.

"Papa, Mama, I hope you found your accommodations satisfactory." Jude kissed his parents on their cheeks then hugged them.

"Your ship, she is so grand, my son." Philippe hugged Jude, thumping him heartily on the back in greeting.

"The men have been working hard to get her in shape and ready for the voyage home. I think some of them desire to return home even more than you, Father."

"I, for one, will be happy planting my feet back on French soil. I miss my home," his mother cried as she turned toward me. "Oh, my dear, you look a bit peaked. Are you feeling all right?" Genevieve said, bringing her hand to my face.

"I think it is a combination of too much excitement and not enough food. I didn't realize how hungry I was until I had a bite of Honore's apple," I explained, leaning over to kiss her on the cheeks.

"Well then, we had better rectify that immediately," Philippe said, taking me by the arm he led me to the captain's quarters where a wedding feast had been laid out on the table.

Anna and Maggie had prepared the room, laying out the food cook had prepared that morning. The table was set with roasted squab, fresh green beans in butter and garlic, baked pears, cheeses, soft rolls dripping in butter and of course, two kinds of wines. It was a feast fit for a king, and I was starving.

I heard Honore call to the men to weigh anchor and unfurl the main sail. Shortly after, I felt the motion of the ship as it began to move away from the docks, bringing me great relief.

Philippe pulled out a chair, seating me at the head of the table as Jude entered the room and, pulling out a chair, he sat at the other end of the table.

"Honore will be here momentarily to join us for lunch. He is just giving the crew orders and launching us on our way," Jude informed us as he sat down.

I nibbled on a piece of cheese for a few minutes until Honore entered the quarters, taking an empty seat in the middle of the table.

Philippe cleared his throat loudly, trying to get everyone's attention. "I would like to acknowledge this momentous occasion with a toast to the bride and groom," Philippe began, as he stood next to me with a glass of wine in his hand. "I wish to start by telling you that my son, Jude, has been a great source of pride and joy in my life since the day he was born," directing his attention to his son at the other end of the table seated next to his mother, Genevieve. "All one has to do is simply look at the man he has become to understand where my pride lays, and for that I am eternally grateful to my beautiful wife who has been by my side for twenty-nine years. But, son, I will be the first to tell you that I could not be prouder of you than I am today when you took this extraordinary young woman to wife." Then Philippe turned to me and raised his glass slightly. "She is intelligent, strong, and dare I say, most comely. May you bear many strapping sons and a daughter that is as beautiful as her mother. My wish is that the two of you live many happy years, celebrating your love for one another. Raise your glasses with me to welcome, Lady Angelina, the Duchess of Bayonne to our family," he finished, then raising his glass higher. "Cheers." This was followed by cheers all around.

I raised my glass to him as tears filled my eyes. I sipped from my glass and wiped a tear that fell with my other hand. Then I stole a look at my new husband as he beamed with pride at the other end of the table from his father's words.

The late lunch was served and I, for one, ate my fill until I was sure the stays of my corset would burst.

After lunch, Anna helped me from my wedding dress and into a simple green velvet day dress with a heather gray collar.

Joining Jude on deck, I found him at the helm of the ship.

"Why are you smiling like that, woman? Don't you know that steering a ship is serious business?" Jude scolded with a half smile on his face.

"I was just smiling because I am so terribly happy today," I replied, unable to stop myself from grinning.

"Would you like to give it a try?" he asked, holding a hand out to me.

"What if I crash the ship?"

"What exactly do you think you might crash the ship into out here in the middle of the ocean?" He laughed then pulled my hand, placing me between the helm and his solid form. "You grip it like so, making sure you keep enough tension to keep the wheel from spinning."

"Spinning?" I gasped, looking at him over my shoulder which only elicited another outburst of hearty laughter from him.

"You will be fine. I'm here, and I promise not to let go of you or the helm," Jude reassured me as he stepped closer than necessary, then leaned down to nuzzle my neck.

Honore cleared his throat loudly causing Jude to slowly straighten up to his full height. "How is it going, Captain, Mrs. Captain? I see you are giving lessons on the very complicated techniques of steering a ship, though I have never quite seen it done that way before." His mocking tone only encouraged Jude further.

"By any chance, have you ever done it this way?" Jude placed his knee between the rungs then spinning me around in his arms and bending me back he cradled me in the crook of his arm planting a passionate kiss on my mouth, taking my breath away in the process.

"No, but I could show you my way if you will just allow me a moment," Honore countered with a chuckle as he moved in to take me from Jude's arms.

"For that demonstration old man, you will have to provide your own Mrs. Captain," Jude informed him as he brought me into an upright position.

"Certainly you can understand that I had to ask."

"I would not respect you if you hadn't," Jude teased back.

"I came to relieve you. Don't you have a honeymoon to start? Honore asked as he placed his hand on the helm to steady it.

"I don't know. Let me ask the missus," Jude said, turning to me as he continued his foolishness. "Mrs. Captain of this beautiful ship, are we on our honeymoon?"

"Allow me to check." Raising my left hand up with its new gold band, I pretended to examine it. "Well, will you look at that, a brand new gold band has been placed upon my hand this very day." I looked up at Jude and Honore giving them both a puzzled and perplexed look. "I do believe that we are," I said in a bewildered tone.

"There you go then, irrefutable evidence that I am married to this enchanting creature and that we are indeed on our honeymoon. So if you will excuse us, we have a bit of business to take care of." And with that, Jude patted Honore on the back several times, then turned to me, sweeping me up into his arms. "Wish me luck," he called over his shoulder.

"Best of luck to you," Honore called out.

My face turned red with embarrassment. "Jude Deveraux, you put me down this instant," I growled under my breath while pushing against his chest.

"You might want to stop struggling or we might take a tumble down the steps."

I looked up just as we came to the steps leading to the main deck of the ship and noticed that no one was working. The entire crew had lined up down the steps and on the deck to witness my humiliation, forcing us to go through the middle of them.

"Jude, I am warning you," I said through gritted teeth while giving him a severe look.

"It is traditional. Would you break the men's hearts by denying them the privilege of wishing us well and seeing us off to bed on this, our wedding night?" Jude purred, with his most rakish yet charming half-smile, stopping at the top of the steps. "Now turn to them and give them a great big smile."

Gritting my teeth and trying to ignore the burning in my cheeks I plastered a smile on my face, then turning to the men I gave an enthusiastic wave and blew them kisses.

The entire ship broke out in loud cheering and clapping as we began walking the gauntlet of men.

Jude leaned down to whisper in my ear. "Here we go and I would suggest that you hang on tight, it can get rough."

Wrapping my arms around his neck, I buried my head in his collar.

Each man slapped Jude roughly on the back as we walked through, calling out their advice all in fun, of course.

"May the seas be rough tonight."

"Be careful that the ship doesn't buck and roll making the rest of us sea sick this night."

One man even had the nerve to call out "If she isn't smiling in the morning you might want to let a real man have a go." For which I promptly bit his neck and heard a rewarding yelp of pain from my beloved.

Finally, making it to the end, the cabin boy held the door opened for us as we entered, then he quietly shut the door behind us.

Removing my head from the crook of his neck I looked around to see the incredible transformation that had taken place since lunch.

The curtains had been drawn and the sconces and candles had all been lit, making the room glow. A white gauzy material hung from the four poster bed, creating an intimate oasis. Red rose petals were strewn about on the satin white bedspread and floor.

"Oh, Jude, it is so beautiful it takes my breath away," I gasped.

"And I thought I was the one who took your breath away," Jude protested while placing me down. "I think you drew blood, you wretched woman."

"Did Anna and Maggie do this?"

"I believe Mother had a hand in it too." Removing his morning coat, he hung it over a chair. "Would you like some wine, my love?" Jude asked from just behind me.

Turning, I found him standing before me in only his trousers holding two wine glasses, the candle light glowing off his bare sun-kissed skin as shadows played against the ripples of his taut muscular form. My heart skipped a beat. Again for the second time in the span of thirty minutes my cheeks burned hot, but this time it wasn't from embarrassment but anticipation of the night that lay before me.

"I think I will forgo the wine, my present view is all the intoxication necessary," I teased as I walked around him, openly admiring his nearly naked form.

Guzzling down both glasses of wine, he carelessly discarded the goblets and raised an eyebrow at me placing his hands on his hips. "Well, Madame, I must say I find your bold looks and brazen behavior shameless," Jude said, trying to sound scornful as he followed my lustful gaze with his crystal blue eyes that sparked with humor mixed with desire. "One might even say bordering on wanton." Catching my arm, he pulled me against his nearly unclad body. "So what do you have to say for yourself?"

"And yet my clothes still remain," I proclaimed while boldly looking into his eyes.

Jude began to slowly pull pins from my ornately styled hair. "Have I ever told you of my desire to be a handmaiden?" The corner of his mouth raised in a half smile.

"No, I don't believe you ever mentioned it to me before," I pretended to be oblivious to his game.

"Well, you see, I thought it would be a very profitable if not rewarding vocation, but it seems when you are a handmaiden you don't get to pick and choose your mistresses." He finished pulling the last pin from my hair and it tumbled down.

"So did you ever get a chance to practice your trade?"

"Well," he began seductively, "I thought maybe you would allow me to practice on you. Have I ever told you that I am very good with buttons?" Jude continued, reaching behind me as we talked and he began undoing the buttons one by one. "Undoing them that is," he stressed the word, undoing, lifting his eyebrows as he gave me a sly look.

"I believe you may have mentioned it to me once or twice," I replied as my hands traced the muscles of his chest working my way down to his stomach. "Anna will be so disappointed that she will soon be out of a job." I teased, looking up at him and smiling provocatively.

"I have no intention of putting Anna out on the street. The way I see it we could share the job. She can dress you in the morning and I can undress you in the evening," he said, finishing with the buttons. He dropped my dress to the floor so that it pooled at my feet. "Everybody wins." He ended by putting his hands in the air as if to say ta-da.

I stood there in my transparent shift with the candle light casting its soft glow over my skin and I could hear his audible intake of breath.

"By all that is holy woman, you turn my blood to liquid fire." His eyes examining every inch of my scantily clad form as he pulled his fingers through his hair trying to gain control.

I placed a finger over his lips. "You talk too much, my love."

I stood on tippy toes and softly at first touched my lips to his, then the kiss became deeper. His tongue slipping past my teeth to explore the warmth of my mouth and, as he groaned, my passion was only fueled. Everything and everyone faded away and there was only us. The world did not exist beyond the glow of candle light.

"You are so beautiful," Jude remarked, lifting his head to look into my eyes.

"I don't believe I could ever get tired of you making love to me. I think that even when I become a very old woman I will still desire your touch."

"And I believe, Madame, that I will never get tired of making love to you. Even when I am old and decrepit my desire for you will only grow," he said, leaning down, passionately kissing my mouth.

23

"GOOD MORNING, MADAME DEVERAUX," JUDE whispered into my ear then nuzzled my neck while his hand rested on my stomach.

"Good morning, Monsieur Deveraux," I said with my eyes still closed. A tired smile played on my lips as I stretched. "I think I rather enjoy the wonderful sound of my new name rolling off your tongue first thing in the wee hours of the morning." I yawned opening my eyes.

"But it is not the wee hours of the morning, my love, it is nearly noon." Jude laughed, raining little kisses on my neck and face. "I swear you have been sleeping for hours. Should I call for Anna and Maggie to bring around breakfast or lunch?" Jude asked, climbing out of bed. He padded across the room to retrieve his britches lying on the floor in the middle of the room. "I, for one, am starving." Slipping on the britches, he patted his muscular stomach.

"I am famished, maybe we should order both," I laughed, sitting up, reaching for my robe lying at the end of the bed.

"As you wish, my love." Jude opened the door to our cabin and called out to James, the cabin boy, "I need you to fetch Anna and Maggie, tell them we are in desperate need of nourishment. Oh, also I need you to bring fresh water straight away."

"Certainly, sir, I will get right on it," James replied as he headed down the hall.

Standing in the middle of the room sipping a glass of water, I couldn't help but admire the beauty of his form as he stood in the door way commanding attention and barking out orders.

Jude turned to find me staring at him. "What seems to be amiss?" he asked with a puzzled look.

"Nothing, my love, nothing at all, in fact everything is perfect." I smiled provocatively at him then turned. Walking to the window I opened the curtains. "Except maybe it is a bit stuffy in here." Opening the window to allow the sea breeze to infuse the room with salt air, I sensed him come up behind me more than felt him.

"So, what shall we occupy ourselves with today, Madame?" He wrapped one strong arm across my front pulling me back into him while lifting some of my hair up to his nose.

"What are you doing with my hair?" I asked, leaning my head against his solid chest.

"Your hair smells like fresh spring flowers. I find the scent intoxicating," he murmured through strands of hair.

"You can thank Anna for that. It's some kind of concoction she puts together when she washes my hair and the secret dies with her when she is gone, because I can't get her to give it up." Turning in his arms to face him, I stood on tiptoes so I could look into his eyes. "I love you so much, and I don't ever want to imagine what my life would be like without you in it."

"Isn't it a good thing that you won't have to?" Pulling me closer with one hand in the middle of my back and the other hand behind my neck, his lips came down on mine gently kissing and exploring.

Several loud knocks at the door interrupted us as Jude, lifting his head but still holding me close, stared into my eyes. "Enter," was all he said while maintaining eye contact.

"I beg your pardon, sir, I thought I heard you to tell me to enter," James apologized, placing the fresh water on the table. "Will there be anything else, sir?"

"No. Thank you, James, that will be all. Would you close the door when you leave?"

"Yes, sir." James turned to leave, holding the door open to allow Maggie to enter.

"I have brought you a tray filled with plenty of food. I made sure the cook knew how you liked your eggs, your grace," Maggie announced as she entered the room bobbing her head to James when she stepped around him with her large tray.

James quietly closed the door when he left.

"Thank you, Maggie, you are a dear for doing that. I am simply starving," I said to her, breaking the spell by looking away first as I peeked around Jude's bare chest.

"Can I get out a dress for you, Lady Angelina? I thought the blue one would be nice today," Anna asked, coming in on Maggie's heels.

"Yes, thank you, Anna, that would be lovely." I winked at her still resting my hand on Jude's naked chest. Anna gave me that all knowing smile and winked back.

"Did you want me to stay to dress you, my lady?"

"No!" Jude answered somewhat quickly then turned around with me in the front as his human shield. "I will be happy to get the lady buttoned up and proper just as soon as we have had some breakfast, if that is agreeable with everyone." He smiled, trying to hide his irritation at being interrupted.

"I could lay out your clothes as well, if you like, sir," Anna said over her shoulder while she rummaged through the cabinet for my blue dress, trying to be helpful.

"That won't be necessary, Anna, but I thank you. Years of military service tends to make one self-sufficient in that way," Jude answered while running his fingers down my spine sending bolts of sensations throughout my body.

Coming out of the cabinet with the prized blue dress in hand, she laid it across the high back chair with matching slip and stockings. "It wouldn't be any trouble." Anna said, looking at him. "If you are certain that I can't be of any help, Maggie and I will be back later to make the bed and pick up the dishes." Walking to the door, she placed her hand on the latch. "I will take my leave then. Enjoy your meal." Anna softly closed the door behind here.

"Well, you were less than hospitable with everyone. What was your rush to send everyone on their way?" I asked, looking at him over my shoulder.

Jude pulled me firmly against him as his manhood involuntarily made itself known. "Truly, Monsieur Deveraux, you are incorrigible. How is a woman supposed to keep her strength up if you won't even allow her to eat a bite?"

"It appears that certain parts of me have a mind of their own," he announced, giving me a sheepish grin, lifting me in his arms as he headed for the bed.

"A piece of toast or a wedge of cheese, I beg of you."

Stopping mid-step he hesitated a moment then headed for the tray sitting on the table, bending slightly allowing me to grab a piece of toast and a hunk of cheese, which I promptly placed together and took a bite. "Oh, this is delicious. Did you want a bite?"

"How can you think of food right now?" he asked, sounding almost incredulous.

"Must I remind you that I am growing a child inside of me, and he is hungry. Nay, ravenous!"

"That is an excellent point." He sat on the edge of the bed with me still in his arms. "Do you really think it's a boy?" Jude asked as he sat thoughtfully a moment.

"The only thing I do know at this very moment is that the child will be ours. So, girl or boy, I will be happy as long as we are together," I replied, taking another bite of toast and cheese. "Are you certain you're not hungry? This is really delicious."

"No, no I'm fine."

"What's the matter, darling, why do you have that look?" I asked.

"I don't think that it has truly hit me until just now I'm going to be a father."

"But you are happy about it, right?" I swallowed hard, suddenly feeling anxious.

"Yes, yes, but of course. It isn't that I would ever be unhappy with a child born of our union." He cupped my face in his hands. "You are the one true love of my life. This is going to happen and I am truly happy." Softly he kissed my lips.

"What shall we name our little one? Do you have any preferences when it comes to names?" I asked.

"Well, I did have a grandmother that I loved a great deal. She died four years ago."

"What was her name?"

"Isabella," Jude said almost reverently.

"Isabella? That's beautiful."

"My grandparents met at Court. My grandfather was a liaison to the French crown. There he met and fell madly in love with the most beautiful woman he had ever seen. Isabella Monique Gerard was attached to the princess's inner circle. After a year of courting her, my grandfather won her over and they were married."

"Isabella is a beautiful name. I wish I had met her."

"She would have loved you very much." Jude cradled me on his lap then pulled me closer.

Loud knocking at the door interrupted us a second time. "Sir, I'm sorry to bother you, but Monsieur Lacroix said to fetch you immediately," James hesitantly called through the door.

"Tell him I will be up in a moment," Jude called back.

"It seems that my presence is required on deck." Jude kissed me again before standing and heading for the clothes cabinet to retrieve a fresh shirt and pants.

Rushing across the floor, I threw off my robe and slipped into the shift Anna had laid out. Then pulling the blue dress over my head, I began buttoning it up.

"And where do you think you are going?" Jude asked when he turned around and found me dressing.

"I want to know what's going on too."

"I need you to stay here, in case there is trouble. I want you to be safe."

"I promise that I will come back if there is trouble, but you have lost your faculties if you think that I am just going to stay cooped up here, wondering and imagining what is going on up top," I said, sitting down in the nearest chair to slip my stockings on.

"Promise me, Angelina, that you will keep your word and return to our cabin at the first sign of trouble." He paused when I gave no immediate response, as I slipped into some shoes. "Angelina Deveraux, promise!" Jude said sternly, raking fingers through his hair, something he always did when he was worried or frustrated, and in this case he was both.

"Yes, yes, of course. I promise," I replied, slightly irritated at his tone. I presented my back to him so he could button my dress for me, then smoothing my hair with my fingers, I grabbed a ribbon, tying it back, then quickly followed Jude out the door.

I had to run to keep up with his long strides. As we hit the deck the bright sunlight caused me to shade my eyes. I grabbed the nearest railing as a wave of dizziness threatened to overwhelm me. *"Oh no, not now, please, God, not now,"* just kept repeating in my head as I took several deep breaths of salty sea air until the dizzy spell passed.

Determination was the only thing that kept me upright as I continued to the upper deck to take my place next to Jude.

Honore was standing at the railing past the helm looking through a hand-held telescoping lens.

"What do you see that has you spooked, old friend?" Jude asked, trying to sound calm.

"It's an English clipper coming up fast." Honore handed Jude the glass.

Holding the lens to his eye, Jude studied the other ship for a few minutes. His spine stiffened and I could feel his uneasiness.

Jude calmly began giving orders to Honore. "When they get closer I want you to bring us about and quietly give the order to load the cannons, but don't bring them out until I give the order. We don't know if they are truly an English patrol or someone concealing their true colors." Collapsing the lens down, Jude turned to Honore. "Tell the men to discreetly load weapons into their belts and tuck a few extra weapons along the port side railings just in case they are needed. We may be in for a fight."

"Aye, Captain." Honore turned and descending to the main deck called out the orders.

The men didn't run around the decks like madmen but, instead, set about calmly and deliberately completing their orders. Like a well-oiled machine every spring, sprocket, rod, and gear had a purpose.

"You need to go below deck and gather my parents and the women in our room. Barricade the door and don't come out until I come to get you," Jude ordered. He watched his men on deck carry out their tasks, barely looking at me. I could see the wheels turning in his head.

"Jude stop! I am not one of your crew and yes, I did promise if there was trouble I would retreat."

Jude quickly turned cutting me off. "Yes, you did promise, and I am telling you that I have an uneasy feeling and something about that ship doesn't sit well with me. So I am asking you to keep your promise and do as I ask." Jude's warning tone telling me that it was more of an order than a request.

"As I was saying we don't know if there is trouble coming, but I will go below deck at the first sign, and I will barricade your parents and the ladies in our cabin, I swear it." I indicated my secret weapon by patting my right hand pocket "And I will take out the first person to step through the door that isn't you."

"Madame, do you still carry that dagger in your pocket?" Jude asked, admiration and surprise showing on his face.

"Anna puts it in my dress pocket every morning without fail. She believes the dagger has saved my life more than once, so now she won't let me get dressed without it."

"I'm just surprised, that's all, but it doesn't change anything. I want you safe—" Jude's tone changed back to serious.

"And I will be," I interrupted.

"Oh, you are a stubborn one," he hissed under his breath. Turning, Jude looked behind us at the English clipper nearly on us. "I guess it is too late now."

"Bring her about port side boys, and raise the doors. Time to bring out the surprise!" Jude barked.

Everything shifted and the ship swung around to her port side and the men stood to the ready.

"Jude, my son, what is happening?" Jude's father asked as he came up the steps. "Your mother is frantic and sent me up to find out exactly what is going on."

"It's all right, Father, it appears to be an English clipper that has been following us," Jude answered, attempting to reassure his father.

"But why would they do that, son?"

"I don't know, but I think we are about to find out."

"Ahoy there, to the Captain of the *Tempest*, I am Captain Alcott of the HRH Marston commissioned by the English Royal Fleet. I would be grateful if you could disarm the weapons and give us permission to come aboard."

"State your business, Captain Alcott, because at present you are interfering with our leisurely voyage home," Jude called back to the other ship.

"Again, I am Captain Sebastian Alcott of the *HRH Marston*, commissioned by the English Royal Fleet, and I am here on official business, and I am asking you to close your cannon doors and stand down, or we will be forced to take action against your ship."

"I am Captain Jude Deveraux of the *Tempest*, and you have no jurisdiction where we are concerned. Permission denied. Be off with you and don't bother us again."

"We are prepared to take action if you resist. I mention this because I was informed that you have women aboard and I am sure that you wouldn't want to see anything happen to them should a battle break out."

"Is that a thinly veiled threat, Captain Alcott? You English have a way of hiding your intentions by talking around things," Jude taunted, causing the crew to laugh.

"Then let me be perfectly blunt, Captain Deveraux. I mean to board your ship by any means necessary, and, if that means an all-out battle between your ship and mine, then so be it. I have my orders." I could see Captain Alcott's face turn several shades of red. It was difficult to tell if it was from embarrassment or sheer anger.

Honore had made his way back and was now standing next to the three of us.

"Do you want me to give the order to attack? I, for one, could use a good brawl today," Honore said under his breath as he leaned in next to Jude's shoulder.

"No, he is right. We have women aboard, and I don't want to chance an all-out battle. Let's hear him out," Jude cautioned.

"Then we throw his English carcass in the water," Honore grumbled, clearly disappointed that he couldn't start a fight.

"Captain, where are my manners? If you throw some ropes over to my men, I would be happy to tie you off so you may come aboard." Jude's jovial tone was masking his uneasy feeling toward Captain Sebastian Alcott and his crew.

I gently touched Jude's arm and our eyes met. "Angelina, stay just behind me. Honore, you are on the other side of Angelina, and if anything happens, you are to drag her downstairs kicking and screaming if necessary." Jude's eyes never diverted from mine as he spoke to Honore.

"Aye, aye, Captain."

Captain Sebastian Alcott was not a large man. In fact, he was a little shorter than I was, but he had a steeliness about him that he wore like a badge of honor. His gray eyes seemed to look through me and his expression never changed. I guessed him to be in his mid-forties, maybe early fifties, and yet he was a fit man. His uniform appeared to have been tailored to conform to his physique like a glove.

Captain Alcott wasted no time making his way to the upper deck with two officers by his side. Ceremoniously he removed his gloves and slipped them under his left arm as if he had practice this move many times. Removing his hat, he bowed to Jude. "Lord Deveraux, Lady Deveraux, I beg your pardon for having to introduce myself in this manner but, as I stated earlier, I am here on official royal business."

"And as I said to you before, you have no real jurisdiction here. I am a French citizen and my father is the Prime Minister of France. In essence, you are on French soil and the English don't have jurisdiction in these waters to stop a French ship in the middle of the ocean. However, I would be happy to offer you tea before you continue on your way."

"The legal lines are not so cut and dry, Captain Deveraux. You see, I have a warrant for your capture, signed by the King of England himself charging you with crimes against the English crown," Captain Alcott pronounced smugly. A humorless smile lined his thin lips that were pursed together as he presented the warrant to Jude for review.

"This is preposterous," Jude said as frustration began to show on his face. Taking the warrant presented to him Jude began reading.

"Let me see that," Philippe said, taking the paper from his son.

"This makes no sense!" Honore burst out, ready to take Alcott on before Jude put his arm out in front of him stopping any further forward progress.

"I would suggest you say your farewells and accompany me to my ship, Captain," Alcott gestured with a sweep of his hand still holding his hat.

"What if I am not amenable to this suggestion of yours, Captain Alcott?" Jude asked, looking as if he were ready for a fight, his superior height towered over the other captain.

"I thought that might be the case, so I have a contingency."

"Exactly what does that mean, you have a contingency?" Jude asked suspiciously. I could tell by his stance he was ready to take Alcott out at the first sign of any move toward me. His hand gripped my arm tighter pulling me behind him.

"May I direct your attention to the mast across the way," Alcott's hand gesturing to the other ship. "You will notice a young man sitting up there with a rifle trained on you, Captain Deveraux." A smug smile formed on Alcott's thin mouth as our eyes caught sight of the young man in question. "Now, of course, the rifle isn't just any rifle, it is what we call a sniper rifle. It is accurate up to two hundred yards and when placed in the hands of an expert it is deadly. Keep in mind that he is a lot closer than two hundred yards, so the bullet will most likely go clean through you and hit your lovely wife standing behind you."

I let out an audible gasp as the full weight of my foolishness hit me like a bucket of cold water. I clung to Jude's arm as tears formed in my eyes. Why did I always have to be so stubborn?

"You may not die from your injury, but she most assuredly would. So, Captain Deveraux, I will leave the decision in your hands." Placing his hat back on his head, Alcott began pulling his gloves on slowly, with a look of satisfaction.

"This states that they are arresting you for piracy, son," Philippe interrupted. "This entire situation is simply ludicrous! Captain Alcott,

I demand you tell me who has brought these false charges against my son?" he shouted, waving the paper in Alcott's face.

"I am certain that I cannot answer that. I only follow the orders given to me. Your son would need to come back to England with us to answer any and all questions we may have." Alcott's now expressionless face made him look less than human as his cold gray eyes stared straight at me. "Well, Captain, what is your decision?"

"We will all go back together. We can turn the ship around and we will all go back together," I argued, taking a step forward. Captain Alcott looked directly at me, his cold grey eyes leaving me feeling chilled to the bone.

"Unfortunately, Madame Deveraux, that won't be possible. Your husband is required to come with us, but I will not allow you to put my men in jeopardy with a possible surprise attack in open water. If we see the sails of the *Tempest* anywhere on the horizon during our journey home, we will be forced to kill your husband immediately without prejudice."

I began to shake, and I could feel myself losing control as my right hand slipped into my pocket. Jude grabbed my arm, pulling my back up against him, trapping my hand in my pocket, then placing his other arm across me from shoulder to shoulder. "Shh, shh, now, *ma belle Ange*," he said, running his other hand along my right arm. "I know you better than you know yourself. What good will it do me to face these bogus charges and come home if I have to visit you in prison for murdering this man who is only following his orders?" Jude's attempt at calming me down did little to stop my apprehensions. He didn't believe what he was saying any more than I did.

Tears began to fall as I turned in his arms and buried my face in his solid chest. "I can't lose you, Jude. It will kill me," I exclaimed.

"You won't have to, my love. I will be back before you know it. They will realize the mistake that they have made and release me. You will see." His words sounded like a lie told to a small child when you don't want them to cry.

"Honore, send someone below deck to get my mother. I wish to say good-bye."

"Jones, send for the captain's mother," Honore bellowed out from the top deck.

"Aye, aye sir, right away," Jones called back as he ran to do Honore's bidding.

"Captain Alcott, I will be coming with you to supervise the humane treatment of my son and to assure that he receives a fair trial," Philippe declared, handing the warrant back to him. "The whole thing is rubbish. Rubbish I tell you."

"Well, I don't think that is necessary, Lord Deveraux," Alcott sputtered, looking for the right excuse. "We wouldn't have anywhere for you to bunk," he insisted.

"Nonsense I can sleep anywhere. I will sleep on the deck or in a long boat if I must, but I will be coming with you! There will be no further discussion on the matter, Captain Alcott." Philippe's face turned red with anger. "I wish to speak to the king personally about these false charges. He and I shared a meal, not two weeks ago, and he never mentioned anything about my son being a traitor or a pirate." Philippe fumed as he left the deck to retrieve some clothes.

Genevieve Deveraux came up the stairs with tears in her eyes as she ran toward her son. "I do not understand what is going on. Why am I being told that you are leaving and you have to tell me good-bye? Has everyone gone mad?"

"It's going to be fine, Mother. I just have to go back to England and clear something up."

"Clear what up, son? I do not understand." Genevieve clung to Jude and put a protective arm around me as well.

"Please, Jude, I have a bad feeling and believe I know who is behind it all." I wiped at my tears with my hand. "Juliette Walters." Just saying her name left a bad taste in my mouth.

"Why would she do such a thing?" Genevieve questioned, clearly confused. "Juliette has been a friend of the family for so long."

"Because she cornered me in the dress shop a while back and threatened me, telling me that I had better leave Jude alone or she would make me pay," I lowered my voice to a whisper now. "She said that she knew Jude's secret and that she would make it known if I married him." I felt sick to my stomach. "It's all my fault that you are in this mess."

"Don't even think that way. You had nothing to do with it," Jude said between gritted teeth.

"If I find out that she is behind this there won't be a rock big enough for her to hide under," Genevieve said, looking like she would kill someone.

"Mama, I need you to do something for me."

"Anything, my son." Genevieve dabbed at her eyes and nose with a white hanky.

"You have to take care of Angelina. She is carrying your grandchild and you can't let anything happen to either one of them. Can you do that for me, Mama?"

Genevieve's started crying again, putting her arms around me. "I will protect her with my life."

"I want to come with you, Jude. If your father can sleep in a boat, so can I." My lower lip began to quiver and I wrapped my arms around his neck.

"I am afraid that women are not allowed on military ships for obvious reasons." Alcott's irritating monotone voice sent me over the edge.

I turned on him as an animalistic growl came from deep inside of me. I leaped at him, ready to tear his dead gray eyes from their sockets. Genevieve, momentarily startled, jumped back as Jude reached out with one large steely arm clamping down on me like a vice lifting me off the ground.

"I won't have you making things worse, my love. Captain Alcott is only following orders. You don't want to add charges of interfering with an officer in the commission of his duties, do you?" Jude said calmly. I could see the resolve in his eyes.

"Jude, darling, I beg you don't do this, don't give up. There has been a misunderstanding," I cried and turned to Captain Alcott. "This is a grave miscarriage of justice. My husband is a good man, you have to believe me. He didn't do this. Please! I am begging you. Allow us to turn the ship around and accompany you back to England," I pleaded, wiping at the tears that now fell freely, wetting the front of my gown.

"Madame, I regret to inform you that your opinion in this matter is not germane, and I fail to see the relevance where I am concerned. I am simply the messenger sent to retrieve your husband."

His arrogant stance grated on me as he raised an insolent eyebrow at me. I was taken aback by his callousness and rendered nearly speechless. "Then I regret to inform you that if anything happens to my husband, I will see to it that you are the last of your kind," I began softly, growling the words between clenched teeth, anger fueling my indignation as I advanced on him. "That every Alcott spawned by you . . ."

Jude quickly grabbed my arm and spun me around pinning me against his solid form with one arm behind me. "Darling, my love." He gave a half-hearted chuckle glancing uncomfortably at Alcott then back at me. "There is no need to finish that sentiment. I am sure that the captain will take excellent care of me," his smile not reaching his eyes as he looked at Alcott again. "My wife can be somewhat dramatic."

I opened my mouth to refute this statement when Jude brought his mouth down hard on mine, his tongue frantically searching out mine. There was urgency in his kiss and my world began to spin out of control. Clinging to him for dear life, my fingers tangled in his hair, sobs mingled with desperation and despair.

Cupping my face in his hands, he forced me to look into his deep blue eyes, now decidedly clouded with unspoken feelings. "I will come back to you, you count on that. Until I return you must do something for me." Jude's hushed voice was gritty with emotion.

"Anything, darling," I whispered, barely able to breathe.

"You must be brave no matter what." Jude's eyes captured and held mine. With my heart pounding so hard, I was certain that my chest would crack open and the organ would fall to the ground, shattering into a million tiny shards.

"But Jude, there must be something more that I —"

"Promise me, Angelina!" His tone stopped my words midsentence. "Promise me that you will wait for me, that you won't give up."

"I will wait for you for an eternity if I have to," I whispered, emotion catching in my throat.

"I love you with all my heart, Angelina, and I will never stop fighting my way back to you. Never!"

"I won't." Unshed tears sparkled in my eyes.

"Honore!" Jude shouted over his shoulder then turned to face his oldest and dearest friend when he heard his footsteps come up behind him.

"Just tell me what you want me to do," Honore said with a heavy heart, his normally jovial manner gone, replaced with a solemn face.

"I cannot leave unless you promise me that you won't leave Angelina's side until I return."

"I promise to guard her with my life, Jude."

Jude reached out, embracing Honore. The love they had was more than mere friendship. They shared a brotherhood born from a lifetime of devoted loyalty. "I have trusted you with my life, but now I find that I must trust you with my future," he spoke quietly next to his ear.

"I won't let you down." Honore's voice was thick with emotion.

"As touching as this scene is, I must insist that we proceed with the business at hand, Captain Deveraux." Captain Alcott advanced on Jude with the two men standing by him patiently. Each man stood at Jude's side, taking ahold of Jude's arms while Alcott led the way. Philippe followed behind them to the stairs leading to the main deck. Jude took one last look back before disappearing down the steps. I stood breathing in and out, my mind spinning out of control.

"Wait!" I yelled frantically, running to the railing then down the steps.

The five of them stopped just before stepping onto the gang plank placed across to the other ship.

"James, run and tell Anna to get the Captain's black wool coat. The double-breasted one. Please hurry."

"Right away, Madame," James called over his shoulder as he ran to do my bidding.

"I beg your patience, Captain Alcott. It will only take a second." I could see the irritation on Alcott's face, but I didn't care.

"I will be fine, my love," Jude assured me as I walked toward him.

"You can never tell when your coat will come in handy. Better to have something and not need it than to need it and not have it, my mother always told me," I stated, trying to make my voice sound as normal as possible, refusing to let Jude's last memory of me be that of a crying, quivering mess.

"Out of the way, boys," James insisted, pushing his way past the men standing at attention in respect for their captain. He ran to me with the coat hung over his left arm. "Here it is, Madame."

Taking the coat from James, I took a deep breath before turning around and handing the coat to Jude, to keep the tears from my eyes.

"Madame, I must insist on inspecting the garment first." Alcott snatched the coat from my hands and began inspecting it thoroughly. When he was satisfied that I had not hidden a weapon anywhere on the coat, he handed it back to me. "My apologies, Madame. I hope you understand the precautions that must be taken," Alcott sheepishly said his face slightly red from embarrassment.

"No offense taken, Captain," I sweetly replied, hoping that I looked appropriately offended. "May I?" I asked holding up the coat.

"Of course, please." He begrudgingly replied, turning his back to stare out at the water.

Taking the small dagger I had palmed in my hand before handing the coat to Alcott, I carefully slipped it into the side pocket of Jude's coat.

"Gentlemen if you don't mind, I would like just one more moment with my husband to say farewell properly before you walk him across the gang plank," I said with more confidence than I was feeling.

Placing the coat across Jude's arm then cupping his face between my hands. "Please be careful with the coat. Anna didn't get a chance to sew that button back on, so be sure you don't lose it." Standing on tiptoes, I winked then kissed his lips.

Wrapping his arms around me, Jude lifted me off the ground then whispered in my ear. "You are a stubborn, determined woman and never cease to surprise and amaze me."

"I will always love you. Keep your promise and come back to me," I whispered as lovers do. "Now go before I lose my nerve and start blubbering like a woman," I said, taking a last look at his face, memorizing everything about it. Closing my eyes, I sent a prayer up to heaven, hoping that my prayers would be heard. But more than that, I desperately needed them answered.

I could hear their footsteps going across the gangplank and I swallowed the sudden feeling of despair threatening to overcome my resolve.

I swallowed hard again as bile rushed up into my throat. I gulped air to keep from dissolving into a puddle of tears when I heard the gangplank removed and the ropes untied. Honore helped Genevieve down the steps from the upper deck, her face ashen and tear streaked.

I turned as the English crew got the sails fully up and the *HRH Marston* pulled away from us. Jude and his father were standing on the deck flanked by guards shackling his legs and hands. The thought that I could not bear to continue watching kept running through my head, but I simply held on to the railing for support. My legs felt like sand when the water rushes the shore, and I knew that any second they would give way and betray me.

Honore and Genevieve came to stand next to me at the railing. I could hear her softly crying as she wiped her nose with her handkerchief. I stiffened slightly when Honore placed a concerned hand on my arm. Like a piece of delicate porcelain, I feared I would shatter, never to be put back together again.

I stood there even after the ship was a good distance off, with my fingers curled around the solid wood railing so warm to the touch, knuckles and fingers white and numb from squeezing so tightly. Genevieve headed for her berth below deck, still softly crying and sniffing loudly, her handmaiden by her side.

Honore loyally stood by my side, watched as the ship swiftly became little more than a distant memory and the southerly winds blew it back to England. I suddenly lurched forward heaving the contents of my stomach over the railing, as Honore's quick hands grabbed hold of my waist. I suspect he feared I would throw myself over the railing in a desperate act of anguish.

Handing me his handkerchief, I obediently wiped my mouth while he supported my arm, guiding me away from the railing in the direction of my cabin. Taking three steps, my legs gave way and I collapsed to the deck, hitting my knees as heartbreak and grief overwhelmed me. The dam of despair broke loose, pouring out the floodwaters of anguish and pain for the world to witness. I could not speak or think, I could only feel agonizing sorrow to the point that I prayed that my heart would just stop beating.

Honore picked me up, cradled me in his arms, trying to sooth my crying as he carried me back to the room that only hours before I had shared with my husband.

Depositing me on the bed, he was unceremoniously pushed aside by Anna and Maggie as they circled around me, certain I had been wounded and in great pain.

I cannot recall the days that followed so lost in my own wretched misery as if I had fallen down a very deep hole, unable to climb out. I did not care if it was day or night, I barely noticed people coming or going. Disinterested in my own needs, despondent and listless, nourishment came when coaxed by patient hands at the end of a spoon.

I wrapped myself in darkness, surrounded by his scent still fresh on my pillows and sheets. I dreamt of him, every joyful essence of his being flooding back in vivid details. Pain started anew each time I awoke to find the pillow empty beside me.

The last day of our voyage, I lay listlessly in bed as Genevieve read to me out loud when Honore came into the room.

"How is everyone today?" he asked, trying to sound upbeat while I continued to lay there unresponsive.

"As well as can be expected," Genevieve answered. "Are we nearly home? I think things will improve when we get settled in."

"We should dock within the next couple of hours. The winds have been in our favor." Honore paced to the window looking out to sea. "Do you think I could get a moment with Lady Deveraux?"

"Of course, but I don't think she will answer you. I have been trying for days now and this is all I get out of her." Genevieve indicated my prone position with her hands. "I will check on lunch. Let me know when you are through and I will come back and sit with her."

"Certainly, but I think she will be up and about soon."

"Now wouldn't that be a splendid trick," she said, stopping at the door with her hand on the latch. She paused for a few seconds then closed the door behind her.

I barely took an interest in their conversation, lost in my own morbid thoughts. Honore sat on the side of my bed stretching out a hand as he felt for a pulse on my wrist. Then he walked over and retrieved a mirror, placing it under my nose. "Aha, just as I thought, it appears that despite your best efforts you are still alive. So don't you think it is time to stop all this nonsense and get out of bed? I mean really, what good will you do Jude if you languish away doing irreparable harm to yourself and his child?" Honore ranted as he paced in front of the bed. "Jude bragged to me about what a spitfire you were and how nothing could stop you. I, for one, am glad he isn't here now to witness this," he continued while my eyes filled with tears. "What, you have nothing to say to that?"

Honore lowered his face until we were nearly nose to nose, forcing me to make eye contact with him. "I should have known that you were just another weak woman. Certainly not the woman Jude described to me." Taking me by the shoulders, he pulled me up and gave me a good shake. "I can't believe that he fell in love with you," he spit the words out as if they left a bad taste in his mouth.

My hand reached out so fast, slapping him viciously across the face.

"Did that make you mad?" he snarled in my face. "Good," he shouted, pushing me back onto the bed like I was a rag doll. Honore stood looking down at me, disgusted, as my eyes followed his every move with contempt. "You act as if you were the only one to lose Jude, you selfish, pampered socialite. Genevieve's only son was taken away and placed in shackles and her husband got on that ship as well. I lost my best friend, who has been like a brother to me. You're not the only one who loves Jude, so get over yourself," he yelled.

"Shut up! Shut up, shut up, shut up!" I screamed at him as I kneeled in the middle of the bed with my hands over my ears, tears glistened in my angry eyes."

Climbing onto the bed, he kneeled across from me. "You're angry. Good. At least you are feeling something." Honore gently reached up and remove my hands from my ears. Still holding my wrist, he looked into my face with compassion instead of disdain. "Feeling something is better than feeling nothing."

I collapsed into him feeling spent, angry spiteful tears fell from my eyes as he held me.

"Jude was always telling me how you smelled of flowers on a spring day. But I have to say my friend did not have a very good sense of smell, because honestly you smell terrible right now," Honore teased, trying to lighten the moment.

I hit him in the chest with my fist. "And you, Honore Lacroix, are no gentleman," I belligerently stated, my cheek still resting on his chest. "Now get out of my bed before someone walks in on us and gets the wrong idea," I argued, pushing him away while trying to sound indignant.

"As you wish, Madame." Honore climbed off the bed, bowed at the waist. "If I can be of further service to my lady, you will let me know," he added, with a good-natured smile retrieving his hat from the table.

"Honore?" I called out to him as he reached the door.

"My lady?" he answered, turning around.

"Will you let someone know that I am starving and really must have something to eat straight away," I hesitated a few seconds then added, "Thank you."

"My pleasure, Madame." A satisfied smile creased his mouth as Honore placed the hat on his head and closed the door.

24

L IFE HAD TAKEN ON A rhythm of sorts as one day blended into the next. My pregnancy had progressed without complications except for the fact that I had grown rather large.

Genevieve and I had formed an alliance out of necessity born of a common goal that had grown into a deeper friendship bonding us together as we worked to free Jude from the Royal English prison. We had spent many hours petitioning the English and French governments to intervene on Jude's behalf.

Honore, residing in the three bedroom guest house, was true to his word, refusing to leave my side for any reason. He recruited a captain to take over his duties on the *Tempest* and Honore took over the running of the business from Jude's office at the chateau. He and I also forged a strong friendship of blunt if not brutal honesty, like a magnifying mirror one holds up to examine flaws. I could count on Honore to always tell me the truth even if it was uncomfortable for me.

The chateau was a grand three-story, twenty-room manor built of white stone imported from Italy. The exterior was trimmed in a local wood painstakingly stained dark brown. The tall windows granted us magnificent ocean views from southern facing rooms and sat on one hundred and twenty acres surrounded by large old trees, rich foliage and meticulously manicured grounds. The manor itself sat back from the cliffs overlooking the Bay of Biscay, with a path cut out of the side of the cliffs leading down to the sandy seashore below.

It had been three weeks since I attempted to walk down to the beach. Because of my expanding girth, the steep climb back up the cliff had become impossible for me to manage any longer. So I sought solace each day by walking out to the cliffs that overlooked the bay to search the horizon for any sign of an approaching ship, hoping and praying that it would bring word of Jude's release.

The arrest and incarceration of Jude had not been made public because of his relationship to the Prime Minister of France, his father, Philippe Deveraux. Gossip of Jude's present accommodations in the Royal Towers had reached the ears of a few of England's aristocrats. King George III of England wished not to risk public scandal associated with such a well-known political family because of the delicate diplomatic balance between the two countries. At the same time, he could not simply ignore the serious nature of the accusations of piracy leveled against Lord Deveraux. As a result, we found ourselves at the mercy of the two principalities and their political stalemate.

Sarah and Jonathan were married in August as planned, then set off for an extended honeymoon to Spain and Italy, sending word that they would be coming to stay with me in early December. I could barely contain my excitement. Each day I attempted to distract myself with busy work but couldn't conceal my disappointment when darkness would blanket the horizon without so much as a hint of white sails in the distance.

Upon rising the morning of December 8 to the sound of gentle rainfall, I had the most marvelous feeling in the pit of my stomach that today would be the day Sarah and Jonathan would be arriving. I dressed in a forest green velvet gown that allowed for my ever-expanding middle. Anna took great care to pile my hair neatly on top with plenty of cascading curls down the back instead of the normal braid I had adopted for convenience sake.

Fresh flowers had been brought in from the greenhouse and arranged with care, while fireplaces had been lit throughout the manor to warm the rooms and chase the chill of the rainy day away.

Cook had been to the market earlier that morning and returned with a beautiful goose and an assortment of fresh vegetables for dinner. The aroma of fresh made bread and pastries floated through the entire manor, enticing me with their delectable delights until I could control myself no longer.

Entering the office with a tray wielding footman in tow, I found Honore nose deep in ledgers and paperwork. "If you would just put the tray down on the table I will pour the tea myself," I instructed, as Honore looked up from his work.

"What's this? You wouldn't be serving up distraction with that tea?" he said with a broad smile as he walked around the desk, rubbing his hands together. "Because, if you are, I will have an extra serving."

"Then I guessed right, when I thought you would be in need of some refreshment about now, and these hot cross buns just came out of the oven and are still warm."

"You are an angel." Honore sat in the chair across from me. "If I had to look at these books another minute I might have gone cross-eyed and stayed that way."

"Then perhaps you should balance the books tomorrow and take the rest of the day off. In fact, I will wager that by the end of the day we will have guests in the house to distract us both," I said, smiling mysteriously.

"Oh, and how can you know this?" Honore asked, giving me that look he likes to give me when I make my mysterious predictions that come true more times than not.

"We will just call it a feeling and leave it at that," I answered, and then took a delicate bite of my pastry.

"You are a most strange woman," he confessed, looking at me over his teacup.

"Will you join me later for a walk? I love a brisk walk after a good rain, everything smells so fresh."

"But it is raining, as you English love to say, like cats and dogs," Honore said, giving me his best aristocratic impression, which always makes me laugh.

"But it will stop," I assured him. "Maybe I will ask Genevieve, she hardly leaves the house anymore."

"Check back with me before you go out. I could use some fresh air, but I really need to catch up on the books today."

"That reminds me, when are we expecting the *Tempest* back?"

"Any day now, in fact the ship was due to off load over a week ago in London. The crew was promised they would be home before Christmas." Placing his cup on the tray, he stood and stretched his back, then reached down to help me up.

"Well then, I will leave you to your work." Taking another hot cross bun before I left, Honore gave me a look of disapproval. "What?" I said defensively. "Don't judge. I don't see you growing a child in your stomach."

"If you are not careful it will be child size when it comes out." He indicated my ever-growing roundness with his eyes.

"Next time I think God should make the men to bear the children, if for nothing more than a little perspective, of course."

"Of course," he chuckled, then walked around the desk, taking a seat.

I wandered out of the room nibbling on my still-warm hot cross bun and climbed the stairs in search of Genevieve and distraction.

Three hours later the rain ended and Genevieve, Honore and I emerged from the house as the sun peeked through the clouds. Glistening raindrops dropped from petals and leaves, leaving puddles on the ground.

The earth smelled of salty sea air that had been cleansed and refreshed from December's mild drizzle.

"Are you warm enough, Angelina?" Genevieve's tone sounding concerned.

"Yes, yes, I am plenty warm. In fact, I was getting too warm with every fire in the house ablaze," I said just a bit impatiently.

"Please slow down before you slip and fall."

"If I hang on to Honore's arm, will you stop fussing over me as if I were an invalid?" I said with a fake smile. Feeling rather peevish, I took hold of Honore's left arm.

"Why are we going out today of all days, Angelina?" Genevieve asked, keeping up with me.

"Because I enjoy the walk and I was feeling cooped up," I called over my shoulder, then looked to my right where I found Honore smirking at me.

"You did not tell her then?" he questioned with a lift of his eyebrow.

"Tell me what?" Genevieve inquired.

"That she had a feeling that today we would be receiving visitors." His skeptical tone irritated me slightly.

"She what?" Genevieve asked, not sure what Honore was talking about.

"Sarah and Jonathan said that they would be here about the first of December, and I have this strange sensation that today is the day. So I have been trying to stay busy and distracted, but I can't stand it any longer, and I want to see if there is a sailing ship on the horizon or some indication that they really could be here today," I rambled on like a crazy woman. "There! I said it. Are you happy now, you doubting Thomas?" I turned to Honore frustrated with him for betraying me to my mother-in-law.

Looking satisfactorily repentant, his big eyes opened wide and his right hand across his heart as if he had been wounded by my words. "Please forgive me. I did not realize I had been sworn to secrecy."

"Turncoat," I teased.

"Is that the reason for the fresh flowers and extra baking Cook has been doing?"

"Yes. As I said it was only a feeling, it may be nothing."

"If nothing else, my dear, the walk will do us all some good." Genevieve reached out to touch my arm. The look on her face was compassionate and understanding, and I smiled.

We walked another fifteen minutes before reaching the cliffs. My eyes frantically searched the horizon a few minutes before I caught the refraction of white sails against a gray and white sky.

"There," I said, pointing a finger in the direction I was looking. "Is that sails, Honore?"

"I don't see anything," Genevieve said, squinting her eyes, trying to make out what I was pointing to in the distance.

Honore pulled out a magnified looking glass from his coat pocket and extended it to the full length. Carefully looking in the directions I had been pointing, he studied a moment then lowered it. "I think you are correct, but maybe…" Putting the glass back up to his eye, his words trailed off.

"Maybe what? What is it, Honore?" I asked, getting a bit impatient, then looking back out toward the horizon.

"I still don't see what you are talking about," Genevieve insisted.

Honore lowered the glass then handed it to me. I put the glass up to my eye. "What did you see, Honore?" I prodded again.

"I think that I see two ships."

"Two ships?" I repeated in disbelief. Then I held my breath to steady the glass and my shaking hands. "I think I see them. Wait . . . yes! There are two ships." I handed the looking glass to Genevieve. "Look out there, just to the right of the tip of the cove."

Placing the glass to her eye, Genevieve moved around quickly.

"You have to move it slower and try to keep your hand steady, or you will never see anything," Honore instructed her.

"How long until they are here?" I asked.

"With the wind at their backs, I would say another two hours if I were a guessing man."

"We better walk back then. There is still so much to get done. Will you harness up the horses and wagons and go down to fetch them?" I asked concerned about the long walk up the hill, as my mind began to work in high gear. "Do you think it will be dark by then?"

"I will take care of everything. You needn't worry about a thing, but I must insist that you slow down," Honore urged, concern etching his voice. He firmly grasped my arm as I headed back to the house. "Genevieve, are you coming? Angelina won't slow down for anyone, so we had better hurry," he called over his shoulder sounding slightly frustrated while maintaining a good grip on my arm.

"Yes, oh yes, there is so much to do," she said, a bit distracted while trying to catch up to us.

Just shy of three hours later, Honore came rumbling up the path with the first of three wagons loaded with people and luggage. I had been watching from a second story window that overlooked the garden path to the ocean.

"They are here!" I shouted over the banister as I headed down the staircase. "They are finally here."

"Angelina, slow down before you take a spill!" Genevieve scolded as I negotiated the stairs too fast.

The door opened as I reached the last step, and the group was led in by Honore.

Throwing my arms around Jonathan's neck, tears of pure joy spilled from my eyes. "I knew you were coming today, I just knew it."

"Let me look at you," Jonathan said, stepping back from me to look at my large stomach. Giving a high-pitched whistle and raising his eyebrows at the sight of my enlarged middle. "A lot has changed in just a few short months."

Sarah hit Jonathan's arm hard, causing him to flinch. "Jonathan Stewart, don't you dare! Angie looks absolutely angelic!" Throwing her arms around my neck, Sarah hugged me so tightly as if we had been separated for years.

"I have missed you so very much," I whispered in her ear.

"I have missed being with you too." Pushing back from me, she also eyed my stomach. "You have simply blossomed since we parted last. Oh, Jonathan, doesn't she just look beautiful?" Tears glistened in Sarah's eyes.

"Yes, darling, my sister simply glows," Jonathan said, exaggerating his words and rolling his eyes. "You know, of course, that if Sarah could have gotten us here faster by blowing into the sails she would have." Turning to Genevieve, he extended his hand taking her hand in his. "Lady Deveraux, you are looking splendid. How has it been watching over my little sister these past few months?"

"Challenging, most challenging at times." She smiled broadly, then looked at me. "She is very stubborn and never slows down," Genevieve said, turning back to Jonathan. "But I have been blessed to have her sweet spirit to keep me company." A sad look came to her eyes which she quickly covered up. "I have enjoyed getting to know my daughter-in-law."

Hearing another wagon pull up outside the door, I tried to look around Jonathan. "How many trunks are the two of you traveling with?" I asked as he blocked my view.

"I may have neglected to tell you about a surprise," he said, taking a hold of my shoulders pinning me in place.

"A surprise!" I squealed.

"Yes, but you are required to close your eyes first," Jonathan replied with a serious look on his face.

"Jonathan Edward Allan Stewart, what are you up to?" I asked, looking at Sarah and then Honore.

"For once don't be stubborn and just close your eyes," Honore ordered.

"Fine! But you are both being ridiculous," I insisted then obediently closed my eyes.

Sarah stepped to my left, and Jonathan held my right arm as they moved out of the way. I heard footsteps stop just in front of me. "Well? Can I open my eyes yet?"

"Yes," my mother said, reaching out to touch my face with her hand.

My eyes flew open to see my mother and father standing in front of me. "Oh, Mother, you are here." I gasped as fresh tears sprang to my eyes again. "Father, I don't believe it." Embracing them both together, I cried in their arms as much from the joy of their surprise, but mostly because I had been terribly homesick and had missed them so much.

"I must say, as a self-proclaimed skeptic I didn't believe her, but Angelina predicted that we would have guests in this home by the end of the day and here you all are," Honore said, breaking the awkward moment as I squealed and then cried again. "Remind me never to bet against one of her funny feelings," he said, pulling a handkerchief from his pocket and handing it to me.

I sniffed then blew my nose and whipped my eyes. "I am just speechless, truly speechless. I would never have guessed that you were coming as well."

"Well, there is always a first time for everything," Jonathan teased.

"I have just been told that dinner will be in an hour," Genevieve announced to everyone.

"Let me show you to your rooms. We won't dress for dinner tonight because there is only enough time to freshen up. I can't tell you how much it means to me that you are all here." Taking my parents by the arm as Sarah and Jonathan followed, I led the way up the stairs and to their rooms.

Dinner had been delicious, made better by the company and lively conversation. Sarah and Jonathan told us all about their wonderful adventures in Spain and Italy, regaling us with stories that made us laugh at their calamity with too much spicy food.

Father, Jonathan and Honore discussed shipping business while the rest of us talked about plans for the Christmas celebrations and impending birth.

After dinner, the men retired to the study to drink port and smoke cigars and further discuss business while the women wondered into the drawing room. Mother and Genevieve sipped on sherry while Sarah and I enjoyed a nice cup of herbal tea. Sarah announced that they were expecting sometime in May.

"Oh, Sarah, that is just marvelous, I am so happy for you and Jonathan." I gushed. "I am glad that we will all be together for Christmas. This truly has been such a wonderful surprise."

"I already told Jonathan that I would be staying with you until the baby comes, if you will have me," Sarah informed me.

"And I will be staying as well," Mother interrupted. "I have a feeling that you will be in need of my help."

"Oh now this is a most wonderful surprise indeed. The only thing that would make this any better would be if I received word that Jude was on his way home as we speak." Tears of joy and sorrow sprang to my eyes as I turned to Genevieve and touched her hand.

"Yes, my dear, that would be a true Christmas miracle," she replied, dabbing at the corner of her eye with a napkin.

I shifted uncomfortably as the baby started shifting and kicking. "I swear when he starts moving around in there it's like an entire team trying to kick the stuffing out of me." Standing to walk, I shifted my weight around.

"It is nice to get a preview of what is to come," Sarah said, shifting her head to examine my large stomach.

"Don't worry, my friend, I can't believe that you will ever be this size, you are much too petite. I am convinced that I am having a boy and that he will come out walking and talking with a full set of teeth," I said with sarcasm, then pushed on my right side where a foot appeared to be poking out.

"Is that your baby?" Sarah asked with complete wonder and amazement.

"I think that is a foot. Do you want to feel?" Taking her hand, I placed it on the same spot.

"That is unbelievable." Sarah's eyes growing wider as she took her other hand to feel my stomach. "May I?" she asked, reaching her hands out before being granted permission.

"Certainly, it is still amazing to me and it is a daily occurrence," I laughed.

"There is nothing like the feeling of life growing inside of you," Genevieve said, a nostalgic look in her eyes.

"Why did you only do it once then, if you don't mind my asking?" Sarah inquired with her hands still on my belly.

"I had a daughter before Jude, but she didn't survive more than three days," Genevieve said then sighed as if she was remembering back. "We tried several times after Jude, but it was not to be, so I just stopped trying." Taking a sip of her sherry, Genevieve seemed to snap out her melancholy as she straightened her back. "Some people are just luckier than others."

"I am so sorry to hear that," Clarisse said sympathetically.

"I have made my peace with it."

"Well, I am grateful that you have been here to see me through everything. I will be the first to admit that I have been homesick, but what has frustrated me the most is the inability to get any news," I said, moving over to the tea tray pouring another cup of tea.

"That reminds me, you needn't fear coming home because of Darcy Montgomery," Clarisse said matter of factly.

"Oh, and why is that?" I asked, caught off guard by her statement as the color drained from my face at the mere mention of his name.

"He was found hanging from a tree in the park on the east side about six weeks ago. It appeared that he had been held and tortured for several months before being displayed in the park for all to see as if they were sending a message."

"What kind of a message?" Sarah inquired.

"Montgomery actually had a note pinned to his coat when he was found." Mother recalled with a shiver.

"Well, what did it say?" I asked, dumbfounded.

"They printed it in the newspaper, and I will paraphrase because I can't remember word for word but it said that the secret society did not like being dragged out into the light of day and that Montgomery's actions were not sanctioned by them," Mother said, turning her attention back to me. "Your father thinks that the secret society wanted to send a message that they would not tolerate disloyal behavior, and they would take care of their own problematic members."

"And what news has there been of my husband in London?" I questioned, looking sideways at my mother, afraid of making direct eye contact in case the news was bad.

"I have heard nary a whisper about him. I attempted to see him a few times, but the only person allowed past the guards is his father. In fact, when I inquired after Jude I was told they didn't have a prisoner by that name." Mother turned to Genevieve with compassion in her eyes. "Your husband assured me that Jude is being treated as well as can be expected."

"What does that mean, Mother?" I asked as my insides twisted with concern.

"It means that he is well and being treated humanely, that is all I know."

"Then I will make the journey back to London to petition the king in person. Darcy Montgomery is no longer a threat to me. Please don't try to talk me out of it, my, mind is made up."

"Angelina, everything humanly possible is being done for Jude as we speak. An ocean voyage with rough seas in your condition would be too risky. My main concern now is for you and your unborn child. And it would seem that I have arrived none too soon." Her eyes traveling to my enlarged belly, she walked over to where I stood uncomfortably.

"But I still have some time before the baby comes. I have plenty of time to make the journey."

"I wouldn't be too sure." Placing her hands on my stomach, she moved them around pushing here and there. "If I had to guess, you will come early."

"I don't understand," I said, surprise showing in my eyes.

"In fact, I would be surprised if you made it to the first week of February." Dropping her hands she stood upright, giving me that all knowing look she often did. I learned to believe my mother without question because nine times out of ten she was spot on. I couldn't help being disappointed just the same.

25

CHRISTMAS HAD COME AND GONE with little fanfare and still my husband sat in the royal towers awaiting word of his fate.

Philippe had sent several letters of the progress that had been made or should I say the stalemate that the two countries found themselves in as they played politics with Jude's life.

Genevieve debated for weeks whether or not to make the trip to London and join her husband to personally see to Jude's welfare. She decided not to go so she could be present for the birth of her first and possibly only grandchild.

I had grown bigger and more uncomfortable with each passing day and my mood had grown even worse with the bad weather that prevented me from venturing out.

I found myself sitting in a chair that faced the large picture window overlooking the stormy seas. Rough waves hit the bluffs with such force I could see the spray of ocean water from where I sat. It had been hypnotic and soothing in a way, watching the lights flashing in the distant sky as lightning strikes cascaded into the water. I had been awake for hours plagued by a nagging backache that awakened me sometime in the predawn hours.

I know that I should have been apprehensive and maybe a bit scared with the impending birth, but I was not. Instead, I felt a calmness wash over me that morning as I awoke knowing all would be made right and that what was meant to be would be. So there I sat, enjoying nature's light show until the house began to awaken and Anna came in to check on me.

Walking across the room Anna deposited a tray on the table, startling me from my meditative state. "Are you trying to make yourself ill? It's like an ice box in here," she said, closing the window with a resounding thud before turning to me.

"No, I was warm when I woke earlier. I guess I didn't realize how cold it had gotten." I pulled the blanket sitting on the back of the chair tighter around my shoulders.

"Are you all right? You look peaked." Anna reached over to touch my forehead then my face.

"Yes, yes, I am fine. I was just so uncomfortable in the bed. It felt like I was sleeping on rocks," I said impatiently, then leaning forward I massaged my lower back and cringed at the pain.

"How long have you had the pain in your back?" Anna seemed to be on high alert all of a sudden.

"I don't know, maybe since last night before I went to bed. All I know is it woke me up several times until I couldn't ignore it any longer. I got out of bed and have been sitting here since." I tried to stand but was unable to get out of the chair by myself. "Could you give me a hand? I seem to be having trouble finding a comfortable position."

Anna leaned down to pull me up and when I stood the pain shot through my back and seemed to radiate in my hips. "Ahhhh."

"You sit yourself back down and I will call for help." Anna wasted no time running to the door as she flung it open, catching Maggie by surprise. "Maggie, fetch Lady Stewart and tell her to hurry. Lady Deveraux is in labor and send someone for the doctor straight away. Oh, and alert the cook and let her know that we need hot water and bring extra linens when you come back. James, just the man I needed to see," Anna yelled to the young man down the hallway. "Bring plenty of wood and build us a fire. Well, off with you now. Don't stand there with your tongue in your mouth. We are having a baby today and we can't have it catching a cold the first day," Anna said, sounding exuberant.

A few minutes later, my room was alive with people.

Sarah was the first to come running. "I heard that the baby is coming," Sarah said, her eager face beaming with excitement. "What do you want me to do first?"

"I don't know, I haven't done this before," I answered, apprehension starting to set in.

"Don't you fear, my lady, we will take good care of you and the little one," Anna said, trying to reassure me.

Genevieve was the next to enter the room. "It is too cold in this room. Where is James? Anna, did you send for James yet?" Genevieve called out to Anna in the next room gathering supplies.

"Don't worry, Lady Deveraux I have taken care of it and I am sure he will be here shortly," Anna said as she walked back in the room with her arms full of things she would need.

Before Anna finished speaking, James arrived with two young men carrying firewood. They quietly delivered the wood, stacking it neatly in the fire box then left. James set about cleaning up the ashes from the day before and starting a new fire.

Mother entered the room like a general addressing her troops before a battle. "You can put the water down by the fire to stay warm and put those bowls over there next to the bed. Honore, we will need your strong back to help Angelina into bed just as soon as the ladies have prepared it," Clarisse said, making her way across the room. She never broke stride as she directed everyone.

"Yes, Madame," Honore said, standing at attention, looking slightly uncomfortable to be in the room.

"Mama," I called out in a voice I barely recognized, sounding more like a scared child rather than a grown woman about to give birth to her own child. Reality didn't hit me until that moment when I heard my mother's voice.

"It's all going to be all right, my angel, I'm here now." Mother's reassuring voice brought tears of relief to my eyes as I reached out to take her hand."

"I need Jude. I can't do this without him." Tears rolled down my cheeks now as much from the pain of loss of him as from the pain of labor that was rapidly threatening to overtake me.

"I know, my darling, but if he were here now he would only be in the way. Once you are safely delivered there will be time enough to worry about your husband."

"Ahhh . . . it hurts!" I said, panting through the pain.

"Honore, your assistance please, we have to get her to bed," Clarisse indicated with a sweep of the hand. "Sarah, Genevieve wash your hands with the hot water. You too, Anna, I will need your help as well.

"Wait!" I said through gritted teeth. "The pain is passing."

"Perfect, we have just enough time to get you in bed before the next one comes," Mother said with a serious face. "Honore, if you will help me get her out of the chair."

When I finally stood upright, I gasped.

"Did I hurt you?" Honore asked.

"No, I don't think you can do anything to me at this moment that would hurt more than these pains, short of cutting off my head, and even then it might be a blessing," I said with a wry smile.

"I'm glad to see you haven't lost your sense of humor," Honore teased.

"I'm standing here before you in my nightgown in labor and my husband is an ocean away. What's not funny about that?" I said with anything but humor in my tone as Honore supported me on one side and Mother on the other side.

"Wait! Ahhh," I said, standing still as another excruciating pain doubled me over.

"Don't push," Mother insisted when she noticed my face turning red. "You have to breathe through the pain. Angelina! Look at me."

Standing at the side of the bed, suddenly a gush of liquid ran down my leg. "Wonderful. Just perfect! Now I have one more thing to add to my growing list of humiliating moments."

"Don't worry, that was supposed to happen and consider that it happened now before you climbed into your dry bed," Mother said, trying to be positive.

"I will take care of that," Anna said, reaching for extra towels.

"Thank you, Honore, for your help, will you go and check on the doctor?" Mother gave Honore a strange look over my head. "See if you can hurry him along."

"Certainly, I won't be long." Honore seemed to fly from the room, closing the door with a thud.

"Maggie, hand us a dry gown if you would please," Mother called to her.

"There is one here," Sarah said, retrieving the gown from the foot of the bed. "Anna thought of everything."

Labor progressed quickly after that and the doctor did not make it in time. The pain was excruciating, and I thought I would die before a copper-colored head popped out. He filled his lungs and let out a cry that could be heard throughout the halls.

Genevieve took the baby from Clarisse and cleaned him off as Mother started pushing on my stomach like she was searching for gold.

"What are you doing? The child is born," I said somewhat indignantly, feeling relieved that the deed was done.

"Yes, and you did a truly fine job of it too," she said, still feeling around my belly. "But I am quite sure that we are not quite done," she finished by closing her eyes and pushing on the left side of my stomach. "Yes, I am certain we are not done."

"What do you mean? Ahhh." I asked doubling over in pain again.

"You are having twins. That is why you were so big."

"Oh my," I heard Sarah exclaim as she came back to my side.

"No! I am not doing this again. Never again!" I proclaimed, still feeling the pain from the last contraction.

"You don't have a choice, this baby is coming one way or another," Mother said, getting in my face, her beautiful, jade green eyes staring into mine. "Angel, listen to me. The baby is turned slightly and I don't know how close the doctor is. I need you not to push. You have to breathe like I showed you before. Can you do that?"

"Yes," I answered.

"Maggie, find out what is keeping the doctor," Mother ordered.

Maggie never even looked back or answered but ran out the door, closing it behind her with a resounding bang.

Genevieve brought my son to me, placing him in my outstretched arms. His crying had ceased and he looked directly at me with cloudy green eyes wise beyond their years when I spoke to him.

"You are so beautiful," I cooed at him. Tears welled up in my eyes and I began to cry and laugh at the same time. "What do you think your father will say when he sees all that red hair?"

"He will say what a fine, strong son you have blessed me with," Genevieve answered, leaning over to hug my shoulders.

"Take him please, Genevieve . . . ahhh." I laid the baby in her arms as the pain came again. "I don't have all day for some doctor to decide that it is time to make an appearance," I said between breaths. "Turn this baby and let's get on with it!" I let out a bloodcurdling scream of pain.

Sarah grabbed my hand, and Anna bathed my head with a cold wet cloth then handed me a sip of water.

"Angelina, I'm not sure about this." My mother seemed to hesitate.

"Just do that thing you do when you suddenly know exactly what needs to be done and let's meet your other grandchild," I said, impatiently waving my hand about as the pain began to abate.

"Then we should wait for the doctor to arrive because that is exactly what I think we should do." Concern etching her forehead Mother wrung her hands together.

"There is no time. The baby is coming. Ahhhh," I gasped in pain. "Do something," I cried out.

"I've seen this done before but you have to listen to me."

"Anything, just do it. Make the pain stop," I cried out again in pain.

"Anna give her some laudanum, just a small amount to take the edge off."

After taking the laudanum, my pain eased some and my head felt lighter. I lay back turned on my side, concentrating on breathing and not pushing. Mother started pushing my stomach and turning the baby in position while Sarah massaged my lower back. Finally, when she was satisfied, the baby was turned enough I began to push. Sarah and Genevieve braced me up from the back because my strength was nearly spent and the laudanum made my head spin.

"Almost there, I can see the head," Mother cried out, encouraging me on.

"Just a few more pushes, Angie, and we will all be meeting the newest Deveraux," Sarah said, as the color started to drain from my face. "Don't give up Angie, you are so close."

"I just need a second. I can't breathe," I said my head began to spin.

"Anna, cold water. Now!" Mother yelled. I could hear the fear in her voice.

"It's all right, Mother, I just need a drink." Gratefully, I sipped the cold liquid feeling it run down the back of my parched throat. "There I feel better already," I said, lying to her.

"The head is there just give me one more big push and . . . she is out," my mother announced, tears of joy flowing from her eyes as she cradled her granddaughter in her hands placing her on my stomach so I could see her while she tied off the cord. The most beautiful raven-haired baby lay sprawled across my stomach crying, loudly announcing her arrival into the world. I reached out my hand to stroke her arm and touch her tiny finger while relief washed over me.

"Do you have a name for her yet?" Genevieve asked as she cried tears of gratitude for the two beautiful grandchildren.

"Isabella. Jude wanted her named Isabella Monique after his grandmother." I could hear words coming out of my mouth but I felt strange, somehow detached from the entire scene before me and then I fell limp.

I saw the look on my mother's face just before everything went dark. I floated above everything and saw her yelling and shaking me, but I could no longer hear her voice.

Honore came through the door with the doctor and Father behind him, but after that I saw a light. The warmth of it drew me nearer, giving me comfort and all I wanted was to get closer because I felt so cold. There was a little boy with red hair standing between me and the beautiful light.

"Hello. What is your name?" I asked, bending down to get a better look at him.

"We never really met before. They call me Charlie." Then putting out his hand, he touched my face and I felt such warmth and joy radiating from him. "I'm your big brother."

My mind refused to understand at first and then recognition began to dawn on my foggy mind. "But how can this be?"

"I watch over you," he said, turning his sweet cherub face toward me. "You have to go back. It's not your time."

"But I like it here. Everything makes sense now," I heard myself whine. "Nothing is working out the way that it should."

"Then you will understand that you're not finished yet, your story is not completed." He held my hand as we walked. His words quieted my mind, and I didn't have the will to argue. "You will see him again."

I wiped at a tear on my cheek then bent down to hug him. I could feel the warmth of his body as he embraced me then closing my eyes, I felt his child like fingers wipe at the fresh tears on my cheeks. I inhaled and he smelled of spring time after a rain so fresh, and clean. Like pure sunlight.

Slowly Mother's voice broke through my unconscious mind. "I'm not giving up on you, Angelina. Come back to me. Please!" she screamed. "Do something. You're the doctor."

"Alas, Madame, there is nothing else that I can do," I heard the doctor telling my mother as he washed his hands in a basin next to the bed.

Had I been dreaming? Had my mind been playing tricks on me? I did not know what was happening, except that there was entirely too much noise to sleep. "Why are you screaming at me?" my voice cracked.

Mother looked over at me in surprise then wrapping her arms around me, she sobbed. "I thought you had left me for good," she whispered in my ear. "I thought for sure you had given up."

"I saw Charlie," I whispered back. "He said Jude will come home."

Mother pulled back gazing deeply into my eyes. "I never had any doubt."

"Can I have some water now? My throat is really dry."

Then Mother started crying and laughing at the same time. "Of course, Angel," she said, patting my hand.

The doctor came over to me, lifting my wrist. He felt for a pulse. "You gave us quite a scare," he said, looking over the top of his glasses at me.

"You think you were scared? Try giving birth twice in one day," I said sarcastically. "Can I have some water, please?"

The doctor looked at me with confusion mixed with indignation.

"I think your services are no longer needed, Doctor. May I see you out?" My father said as graciously as he could. "Maybe Cook would be kind enough to put together a plate of something for your long journey back.

"Yes, thank you. That would be most kind of you," Doctor Morel said as he gathered his things, quickly stuffing them in his black leather bag. He followed my father from the room. Stopping to look back at me one last time, he adjusted his glasses on his nose and shook his head. "Most unusual."

Anna helped me to sit up, placing pillows behind my back as Mother handed me a glass of water. Genevieve placed my son in my arms wrapped in a fresh blanket as Sarah sat on the edge of the bed with little Isabella cradled in her arms. They had both been washed and clothed in white gowns.

Both babies were small in size but well formed, one with copper tufts of hair and the other with raven locks like her father. Looking into my son's eyes as he looked into mine, a shiver ran up my back. His green eyes with blue flecks looked back at me with such wisdom. "I want everyone to meet Charles Philippe Deveraux but we will simply call him Charlie." I looked at my mother as I made the announcement and saw the tears shinning in her eyes.

I motioned for Sarah to hand me Isabella as well. She gently placed her on my lap next to Charlie. I marveled at the two of them laying side by side, my little miracles so different in appearance and yet the same in essence. Isabella, with black hair and jade-green eyes, and Charlie, with his copper-colored hair and blue-green eyes, how beautiful they were.

Bringing them to my face, I inhaled and I swear they smelled of pure springtime and sunlight. My joy was full and my heart overflowed as tears of joy flowed from me freely. I could feel my brother Charlie in the room with me and the last words he said to me, "You will see him again," made my happiness nearly complete.

"Oh, what a joyful day it will be indeed when your father meets the two of you," I whispered quietly.

26

WO WEEKS HAD PASSED SINCE the birth of the twins and we had gotten into a nightly ritual. I would feed one and then the other, cradling them together in bed with me and the three of us would meld into the other. At some point, Anna intuitively knew to quietly move Charlie and Isabella from my bed, placing them together in their cradle in the next room.

The two of them would only sleep if they were snuggled together in the same bed touching one another. Once when they had been crying and inconsolable, Isabella reached out her hand and the mere act of touching her brother calmed her and she fell asleep. After that, I insisted that they be placed together when they slept.

I had fallen asleep after the ten o'clock feeding, determined to care for my children myself without the aid of a wet nurse. Exhaustion was beginning to set in from the constant feedings. If not for Mother, Sarah, Genevieve, and Anna tirelessly taking turns helping with the twins, I would have never been able to survive. They changed diapers and clothes, and rocked the babies to sleep while I rested or ate.

The soft candle light glowed from the night stand next to the bed and I heard Anna enter the room picking up Charlie then walking from the room only to return to retrieve Isabella.

I remember not opening my eyes because I was having the most wonderful dream of Jude. I dreamed that he had returned to me and so vivid was my dream that I swore I caught the scent of him. Like an ocean breeze, tantalizing and strong, the smell of him filled my senses, and I snuggled even deeper into the blankets sighing with pleasure.

I could feel the warmth of him settle in next to me, and I sighed again as his arm wrapped around me in the familiar way he always did when we lay down together. The strength of him and the scent of him filled my being so completely that tears sprang to my eyes, and I cried for a moment.

My longing and desire for him made this dream so real I turned toward the warmth that radiated from behind me. Surely exhaustion mixed with delirium caused my mind to play tricks on my senses.

I opened my eyes just a crack, afraid that the apparition haunting my dreams would fade away in a puff of smoke, leaving me with the realization that it was all just a dream once again.

Instead of fading into a cloud of smoke, like all the other dreams of Jude, I found him there on the pillow next to me. Slowly reaching my hand out to touch his face, his crystal blue eyes stared into mine.

Could this be true? I dare not hope. I held my breath and touched his lips and then his stubble, weary face. It was warm and pliable unlike the dreams before and my heart quickened. "Am I losing my mind? Have I finally lost all touch with reality?" I spoke out loud, certain that my mind was playing me for a fool.

"No, my love, I have returned to you as I said I would." His blue eyes sparkled with emotion. "I can't tell you how many times I have dreamed of holding you in my arms again."

"How is this possible?" I stammered. "What happened?" Sitting up in bed then getting to my knees to get a better look at him.

"It seems that the mysterious witness against me vanished without a trace. The king had no choice but to set me free. Without a witness, there was no case," he answered, propping his head on his hand.

My eyes drank in every inch of him as he lay in his trousers and open shirt. My hands started to touch him, examining for anything that might be amiss. "Did they torture you? Were you hurt?" Concern laced my words.

"I am fine." Taking my hands between his larger ones, he brought them to his lips. "You have been busy in my absence. I return home for the birth of my child and find that not only did you not wait but you gave me two children instead of one." His eyes searched my face, his humor now replaced with a look of concern. "I should be asking you how you fared."

"I have been here luxuriating in all the comforts of home while you languished in a dungeon. How can I complain when I feared for your life every single day?" I cried.

Coming up on his knees to kneel in front of me, he wrapped his arms around me to bring me closer, then tipped my head up with his hand. "My accommodations were not so dire, my love, I was treated more as a political prisoner rather than an enemy of the crown. My father saw to that. As for my treatment, well, let's just say I was not fed gruel and stale bread. I was questioned a few times, but my story never wavered, and I was never tortured. I have all my fingers and toes intact," he added, displaying his hands as evidence, "as well as all my other parts," a large smile assured me that he was functioning and ready for action.

Relief washed over me as exhaustion, mixed with gratitude, set in. "As tempting as your randy offer may be, I have been dealing with a couple of starving beasts of my own. They are always ravenous, so if it is all the same to you, I will forgo the home-coming celebration I have been dreaming of." I touched his face and then his lips with my finger as I searched his face, "Only for a little while, my love." I laughed, grateful he was home.

"I will wait as long as it takes, even if that means forever, my love." Bringing his lips to mine, we kissed passionately.

"I don't believe it will be nearly that long, my love."

A Preview
Isabella's Heart:

The Sequel and Continuing Saga of Angelina's Secret

IVING CALEB PERMISSION TO ATTACK first, I gestured with a wave of my hand. Daughtery attacked and I easily parried, then countered back, with an attack of my own, forcing him to retreat several steps. Jabbing Caleb in the chest area with the dulled end of my rapier, I hit my mark. The crew standing around on deck, jeered, calling into question the first mates manhood. He took it all in good fun, but attacked with more zeal and vigor the next round.

Resetting, we began again trading attacks and parries back and forth for about twenty minutes. We began to perspire with all the physical activity, so Mr. Daughtery decided to call for a small break. Slipping his coat off, Caleb deposited the garment with a crew member.

I removed my coat as well and wiped my forehead with the sleeve, before depositing the coat on a pile of ropes. Noticing that the rowdy crowd of men had suddenly gone silent, I looked up to see what had caused it.

That's when I came face to face with the unsmiling, yet ever handsome, brooding Captain Townsend.

"How about we engage in a real dual, my dear?" the captain challenged, his voice seductively deceiving as he broke the tension between us by giving me a half smile. His blue eyes seemed to spark like the sky during a thunderstorm, causing my breath to catch.

Dumbfounded for a moment, as my mind scurried to assimilate and assess the situation, I asked for the only thing that came to mind, "May I please have a drink of water first?" I queried, locking eyes with him.

"Since you asked so nicely," Captain Townsend said, with a sardonic smile. "Rogers, fetch Lady Isabella some water," he bellowed in my face while maintaining direct eye contact.

Mr. Rogers ran to do the captain's bidding, bringing me a ladle full of fresh water. He handed it to me, and I gratefully sipped it slowly trying to buy time.

Realizing what his friend had in mind, Caleb stepped forward. "Aiden, I must protest. What you are proposing is wrong," he said sternly, as the casual exhibition turned serious and the crew of rugged mercenaries looked on in disbelief.

"Anyone can have a leisurely game of back and forth exchanges for fun or even show, but your enemy is not going to follow the rules, nor will they give you a chance to catch your breath between bouts," the captain said, putting his hand up to stem the flow of any further protests from Caleb.

Turning his back on Caleb so he could focus his full attention back to me, Townsend continued to speak, but this time he was playing to the crowd, who had gathered for the show.

"Although you and my first mate here seem to know your way around a rapier, we are going in with swords, Lady Isabella. Of course, if you would prefer not to continue because you are too tired. . ." Townsend said, leaving the question open ended as he gave me a patronizing smile. Then turning his back to me, Townsend faced his crowd, as they began to jeer and yell loudly.

Paralyzed by indecision, and the dangerous glint I witnessed in Townsend's eyes, I chewed on my bottom lip, still trying to think clearly.

Turning about in a circle, while shrugging his shoulders, the captain truly was a showman, as he expertly worked the crowd of men up into a frenzy. As if to say the show was over, the captain looked at me and smirked, then shrugged his shoulders as he turned his back to me again. "Well, lads, I do not think the lady is truly up to the challenge. I would suggest you all return to work." Some light laughter erupted as the men slapped the captain and first mate on the shoulder and turned to resume their duties.

I picked up the two sabers and weighed them both in my hands, then choosing the one in my left hand, I threw the other at the captain's feet. The blade landed with a loud clank and skidded to a halt against his shiny leather boots.

Turning around, Captain Townsend's jovial smile quickly faded as he noticed the sword in my hand. Then slowly looking down, he scoffed, and bent down to retrieve the sword at his feet.

"It seems I was wrong, lads," Townsend announced loudly between clenched teeth. "It would seem the Lady has a backbone after all."

The thought flashed through my mind that these blades had very sharp edges and were void of guarded tips for safety purposes. I quickly pushed the thought from my mind and remembered that I truly had a reason for being here my brother and I would never turn tail and run from anyone, especially someone as smug and self righteous as Captain Aiden Townsend.

We walked in a circle like two wild beasts at the ready, each taking the measure of the other. The tension was thick as everyone on deck fell silent again.

Caleb again tried to protest, but Captain Townsend gave him a look that silenced him at once. I felt like I vibrated with the silent tension that existed on deck as I prepared my strategy.

I made the first move while Townsend still looked at Caleb. Thrusting my sword, I caught the captain off guard by cutting the button from his woolen coat.

Lifting his eyebrows in a manner that could have suggested either a question or a challenge, Townsend licked his lips and gave me a smile. It was not a pleasant smile, in fact it wasn't a smile at all, but a grimace meant to warn me of the impending danger ahead.

The crew suddenly went crazy. They shouted and jeered again as I heard money called out and odds exchanged. The captain lunged forward, and I deflected the attack with my sword, easily stepping to the side and swinging. We exchanged thrusts and parried back and forth, moving around in our tight little circle for several minutes. I refused to back down or give an inch as he pressed his advantage of height and strength, pushing me back against the masthead.

I sidestepped him as he swung his sword, and then pulled up short at the same time as I ducked. I figured it was his way of giving me a warning. But I didn't need a warning because I was playing for all the marbles in my brother Charlie's bag.

Knocking Townsend in the stomach with the hilt of my sword, I stepped to his right and repositioned myself to the ready. The sardonic smirk was back as he lunged at me, taking several heavy swings with his sword, and nearly knocking me over. We locked swords, and he came in close, growling under his breath. "Do you concede?" he asked, holding tightly to my free hand, keeping me momentarily still.

"No!" I said, that one word dripped with derision from my lips.

Not giving him a chance to reset, I pushed off from him and swung hard, forcing him back. The surprise I saw in his eyes was gratifying, if only for a split second, before regaining his composure and retaliating in kind.

He forced me back as he went on the attack, and I caused several crew members to scramble for safety, as I beat a hasty retreat.

A low animalistic growl escaped my lips as I attacked in frustration. My muscles were beginning to burn in my right arm, and I let my guard down for just a second. That was all it took. The captain's sword inflicted a nasty gash on my left arm, several inches below the shoulder.

A small cry escaped my mouth. Captain Townsend froze in mid swing, and then lowered his weapon. The smugness instantly drained from his face, replaced with concern.

Maria made her way to the deck, drawn by all the commotion and noise. I heard her gasp and I looked at her for a split second, but I didn't really see her. My mind was already going through the evasive moves

I had been taught. Maria closed her eyes and began to pray, as the entire crew on deck fell silent.

Then I remembered the reason I was there, on that deck, in the first place. Looking down at my arm, I could see the cut was deep and the blood had begun to flow from the gash. This was no time to wallow in my pain. Moving my arm to make sure it was still of use to me, I blocked out the pain, and concentrated instead on the moves I intended to make.

I turned my full attention back to the captain and gave him a murderous stare. I felt something snap inside of me. Like the floodgates being opened, all I could see was Townsend. Everything and everyone else faded away.

The captain wore the strangest look on his face as I raised my sword above my head and set myself to the ready.

Narrowing my eyes at Townsend, I prepared myself to fight, as if it were a matter of life or death.

I was fighting for my brother's life!

"I think it is time for you to concede," Captain Townsend stammered as he lowered his guard. "Look, your arm is hurt and —" the captain said, pointing at my arm with his free hand.

Cutting him off, I lunged at him, and he deflected my blade, but stumbled backward several steps, while still attempting to reason with me. I refused to hear him out. I was now focused on the task at hand.

"I thought you said you knew how to fight," I taunted, causing the crew to go crazy again. "Or perhaps *you* would like to concede?" I jeered.

Aiden lunged and half heartedly swung his sword, which I easily blocked. Lunging back in turn, I managed to put the captain on the defensive. Seeing a moment of hesitation from him, I delivered a kick to his lower left leg, throwing him off balance. He grunted and fell to the deck onto one knee.

I circled around behind him as my breath seemed to come in harsh, angry gasps. Giving an extra push with my booted foot in the middle of his back, I managed to knock him down on all fours.

The captain snorted in frustration and pounded a fist into the deck in a show of anger of his own. Then slowly rising to his feet, he looked over his shoulder at me, and I saw something in his eyes besides surprise at my underhanded tactics it was determination.

Growling somewhere deep in his throat, Captain Aiden Townsend looked like an angry bull preparing to charge. Turning towards me he lunged, slashing with his sword, a move I had anticipated and easily sidestepped, deflecting his emotionally fueled advances.

This caused another loud outburst of laughter from the crew.

We circled each other again, both of us taut and on edge as we lunged at one another, simultaneously locking blades. Aiden's left arm snaked out and grabbed a hold of my waist.

Pinning me tightly against his larger frame, our swords rested between us. "You need to concede, and I will allow you to save face," Townsend said between clenched teeth. His rage was clearly manifested by his ragged breathing as he leaned in even closer to my face, to emphasize his displeasure.

"Your hubris is astounding, sir, or is it that you are worried that you might be bested by a woman!" I sweetly asked, just before stomping on the instep of his foot with the heel of my boot.

"Ouch!" he yelled. "Why you little—" he began to say, before letting out another growl of displeasure.

I pushed off from him when he was momentarily surprised by my move, and my blade caught the back of his hand, when we came out of the clench. Looking down, he couldn't believe what he saw. The back of his right hand was bleeding from a two inch gash.

I didn't give him time to ponder whether I had done it on purpose. I immediately lunged at him, and our swords clashed back and forth as we took turns attacking one another.

I was physically tired and backed up, trying to step out of his reach, but he was relentless. Stepping back several more feet, I soon realized my mistake when I came up against the masthead once again.

Quickly dropping his blade to block me, I found myself trapped as I quickly shifted, attempting to turn to my left.

Raising my arm high above my head to strike back at the captain's trap, he gave my blade a mighty blow, knocking it easily from my tired hand. Moving quickly, he pinned my right arm above my head, with his left hand, trapping my body between himself and the masthead.

I found it difficult to breathe as he pressed his hips against mine in a show of superiority. The crude shouts of encouragement from his crew made my cheeks turn crimson. He leaned his face down close to mine as if we were merely lovers exchanging lurid thoughts of what we might do to one another later.

He smiled seductively and I could see he felt self assured of his manly prowess. "Do you concede now?" he purred in my ear. His mouth was now so close to mine, I thought he meant to kiss me.

"Are you truly so sure that you have the upper hand?" I said, tilting my face up just a touch more toward his, just to show that I was not intimidated by him.

"If this had been a real fight, my lady, you would be walking through those pearly gates to greet Saint Peter, by now," he retorted with a smug smirk and a small chuckle to top it off.

"Oh," I said, feigning surprise and shock. "Then this must be when I shout out loud and clear so everyone can hear me say that I concede," I continued, attempting to play coy, as I dropped my eyes downward.

"That would be the customary thing to do," he said, as his continued smugness radiated from every pore.

Looking down to where his hips connected with mine, I made a slow but assessing trail back up to the captain's eyes. Giving him a shy smile I sweetly asked, "I was wondering if you could point that thing in a different direction. I hear they can be dangerous."

"Only when placed in the hands of amateurs," the captain purred seductively again.

"And what if I said I had a little surprise of my own, just for you?" I sweetly retorted, pressing my chest into his as I seductively smiled up at him.

He chuckled again, and moved his face to my ear as he inhaled deeply of my scent. "Mmm... What a delicious and unexpected occurrence. Perhaps we could discuss the matter over dinner tonight in my private quarters," Aiden purred again. Locking eyes with the rakishly handsome captain, I raised my eyebrows. Then giving the captain a seductive smile, I chuckled in response. "Oh Captain Townsend, I find men as a whole an easy lot to manipulate," I retorted. "And if this had been a real fight, you too would be walking through those pearly gates to greet Saint Peter himself, having been unmanned by a woman," I said, pressing the tip of my dagger into the delicate fleshy parts of his crotch, for emphasis.

"Ouch!" he growled, squeezing my pinned wrist tighter, as he backed his hips up a couple of inches to avoid another nasty poke from my dagger. "You don't fight fair," his angry tone told me he was not pleased by my unorthodox tactics.

"And neither will the enemy. I believe those were your words, were they not, Captain?" I said smugly. "So I have only one question for you, Aiden, are you ready to concede?" I asked, giving him a wicked smile.

Authors Note

Thank you so much for reading my book. If you enjoyed it please consider posting an honest review on Amazon (https://www.amazon.com/Diane-Merrill-Wigginton/e/B00MS5NV38) and Goodreads (https://www.goodreads.com/book/show/34318579). Please feel free to visit jeweleddaggerpublishing.com to sign up for new book releases or to contact me. It would really mean a lot to me. Thank you.

Diane Merrill Wigginton

Printed in Great Britain
by Amazon

37750688R00189